GHOST MARINES

BOOK 3

DEVOTION

Colonel Jonathan P. Brazee
USMC (Ret)

Semper Fi Press

A Semper Fi Press Book

Copyright © 2019 Jonathan Brazee

ISBN-13: 978-1-945743-32-0
ISBN-10: 1-945743-32-8 (Semper Fi Press)

Printed in the United States of America

Acknowledgements:

I want to thank all those who took the time to offer advice as I wrote this book. Thanks first goes to Micky Cocker, James Caplan, Kelly O'Donnell, Robert Burnham, Fraser Butterworth, and Jim McNeil for their editing. And thanks to my friend, retired Marine Craig Martelle, who besides being a valuable sounding board, helped me with the Imperial Marine Corps collar device as well as the book's blurb. A special thanks goes to fellow writers Lauren Jankowski and Karen Herkes for exposing me to more of the many facets of the human condition. Finally, I want to thank Melton A. McLaurin for his book, *The Marines of Montford Point: America's First Black Marines* and Henry Badgett for his book, *White Man's Tears Conquer My Pains*. Without these books, *Ghost Marines* would not have been possible for me to write.

A few hours after I wrote the above acknowledgments, I found out that Mr. Badgett passed away a week ago on April 24, 2018. RIP, sir!

DEDICATION

This book is dedicated to the Sergeant Major Gilbert "Hashmark" Johnson, USMC.

October 30, 1905 – August 5, 1972

PRAXIS

Chapter 1

Mother help me . . .

Sergeant Leefen a'Hope Hollow, Imperial Marines, was awash in pain, converging from every cell in his body to blossom right behind his eyes. He almost cried out as he gasped for air.

Slowly, his mind started making sense of what was happening, and he remembered.

They said it would hurt, but by the Mother, I didn't expect this.

He rhythmically started squeezing the small bulb that had been secured in his right hand, and almost immediately, relief started flooding into his arteries, like a cool breeze off the snow-capped Silver Range on Home. Each pulse forced the relief farther, deeper, until at last, it reached the nexus of pain behind his eyes, and mercifully, the agony faded into a misty memory.

He took one more deep breath, then hesitantly opened his eyes. Not that there was much to see. A single bio-strip illuminated the inside of the cocoon, revealing a mechanical—yes, mechanical—timer. Leif eyed it suspiciously. Home was not the most technically advanced planet in the empire, but even coming from there, trusting his life to a mechanical contraption made him nervous. He'd feel a lot more confident with something higher tech . . . as in anything from the last millennia or two.

Leif understood the reasoning. His cocoon was completely inert, without an energy trace. His body put off the most energy, more now that he was brought back from chill-sleep. Hopefully, it wouldn't be enough to alert anyone on the planet's surface. If he ever got there, something that was far from certain in his mind. The cocoon had wakened him, but that was a long way from getting him down to Praxis' surface.

The civilian tech rep aboard the freighter had crowed about the high tech that had created the cocoon as he'd stuffed Leif into it. According to the guy, it was better than the finest Rolex or Ling Na craftsmen could hope to make, a tribute to mechanical genius.

It's not telling time, though. This thing's got to get me down on the ground.

There wasn't anything Leif could do about it, though. He was out of the loop and had to trust his cocoon to get him down in one piece and in the right place. Not only him, but the other 15 Raiders. Each of them had been "shot" from the freighter/special ops ship on its way to deliver a legitimate shipment to Warbler Station on Praxis' moon. If the freighter's aim was true, the calculations accurate, and the cocoons worked as promised, both teams would land in the same area throughout a single night, hopefully mistaken for debris from the local meteor shower if they were picked up at all.

Leif stretched himself. The tallest member of the platoon, it had been a tight fit for him, and his muscles and joints were stiff. He fingered the IR-77 Stahlmont strapped to his left thigh, his finger touching the power button. He doubted that anyone on the ground was scanning for them, and if they were, that they could pick up the weapon coming online. But orders were orders, and it wasn't as if he had a target where he was now.

Without much to see, he kept his eyes fixated on the timer a few centimeters from his face, watching as it counted down to the number the tech had scribbled down with a stylus. He'd been in the cocoon for seven days, long after the freighter had been denied docking rights and departed. Now, within a few more minutes, he'd know if he'd reached the planet's atmosphere.

A small bump made his heart race, but it was a welcomed sign. More bumps, then buffeting took over. He had reached Praxis' thermosphere and was entering the mesosphere. That was good news, but he'd have given a month's pay to know if he was on course. Most meteors burned up in the mesosphere, and as the heat started to build up in the cocoon, he knew he had to be leaving a trail in the night sky.

The tech assured him that the cocoon would survive entry, parts of it designed to ablate away, slowing him down, and giving him cover from surveillance. The cocoon would drop 2/3's of its mass before it hit the troposphere and he would . . . he didn't really want to think about that.

Instead, he watched the timer count down, grunting as the more severe jolts jerked and battered his abused body. When it hit 20 seconds, he tensed his body, pulling his arms in tight, squeezing his eyes shut . . . and waited. Nothing happened, just more shaking. Thinking things must have gone to shit, he opened one eye, ready to hit the manual release, when the cocoon split open, sending him spinning into the night sky. The centrifugal force splayed his legs out, almost wrenching them from his hip sockets, and his facemask was twisted askew.

Don't panic. You've done this part before. Just let the suit take over.

He brought his legs back and held his position as his suit fed out tendrils of fabric that both slowed and stabilized him. Within twenty seconds, he was in flight mode. Leif released the tendrils, and spread his arms, reveling in the feel of control. He didn't know if he was in the right location, but he wasn't going make a crater in the ground below, and that was a win in his book.

He took a quick look around for the others, then laughed at himself. They were all coming on their own, not in some sort of coordinated assault. For him to spot one of the others would be more than surprising. But he did have to figure out where he was. There were scattered lights below him, but it was the red flashing light—three flashes, pause, two more, pause, and back to three—at the top of Mount Cassius that gave him his bearings. He tucked his head down and located the lights of Red Mud, then the blue wind turbine lights of the power station that provided energy for the entire valley. Leif adjusted his course for the dark area just to the south of the power station. If everything worked out as planned, sixteen Raiders would rendezvous there for their mission.

Leif hadn't been in the Marines a long time, but he'd seen action, and things rarely worked out as planned. Hopefully, they could all get to the ground in one piece.

At 2,000 meters, Leif popped his foil. He'd glide the rest of the way in, hopefully unnoticed. The wind whispered over the polytrilene wing as he flew over a silent landscape.

Up this high, he could make out the outline of Mount Cassius and caught a few glints of moonlight off of the Huang River. The lights on the wind turbines gave him perspective as to how high he was. But the closer he got to the ground, the more he realized that he couldn't see shit. His DZ, below and ahead of him, was a dark mass of forest. Wyntonans could see better in the darkness than humans, but that didn't mean they could see well, and he didn't fancy plunging into the trees blind. That was a good way to get injured and get dropped from the mission. Directly below him, the ground was lighter, a single yellow light farther ahead.

Maybe a farm?

"I'm going in," he muttered, pulling hard on his left control line to spiral in. Better a field than the trees, and he could hump it in from there. Flattening out and bleeding speed, he prepared for an elegant landing . . . and got knocked face-first into a tightly packed field of two-meter-tall gencorn, crushing 20 or 30 of the stalks. He broke off a few more as he scrambled to his feet, shucking his wing before the light breeze could catch it.

He looked over the tops of the corn toward the farmhouse in the distance, pulling his Stahlmont out of the thigh scabbard and powering up the weapon. During their mission order, the S2 had told them that local farmers often had sensors protecting their fields. Leif didn't know the relative value of corn and whether it was worth the cost of sensors, so he froze, watching for any sign that his landing had been noticed. After a long minute without any sign of alarm, he figured he'd dodged that bullet.

Now that he was on the ground, he dropped his O2 tank, helmet, and flight suit and rolled them up in the wing before shoving the entire bundle amongst the corn stalks. The wing would decompose within six hours, but by then, their presence wouldn't be a secret.

One way or the other.

He took a huge breath of fresh air, filling his lungs. He wasn't fond of canned air, even onboard ships with all their scrubbers. Fresh air, even with Praxis' lower O2 concentration and a few weird trace gasses, was far more preferable. He felt more alive, more alert.

Don't just sit here dawdling, Leefen, he told himself. *Get a move on.*

With one last look back at the farmhouse and a silent apology for the damage to the crops, he pushed through the gencorn and out to the treeline.

He had a rendezvous to make.

****

Major Loreen Kim, the raid commander, gave the signal, and the fifteen Raiders, (fourteen Marines and one Navy corpsmen) started threading through the forest toward their objective. They had dropped fifteen Raiders, but Doc Watson, First Team's corpsman and demo expert, never made it to the assembly area. Leif hoped she had been merely off-course and was on the ground out there somewhere and in one piece. The mission couldn't wait, however, and they had to move out.

Timing was essential for success. A Marine Expeditionary Unit, close to 3,500 men and women, were about to enter the system, and the raid force had to secure their objective before then. Made up by First and Third Team from the First Marine Special Operations Battalion (Provisional)'s Charlie Company, the raid force had a precious few hours before the Novack insurgents realized they were under attack and could begin to conduct their threatened reprisals.

In other words, to kill their hostages.

After the failed coup against the emperor and empress, the six clans that had rebelled lost their charter and were officially disbanded, their holdings turned over to the planetary residents or reverting to the crown as trusteeships. The Yamanaka Clan sacked and imprisoned their leader and petitioned the crown to regain their status, which was supposedly under consideration. The other five did not fade quietly into the night. The Jin Longs, still immensely powerful with tentacles inextricably intertwined in the empire's economic fabric, were conducting a PR campaign and becoming cozier with the sassares Hegemony. The New Alignment Group—the Novacks—were more direct. Led by the Fremont Clan that still had significant individual wealth, those resources could buy hired guns. Stripped of ten of their eleven worlds, and with an imperial governor on Galveston, they weren't technically at war with the empire, but Novack funded mercenaries, made up almost exclusively from former Novack militia, were conducting raids and acts of piracy.

And that led to the current mission. Praxis had been one of the Novack worlds stripped from them, and one where the residents had long benefited from their former alignment. A majority, perhaps as high as 70%, supported Galveston, which in and of itself was acceptable. During their mission operations order, the battalion S2 told them that the emperor fully expected some of the old ties to reestablish themselves, and the hope was that by doing so, a more stable empire would come out of the mess that the coup attempt left.

But the Novacks were not willing to let their former holdings drift back to a new grouping, even with the Fremonts in positions of control. They wanted to make a statement, that their planets were illegally stripped from them by an overreaching emperor.

Which was utter radlishit, as far as Leif was concerned. They were foresworn, revolting against the emperor in an armed coup. Let them reap what they sowed.

Former Novack militia, led by the self-professed "General" Robles, a former lieutenant colonel and Praxis native, seized control of the local government, taking the imperial staff prisoner, along with "collaborators" and non-humans, and proclaiming Praxis an independent, Novack world. The imperial governor and 93 prisoners of note were being held at Robles' headquarters as human shields.

Another 200-plus hostages, mostly those citizens who'd taken jobs with the new imperial staff and non-humans, were being held at a former militia base. Robles had threatened to execute them should the imperial military attempt to intervene. It was the Marine special ops mission to protect those prisoners until a Marine battalion arrived to take the base and put down the insurgents.

With most of the planet's population either ambivalent at best, vociferously supportive at worst, it rendered the Marines' mission as one in enemy-held territory. The raid force could not afford to be detected as they silently glided through the dense forest to their objective.

****

The guard had his face buried into his scanpad. Leif shifted the crosshairs of his scope off the man's chest and to the pad, his scope adjusting to the light. Three children were looking across a river at another child who was crying. A golden, long-haired dog with the three children leaped out into the river, fighting the current to cross it. A moment later, it led the crying child, arm latched around the dog's back, into the water and back across to join the other three.

Leif shrugged. Not many of the humans' flicks appealed to him, and this one looked particularly sappy. He raised the crosshairs again, and as the scope adjusted, he was surprised to see the guard wipe away what had to be tears. For some reason, that surprised him. The man was a traitor, someone there to kill the hostages, but he was moved by some dumb flick? He shook his head.

Not that he'd hesitate to pull the trigger if it came to that.

"Looking good, Fort," Staff Sergeant Lars Silva—Puff—whispered behind him.

Leif took a quick look from where he was laying on a small rise, only his head and shoulders visible to anyone in the camp. Corporal Forintik, Second Team's lone qiincer Marine, had stripped down to a skin-tight unitard that left nothing to the imagination. She gave the big heavy-worlder a middle finger.

The unitard had dampening characteristics, but that wouldn't mean anything if the guard looked up as she flew in. And that was why Leif had to be ready to take the man out if he saw the qiincer—before the Novack could raise an alarm.

Without any way to communicate with the prisoners, someone had to get to them and let them know what was going down. The only way to minimize casualties would be to get them ready not only to act, but to act quickly and in unison.

Bird—Sergeant Anthony Garaumndi—had scanned the area outside of the fence and detected ground sensors, which had been expected. But a qiincer could fly over the fence without setting them off. There were very few, if any, qiincers on Praxis, and the raid force was making a huge assumption that the militia would not be prepared for a 45kg qiincer flying just over the fence.

Assumptions were dangerous and had a habit of blowing up in people's faces, but if she were detected, Plan B, which involved a much more active assault, would be initiated. Leif gave Forintik a 50/50 chance of getting in without being seen, and he thought he was being generous with that. The insurgents might not be Marines, but he couldn't imagine any military force leaving such a gap in their defenses.

"Five minutes," Silva said, tapping Leif's leg.

Leif tossed a small evergreen cone at Sergeant Wynn Lerner—Skate—then mouthed "Five minutes." She nodded and passed that on to the gunny. Lerner was the only member of the team who hadn't been with them since formation. She was a replacement for Ariel Fruhstock, who hadn't made the cut during the battalion's shake-down training. Leif still didn't know quite what to make of her. She was a competent Marine, but Leif didn't feel a personal connection with her. With only eight in the team, it was vital that all of them meshed into a single working machine if they were going to succeed in the field of battle.

Hopefully, this mission, their first since the battalion was stood up, would create the bonds that only combat could form.

If we succeed, that is. Come on, Leefen. Focus on the mission and don't worry about Skate.

He looked down his scope again. The guard was still engrossed in his scanpad. Leif let his thumb gently stroke the safety. One quick flick, a gentle touch on the trigger, and the guard would be dead. At only 234 meters, there was no way he could miss.

Sometimes, he wondered at how he could so readily accept the idea of killing a sentient being. He was a civilized person, from a race that had turned away from warfare, after all. This was not one of those times, however. The man on the other end of his scope had chosen to keep innocent civilians prisoner and had accepted that his mission was to execute them if the empire landed to take back the planet. Leif wouldn't take joy in killing the man, but he wouldn't lose any sleep over it if he had to.

His musapha stirred within him for a moment, but without conviction, and he was able to damp it down with barely an effort. His people may have recently given up on war, but millions of years of evolution had created his mistress, proof that his kind were not inherently pacifists.

He felt more than heard Forintik get ready behind him. In a moment, the mission would kick off. Like any operations plan, this one was rife with details and coordinating measures. But the overall plan was simple in concept. Second Team would send in Forintik to warn and prepare the prisoners for the breakout. Thirty minutes later, First Team would initiate an assault on the other side of the camp, focusing the attention of the defenders, but never creating the breach that would kick off the prisoners' execution. Second Team would breach the fence in the back and try to get as many of the prisoners out before the insurgents could react.

There were more details than that, of course, and it could go down just as planned. If Leif was a betting man, however, he'd lay money that things would deviate from script. They always did. And if—*when*—they did, Leif and the others would adjust on the fly to make sure the commander's intent, to rescue the hostages, was accomplished.

"Stand by," the captain whispered.

He heard a whisper as Forintik unrolled her wings and waited for the pseudo-haemolymph to pulse through the vascules, giving the six wings rigidity. He brought his crosshairs to the base of the guard's throat, the soft, low buzz behind him telling him that Corporal Fornitik was taking off. He caught a glimpse of her with his peripheral vision as she flew past, but he kept his eyes locked onto his target.

The man was still engrossed in his scanpad while Leif silently counted down the seconds. At thirty, he started to relax. Forintik must have made it. He started to shift his line of sight to see if he could spot her when the guard looked up, then shouted out "Hey!"

Leif's heart lurched to his throat, and he brought his aim back on the man's throat, his finger twitching to press the trigger, but something held him back. His forefinger froze, barely touching the small red button that would send the round downrange.

"What's going on?" Silva asked. "Did she get spotted?"

"I need to take a piss," another voice shouted back, probably too quiet for the humans to hear, but audible to him.

Leif held up his right hand, palm forward. He swung the scope around, catching a figure leaning unsteadily against the building, one hand holding him up, the other at his crotch.

"Do it in the fucking latrine, Will," the guard yelled out.

"Too far away," the man pissing said, slurring his words. "You just stand post. You're not the bloody hygiene police."

The guard mumbled something that Leif couldn't catch before he went back to his scanpad.

"Just someone taking a piss," Leif said, turning to the skipper. "I don't think they saw her. But, that guy's drunk."

"Are you sure?"

"Positive."

The team leader hesitated. This was something that the major and Team 1 should know, but was it enough to break comms silence?

He crept up to join Leif, then flipped down his NVDs. The guy taking a piss was just then pushing himself off the wall before he stumbled back toward the front of the building.

The captain watched for a few moments, then said, "Keep an eye out. Let me know if you see anyone else who looks drunk."

"Roger that."

The captain patted Leif's back and then low-crawled over toward Lerner. With only three sets of eyes on the target, he'd want each of them to look for more signs of drinking. Enough drunks could shift the probability of success dramatically.

The drunk had teetered around the corner of the building and disappeared from sight. If the guy had to piss that badly that he couldn't make it to the latrines, however, Leif doubted that the man had wandered far. As sure as a grazpin could hop, the man would have come out of the same building.

Leif strained his ears, picking up some muffled sound, but he couldn't make out words nor tone.

He turned over and whispered to Silva, "Puff, give me your long ear."

The staff sergeant pulled the long-range listening device from his cargo pocket and tossed it up to Leif. The PPL-31 was a compact, 450-gram wonder that could not only amplify sound, but also pick up vibrations on windows, walls, or almost any surface, then combine both sources into an intelligible output. It, along with the bigger PPL-37, was the most effective passive listening device in the Marine Corps.

Leif pushed the earbuds as deep into his ears as he could. They were made for human ears, not wyntonan, so they did not fit snugly, and he made yet another a mental note to figure out something after they got back to make them secure.

This time, I'm going to remember.

There was a simple optical sight on the top of the hand-held device, and he aimed it at the side of the building. Almost immediately the sounds of partying reached him. There were too many inputs for him to make out much of what was being said—with more time, the long ear's filters would start to separate the voices—but the tone was clear. The insurgents were having a good time.

The captain crawled back from the gunny, and Leif motioned him over.

"What do you have?"

"Partying. Lots of it," Leif answered, handing the long ear to the team leader. "Building G," he added, using their own internal designation for it.

Captain Dubois took the listening device, crept up to where he could see the camp, and aimed it.

"I can't make out what they're saying."

"It's the tone. They're feeling no pain."

"Are you sure?"

"Sure as I can be."

The team leader looked across the open area for a moment, then said, "OK. I've got to let the major know."

He scooted back down the slight rise to join Silva in the depression.

Breaking comms silence was always a risk. The Raiders were not a normal infantry unit, however. They were given the most advanced gear available, even gear that was not cleared for open use. The raid force comms were ultra-low frequency, far below most communications nets. This allowed for low power usage and could be disguised as coming from routine sources such as power plants. Even if the broadcast was detected, the hope was that it wouldn't be recognized as communications.

Leif tossed Silva his long ear, then kept scanning the camp. Forintik should be with the prisoners by now. There had been a real chance that there were quislings in with them, people loyal to the Novacks and there to keep an eye on them, but that was a chance they'd had to take. With no hue and cry being raised, it seemed as if that was paying off.

"Leif," the captain hissed.

Leif turned back, and the team leader was motioning him over. With one last look at the camp, he slid down the rise. He was too tall to stand up, even in the depression, so he knelt beside the captain, waiting until Gunny Dream Bear joined them.

"Change of plans."

Of course. There always are.

"The major wants us to get inside the camp and secure that building once they initiate their assault."

"Inside?" Gunny Dream Bear asked. "How? We've got sensors between us and the fence. And there's the guard there."

"There's been some activity over on the north side of the camp. About 250 meters from us. Someone's been taking out trash to a burn pit. You two are going to take him out, then use his path to get inside."

Leif and the gunny turned to look at each other. Leif was tall, slender, and pale. He certainly couldn't pretend to be the insurgent returning from the burn pit. That would have to be the gunny. If they got that far. If the insurgent was still there. If they managed to take him out.

Too many ifs.

"Needless to say, but I'll say it anyway. Complete silence. You cannot be detected. And this: you've got twenty minutes. We can't push this back any further."

Or we start running into the dawn, I know.

"Any questions?"

Yeah, about a million of them.

"No," Leif said instead.

They were Raiders, the Corps' best. They'd have to figure it out as they went.

"Then get going."

Leif and Gunny Dream Bear slipped back from the edge of the trees, then bent around in a slow, careful jog, making a crescent as they paralleled the camp fence. Leif sniffed, smelling the putrid smoke of the burn pit long before they reached it. He was surprised that anyone on a human world used burn pits. On Home, back at Hope Hollow, sure. If it wasn't compost or recyclable, it got burnt. But here?

The two slowed down as they got closer. Leif caught the tiniest flicker of light through the trees and motioned the gunny to halt. This was why the captain had picked him. He might not be able to bluff his way into the camp, but he was a ghost when it came to movement, able to move with a silence that belied his size.

"Ghost" was still a derogatory term some humans used, but within the team, it was a compliment.

Leif glided through the forest, silent as a wraith. Within 30 seconds, he spotted his target. The insurgent was putting trash cans back on a small cart, embers from the pit rising in the air, dots of glowing orange. The pit was 15 meters from the edge of the trees, in full view of the camp. A trampled path led up to a small gate where a guard stood, a dark shadow with the camp lights behind him, the red glow of a cigarette in his hand.

Leif had to act quickly. He couldn't just shoot the man. His Stahlmont was relatively quiet, but the crack as the round exited the muzzle would reach the 100 or so meters to the guard on the gate. No, he had to cross the 15 meters in the open and take out the insurgent before the man could raise the alarm. His musapha started to stir, but he slammed it back down. This was not a time for brute force.

Without thinking, he drew his vic from the sheath on his left calf. Soldiers of all types carried blades, but it was almost unheard of to ever use one in battle. Leif had already used this one, his gift from Soran, when he killed the empress' brother. No, it looked as if he needed its bite once again.

Leif didn't hesitate. As the insurgent bent over to grab his cart by the handle, he moved, covering the 15 meters in an instant. The man must have felt his presence, however. He dropped the handles and started to turn just as Leif crashed into him, one long arm reaching around to grab the man's chin and covering his mouth, pulling up and back, while with his left, plunging the vic in deep. He felt the tip of the wyntonan traditional blade skitter across bone before it found the gap between the vertebrae, cutting through the spongy disk and severing the spinal chord, cutting off the scream before it had a chance. Hot blood spurted as the man went limp in his grasp.

He slowly lowered the body to the ground behind the cart, eyes locked on the guard up ahead. The cherry of the cigarette never wavered.

There was a rustle behind him as Gunny Dream Bear joined him behind the cart.

"Help me," he said, as he started to strip off the floppy hat and fatigue blouse from the man.

The blouse was covered with blood, but Leif helped pull it off, all while lying on the ground behind the scant cover of the trash cart. Within moments, the gunny had slipped on both. The amount of blood was appalling, and Leif was sure the smell alone would betray him, but the gunny had to do something. A spec ops Marine did not look like an insurgent, even in the dark.

"If I secure the gate, get your skinny ass up there with me ASAP," he told Leif. "Until then, lay low."

He slid his rifle into the cart before standing up, pulling out one of the trash cans, and dropping it in front of Leif and the body.

Not much cover.

He wondered if he should crawl back to the trees. But the gunny was already on the move, casually pushing the cart up the path to the gate. Leif turned his head, left side of his face in the dirt, so he could watch, and slowly pulled his Stahlmont up, finger on the safety. Gunny Dream Bear didn't look like an insurgent, and Intel thought there were only 30-40 guards in the camp, few enough so that they would all know each other.

As the gunny pushed the cart into the circle of light on the gate, the guard said something that Leif couldn't catch. The gunny lifted a hand in a casual wave, but the guard realized something was off. He started to unsling his weapon as he turned to face the Marine.

Leif pushed up to a kneeling position, taking aim, but the gunny was quicker. I single pulse of light reached out, hitting the guard in the head. The man dropped his rifle and went to his knees, hands reaching up to cover his face. That was all the gunny needed. He vaulted past the garbage cart and pressed his PK-9 up against the man's temple and fired, sending a powerful laser to cut through flesh and bone.

Leif was already moving, running forward to join the gunny, who was already opening the gate. He gave his PK a quick pat as Leif reached him before holstering it, turning to give Leif an expectant smile. Leif gave a shrug and nod of acknowledgment.

With options to carry almost any weapon available, Leif and the gunny had argued over the PK's efficacy. While it packed a powerful punch, the laser was easily defeated with even rudimentary body armor. More than that, the small powerpack was good for only three half-second pulses before it had to recharge.

But the gunny had taken out the guard, managing a tricky shot to the face, and taking the man down before he was able to finish him off. Leif, with his vic, would never have been able to reach the man quick enough to silence him. He'd have had to use his own Springfield .45 or Stahlmont, both of which could have . . . probably *would* have . . . alerted someone inside the camp. Leif felt more confident with physical rounds, be they slugs or darts, but gunny has just proven that energy weapons had their place in the armory.

Marines loved to discuss weapons, but now was not the time. Leif pulled the guard's body up against the gate, trying to make it look like he'd taken a seat. It wasn't great, but it was better than leaving him lying on the ground. Gunny Dream Bear pointed back in the direction of Building G, and they both started jogging behind the line of buildings. These were barracks, back when the camp was fully occupied by Imperial Army engineers. Now, most of them were dark and silent. At least one was occupied, however, the flicker of light from a holovid reflecting off the windows, and twice the two had to stop and hug the back walls as insurgents walked by, but within two minutes, they had reached their target.

The windows were high and on the small side, barely large enough for a smallish soldier to crawl through. Leif was tall enough to see inside, so he carefully looked in one of the windows, taking the scene in with a glance before pulling back out of sight. There were at least 15 insurgents inside the building. Racks had been pushed to the side, and a table set up with drinks and food in the middle. A keg of Dynx was at one end of the table, an insurgent filling a stein. Leif knew there was a fully furnished E-Club in the camp, so if this building, back in the empty part of the camp, was being used as a party site, then it was undoubtedly because this was an unauthorized celebration.

"I've got fifteen or so, partying hard," he whispered to the gunny. "Most look pretty sloshed."

"Back here, I'm betting this isn't an authorized party," the gunny said. "All the better for us."

He motioned Leif to follow as he made his way to the back of the building where a burnt-out light hung above a single entrance. Hugging the wall so the guard on the fence couldn't see them, they crept up to the door. The gunny took out a slap tie, the ubiquitous fastener that could do anything from attaching a canteen to a belt to securing a prisoner. He wrapped it through the hasp on the door before connecting the ends, giving it a slight tug. No one would be coming out through that door unless they broke it off the hinges.

They sidled back, then along the wall, keeping the building between them and the guard, until they reach the front and crouched. Gunny checked the time and said, "Four minutes."

It was a long, long four minutes.

At last, the sounds of firing broke out toward the front of the camp, several hundred meters away. Immediately, Leif secured the front door with a slap tie. The sound of partying kept going for a few moments before someone either called those inside or the insurgents figured out something was up. The sound of music cut off, and someone tried to open the front entrance, then kept on trying when it wouldn't budge, jerking it with force. Shouts replaced the sounds of fun, and then door shuddered as someone hit it with full force.

"Take out the guard," the gunny told Leif before he fired a single high shot right through the door in warning.

Leif hadn't seen any weapons inside the building, but he wasn't taking any chances. He bolted past the door, minimizing his exposure, and stopped at the corner of the building. His mistress threatened to make an appearance, but experience gave him much better control now, and he easily blunted her.

He took two deep breaths, then led around the corner with his Stahlmont, exposing only his head and shoulders. The guard had stepped back from his post and was facing the building, looking unsure of himself. At 20 or 30 meters away, he was dead meat. All Leif had to do was press the trigger.

"Drop your weapon!" he yelled instead, stepping out, his rifle trained on the insurgent. "If that muzzle so much as twitches, you're a dead man."

The insurgent didn't even hesitate. His rifle fell to the dirt with a thud.

"On your face!"

He dropped almost as quickly.

Leif ran up and kicked the man's weapon away, then grabbed him under one arm and dragged the unresisting insurgent back to the guardpost. He pulled out another slap tie and bound one of his prisoner's wrist to the frame.

"Who . . . who are you?" the man stuttered out.

"Imperial Marines, that's who. Now shut the hell up."

There was a crash of glass behind him, and Leif wheeled around. A head and arm emerged from one of the windows. Leif fired a single shot at the top of the window, shattering the frame, and the insurgent ducked back inside.

"We're coming in," the captain passed on the comms, the blackout forgotten.

Leif looked up as the rest of the team came running up out of the dark. The contingency plan was for doc to blow a hole in the fence, but Leif kicked the gate open, and the team ran through, taking an immediate defensive posture.

"Any of them get out?" the captain asked, pointing at the building, but sparing a glance at Leif's prisoner, who was studiously avoiding his gaze.

"No. Maybe fifteen inside."

"Make sure they stay that way."

He got the other four up and moving, heading to the former supply shed that was now being used to house the hostages and where Forintik would hopefully have the prisoners ready to move as soon as they took out whatever guard was on them.

"I've got the east side and the entrance covered," the gunny passed to Leif. You OK with the west and back?"

Leif shifted his position by a few meters so he could see the back wall of the building. "Roger that. I've got it covered."

"Be ready to pull back as soon . . . shit, here they come."

During the rehearsals, it had taken the full team, including Leif and Gunny Dream Bear, seven minutes to take out the guards, gather the hostages, and get them back to the fence. It had only been about a minute since the five had entered the camp, but there they were. A mass of people was hurrying toward them through the camp, Doc and Silva in the lead.

Leif pushed open the gate, as the first of the hostages reached them.

"No guards," Silva said as he passed him. "They bugged out."

Leif scanned the area.

Bugged out or joined the fight with First?

If they had just bugged out, then they would be out there armed somewhere, and he doubted they could miss the 200 hostages that were bunching up to get through the gate. If they decided to try and stop the escape, then Leif had to spot them first.

Two-hundred scared and excited people took almost four minutes to file through the gate, and Leif wondered if it would have been better to go with the original plan and blow a bigger hole through the fence. But finally, the last of them were through and moving en masse to the assembly area, lead by Silva and Doc.

Leif was about to follow when Captain Dubois came on the net. "Change of plans. Cub, take Fort and Bird and get the hostages out of here. Skate and Leif, stay here with me. Resistance is light, and First is going to assault through the camp. The three of us are going to keep our friends in the building locked up and dissuade anyone else thinking of slipping out the back. We're going to make sure there's no pursuit."

Leif checked the time. The Marine company was scheduled to land and take the camp in 27 minutes. The plan had been for first to keep up pressure at the front of the camp while Third Team moved the hostages as fast as they could, laying a few bounding ambushes to slow down pursuit until the rifle company arrived. Leif was out of the loop with what was happening with First Team, but evidently, enough had changed so that the major felt they could assault through.

"How many of you are there in the camp?" he asked his prisoner.

Leif wasn't ITT, and the SOP was not to talk with prisoners, but he wasn't a super fan of Standard Operating Procedures. War was never "standard."

"I don't know—"

Leif took a menacing step toward the man.

"I mean, I'm not sure. The officers and the chiefs, except for Master Chief Sergeant Limon and Sub-Lieutenant Walsh, I mean, they're at the cordon commander's birthday party. You got the off-watch in there, and my regent sergeant," the man said, pointing with his free hand at the building. "He told us we'd be OK out here. So, just the on-watch section."

"And how many is that?"

"Eleven. We've got eleven posts."

And we took out two of them. Ten insurgents. Fewer if Razor took out any.

Razor was First Team's sniper, and he was deadly.

No wonder the major thought he could end this right now. If . . . he looked down at his prisoner . . . *this guy is telling the truth.*

The man was nervous, but not unreasonably so given the circumstances. But still, would anyone be so open to giving out information? And all of this seemed too good to be true. The officers and senior staff just happened to be off at some party?

"I hope you're telling the truth," Leif said as he fingered the trigger on his Stahlmont, eyes scanning the darkness for any threat.

****

"Glad you could make it," Leif told the staff sergeant as the Marine led his squad up to him.

"My lieutenant told me you've got some prisoners?"

Leif waved the muzzle of his Stahlmont toward the three insurgents slap-tied to the guardhouse. The guard hadn't been lying. The camp had a skeleton crew. Five of the insurgents had been killed or wounded by Razor and the rest of First Team. With the 18 Leif and the gunny had taken out—two killed, one captured, and fifteen trapped in the building—that left seven effectives before First Team entered the camp itself. Three more had been taken out of the fight, and two—Sub-Lieutenant Walsh and a regent sergeant—had tried to slip out the back gate, only to be nabbed by Leif and the captain. Two more were probably hiding out somewhere in the camp, but that was a problem for the infantry company.

"Three OPW's? Not bad," the staff sergeant said.

"And another fifteen in the building."

The entire squad swung as one toward Building G, weapons ready.

"They haven't quite surrendered, but we'll leave that for you guys."

As if on cue, a muffled shout reached out to them, "We are going to fuck you assholes up. Let us out!"

"Not the most diplomatic way of trying to convince us, but you know insurgents . . ."

The staff sergeant laughed and said, "Not too bright. But then again, are they ever? Let me find out what the lieutenant wants to do."

He looked up with the vague look of someone on comms.

A wyntonan private stepped up to him while her squad leader was getting his instructions. She hesitated, cleared her throat, and said, "*Daya*. Are you Leefen a'Hope Hollow?"

"*Daya*. And yes, that's me."

Her face broke out into a smile and . . . *hero worship?*

"I am honored. Karanun a' Red Rock."

Leif raised his eyebrows in surprise. Red Rock was a neighboring village back in the Silver Range. He knew her people.

"From my heart, it is I who am honored," he said, the standard response.

Who would have thought that I'd meet someone who's almost kin, way out here?

"Hey," she said, turning around to the others. "This is Sergeant Leefen a'Hope Hollow."

"No shit?" one of the humans said. "Like the Imperial Order of the Empire sergeant?"

The humans started to gather around when the squad leader shouted out, "As you were, Marines. The camp isn't secure yet. Eyes front.

"Sorry about that," the staff sergeant said to Leif. "Uh . . . the lieutenant's bringing up the rest of the platoon, and we'll make sure our friends in there don't cause any trouble. Do you want to come with us while we secure the bad guys?"

Leif was pretty familiar with humans by now, and he was sure there was a hopeful tone in the staff sergeant's voice. The man wanted Leif to join them. They'd come a long way since the first 50 People had enlisted in a resisting Corps.

Leif had been about to beg off. With the arrival of the company, the Raiders' mission was over. The captain had told him to stand by, and they'd lead a platoon to the assembly area and turn the hostages over to them.

The staff sergeant was trying to be nonchalant, but Leif knew what he hoped for. Which was mind-blowing to him.

"Skipper, how much time before we take off?" he passed on the team net.

"About twenty mikes. Maybe thirty. As soon as the grunts cut loose a platoon."

"Roger that," he said before turning back to the staff sergeant.

"If you're ready before twenty mikes, I'd be honored to join you."

ISS KONINGSDAM

Chapter 2

"So, what are you going to do if he's out of reach?" Gunny Dream Bear asked, turning Lief's vic over in his hand, closing one eye and staring down one edge, then the other. "Throw it?"

The wyntonan vic as a short, triangular blade, heavily weighted to the back. Presented to proven *serta*—warrior knights of old—it was made for punching through ancient wyntonan armor, not for throwing. It might knock some sense into a head if it hit, but it would hardly fly true, point first.

"Not that it did you a lot of good, Cub," Leif said, refusing to answer directly. "Took you two shots with your PK. And you were lucky. That guy had Class 3 armor."

"Which is why I went for the head," the gunny said. "Double tap."

Leif shook his head. The PK was effective against organics and most inorganics, but any modern armor better than Class 2 could divert the beam.

"If he had on his helmet with the face-shield—"

"Which he didn't, Leif. Case proved."

"And 'case proved' with my guy," Leif said. "Twice now."

"True enough. Newbie's luck," the gunny said before starting to hand the blade back.

Silva intercepted it first, then with an underhand motion, stabbed the air a dozen times in two seconds.

"Can't do that with a PK, Cub," he said. "You need a shiv like this to perforate a snitch."

Shiv?

For the hundredth time, Leif wondered about the Marine's background. He continually made references to prison slang, but if he'd really served time, Leif didn't think he'd been able to enlist, much less get into the Raiders.

"Don't need to, Puff. Once is good enough," the gunny said.

"Twice," Leif corrected.

The staff sergeant was right, however. Depending on the setting, the gunny's PK was good for two or three shots before the capacitors could recharge.

Silva flipped over the blade, grabbing it by the blade, then kneeled, bowing his head and offering the vic to Leif over a bent arm, like a medieval human knight.

"Take yon dragon's tooth, oh swordmaster."

Leif snorted, but retrieved his blade, wiping Silva's finger oil off of it before slipping into his calf sheath. At least he had it with him. The gunny's PK was in a shipping container somewhere, on its way back to Iwo.

Not that he was complaining. Compared to the trip out to Praxis, anything would be a step up, but the *ISS Koningsdam*? A luxury cruiser? The fact that they were four to a room in steerage was nothing. It was still hard to believe their luck, but the brass wanted them to stay off the horizon, and traveling as civilians to get them back had been deemed "mission essential."

Silva straightened, but not before grabbing his lower back and grunting. He'd landed hard during the drop, refusing to let anyone know during the mission.

"Leif's got two with his freaking knife, Cub. What's your tally with your PK?" Doc Yeltsov asked, not looking up from her scanpad.

"Just the one," the gunny said, nonplussed. "I prefer to take them out at a distance."

"Now, that I can agree with," Leif said.

"I'm so happy you do, *Sergeant*. I don't have to change over now."

Leif just rolled his eyes. This wasn't the first time they'd argued over weapons, and it wouldn't be the last time. It seemed to be embedded in every Marine's DNA.

"You know, that is the second guy you've shanked," Silva said. "I think that finally calls for a team name."

"Not again," Leif muttered to himself.

Rank was rarely used within each eight-person team, and all of the humans went further with nicknames. But for the two non-humans, Forintik was simply "Fort," and Leif was "Leif." He couldn't quite understand why humans wanted to change their names like that. He'd accepted Leif instead of Leefen due to long use and the humans' difficulty with the aspirated "n," but he'd resisted any other attempt at giving him a nickname.

"Shivmaster? How's that?" Silva asked excitedly. "Or just Shiv? Maybe Blade? What do you think?"

Leif knew he wasn't asking him. By some ancient human tradition, the person getting nicknamed had no say in the matter. More idiocy. Leif knew that if he ignored the staff sergeant and refused to respond to whatever crazy name he came up with, Silva would eventually give up . . . until the next time.

"How about—" Silva started before Doc interrupted.

"Take a look at this," Doc said, projecting her scanpad so the rest could see.

It was a news report of the mission on Praxis, except it left out quite a bit. The talking head described the mission from the time the battalion landed and took down the insurgents. No mention was made of the Raiders.

The talking head turned it over to a reporter on the ground, who had the battalion XO with him. The major gave a short account of the overall mission, noting that the assault had been conducted so swiftly that only a few hostages at General Robles' headquarters had been lost, and none at the auxiliary camp—the camp the Raiders had secured. All told, three Marines had been KIA, while hundreds of insurgents had been killed or captured.

Leif glanced at Doc, who had her mouth tensed into a tight frown. Three battalion Marines had been KIA. One Raider, Doc Watson, had been killed when his cocoon malfunctioned during entry.

The four of them knew their mission was being kept out of the public view. The Raiders existence wasn't completely secret. They weren't officially operational yet and wouldn't be until they were commissioned. Their training, along with this first mission, was all classified as their SOP was still being developed. They didn't expect public accolades, but that didn't mean they liked seeing the battalion take all the credit.

The stream cut to the next story, and Doc turned her scanpad off.

"Sorry about Doc Watson," gunny said quietly.

The two corpsmen had been very close. Doc Yelstov shrugged, then said, "No big thing."

But Leif knew it was a "big thing." He'd been there before, losing people close to him.

"Hey, what say we go get some chow?" Silva asked, breaking the silence.

"We just ate two hours ago," the gunny said.

"So? It's free-flowing feed here on this cruise. And it's damned good shit, even in here with the peons."

He had a point. Leif was now used to human food, and he didn't often rely anymore on his spice mix to make it palatable. But the ship's spread was excellent, and they even had passable wyntonan dishes.

"And what else are we going to do? Go mingle during afternoon tea in the piano conservatory," the staff sergeant added, effecting what Leif figured was supposed to be a high-class snobbish tone.

Gunny Dream Bear snorted, then said, "Why the hell not? The Big Green is paying mucho dinero for the trip, so we might as well get their money's worth out of it. We'll be back on Iwo soon enough, ready for our next mission."

Nothing truer than that, Leif thought as he joined the others to go stuff themselves with civilian chow.

IWO JIMA

Chapter 3

"He's not even looking at me," Leif complained as his son cooed and reached for something out of cam view.

"That's because you're on the 2-D," Soran said, shifting Jord to her hip and trying to get him to focus on the screen. "If you'd holo, he could focus on you better."

"Just trying to save money," Leif said.

That probably wasn't the main reason he was on the flat comms. True, the 2-D was cheaper than a holo; however, there were free options. The base ISO provided free comms home, but there wasn't an ISO at Camp Navarro, and he'd have to take the shuttle to mainside. Four hours back-and-forth and waiting for a slot, all for a ten-minute call had not seemed too optimal, especially after water-insertion training all night. To top it off, he had the duty starting at 1600, and he'd be up all night again.

After watching his son ignore him, however, he'd wished he'd either sprung for the holo or gone to mainside. Jord was already growing too fast for belief, and that made him question, for the thousandth time, if staying in the Corps was the right thing to do. He was a father now, and he belonged with his family. He shouldn't leave Soran alone to raise the little guy.

Not that she was completely alone. Family banded together out in the Silver Range. Soran had lost both parents in the slaver raid when they were tri-year threes, but Leif's mother had taken his *ishta* in, and there were plenty of cousins, aunts, and uncles around to help out.

"Speaking of saving money, are we in the system yet?" Soran asked.

"Jord yes, you no."

She furrowed her brows in the wyntonan expression of disdain. "You're out there serving the empire, and they can't get the records straight?"

Leif sighed. Jord, as his blood child, had been straightforward. However, with Soran, things had grown a little complicated. Out in the Silver Range, and even in the central plains, wyntonans didn't officially marry, at least in the same way most races in the empire did. *Ishtatanta* was something between two people, not anyone else's concern, particularly the government. With multiple races within the empire, and with many different human beliefs and cultures, the government was used to handling different norms, but the Corps had been human-only until six years ago, and Leif was the first wyntonan Marine to be bonded. However, when he'd tried to register Soran and Jord as his dependents, some civilian paper-pusher had read up that wyntonans didn't "marry" until at least their third cycle, so Leif and Soran couldn't be married and were obviously trying to scam the system.

Wyntonans usually didn't enter *ishtatanta* until at least their third cycle, and maybe beyond that, but with Leif in the Corps, the two had entered *haspe* after their first pairing, and when their second resulted in Jord, they'd made it official.

Master Sergeant Axios, the battalion admin chief, had promised to get it straightened out, but until it was, Leif's FAP, his Family Allowance Pay, was being withheld.

Leif was sending as much as he could out of his basic pay, but the extra would sure be welcomed. It was bad enough for him to be gone, but both Soran and he hated relying on family for financial assistance.

"Top Axios thinks it'll be soon. They're just waiting for the response from the imperial liaison."

"Them," Soran said with a snort, shifting Jord to her other hip, leaving no doubt as to her opinion of the bureaucrats back in the capital. "You've got friends in high places," she added. "Why don't you use that?"

Leif fingered the small gold pin, the head of a lioness and crossed swords that marked him a Knight Extraordinaire under the patronage of the empress. He knew he could make the call. Not to the empress herself, of course, but to one of her many staffers, and that would cut through all the bureaucratic bullshit. But that seemed beneath the honor of being a Knight, using it for personal gain. His full title was Knight Extraordinaire, Protector of the Empire, after all.

"I'll check again and see where we are," he said, putting his *ishta* off.

She furrowed her brows again, even if not quite as much as before.

"Well, you do that. And I'll let you go. Your son needs changing," she said as Jord's little face scrunched up and he started to wail.

"*Adaon*," she said, reaching up with one hand to touch the cam pickup.

"*Adaon*," Leif answered, reaching up as well until her image faded.

He watched the empty screen for a moment before he surged to his feet and took off for the CP and admin. Leif could face down insurgents and rebels without fear, but sometimes—make that usually—his *ishta* scared the shit out of him.

Chapter 4

Battalion, Atten . . . HUT!" First Lieutenant Natasha Limon, the battalion adjutant shouted out, as three-hundred-and-twenty-two members of the First Marine Special Operations Battalion (Provisional) snapped to attention.

Lieutenant General William S. Chen, III, Commanding General of Marine Corps Home Command, returned Lieutenant Colonel Malante's salute, then performed an about face. In the single set of bleachers, a small group of dignitaries sat, led by the emperor's *pinkerness*, Sept-Minister Constantine Iaxi. To his right was the Navy Deputy Director for Special Operations, and to his right, the newly appointed Assistant Minister for Special Operations (Marine) Juliette Montrose, the battalion's direct civilian boss.

Many . . . almost all . . . of the Raiders were puzzled by the selection of the older woman being the civilian head of Marine Special Ops. Pushing 70 years, she was heavy-set with a short bob of hair that framed her round face. "Matronly," was one of the politer terms used. Leif was in lockstep with the majority here. The Raiders were the cream-of-the-crop, the most capable, elite warriors the Corps had, and even though they weren't officially commissioned yet, the members of the battalion had already adopted an élan that might seem arrogant to others given their single combat mission to date. To the Raider, it wasn't arrogant, just simple confidence.

Colonel Jorge Petronas, the Deputy Chief of Staff for Special Operations, sitting next to the assistant minister, was far more accepted. With two Golden Lions, the "War Eagle" was a proven combat leader with a sterling reputation. Whipcord lean with a large, hooked nose, he reeked of derring-do. He'd joined the Raiders during several exhausting training missions and run more than a few of the Marines into the dirt during PT, yet he answered to the older woman? For the thousandth time, Leif realized that he would never understand humans.

"Marines and sailors, His Imperial Majesty, Forsythe the Third, Protector of the Empire and Servant of the People," the adjutant announced.

The dignitaries stood as one as the holopad set up on the parade deck flickered. The image of the young emperor appeared for a moment, then disappeared. Twice more, he appeared before fading out. One of the general's minions ran out, reset the mod-socket, and finally, the emperor's image solidified.

"Well, I'm glad this is just a hologram," the emperor said, looking awfully young to be the head of the empire, "And I'm still in one piece."

With the battalion at attention, no one laughed, and the emperor continued, "Well, then, since I'm here now, let's get on with this."

He straightened up and seemed to age, as if he was absorbing gravitas out of the atmosphere. "Your majesty?" he said, turning to look at someone off the holocams.

The holo flickered again, and the adjutant announced, "Her Imperial Majesty, Jenifer the First, Keeper of the Flame and Servant of the People," as the image of the empress stepped up beside her husband.

Leif glanced out of the corner of his eyes to the platform. He hadn't expected the empress to attend the commissioning, and his heart skipped a beat. Leif respected and admired the emperor, but the empress held a special place in his very being. After the fight on Irugwa Island, he and the rest of the surviving Marines had become intimately connected with her.

No, that isn't right. It wasn't just fighting together.

The empress could have left the emperor at any time, but she'd chosen to abandon family for her oath and the good of the empire. Leif could empathize. He was a long way from home, away from Soran and Jord, away from his family, because of his oath, because he believed in what the imperial couple was trying to do.

The small gold lioness head Leif wore on his collar felt warm and substantial, far more than its meager mass could explain.

The empress stepped up beside the emperor—not a pace behind, but alongside him, as an equal partner.

"Marines and sailors of the First Special Operations Battalion, I am sorry we cannot commission you in the manner you deserve," the emperor said. "And I wish the empress and I could be there with you in the flesh and not only in the spirit."

With the secrecy still surrounding the unit, no one expected the imperial couple to travel to Iwo Jima from Earth. They were rather hard to ignore.

"You have already proven the mettle of your steel, however. Not that I had any doubts you would. All of you are drawn from the finest the Corps has to offer, so I expected no less when you were called to duty even before you were officially combat ready. And I expect—no I am positive—that you will be called on to defend the empire and her citizens again. We live in turbulent times, yet it is our duty to enable each citizen to enjoy a peaceful, prosperous life.

"As I look out over you, my chest is bursting with pride. You are what makes the empire strong, and you are the ones that will keep it alive in troubling times. Our armed forces are the shield behind which we take cover, and we sleep well at night knowing you are on watch. And I—"

The empress nudged the emperor, who stopped for a moment, then looked sheepish, showing his age again. He smiled and said, "The Empress Jenifer warned me about getting on my soapbox. I've been briefed that there are forms to be followed, and those don't include me giving speeches.

"So, let's begin," he said, clearing his throat. "Lieutenant General Chen, I charge you to act in my stead."

The commanding general saluted the hologram, then performed an about face. From behind the single set of bleachers, Private First Class Hexter Bon-Kingury, the junior Marine in the battalion, marched forward carrying a furled flag. Bon-Kingury had been a professional pitchball player of note who had quit the sport and enlisted after the attempted coup. He may not have much experience yet, but he was as old as Leif and an amazing athlete.

The PFC marched forward and presented the colors to the commanding general. The general took it and with a twist of his wrist, the flag opened up, a brilliant red with gold piping, the Marine Corps emblem centered with the words, "First Special Operations Battalion" emblazoned over it.

Leif felt his throat catch. Except for the wording, it was no different than any other unit colors in the Corps. But it was different for him. He'd been proud of being in Third Battalion, Sixth Marines, taking his place in a long line of Marines going back for centuries. This time, he was there for the creation of a new unit. He was a plank-holder.

The general stood for a moment, the colors held diagonally across his chest, before with a snap, he thrust them out. Lieutenant Colonel Malante reached out and took the colors and looked to the imperial hologram.

"I am going off-script here, if you will allow me this privilege," the emperor said.

There was a slight group twitch. They'd rehearsed the simple commissioning ceremony five times, and this was a surprise.

"Assistant Minister Montrose, if you will," the emperor said, turning his hologram to face the observers.

The assistant minister stood, and carrying a black package, marched up to the general.

What is going on? Leif wondered.

The emperor was supposed to declare the battalion commissioned, no longer "provisional." They wouldn't hide any longer in plain sight as a support unit of some kind.

The general took two steps to the right as the assistant minister stepped in front of the battalion commander. She said something to him, and with only the slightest hesitation, lowered the top of the colors to her. She opened the package, and something silver and red fluttered.

"Oh, wow," Silva whispered beside Leif, breaking the silence.

The assistant minister attached the fluttering gray streamer to the top of the colors, and the battalion commander raised them.

"I realize that you were not commissioned yet during your last *training* mission," the emperor said, finally breaking through the discipline and receiving a small laugh. "And the commandant told me that as a provisional unit, you could not rate a battle streamer. But as the emperor, I can pull a little weight of my own, so I insisted.

"Marines and sailors of the First Special Forces Battalion, I now declare you commissioned. You are officially on duty, Raiders. Always faithful, always forward!

"Lieutenant Colonel Malante, if you would present your colors to the men and women of your command?"

The CO of the battalion turned around and held the colors high over his head with one hand as three-hundred-and-twenty-two throats erupted in cheers.

SUNRISE

Chapter 5

Three weeks after commissioning, Charlie Company debarked the trucks in front of their new barracks at the vast Fleet Naval Base, Sunrise. The posting took the rank and file by surprise, but with Second Special Operations Battalion already standing up for training, the Marines and sailors should have realized they wouldn't be sitting on their butts back on Iwo, just waiting for a mission. The Raiders were intended to be proactive, not reactive.

FNB Sunrise was the largest military facility in the quadrant, located on the economic center of gravity for what used to be the New Alignment Group: the Novacks. After the attempted coup, the Fremont Clan was stripped of their holdings, and a provisional government of local bureaucrats and business leaders was formed.

The imperial fleet operated out of Mbangwa Station in orbit, but the bulk of the base's facilities, specifically the heavy manufacturing, supplies, weapons storage, and family housing, were on the planet's surface. Shuttles and two huge magrail launchers supplied the ships and station.

During the coup, two of the Navy ships at Mbangwa declared for the Novacks, but the rest remained loyal or were able to put down Novack sailors' attempts to take them over. It became a standoff with 21 ships in imperial control, the two rebel ships, and a sassares dreadnaught that was in the system. No shots were fired.

Down on the planet's surface, however, Novack militia, aided by the civilian security, stormed the base, taking over most of the heavy manufacturing facilities and Class I, II, and IV supply warehouses. Captain Knute David, the base commander, collapsed his defense to protect the magrails and the the Class V and VII, the ammunitions and weapons, gathering SeaBees, admin sailors, military police, clerks . . . anyone he could grab. Despite being overwhelmingly outnumbered, the small force was able to hold off the Novacks until the defeat of the coup on Earth.

Captain David and three of his sailors were awarded the Imperial Order of the Empire for their actions. All but EC3 Winella Vought's IOS were awarded posthumously.

The Fremonts were no longer in power . . . officially. However, they had their fingers everywhere, and forensic accountants could not locate and freeze all the clan's funds. Horatio Fremont, the scion whose abject theft of imperial funds set the coup in motion, was still at large, almost assuredly being protected by the planet's citizens. There were small outbreaks of domestic terrorism, attacks on infrastructure designed to both gum up the works and convince the people that they had it better when the local Fremonts were in charge instead of a distant emperor, one who had spurned a Fremont bride to join him on the throne.

The emperor had refrained from punishing the populace of the former Novack holdings, but he was adamant that the planet was not going to collapse into anarchy. The base had been damaged, and it was not secure. He sent a detachment from the Fourth Naval Construction Battalion to lead the rebuilding of the base facilities. The Seabees were in charge, but the bulk of the work was to be contracted out to companies from planets that had supported the throne.

This proved to be a bone of contention to the local firms, however. Leif didn't see the problem. The locals were the ones who stormed the base, and as they still held allegiances elsewhere, they could not be trusted. There was a saying in Uzboss, the main wyntonan language, *lidet a'for diddad hoter'an*, which translated almost precisely to the human phrase, "you reap what you sow."

Until the job was finished, the base had to be secured, and so the Second Battalion, Fourteenth Marines, was sent to join the 55th Imperial Reserve Military Police Regiment from Knot's World that had been recalled to active duty. And now, with the Raiders duly commissioned, Charlie Company was joining the mission.

"OK, you've got your room assignments," Gunny Xan shouted out to the loose formation. "Get your gear inside and be back out here in thirty. I should have word for you then."

No one knew yet exactly what their mission would be, but as Leif picked up his seabag and slung it over his shoulder, he looked out over the base. It was bustling with activity, but nothing in that activity interested him. He was not an engineer. He probably couldn't build a wall to save his life.

But I can sure blow one up!

He just hoped he wasn't going to be bored.

Chapter 6

"Glad to see how much they love us," Doc said as they looked out the fence to where several hundred protestors were gathered, signs decrying "Stop Imperial Subjugation," "No Colonies," "Marines Off," and other like messages rampant.

Leif grunted. He'd never been hurt by a sign, no matter how vigorously it was being waved, nor how loud the chanting. To him, they were a curious sideshow, nothing more.

"You'd think they'd like having the power given back to them instead of being used to line the Fremont's pockets," Silva said.

"They *are* the Fremonts, or at least those who profited off of them. Look at the ones on the right, the ones against foreign workers," Fort said. "Do you think those people care about anything else except for the fact that their companies didn't get any of the repair contracts?"

The others turned to her as one. Fort was not quite as taciturn as PFC Hkekka had been, but she was still a qiincer, and this might have been the longest couple of sentences she'd said at one time since joining the team.

"Get some, Fort," Doc said.

The qiincer Marine was right, though. While disdain for the empire was widespread, and while there was more than a little resentment that the Marines had been inserted into the situation on Sunrise, it was no secret that the protests around the base were largely organized by the old guard. The spiderweb that was the Fremont clan and their allies wanted things back to how they were, and their old business adversaries wanted their time at the feeding trough. For once, their interests were aligned, and that interest was keeping the money in Sunrise hands, not in those of shareholders spread across the empire.

With the influx of "aliens," mostly tokits and alindamirs, jobs that the locals thought were their birthrights were being filled, and the flames of resentment were being fanned into protests and marches.

No one knew how things were going to play out. There had been no real action taken against the base or the personnel since the MPs and 2/14 arrived, but the protests had been growing. The media had started to arrive, including JBS, the sassares-backed network.

And now the Raiders were on the scene. They were the break-the-glass emergency response, ready for whatever was required of them. The problem was that no one knew what that requirement would be. They were a new shiny tool in the generals' toolboxes, but Leif wasn't sure that anyone knew how to wield them.

Chapter 7

"Sorry your albino-ass makes you stick out," Silva said as he wrapped his khasa around his shoulders.

Leif gave him the finger, then said, "And you think you look like a reg in that thing?"

"Impossible to hide my manly physique, true, but I'll pass."

He's probably right.

The tan and brown khasa, a loose cross between a coat and a shawl, did an adequate job of hiding the staff sergeant's bulk. Not that it mattered that much. There were heavyworlders on Sunrise, after all, so his presence wouldn't be that noteworthy.

With their mission still unclear, the major wanted the Raiders to get the lay of the land, so-to-speak. Dressed in civilian clothing, they were leaving the base in groups of two or three to wander around Prestonville, listening and observing. The Raiders weren't Marine Recon, whose mission was to gather military intel, but understanding the city and the mood of the people would come in handy for any mission that did come down the pike.

But a 205-cm-tall wyntonan on Sunrise was almost as conspicuous as a 100-cm qiincer with unfurled wings. That little fact seemed to have escaped the mission planners. So, when the teams were supposed to blend in, the company's four qiincers and six wyntonans were restricted to the base. They wouldn't leave unless the teams were going out as a unit and in uniform. Hexter Bon-Kingury was restricted to the base as well, at least until the beard he was growing filled out. "Ball" had been too well known in his former life as a professional pitchball player and could—probably would—be recognized by some sports fan.

Gunny Xan had assured them that the Corps had ordered holovid-quality makeup that would help them blend in, but that was going to take a few days to arrive. In the meantime, the eleven of them were to help him and Sergeant Willis set up the company office.

"You ready?" Silva asked Doc.

"Been ready."

"Then, let's get out in the ville and see what's up," he said with way too much enthusiasm.

"You're not going out on libbo," Leif said, unable to keep the disdain out of his voice.

"No, but if we have to grab a beer, you know, just to blend in . . ."

Silva slapped Doc on the back, and the two started to step out of the team hut before stumbling to a halt. Silva bent over and picked up a small package that had been on the ground outside the hatch, turning it over in his hands until he read the label attached to it.

"Hey, this is for you," he said, tossing the package to Leif, who snatched it out of the air with a long arm.

It had his name on it, but nothing else. Not who it was from, nor what it was. Which was strange, and strange on a mission where the Marines were not welcomed was not a good thing.

Leif shook it, holding it up to his ear, but that told him nothing. He looked at Fort, but she just shrugged. He knew whatever it was, it wasn't official from the chain of command, and he also knew that he should give it to the MPs to have them check it out. But curiosity was welling within him. He held it to his ear and shook it again.

It doesn't sound lethal.

His mind made up, he took out his vic and sliced open the seal. Out tumbled a small packet, and the smell of spice rose up to tickle his nose.

He automatically took a deep sniff, savoring the depth and nuances of the spice. It wasn't one of Granny Oriano's mixes. In fact, it was a fairly commercial variety, like the spice mixes made in factories that supplied most of Home's citizens. But it wasn't bad, and Leif's dwindling supply of last year's Hope Hollow mixture was almost gone. He licked a finger, dipped it in the mix, and placed it on his tongue.

Not great, but good enough. But who the hell left it here for me and why?

It wouldn't be one of the other wyntonans in the company or with 2/14. Spice was part of their culture, to be shared openly, not to be left anonymously.

He walked over to the hatch and looked out. There was the normal bustle, people and equipment going back and forth. No one, as far as he could tell, was paying him any attention.

"Hey, Leif," Sergeant Willis passed over the p-comms. "Gunny Xan's on the warpath. He wants to know where you are. You were supposed to relieve Jetta five minutes ago."

"Right. I'm on my way," he said as he sealed the packet and slipped it into his pocket.

A mystery, but I'll find out who left this.

Chapter 8

The tokit was hung upside down, a rope attached to his ankles. He'd been beaten, his face too damaged to make out his features. A single sign, bloody and tattered, had been tacked to his chest: *Go Home, alien!!!!*

Gorge rose in Leif's throat, and his musapha threatened an appearance. If he knew who'd done this, he'd let his mistress go. He'd let the rage engulf him and render vengeance.

"I found him here like this," the civilian said, his voice low. "This isn't us. Novacks. I mean, I don't like these tokits none, taking our jobs and all, but he don't deserve that."

The man, Frank Gandy, had walked up to Gate 5, telling the guards he had something to show them, but refusing to say what it was. Twenty-minutes later, Third Team had been dispatched to find out what the man wanted them to see. If he really wanted to show them anything, that was, and not lead the Marines into an ambush.

Looking at the murdered tokit, Leif wished it had been an ambush. He could fight that. What could he do here?

Tokits were . . . well . . . tokits. Not only humans considered them as barely tolerable among the Mother's children, connivers at worst, cheap labor at best. They scraped and struggled to make a living, smaller and less physically capable than most of the other races. Once released from the bonds of their single planet, they spread throughout the galaxy, making up vast ranks of menial labor and taking jobs no one else wanted to do.

But without them, without their willingness to die for a cause, the coup against the throne probably would have succeeded. Leif had never given tokits much thought before. They were just part of the landscape, but he admired them now.

Not that that made a difference. No person: tokit, qiincer, alindamirs, human, tost'el'tzy, hisser . . . deserved to be strung up like that. And why?

"Why did you come to us?" Captain Dubois asked. "You've got your police."

The man looked down, refusing to meet the skipper's eyes. He cleared his throat, then said, "If I did, it would probably be, you know, shoved under the rug. But you, you're imps, so you gotta take care of this. You can't ignore it, right?"

The captain looked long and hard at the man. The local sounded sincere to Leif, but he could never be sure with humans. It could still be some sort of elaborate trap.

"Uh, you're not going to tell anyone I came and got you, right?" the man asked.

The captain shook his head. Mr. Gandy had been scanned, of course, when he had approached the gate, so they knew his identity. With the general tenor on the planet at the moment, he wouldn't want to be seen as a collaborator.

"Skate, call it in," the captain said, his mind made up. "Tell them what we found, and that we need a forensic team from the MPs here. It looks like the scene's been sanitized, but you never know."

"Can I go now?" Gandy asked.

"Yeah. But we might have to contact you later. And thanks."

"We're not monsters, sir," the civilian said.

He hesitated, his mouth opening again to say something, but he shook his head and cut it short before edging to the alley entrance. He carefully looked both ways before slipping out and disappearing.

"You think this is all on the level?" Gunny Dream Bear asked the team leader.

"I think so, but I don't trust any of them. Full defensive posture while we wait for the MPs."

"Leif, Bird, take the entrance," the gunny told them. "Weapons ready, but not brandished."

Leif gave the tokit's body one more glance before he joined Garamundi at the mouth of the alley. Novacks were going about their business, lost in their own worlds, trying to live their lives. Someone out there did this, though, and that was something Leif was not going to forget.

Chapter 9

"So, you don't stab the wasilla?" PFC Terry Bon-Kingury asked. "You place the butt on the ground and hope the thing runs up it?"

"Pretty much, yeah."

"Icicle balls, Leif. Icicle balls. And if you miss?"

"Sometimes you win, sometimes the wasilla wins."

Bon-Kingury mimed placing a spear on the ground and holding the tip out, squinting his eyes as if he was watching a wasilla charge.

"I'd like to give it a shot. Think I could do it?"

"Hell, Ball, you know you could."

Leif wasn't blowing smoke up the human's ass. Bon-Kingury, "Ball," was the most physically impressive human Leif had ever met. He wasn't huge, but his body was a machine. He'd been a star forward in the pitchball prime league before he quit to join the Marines, and everyone knew he was going to make waves in the Corps as well.

"But would they let me, you think?"

"That's the question, now, isn't it? After that damned tourist . . ."

A month before, a rich human kid, an heir to one of the clans, had snuck into one of the wasilla ranges at a conservation park near the capital to bag a trophy, as he called it, and then streamed it live. It hadn't gone well, even when he'd dropped his spear and pulled out a massive handgun, and his death had been viewed over a billion times.

Elder Brynttyon, a long protector of wyntonan culture and traditions, had pushed the rest of the council to consider ways to keep the preserves closed off to non-wyntonans. Bon-Kingury was known and had fans on Home, but as much as Leif liked the human, an a'aden hunt was not for tourists.

"That guy was an idiot," Bon-Kingury said. "Got what he deserved. And I understand how you wyntonans must feel, some human trying to make light of your traditions. Still, what a way to prove yourself. Not that asshole. I mean, to do it right, following your traditions."

"Not many of us are still doing it, though. Times are changing."

"But you did, my man," Bon-Kingury said, giving Leif a hard shot to the upper arm. Icicle balls."

"And Gunny's going to have our balls if we don't get this inventory done," Leif told him as he opened the next container, trying not to wince as his arm protested.

Leif had gotten to know Bon-Kingury pretty well over the last few days while on the gunny's working parties for those restricted to the base. The work was mostly mindless, so they encouraged conversations to stave off the boredom.

"Aye-aye, Sergeant," the PFC said in his best "recruit" voice, coming up to an exaggerated position of attention and saluting. "Can't get the gunnery sergeant upset now."

"Eat me," Leif said with a laugh.

Ranks didn't carry the same weight within the Raiders as they did throughout the rest of the Corps. Everyone knew each other's ranks, of course, and the command structure followed it, but there was a degree of easy camaraderie that transcended that structure. It had taken Leif awhile to get used to it, but it was second nature to him now. Bon-Kingury was extremely capable, and he was already a center of mass within the company. He was one of those figures that stood out, someone who was going to go far in the Corps. He'd confided to Leif that after his enlistment, he wanted to get commissioned, but pretty much every other Raider already expected him to become an officer.

More than his obvious capabilities, Leif just liked the man. He was another reminder that no matter their differences, humans and wyntonans really weren't that far apart. The human phrase, "brother from a different mother" came to mind. Bon-Kingury *was* a brother, for all intents and purposes.

But now, these two brothers had work to do. He hadn't been exaggerating when he said Gunny Xan would have their balls if they didn't get this done.

"Scan," he told the PFC.

Bon-Kingury ran his wand over the opened case, looked at the readout, and then said, "Two-hundred-and-twenty-one."

"Check," Leif said, comparing the number to the one displayed on the case counter.

"And now, because we don't trust our scanners, we count," Leif said. "Let's get at it."

It wasn't so much that the scanners didn't work, but that there was a problem with supply "evaporation" aboard the base. With the government price tag on the GG-31's in the case, even higher on the black market, it was worth the risk to grab a few, then spoof the scanners to indicate a full container.

"One, and a two, and a three . . ." Bon Kingury started to count.

Leif looked down the containers the gunny wanted hand-inventoried before chow and sighed. It was going to be a long, long afternoon.

Chapter 10

The Sierra XS screamed around the corner, polymemfoam tires screaming in protest as they kept the truck on track. Leif, braced his legs against the firewall, his Stahlmont trained outboard at the frightened eyes of Sunrisers as they jumped out of the way. Another truck followed in its trace.

The call had come in only twenty-two minutes before. Fox Company, during a routine patrol to the sector power relay station, had the big man himself trapped: Horatio Fremont, the ex-heir-apparent to the Fremont Clan head and whose arrest warrant had touched off the attempted coup.

He'd undergone extensive modification and was unrecognizable to the naked eye, but not to the drone-mounted surveillance AIs that bird-dogged the Marines on their route. The former heir hadn't been able to resist watching the Marines move through the vast Jericho Housing Complex, and he'd revealed just enough for the AIs to identify him.

Orders were immediately sent out for Fox to continue on its patrol route for the moment, but instead of moving on to the relay station, they were to start to bend to the west, providing a blocking position. A fleet of microdrones joined the orbital surveillance platforms to cover every square centimeter of the complex. The noose was tightening, and the Fremont had nowhere to go.

"House calls," or snatch missions, were an essential component of the Raiders' overall mission statement. The infantry battalion commander was probably beside herself, that she couldn't just send in her Fox Company, but this was why the Raiders were on the planet. They gave Colonel Tähevӓli, the operational commander, more tools in his toolbox.

Third Team, except for Fort, had been in the gym when the call came. Thirteen minutes later, they were in their war gear and aboard the civilian bongo truck, joining the rest of the First and Second Platoon as they raced through the city while getting their operations order dropped into their Battle-Is, their Battle Interchanges. The company had nine "snatch in the boxes," nine hip-pocket snatch operations that they could adjust as need be. Major Quinlan implemented Charlie-Four, while he and Major Kim, the raid commander, adjusted on the fly for the particulars.

The Sierra XS sped around the next corner, the standard installed governors overridden by the Marines. They might be typical commercial trucks bought on the open market, but the Marines needed to be able to push the envelope.

A blue light flashed on his face shield, and a moment later, the updated plan appeared. It was pretty much as Leif expected. A diagram of the target building appeared. First, Second, and Third teams were to approach the target from three different directions, while Second Platoon's Second and Third, who were standing by back on base, were to make an aerial assault, landing on the roof and pushing their way down. With First Platoon on the ground floor, Fremont should be trapped and captured as Second Platoon made their way down.

"Everybody got that?" Captain Dubois asked. "Give me a verbal."

"Roger that," Leif said, taking a moment to study the plan. As expected, he was in the breaching team, providing security to Doc as the corpsman made her breach. From there, things would become more fluid as the situation progressed.

"You OK?" he asked Forintik.

She didn't look OK, but she gave him the weird-looking thumbs up that qiincers used, forefingers half curled and spread apart, thumb crocked out at an angle. For a race that could fly, she had a delicate stomach, the lurching of the vehicle was getting to her.

"Two minutes," the captain said.

The Sierra XS whipped past an MP checkpoint, the soldiers waving the vehicle through. It felt weird to be rushing to a mission in a civilian vehicle. If the intent was to blend in, then they were failing miserably. No bongo truck would ever be driven this recklessly.

The target building looked like each of the other 96 buildings in the complex. Eight stories tall, they were utilitarian despite a valiant attempt by some long ago architect to give the facades a little character. Too many years turned what might have been art nouveau into something stodgy and tired.

Come on Leefen! It doesn't matter what it looks like. Focus on the mission!

The two trucks swerved to a halt at the main entrance, and the eight Marines piled out, Leif and Doc rushing to the main entrance. To his left, Leif caught a glimpse of First Platoon's trucks pulling up, and overhead, the first team from Second Platoon flashed by, heading for the roof.

Leif had to resist watching them and focus on Doc. Truth be told, he was a little jealous of Second Platoon. While all of the Raiders were monopod qualified, Second was the designated airborne platoon, and they regularly trained in the small, single-person flying platforms. With First being the general-purpose platoon, and Third being the waterborne platoon, Second had by far the most enjoyable specialty.

Doc finished scanning the door, and she turned around just as it opened. Leif lunged forward, Stahlmont at the ready as a young woman with two young children in tow stepped out. The woman halted at the sight of the two Marines, almost retreated back inside, then grabbed the two youngsters by the hand and pushed past Doc.

"Clear," Doc said belatedly as the woman hurried her kids down the steps.

"Use it," Captain Dubois said.

Marines, as a habit, did not breach buildings by going through doors. They liked to make their own entrances. But this was a civilian building, one where imperial citizens lived, and their standing orders were to snatch the target while leaving as small a footprint as necessary.

Which was getting more difficult as the seconds ticked by. Their arrival hadn't gone unnoticed. Sunrisers were starting to gather, watching the Marines.

"Hey, what're you imps doing?" someone shouted out.

"Inside," the captain passed on the team net.

Leif burst past Doc, taking a knee and covering the long ground-floor hallway. A door half-way down opened, a male face peeked out, then disappeared back inside. The security lights framing the door switched to red.

"Coming in rear," Sergeant John Runcian from First Team announced. A moment later, the entrance at the back of the long ground floor hallway opened, and two Marines slipped inside.

"I've got you in sight," Leif told him.

"Coming in right," Silva said, slipping in behind Leif, then moving to the right. The rest of the team entered the building, taking up a hasty defensive posture.

"Commence Phase 3," Major Quinlan passed from the command center back on base.

That initiated two separate actions. The first was that the two platoons would now start a search of the 48 apartments in the building. With twelve four-person teams, two would secure the hallways while ten would clear the rooms until they found the target. Outside the building, Fox Company and the MPs would start to collapse the perimeter, securing the area. Fremont was trapped like a grazpin in a snare.

Leif, Doc, Silva, and Gunny Dream Bear stepped up to apartment 1A. "Imperial Marines. Open the door!" Gunny yelled out.

There was no answer, and the security indicator surrounding the door shone a steady red.

Not a problem. Marines weren't law enforcement, and they had no power of arrest, but they had access to the same equipment as the police. Doc pulled out her police-issue lock-null, aimed it at the intake lens at the top of the door, and activated it. The lights around the door cycled red for a few moments, then shone a nice, bright green. With a click and soft hiss, the door opened a few centimeters.

"We're coming in," the gunny yelled out as Leif pushed open the door with the barrel of his Stahlmont and rushed in, followed by the other three and a small nanodrone.

A middle-aged man with a growing paunch and a sickly pallor, clad in his underwear and a long-sleeve T-shirt jumped off his couch with a squeal, then ran behind it. The smell of old, rancid food stung Leif's nostrils.

"You can't come in here!" the man shouted. "This is private property."

Silva stepped to the middle of the room and ran a scan, slowly turning around in a 360 as he read the readouts. He stopped, looked at the gunny, then said, "One body."

Leif kept his weapon trained on the trembling man while the gunny checked the readout from the bio-nanodrone.

"Not our target," the gunny said. "Move out."

"Hey, what about the damage? Who's gonna pay for that?" the man yelled . . . but only after they had left and were ready to enter the next apartment, which turned out to be empty.

Their third apartment had five people—two adults, a young girl, a baby boy, and an elderly woman—who stood together while Silva checked for anyone else and the nanodrone confirmed that none were the Fremont heir. Leif kept glancing at the baby, wondering what he'd do if he was back in Hope Hollow with Soran and Jord, and someone came barging into his home. He already knew what it felt like to be invaded when slavers had come to capture him and the rest of his village, only to be saved by the Imperial Marines. This time, it wasn't saving that the Marines were doing.

Come on, Leefen. It's not the same thing at all. We're not trying to enslave anyone.

It was true, but he still felt a pang of guilt as he watched the man's hand drift over to protectively cover the baby's chest while the infant slumbered on, oblivious to the drama.

He felt relieved when the gunny declared the apartment clear, and they leapfrogged past Second Team to the third floor. But it was more of the same. Sullen or frightened people, but no Horatio Fremont. Within twelve minutes, the building had been cleared. The mission was a bust.

Major Kim called in the MPs and turned the building over to them. They'd interrogate the residents and try to find out what happened. All of that, however, was out of the Raiders' control. They loaded their vehicles and returned to the base, disheartened that their first real mission had failed.

It wasn't until the morning brief the next day that they were told the heir had been in the building but had escaped out of a sophisticated tunnel whose entrance was under the food processor in Apartment 1A, the first one they'd checked. Using retrograde DNA sniffing, the forensics team determined that the Fremont heir had most likely escaped just as the Marines were arriving at the building.

They'd missed the asshole by seconds.

Chapter 11

"Anything else I need to know? Anything support you need?" Assistant Minister for Special Operations Montrose asked.

Leif couldn't imagine that he'd thought the minister "matronly" back at the battalion's commissioning. If her steely gaze didn't reveal the fire within the human female, then the sharp, to-the-point questions during her brief would have.

She wasn't in political cover-her-ass mode, which was what everyone thought when she unexpectedly arrived the day after the failed snatch mission. Her questions over the last two hours, however, were not targeting blame, but how to improve the company's capabilities. And she asked the right questions, revealing an understanding of what the Raiders were supposed to do.

"You heard her. Any saved rounds for Minister Montrose before we take off?" Colonel Petronas asked. It was obvious that the battle-hardened Marine respected his civilian boss, taking on a protective posture. Leif was getting the feeling, however, that the minister didn't need much protection.

"Yes, ma'am," Gunny Xan said. "It's kind of routine, but we're still waiting on several shipments. We need the XM-151 maintenance kits. We can't get the 151's operational without them."

"And do you need them to perform your mission, Gunny?"

"Well . . . it would help—"

"Then it isn't routine, now, is it? You need them."

She turned to Colonel Petronas and said, "Find out what's happening and get it done."

The colonel nodded and whispered into his collar-mic.

"Anything else?" No one said a word. "You've got me here for another few minutes, so make use of it."

"I do have one more thing, ma'am," Gunny Xan said. "We had to order some make-up kits, stuff that isn't in the system. They were supposed to be delivered two days ago, but they're held up at NSB No Regret."

The assistant minister shifted her gaze to the wyntonan and qiincer Marines for a moment before telling the colonel, "It's those supply types. They want to get the kits in the system before they're sent out to the using unit. Get Master Sergeant Smith on that, and if he gets any pushback, I'll call Rear Admiral Baker myself. I want those kits here by tomorrow so everyone can blend in when necessary."

Silva gave Leif an elbow-nudge. Not only did the minister already know what the kits were for without being told, but she was also going to go head-to-head with the sector supply chief. Over make-up kits.

The rear hatch opened, and a sergeant stuck in his head.

"Is it time, Sergeant Abdalla?" the minister asked.

"Five minutes," the sergeant said.

"Well, Charlie Company, thank you for your attention, but I've got a ship to catch. I'll try to get back here when I can, but in the meantime, if there's anything I can do to cut through the bureaucratic BS, or if you've got a better way to do things, let me know. I work for you."

She turned to the company commander and asked, "Major Quinlan, if you'd walk me to the shuttle?"

The entire company jumped to attention as the minister, Colonel Petronas, and the company commander walked up the aisle to where Sergeant Abdalla waited. They held their silence until the hatch closed behind the minister, then broke out into conversation.

"What do you think?" Silva asked Leif.

Leif stared at the closed hatch for a moment. The minister knew her shit, that was for sure. And she seemed willing to fight for the Raiders, making sure they had what they needed to accomplish their missions.

And she didn't need any of the trappings that many human officials seemed to require. She'd come all the way to Sunrise with only a colonel and a sergeant.

What do I think?

"I think I'm going to like her, Puff. Yeah, I'm going to like her a lot."

Chapter 12

The assistant minister was as good as her word. The next morning, Gunny Xan had his XM-151 maintenance suite, and the wyntonan and qiincers had their make-up kits. Only, "make-up" seemed too tame of a word. What they had were full theatrical stage kits.

"Montik, you really do look like a human, Leefen," Ronan a'Shallows said, standing beside him. "And here I always thought you were a good-looking aden, and now you have to go ruin it. What's Soran going to say? Or better yet, little Jord?"

"I'm going to send her a holo, so we'll know soon enough," he told the wyntonan corporal.

He knew Ronan was just giving him grief, but she was right. He did look human, and it freaked him out more than a bit. The toner darkened up his skin just enough to fit in among the various shades of humans, but instead of an even coloration that he expected, something that would look artificial, the nanites in the spray had variations in the color that molded to his facial features. His cheekbones were slightly ruddier than the rest of his face, and there were imperfections that made his skin look natural. The ruddy blush crossed over the prosthetic nose that molded to his own flat nasal bridge, making him look like a bird-of-prey. He'd been concerned that the elongated nasal passages would interfere with his breathing, but after a few test sniffs, he could almost forget that the fake nose was attached.

A long, scraggly brown wig covered his own snow-white hair, and contact lenses gave him surprisingly human-looking eyes. Add a few pads added to the inner lining of the jacket, and he could pass for a tall, somewhat lean human.

"You ready?" he asked Forintik.

"She's been ready for ten minutes," Skate answered for the qiincer. "We've just been waiting on your slow ass."

Forintik stepped into the center of the room, and Leif would swear that she seemed nervous. With her complexion and face more in line with humans, all she'd needed were ear caps to hide the points. Her problem was her proportionally broad chest and the bulge of her wings. With her pronounced musculature, the experts had decided that the qiincer she would become a human he. She hadn't taken it well, but Leif could see that the gender shift had been a good choice. Lifts raised her height, and she looked like a short human male gym rat.

The wings, which had seemed like the biggest problem, were actually quite easy. Furled, the wings were a bulge across her back. Instead of trying to disguise them, the experts had decided to hide them with a simple backpack.

"You look . . . human," Leif said.

"Yeah. Sucks, doesn't it," Forintik said with a trace of her old sarcastic self. "I don't know how they put up with it themselves."

"Hell, Fort. You look almost good enough to date," Skate said. "Almost."

"If you're done, how about getting out of here so the rest of us can get ready," Ronan said, giving Leif's chair a kick.

"Wait. I want a holo," Skate said, grabbing a scowling Forintik by the shoulder and pulling her in to stand by Leif.

She tossed her scanpad to Ronan, then stood between her two teammates while Ronan snapped off four.

"OK, now, let's get out in the ville," Skate said. "Like the captain said, just a stroll, taking in the sights, getting a feel for the locals."

She gave her scanpad a quick look to check the holos before sliding it into the case on her belt.

"Hey, forward me a copy, OK?" Leif said. "I want to send it to Soran."

"Sure thing."

Both Leif and Skate turned as one to look at Forintik expectantly.

"OK, OK, forward me a copy, too. Not that I'll ever look at it."

Skate put her arm around the qiincer's shoulders and pulled the smaller Marine in close, giving her a kiss on the top of the head. "Ah, we'll make a human of you yet."

Forintik gave her a wicked shot just below the ribs that cut the human's laugh off short.

Leif ignored them. He'd been getting a little tired of working for Gunny Xan while the rest of the team, except for Forintik, had been outside the wire almost every day since their arrival, while he'd only been outside for the two missions. He was looking forward to the change of scenery, and without the stress of an op.

****

Four hours later, Leif was back on base, stripping his human disguise. Their patrol, as the team was calling the excursions, had been non-eventful. They'd wandered around, stopping at two cafes, just soaking up the atmosphere.

It had been a pleasant, if somewhat boring, afternoon. The population might be antagonistic to the imperial forces, according to Intel, but Leif saw none of that. He heard no plotting, he spotted no furtive insurgents. Just humans going about their business. If he squinted his eyes hard—real hard—he could be back on Home in any of the plains cities.

These humans were no different than the rest. If they'd been born on Earth, Garden, Saint Croix, or any of the other worlds, they'd probably be loyal to the emperor and critical of the Fremonts. But since they'd been born or immigrated to Sunrise, their allegiance was to the clan. It was all a geographic crapshoot.

That didn't make the Sunrisers right, though. The images of the murdered tokit were still burned into Leif's brain. The Sunrisers might act civilized, no different than anyone else, but some of them, at least, were evil incarnate.

Chapter 13

Not everyone on the planet was evil, Leif had to admit. Some, maybe most, had a core of good within them.

One such human was the reason that the platoon was out in force. An anonymous warning had been passed to the Marines that an incident was planned at the Creighton Industries' shift change.

Creighton Industries was one of the empire's largest construction corporations and had been for over 400 years. The CEO, Tess Singh, was a staunch supporter of the Granite Throne, so no one was surprised when the corporation had won several of the contracts to rebuild the base. Like most of the off-planet bid winners, CI made heavy use of tokits and less of alindamirs for unskilled and administrative labor. Without the facilities on base to house just shy of a thousand tokits, CI had rented out the Highland Arms, a barely-two-star, 180-room hotel that had seen better days.

The hotel had been the target of sporadic protests, and the MPs had created a post at the front entrance, manned by two soldiers at a time. It the tip was true, however, what was planned went far beyond a simple protest. The players wanted action that would hit the newslines, and hopefully result in the tokits refusing to work or being taken off-planet by the company.

Colonel Tähevali had orders from the force CG back on Ganymede to not only stop the planned attack but do so in a very obvious and lethal manner. He wanted a message sent.

Sending in a Marine rifle company would thwart any planned attack, but it wouldn't be lethal. Not many terrorists were stupid enough to take on the Marines. If Golf Company was deployed around the hotel, the terrorist would just fade away and plan their next attack, and next time, there might not be any do-gooders to warn the Marines.

That left the colonel with a problem. He had to let the attack commence, but protect the CI workforce AND kill or capture the terrorists. Luckily, he had a covert force that could blend in with the populace, yet be in position to take action: Charlie Company. First Special Forces Battalion.

Leif scratched at the brown wig on his head and downed the last of his tea. He was sitting at a small sidewalk cafe. Scattered around him was the rest of Second Platoon, all strategically placed around the back of the hotel where the buses picked up the next shift before bringing back the off-going shift. First Platoon was spread out along the route to and from the base, while Third Platoon was in front of the hotel.

His Stahlmont was heavy on his thigh, hidden by the long tan greatcoat he'd chosen. The lump of his weapon seemed obvious to him, but no one had given him a second glance.

He raised his hand and half coughed, half shouted out, "Can I get a refill?"

Leif was conscious of his accent, sure it would give him away as being a wyntonan, and he tried not to talk much, and when he did, he attempted to disguise his voice. The barrister just nodded, however, and filled a new cup before bringing it over. Like almost all human planets in the empire, Sunrise was home to people from across the empire, many where Standard was not the lingua franca. Leif might have a wyntonan accent, complete with his rasping aspirations, but evidently, it didn't scream wyntonan to the average human.

Leif blinked into the credit reader. The first time he'd had to pay for something, he'd almost panicked, but the contacts that made his eyes look human were coded to a fake account. That wasn't supposed to be possible, but Gunny Dream Bear said it was right out of the IIA's handbook. Leif didn't know how the spooks managed it when accurate payments for goods and services were the very foundation of the empire, but it worked. Leif was not on the hook for anything he bought when in disguise and outside of the wire.

From his seat, Leif had an unobstructed view of Mazalan Street, down which the buses would be picking up the new shift. Already, tokits were gathering outside the back entrance.

"Buses are inbound, ETA four minutes," Captain Dubois passed. "Keep alert. This could still be a trap."

The Marines of Second Platoon realized that they were waiting in what would be an effective killing zone should the "warning" turn out to be part of an elaborate ambush designed to take out a Marine force. High buildings provided platforms for plunging fire into the street and sidewalks, giving the ambushers multiple avenues of escape before reinforcements could arrive on the scene. Nanodrones were scanning the area, but there were ways to defeat them.

A flash of motion four stories up in an apartment building across the street caught Leif's eye. He reached to place a hand on his Stahlmont.

"Building Delta, four up, three from the right. I've got a window opening."

A hand reached out holding what looked like an old cyclonic handgun, a round cylinder protruding under a barrel, but just as Leif started to shout out a warning, the woman tipped it forward, and water poured out into the window box.

"She's clear. Just watering her flowers," Forintik said from her position on the roof of the hotel.

Calm down, Leefen. You don't need to be knocking off civilians here.

This wasn't Leif's first rodeo, a term the gunny was fond of saying, and he'd been in heavy shit before. Yet, he was nervous each time he faced a fight. Once it started, his warrior self kicked in, but the waiting drove him crazy. He took five deep breaths, then emptied his cup of tea, scalding the roof of his mouth and making him grab the glass of ice water and take a swallow. He looked around to see if anyone noticed.

"Two minutes," the captain passed. "No sign of aggressors on the way in."

Not that anyone had expected the empty buses to be hit. If there were going to be an attack, it would be where tokits would be victims. The terrorists would want blood, not just wrecked vehicles.

Leif sat up straighter, scanning the Sunrisers around him. The CI work shift corresponded with the overall planetary work shift. Humans in the cafes that dotted the sidewalk were finishing off their coffee or tea while others walked purposefully to their places of work. The morning rush was in full swing. The battalion's threat AIs back on base were busy analyzing the incoming data, trying to spot the human tics and traits that indicated nervousness or aggression. Leif pulled up the feed on his remote Battle-I—his spec ops model encased in a Sansui civilian scanpad frame—but the shifting percentage figures were overwhelming, and he turned it off.

"Here they come," Forintik passed, and a moment later, eight buses turned the corner and came to a stop behind the hotel. Many people ignored the buses as they hurried to their work, but more than a few people looked up at the buses with scowls or other expressions of distaste. No one within Leif's field of vision seemed about to do anything about them.

With the buses arriving, the rest of the tokits on the shift streamed out of the hotel, and that brought more looks from the humans passing by. Tokit were talkative, garrulous beings, and they only spoke Standard when needed. Their trills, whistles, and clicks filled the air as they pushed and shoved en masses to board the buses. The drivers—all humans—did not attempt to bring any order to the mob. They'd probably been doing this since the CI arrived on the planet, and they knew better than to try. Tokits seemed disorganized to other races, but they also seemed always to get things done.

But you could be a little more organized here, guys.

Transitions were always danger areas in combat. The quicker the tokits got on the buses, the quicker the drivers could start driving, and that would make any attack that much more difficult. Now, with hundreds of tokits pushing and shoving, half on the buses already, half still outside, they were a much more vulnerable target.

"Viper-two, we've got two ghosted vehicles inbound and heading your way along Cranston," First Platoon's Major Wixli passed on the net.

"Are you engaging?" Captain Dubois asked.

"That's a negative," Colonel Tähäveli passed, overriding the major. "We need overt action on their part."

Leif shifted his body to take in the intersection of Cranston and Mazalan. A "ghosted" vehicle was one where the ID transponder wasn't working. A single vehicle *could* have a bad transponder. The chances that two just happened to have malfunctioning transponders was too small to consider.

Leif pulled up the feed. Two Omato Sunbear multis were pushing down Cranston, going around vehicles by heading down the oncoming lane. One of the nano-drones dipped lower, and the feed showed darkened windows.

"Viper-two, there are four, I repeat four bodies in the lead vehicle, and four, I repeat, four bodies in the trail vehicle," someone from the CP passed over the net.

"This looks like the real deal, but they must show active aggression for you to engage," the colonel passed. "They have to fire or exit the vehicles with weapons in hand."

Leif understood their ROE, but he didn't have to like it. If those two multis were coming in to attack the tokits, and he was positive that they were, then the safest option was to take them out from orbit. But if the Navy did that, no matter the evidence they had, it would be reported in the media as "Imperial forces murder Sunrisers." The Marines couldn't assume intent. They had to see overt action. And that meant that some tokits, at least, were at risk.

"Get ready. Assume your positions."

Leif stood up and moved to the edge of the sidewalk. Each of the Raiders had specific positions that gave the teams the best coverage of interlocking fires. He unbuttoned his great jacket, the slight breeze blowing it open as he placed his hand on the butt of his Stahlmont. An image of a holo he'd watched a few months back flickered through his mind. It was an historical, placed in the American Old West of the 19th Century, the sheriff of some small town standing in the street, waiting for the arrival of the bad guys.

But that was then, this is now.

The two vehicles, barreled around the corner, the trail vehicle sideswiping a taxi. They headed right at the buses, swerving to a stop.

"Now!" Captain Dubois shouted.

Leif dropped his jacket to the ground, revealing a black long-sleeve tactical shirt with "IMPERIAL MARINES" emblazoned across the back, as he snatched up his Stahlmont from the thigh holster. Power pulsed through it, making it jump as if alive.

Two humans in common blue work jumpsuits jumped out of the rear passenger door, one with a military-style rifle of some kind, the other with a rocket-in-a-box launcher that he started to bring to his shoulder as he swung to face the tokits.

He never got it up. Leif's first round hit him high in the chest, and as he dropped the launcher, a look of surprise spread across his face as if he couldn't believe he'd been shot. Leif's next three rounds dropped him. Before the man's body hit the street, Leif had shifted his target and stitched the side of the second man.

Firing broke out, followed an instant later by human screams and tokit trills. Leif ran out into the road to get in position to engage the attacker getting out of the other side of the vehicle, but too many humans were running in terror between them. He couldn't engage.

A broad-shouldered body ran forward toward the Sunbear, knocking people out of the way as he shouted, "Get down, get down!" Leif caught a glimpse of an attacker's face as she swung around at Silva, but he still didn't have a shot.

The attacker shifted her aim from the tokits to Silva, but the Marine was quicker. Having bodily cleared the way of civilians, he fired a single shot from his BBK-40. At only 20 meters or so, the ramdarts were unstoppable, and they destroyed everything from the chest up, splattering the multi with blood and gore.

The driver's door started to open, and a head appeared before it slumped back inside.

Thirty seconds after Leif killed the first terrorist, the firing stopped. The screams and trills did not as humans and tokits continued in a panic. Leif ran up to the Sunbear and kicked open the driver's door, Stahlmont at the ready, but the man was dead, the side of his head gone.

"Vehicle One clear!" he shouted out, followed an instant later by PFC Bon-Kingury's, "Vehicle Two clear!"

Most of the tokits were still struggling to push back through the hotel door, creating a logjam. Humans were either still running or beginning to raise their heads from where they'd dived to the ground.

"Doc, see to the tokits!" the captain passed over the net. "We've got at least one down."

Over by the first bus, a tokit was sitting on the ground, keening while holding her upper arm. Blood streamed down it, staining her lilac jumpsuit. Two others hovered beside her while still more had their faces pressed up against the bus window as they watched.

By delaying their response until the terrorists had shown their hand, Leif had feared many more would have been killed and wounded. If it was only the one who had been shot, while tough for her, he'd take that as a win. But now wasn't the time to dwell on that, or on the wounded tokit. Just because there had been two vehicles in the attack, that didn't mean that there weren't anymore. Terrorists throughout the ages often used one attack to gather victims for another attack. Leif and the rest could not afford to let their guard down.

"Nice shooting," Silva said, pointing to the two Leif had killed, their bodies untouched from where they'd fallen.

"You didn't leave much of yours," Leif noted.

Silva patted the stock of his BBK-40 and said, "Yeah, kinda overkill, I guess."

The sassares weapon was typical of the race. It packed a big punch, but it was clunky to reload and had only limited range. The Raiders were like the Navy SEALs in that they had a wide discretion with regards to weapons choice, but Leif didn't know anyone who carried a sassares weapon. He'd been dismissive of it, as most Marines were of anything sassares, but he'd have to rethink that given how effective it had been.

"Not one of us scratched," Silva said.

They hadn't worn armor, and that had been a minor concern. Even with their new kit, it would have been difficult to hide that as they waited.

"None of us, but a tokit got hit."

Silva looked back to where Doc was patching up the victim, and he shrugged.

"Only one. That's a lot less than would have bought it if we weren't here."

Leif fought back the frown which threatened to make an appearance. Silva was telling the truth, Leif knew. But his friend's cavalier attitude toward the wounded tokit was so . . . so . . . so human. If it wasn't one of them, it didn't matter.

He wasn't blaming Silva. The staff sergeant was a heavyworlder, sometimes subject to discrimination by the regs, and he didn't seem to have a problem with either Leif or Forintik. It was just something deep inside all humans, and it probably explained the "manifest destiny" that seemed to prevail among them.

Humans and sassares alike. Maybe that's why they rule most of the galaxy between them.

He shook his head and scanned for a follow-on attack. But there wasn't another one. Twenty minutes later, ten minutes after the first of the news drones arrived, and fifteen minutes after the tokits seemed to notice Leif, in particular, the MPs arrived to take over the area.

Leif wasn't sure why he was the center of attention for many of the tokits. He'd been told that he was somewhat of a noted figure among the race after both the rescue on the slaver ship and then the fight on Irugwa Island, and he'd often posed for holos with them outside of Camp Navarro, but he was still in his human get up.

Can they recognize me?

He could barely tell one tokit from another.

"Let's load 'em up," Gunny Dream Bear said, making a circle with one raised hand. "We've got a debrief with the colonel at eleven-hundred."

Colonel Täheväli had watched the entire operation play out from numerous feeds. He probably knew more of what went on than any one of them. But the military was the military, and no operation was over until the debrief.

Leif checked the time as he ducked his head and stepped into the cattlecar. Hopefully, he'd have enough time to get out of his makeup and get a bite to eat before he was trapped in the who-knows-how-long-it-will be debrief.

Chapter 14

"They're banning a'aden hunts," Soran said the moment their images coalesced.

"What?"

Leif had expected a hello, we miss you, we love you-type comment, but where was this coming from?

"They're banning a'aden hunts. No more after the first of the year."

"I . . . what . . . where in the Mother's name did this come from?"

"The Council of Elders just announced it two days ago. I'm surprised you haven't heard," Soran said, shifting Jord to her other hip.

"We don't get much news from Home out here. Mostly human stuff. But back to this. No more a'aden hunts? Why?" he asked, totally perplexed.

The council says it isn't civilized, and that other races think it's cruel."

"But the wasilla, they come when they hear the beaters. They want to fight. And we don't usually kill them. More of the People die in the attempt."

"All the more reason, they say, to bring us into modern times."

"It's been a tradition for thousands of years," Leif protested.

Soran scowled. "Don't you think we've said that? The Silver Range is up in arms, but the council is firm on this. The Mother help us if we seem too barbaric to mix with civilized folk."

Leif had to sit back to let it sink in. A'aden hunts were ingrained into the People's cultural inheritance. True, fewer and fewer were partaking, but that was a personal choice. Even out in the Silver Range, fewer ada were making the transition to aden by hunting a wasilla, armed with only a spear.

"Did the humans force this down our throats?" Leif asked, anger starting to burn in his chest.

"From all account, not technically," Soran said.

"What does that mean? 'Not technically?'"

"Well, GWT did a documentary on it. Went out on two hunts. The coverage was more than slanted, and the social media response was not good. More than 80% negative."

"Social media? Who cares about that? This is our culture. Did the imperial government step in?" Leif asked, afraid to hear Soran's response.

"No, it was the council, led by Elder Hordun. He says it will help us fit in better."

Elder Hordun? *That's a surprise.*

Leif had met the elder three times now, the first when they were still on Home and about to leave for boot camp. Still young for an elder, it had been obvious that he had aspirations. But this made no sense.

"What about Elder Loroton? Elder Brnttyon?"

Elder Loroton was from the Silver Range, and Elder Brynttyon had long been the keeper of wyntonan culture.

"They fought it, from what's leaked out. But the council has decided. Unless . . ."

"Unless what?"

"Well, some people have reached out to me. If you were to address it, that could sway sentiment."

Leif stared at his ishta in shock, his mouth dropping open.

"Me? Why the montik would that matter?" he asked, confused.

"Because you're, uh, you've become kind of a symbol of the People succeeding among the humans. The call I got, it sort of suggested that if you were to speak out against the move, there might be enough sway to change the council's mind before the new year."

"Who called you?" Leif asked.

"I can't say. I gave my word," she said, suddenly refusing to meet his eyes.

This was all too much for him. They were banning a'aden hunts, and now his ishta was keeping secrets from him?

The ember of anger inside of him threatened to burst into flame.

Leif was living as a human, but he wasn't human. The only things that kept him sane were his family and his cultural anchors. Each time he sprinkled spice on his food, it was more than making it palatable—it was keeping him in touch with the People. Each time he honed his vic, it connected him to the People's warrior past. These things kept him grounded as to who he was. He'd never be a human, and now a core principle of what it meant to be wyntonan was being snatched from him.

Jord shifted in Soran's arms, one hand reaching up to play with her ear.

What will he do? What will my son do to become aden?

From the instant Jord was born, he'd known that his son would face a wassila. There had been no question. Jord would be a proud aden who earned his position in society. Now, he was being told it was forbidden?

"Jord," he said.

Soran looked up, and Leif could see the tears in her eyes.

"Yes, I know."

He stared at his ishta, wishing he could reach through the screen and comfort her. He knew he should say something, to assure her that he knew this wasn't her fault, but nothing came out.

Finally, after too long a silence, he asked, "And I supposedly carry weight with the People?"

Just saying that out loud made him realize how ludicrous that was.

Soran sniffed, rubbed the tears from her cheek, and nodded.

Marines didn't express political views while they were still on active duty. They served the Granite Throne, and since the throne served all the citizens, the Marines, in turn, couldn't take one side of a position or the other.

Would that matter for something like this? Not that I really could make a difference. That's just a fantasy someone dreamed up.

"What do you think I should do?" Leif asked.

"Jord," was all she said.

Meaning Jord's cultural history was being snatched from him. Meaning he should speak up.

But could I? As a Marine, as a Knight Protector, do I have to keep neutral when I am so against this stupid decision?

He didn't know the answer to his questions, but he did have access to the empress' staff. He could at least find out if he'd be allowed to make a statement.

"I have to think about this, Soran. I don't know if I can. I'll call you tomorrow," he said, reaching to cut off the feed.

He caught a glimpse of her starting to protest before the holocast went dark.

Chapter 15

"Do you know what this is about?" Leif asked PFC Bon-Kingury as they took their seats in the classroom.

The PFC might be the junior Marine in the company, but he had a knack for being in the know. This time, however, he was evidently in the dark just as much as the rest of them.

He shrugged his shoulders and said, "Major Quinlan got a call to go see the colonel, and he called back telling us to wait for him here. No word why."

Leif had been prepping for a trip out in town, his skin toner half-applied when the word came down. With the major limiting the numbers of them out beyond the wire at any given time, he hoped that whatever this was wouldn't knock him out of the rotation. With training limited to half-a-dozen Class 6 battle sims in a secured warehouse, he looked forward to his recon patrols out in town. They weren't the same as going out on libbo, but they still cleared the mind to an extent.

The hatch opened, and over a hundred heads swung in unison as the Raider commander entered, followed by a young human female dressed in what his friend Lorrie sarcastically referred to as "safari chic." The major had a slight scowl etched on his face as he made his way to the front of the classroom, while the woman scanned the company with a look of . . . superiority? Amusement? Leif wasn't sure, and he wasn't going to ask one of the humans if they had a better take on her.

"Charlie Company, this is—" the major started before she held up a hand and stopped him.

She took out a small white wand out of her waistpack, held it out in front of her, and slowly waved it over the assembled Raiders. She checked the base of the wand, nodded, and slipped it back into her pack before looking up and smiling.

It didn't seem like a friendly smile to Leif.

"What Major Quinlan was about to say is that I'm Special Agent Tambor."

Leif wasn't the only one to look around the classroom at his fellow Raiders, feeling a slight blush of guilt.

But I haven't done anything wrong!

The Raiders had been given a significant amount of freedom in conducting their missions, and with their very existence still not widely promulgated, and their missions classified, that left room for abuse. A team from Bravo was now being held in the brig on Iwo while waiting their courts-martial. While on a training mission in Torrington, the capital of Westerly, they had decided that they might as well live it up at the Westin Sky Needle, where the cheapest rooms cost more per night than a Marine captain made in a month. Even then, they might have gotten away with it if Gunny Gilbert hadn't tried to put in a reimbursement claim for a night's entertainment at a strip club.

The entire battalion had been read the riot act, and all expenses were being scrutinized at the company level before being turned into battalion.

The captain said ordering the tea was OK, Leif told himself, thinking back to the mission to foil the attack on the tokits.

Then there was the matter of the little gifts showing up for him. Could that be getting him in trouble?

He evidently wasn't the only one who was wondering. Several Marines were whispering to one another.

Leif settled in his seat and locked his eyes on the agent, hoping that she wouldn't be looking for him to catch his eyes with her predatory stare.

"It has come to the attention of our special agent in charge that you Marines have been taking a clandestine approach to familiarize yourselves with the lay of the land," the human said. "This will stop immediately."

What?

"You are not the professionals here, and we don't need you fucking up our operations by bumbling about like bulls in the proverbial china shop."

Leif was confused. NIS had operations going on?

Well, of course, NIS had a presence on the base. With the sheer mass of military supplies on the base, there would always be "erosion." NIS would be tasked with if not halting that completely, then at least minimizing losses and taking down enough of the perpetrators to make others think twice about doing the same.

But what did the Raiders have to do with that?

"The agent-in-charge has authorized me to tell you this. Sunrise is not firmly entrenched in the empire's embrace."

"No shit," Bon-Kingury muttered.

"Aside from the obvious, there have been foreign fingers dipping into the scene here, keeping things stirred up, and there are indications that something else, something bigger is in the works.

"We've got our assets in place, and we'll succeed in rooting out the rot. You, on the other hand, will stay here on the base like good little Marines, in your uniforms and out of our way."

She broke into a huge smile, while beside her, Major Quinlan scowled even more. He didn't say a word, however, so whoever this human was, she was the one in control.

She's not NIS. She's IIA, Leif suddenly realized. *She's not worried about military supplies growing feet and walking off-base and into the local economy. She's doing spy shit.*

"So, to sum up. You do your Marine shit, and you leave the clandestine work to the professionals." She turned to the company commander and said, "See to it, Major," before striding back to the exit, well aware of the 138 sets of eyes locked on her, and from all appearances, reveling in it.

Dead silence reigned until the hatch closed behind her, and the company broke out into a hubbub.

"Foreign fingers?" Leif asked, already knowing the answer.

"Sassares," Bon-Kingury said. "Who else would it be?"

Major Kim, sitting the front row, stood up and asked, "Is this for real?"

"Yes, it is," Major Quinlan spat. "This is coming down from the highest levels."

"This is bullshit," Major Kim said, to everyone's agreement. "They are the professionals, and we aren't? They just don't want the competition."

"Doesn't matter. We're standing down. This is coming from Iwo. From now on, unless we get clearance first, we're in uniform."

There was a rise in the noise level as people tried to talk, but the company commander held up his hand, palm outwards, to silence everyone.

"This isn't open for discussion. You're Raiders, damn it. Start acting like it. We'll do our job like we always do!"

"Always faithful, always forward!" someone yelled from the back of the classroom.

A chorus of ooh-rahs greeted him.

The major was right. They were Marines first and foremost, and they'd salute smartly and march on, ready for whatever mission came down the pike.

Leif stared at his right hand for a moment, the one that had already been tinted to human coloring.

"Fuck it. I look like shit as a human, anyway."

Chapter 16

It took only two days for the Raiders to find out what "foreign fingers dipping into the scene" meant. Arms were being smuggled onto Sunrise. Several shipments had already arrived, and another was scheduled to land in the remote hills of the McHenry Range, some three hundred klicks from Prestonville.

And for all of Special Agent Tambor's arrogance, the IIA didn't have the manpower nor training to take concrete action. In normal circumstances, the local police would act on the intel the IIA developed, but on Sunrise, there was a significant lack of trust in Sunrise law enforcement. From the mission brief, while it wasn't explicitly stated, Leif got the feeling that the members of the police were on the receiving end of at least some of the weapons.

There were two forces on the planet, however, that did have the training, muscle, or legal authority to step in: the MPs and the Marines.

Legally, using the Marines to stop the smuggling was on shaky grounds. The MPs didn't have the same restrictions. But no one equated the combat prowess of the MPs with the Marines. They simply were not trained and organized for combat-type operations.

There was a workaround. A single squad of MPs was tasked to seize the incoming shipment. Alone, that would be a tall task, but with a Marine battalion for "security," they shouldn't have much of a problem.

Of course, the Navy could simply intercept the ship coming in, but at least three others had already slipped past their security lattice surrounding the planet, and even if they intercepted the ship, that wouldn't nab the recipients on the ground. The brass wanted a clean sweep, smugglers and terrorists.

The vaunted IIA didn't even know who the smugglers were. Over the centuries, smugglers had remained at the forefront of getting in and out of places unnoticed. But with the heightened security around Sunrise, run-of-the-mill smugglers should have been spotted. That meant that either some of the high-tech outfits had been hired, or, more likely, that the sassares were doing more than providing the funds or weapons. They were directly involved.

"Ten minutes!" Gunny Dream Bear shouted as the team prepared to move out.

As Leif checked his charge, his musapha gave him a little reminder that she was there, waiting to make an entrance. Facing sassares excited him. He'd proven himself against humans, but this would be different.

Not that the Raiders would be facing them. The point of main effort here was Second Battalion, Fourteenth Marines. This was their show, and they were the correct choice. If there were sassares on the shuttle, it would be the infantry Marines who would be taking them down—alive, hopefully, but dead if it worked out that way.

The Raiders were still part of the mission. Just under eleven klicks away from the clandestine landing pad was a "wilderness" camp, one of many scattered throughout human space where camp-goers learned self-reliance and how to live off the land. These camps had become quite popular over the last 20 years among the more affluent worlds. This particular camp probably fit the pattern at one time. It had a more sinister purpose now, though, developed over the last year. The camp-goers were learning more martial skills. If the intel was correct, and Leif had no reason to doubt it, many of the "camp counselors" were former Marines who'd either quit or were kicked out when sides were drawn during the coup attempt.

No one knew if the camp-goers would react if the arms smuggler was seized, and the Raiders were to be a blocking force to *dissuade* them, with as much force as necessary, should they try to rescue the ship and weapons.

As the team waited to move out, Lerner hit herself six times in the chest. Never five times, never seven. Always six.

"You ready, Skate?" Leif asked her.

"Ooh-fucking rah, yeah, I'm ready!"

The latest join to the team, taking the place of the unlamented Ariel Fruhstuck, the sergeant had fit in well. Her enthusiasm was contagious.

"How about it, Fort?" she bellowed across the room. "You ready to show these boys how to kick ass?"

The qiincer gave her a double thumbs up. For a qiincer, that was downright sociable.

"Let me check you," Leif said, pulling Lerner around. She slightly bounced from one foot to the other, stretching her neck from side to side as Leif pulled and tugged on her battle rattle to see if any of it was loose. Loose gear could make a noise at the worst possible moment.

"All good," he said. "Now check me."

She was a little rougher on his as she went down the checklist, but a moment later, she pounded him on his back. They were ready.

"Five minutes," the gunny said just as the hatch was thrown open and Silva barged in, dangling a struggling tokit from one meaty hand.

"What the hell, Puff?" the gunny asked. "We don't have time for your ball-jacking around."

"I caught this tokit sneaking around when I was coming back from the head," Silva said, putting him down, but keeping a firm grasp of his collar.

That caught the attention of the rest of the team. It was taken as fact that the body of civilian workers allowed on the base was rife with Novack spies, eyes that sought out information and kept an eye on Marine and MP movements.

"What were you doing outside the hatch?" Captain Dubois demanded, kneeling in front of the tokit so their eyes were level.

The tokit looked around fearfully at the Marines looming over him, his mouth gaping, but not making a sound.

"I asked you a question," the captain said, steel in his voice. "What the fuck were you doing?

The tokit, still in Silva's grasp, looked around the room, then raised a shaky hand to point at Leif.

"Him!" he squeaked out.

What?

Leif took a half-step back in surprise.

The captain looked up at Leif, then back at the tokit. "What about Sergeant Hope Hollow?"

Yeah, what about me?

The tokit reached under his shirt, and six Marines immediately pulled up their weapons. Silva reached forward, pinning the guy's hand inside his shirt.

"Freeze," he yelled, eliciting a squeak from his prisoner.

"It's for Sergeant a'Hope Hollow," the tokit said, eyes round in fright.

Captain Dubois lowered his M-123, then reached inside the tokit's shirt, withdrawing a small, wrapped package with Leif's name written on it, just like the others that had been left for him over the last three weeks. The captain took it, shook the package, then shrugged. He looked to Leif who nodded and tossed it to him.

Leif pulled open the top, catching sight of a familiar logo. He had no idea how the tokit, on Sunrise, had managed to score a bag of *Otypisus* chips.

Greens. Not the reds, but still, I haven't had Otypisus in years.

"It's a snack food, from Home," he told the others.

He pulled the bag out from the wrapping, and something else fell out to clunk on the floor. Leif bent over and picked up the small copper-looking oval attached to a thong. About 15 millimeters long, it had a stylized image of a female tokit's face, crossed lightning bolts behind her.

"What's this?" he asked.

"The *Nonnana*," the tokit said. "For luck. To protect you."

Leif was only tangentially aware of tokit religion and mythology. They had one central belief that was embraced by seemingly the entire race, and "Nonnana" was something like a goddess. She wasn't quite the Mother of the wyntonans, the Progenitor, God, or any of the other mono-deities of the humans. One of many, the best Leif could recall, like the wyntonan gods of old or the human Hindu pantheon of deities.

"Why are you giving me this?" Leif asked the tokit, stepping forward. "And why all the other packages?"

"We have *thynot* to you," the tokit said, calming down.

Leif had no idea what "*thynot*" meant, and he looked around in confusion.

"That's their honor debt," Fort said.

"Why do you have this . . . *thynot*," Leif asked, his tongue tripping over itself as he mangled the word.

The tokit smiled and shrugged, a very wyntonan (and human) gesture.

Leif knew he was popular among the tokits back at Iwo, both for his role with 2/4 in rescuing hundreds of tokits from slavers, and later after his role in the attempted coup. He'd often have to pose with them for holosnaps when out in the ville. But the idea that this went beyond the units involved, that it could follow *him* out to Sunrise, was mind-boggling, to say the least.

"Skipper, we need to go," Gunny Dream Bear said.

The captain looked deep into the tokit's eyes for a long moment, then turned to Leif and asked, "What do you want us to do with him?"

Me? This is my choice?

The tokit was staring at him, but no longer afraid. He was calm, as if he knew what Leif would say. If this was some sort of con, if this was part of some diabolical plan, then tokits on both Iwo and Praxis were playing an extremely long game.

Leif opened the bag of Otypisus chips, removed one, and ate it. It sure seemed like a real chip, and he wasn't gagging out his life while some fast-acting poison killed him.

"Let him go," Leif said, sure of himself.

Silva looked at the captain who nodded and let go of the tokit, who bowed several times, trying to target each of them, before he stepped out of the hatch and disappeared.

"I never got his name," Leif said as he slipped the thong and good luck medal over his head.

Chapter 17

There was a whisper of displaced air over the team and a distortion, like heat waves over desert sand. The smuggler was coming in for its landing.

Leif knew that ships could "bend" light around them to hide from sight, but seeing it—or *not* seeing it, more accurately—was impressive. He hadn't realized that so much tech, cost, and effort went into smuggling. This wasn't like the holovids, where smugglers were generally portrayed as dashing, semi-good guys, just trying to avoid excessive tariffs and other taxes. Dual-purpose ships that could traverse space and land on a planet were inefficient. Add the stealth modes and the high cost for getting caught, and only the most valuable or illegal goods were smuggled in this surreptitiously, avoiding customs and law enforcement.

Second Battalion, Fourteenth Marines were already lying in wait around the LZ, ready to pounce once the ship landed. Two Navy Lancer fighters were on standby at the base, ready to move as well to help convince the smuggler to stand down once the Marines made their move. As a backup, no fewer than six Shrike anti-air teams were ready to bring down the ship if it tried to flee. The smuggler didn't even have to land for them to spring into action. Even if the pilot smelled a trap, the ship was already within range of the shoulder-launched missiles.

Charlie Company had set up a simple blocking position, an L-shaped ambush, along the road between the militia training camp and the LZ. If the campers decided to react, they'd be heading into a kill zone. Defensive postures like this were not the Raider forte, but they were Marines first and foremost. This was like breathing to them.

Leif looked down his PDF, his Principle Direction of Fire. He'd traded his trusty Stahlmont for a basic M-58 MAW, Medium Automatic Weapon. The canister-fed weapon could put out 660 rounds-per-minute, and he was positioned to pour enfilade fire along the advancing Novacks.

If they were smart, they'd stay buttoned up at their camp. But humans, for being so successful, often showed a surprising propensity for doing stupid things. Silva gave them a 70/30 shot to try and come to the rescue. Leif thought that was about right, but Silva wanted to put money on it, so they'd bet ten BC, Silva saying they'd come running, Leif that they'd be smart and stay put.

One of the options had been for the Raiders to launch an assault on the camp simultaneous to the seizure of the smuggler's ship to pin them there, which would have been the choice of most of them, but Colonel Tähevӓli wanted to limit the operations moving parts. The objective was the ship, not a bunch of wannabes out playing soldier in the woods.

"The target has landed and is shutting down," Major Quinlan passed on the company net. "The Lancers are scrambling, and two-fourteen is closing in. Let's see if the militia wants to play."

Leif looked over and caught the eye of Silva, eight meters to his right. The staff sergeant, a huge smile breaking the camo pattern on his face, gave him a thumbs up.

With the ship's power-eating engines shut down, Golf Company would initiate the assault. This was the key action in the mission. While no one knew the make and model of the smuggler, most ships needed time for the engines to come back online. The Marines of Golf Company needed that time to spring the trap and capture the ship. The trucks lined up to pick up the cargo could flee, of course, but Fox Company was positioned to pick them up.

Leif started a timer on his Battle-I. Golf Company had been given six minutes to secure the LZ and capture the ship. The burning question was if the smuggler would still be there.

The Navy Lancers were slower in an atmosphere, but they'd be over the LZ in eight minutes. If the smuggler ship took off before Golf could capture it, and if their Shrike gunners didn't bring it down, the Lancers would make sure it didn't leave the planet's atmosphere. One way or the other, those weapons were not going to make it into the insurgent's hands.

Leif checked the swing of his MAW. He'd already checked it a dozen times over the last thirty minutes, and no tree or other obstacle had popped up in the meantime to block its movement, but he was getting antsy. The waiting was the hard part. His musapha stirred as if it was waking from a long slumber.

Calm down, Leefen. If they come, they come, and stressing out isn't going to make any difference except screw you up.

He settled in to wait, taking timed breaths to slow his heartbeat.

He was almost surprised when Major Quinlan said, "Golf is in the LZ. There's no resistance from the Novacks."

That was a little surprising. No one expected the truckers to put up much of a fight, but there had to be soldiers there for security there, too.

Leif looked over at Silva who held up seven fingers, then three, then pointing at Leif and holding up ten. He was holding firm on his bet, and he was digging it in. He was probably right, but Leif couldn't let him trash-talk (trash-gesture?) like that. He flashed ten fingers, closed his hands, then flashed another ten. Silva smiled and nodded, accepting the doubling of the bet . . .

. . . which Leif lost less than two minutes later. Navy orbital surveillance, Marine drones, and the IIA's asset inside the camp revealed that the "campers" were grabbing weapons and scrambling for their vehicles.

"We are live," the major passed. "We know what to do."

Leif couldn't help it—he checked the swing of his MAW yet again as he felt the familiar surge of excitement flow through him. His mistress shot forth a questing tendril, but he pushed her back down. He wouldn't be needing her for this fight.

The camp was less than two klicks down the road, and in the distance, Leif heard the growl of a fossil fuel internal combustion engine. It wouldn't take them long to reach the ambush. Microdrones tracked the makeshift convoy as it approached.

"Rocket, you are cleared to fire," the major passed.

Gunnery Sergeant Julia Winnimuka, First Platoon's Team 3 designated sniper, was 400 meters to Leif's left, at the base leg of the L. Armed with an old bolt action .50 caliber slug-thrower, her mission was to take out the lead vehicle. Leif started squeezing and releasing his MAW's pistol grip as he waited for her to take the shot.

The first vehicle crested the far hill, 743 meters from the base of the ambush. It was a Dowd Summit, a locally manufactured SUV. An insurgent sat half-out of the front passenger window, his legs inside the cab, as he brandished a modular weapon. Dust plumed behind the Summit as it raced down the slope. Two more vehicles, then another three followed. Six vehicles. Four or five in each one. Maybe 30 insurgents, to face 138 Raiders. It was possible, even probable, that more were coming, but that was all that were racing toward them at the moment.

At 300 meters, when the lead elements had already passed Leif's position, a single shot rang out. Leif could hear the clunk as the big round tore through the engine block, and the Summit swerved to the side, crashing into the raised berm.

"Drop your weapons and come to a halt," the major shouted through his amplifier. "We are Imperial Marines, and we've got you surrounded."

Not exactly true, but with them in a depressed kill zone, they might as well be surrounded.

Four of the vehicles started to slow down, but the second in line sped up, trying to bypass the stricken Summit. A moment later, another single shot rang out, the second vehicle stopped dead.

Now was the moment of truth. The campers wouldn't know how many Marines they were facing. If they thought it was just a squad, they might try to fight. The major had taken that into consideration.

Their ROE was to attempt to stop the reinforcements, first by a show of force and a demand to halt. These were still imperial citizens, despite their hatred of the empire, and no one wanted to encourage more people to join a resistance movement. So, the warning shots were given, and the major asked them to surrender.

To make the demand a little more convincing, Second Platoon rose up as one, revealing their position. This was a thorn in the craw to the Raiders. The idea was to remain in defilade and neutralize any threat, not exposing themselves to fire.

Leif thumbed off the safety as a couple pairs of hands were thrust out of various windows.

"Come out of the vehicles," the major ordered. "Slowly."

One-by-one, four, then five doors opened, and bodies started coming out. Some went right to their faces in the road while others stood still, hands raised above their heads. The doors of the second-to-last vehicle, a bright red Dowd Alpine with bright yellow and orange flames painted along the bottom, remained closed.

"In the Alpine, show us your hands and then get out!" the major said.

Leif shifted his aim to the Alpine, but surrendering insurgents were in his field of fire, effectively blocking him.

Finally, two of the windows opened, but instead of hands, two barrels appeared, spraying fire as Second Platoon Marines hit the deck. Leif had no shot. If he'd fired, he'd hit the surrendering Novacks.

Second Platoon sure had clear fields of fire, however. From their bellies 30-60 meters away, they poured concentrated fire onto the Alpine. The fancy paint job disintegrated under the withering barrage, and the vehicle lurched downward as the tires were blown away.

Surrendering Novacks dropped to the deck, hugging it in an attempt to get small.

"Cease fire, cease fire," the major passed over the amplifier. "All Novack combatants, do not move a muscle if you want to live to see another day. Comply with all orders."

Second Platoon's four teams, 32 strong, got back to their feet and made their way into the kill zone while First and Third Platoons provided cover, waiting for the slightest twitch from the Novacks. With a smoking wreck of an Alpine as a reminder of the futility of resistance, the prisoners were extremely compliant as the Raiders zip-tied their hands behind their backs before dragging each one to the sitting position.

The smuggler ship was declared secure before all the Novacks were zip-tied. The Raiders captured 22 Novacks, the battalion another 31. Not one Marine had been wounded. The big question in everyone's mind was if there were a sassares aboard the smuggler. If there was, that wasn't being passed over the net.

Leif was still full of nervous energy. He hadn't fired his MAW, so it had had no outlet. Once the final Novack was secured, he and the rest of First started to move forward to take a blocking position across the road. With more than a hundred Novacks at the camp, the 22 prisoners and four dead were barely a fourth of the camp. Until the ship and its cargo were taken back to NAB, the Raiders needed to make sure the Novacks in the camp stayed there. The two Lancers that buzzed the camp low and slow were pretty decent exclamation points to that end.

"Twenty BC, Leif," Silva said as he came up alongside of him. "Twenty sweet BC."

"What about the rest of them. They coming?" Leif asked in a sour tone.

"Them. Nah. Too scared."

"I say they'll come. Double or nothing," Leif blurted out.

"Double or nothing? You're on."

Leif had hoped the Silva would have said the rest of the Novacks would come so he could bet the opposite. He didn't think the remaining Novacks would stick their noses outside of the camp, but there was no way he was going to let Silva take 20 BC from him without a fight.

Chapter 18

"Look at her face," Sergeant Lerner said, launching a wadded-up napkin that passed through the image, momentarily making it flicker. "She's pissed that she has to slum it with the Marines and explain why there wasn't a sassares on the smugglers' ship."

The operation hotwash was being held at the temporary CP, but with close to 1800 Marines and sailors, most of the 75% that were not on post were watching back in their quarters, with only the officers and senior staff there in person.

Lerner was right, though. Special Agent Tambor did not look happy. She'd been so sure that there were sassares on the ship, and she didn't strike Leif as the kind of human who could take being wrong so publicly.

There wasn't a sassares, but there had been a nyx, one of the second-tier races within the Hegemony (only one race was first tier: the sassares themselves). The nyx rarely ventured into imperial space, and given their subservient position to the sassares, Leif thought her presence was telling enough.

They'd never find out anything from the nyx, however. She committed suicide as the Marines boarded the smuggler. The humans meeting the contraband cargo and two alindamirs on the ship were being held by the MPs on base while imperial interrogators were finding out what they knew. Maybe the IITs already had what they needed. A full day had passed since the seizure, and whatever they found would almost certainly never make it down the chain to the teams. They had no "need to know."

The cargo aboard the ship had proven to be interesting, far more so than Special Agent Tambor's obvious attempt to cover her ass. Leif had helped unload some of it off the trucks and into a warehouse. Some were common weaponry found throughout the empire, the Hegemony, and even the far-off Leera Ascendency. Other containers were packed with equipment whose functions were not so obvious. And that was a puzzle. If the equipment was valuable enough to attempt to smuggle it in, then what was it?

None of the Marines in the battalion were qualified to examine the equipment, so engineers from Mbangwa Station were due down any time now to figure out just what they were. If they were weapons of some sort, then the Marines needed to be aware of their capabilities, and so that, at least, should be promulgated downhill to the rank and file.

"How much longer is this going to be?" Silva asked.

"We haven't even gotten to the Ops O yet," Gunny Dream Bear said. "We're here for the long haul. Just be glad we're not at the CP."

"Amen to that," Garamundi said, scratching his crotch.

As was normal for her when they were in their team hut, she'd stripped off her utility trousers and was down to her skin-tights. Not Marine-issued skin-tights. The polymem shorts were lavender with bright orange and black butterflies. Non-reg, but no one cared.

"Are they going to at least hold chow for us?" Silva asked.

Gunny rolled his eyes and said, "Every swinging dick is at the CP or watching the holocast. They're not going to throw out all the chow if we go long."

"So, they're holding it?" Silva asked.

Leif threw his empty Otypisus bag at his friend, bouncing it off his head. At least he'd been able to snack. He'd offered the others the chips that the tokit had left for him, but evidently, they didn't tickle human palates. He didn't care—all the more from him.

"What did the gunny just say, Puff?" Leif asked him.

Alarms blared, cutting off his reply. The team jumped up, scrambling to get dressed. Above the holopad, the image of Special Agent Tambor froze, a confused look on her face.

"Condition One-Alpha, Condition One-Alpha," the alarm blared.

The base was under attack.

Chapter 19

Leif and the rest of the Marines donned their battle rattle on the run as they bolted out of their barracks and to their positions while their Battle-Is crackled with orders. Smoke rose from the East Gate, and fire resonated throughout the camp.

Silva and Leif jumped into the fighting hole alongside their post, a few rounds hitting near enough to them to splatter Silva with dirt. As they'd run, the two had been taking in the display on their Battle-Is, but now they had direct visuals. The East Gate was 200 meters to their right. They didn't have a clear view to the area directly in front of the gate, but the two could see the remains of three vehicles. Scattered farther out, three trucks were stopped, and dismounted troops were firing into the camp, trying to cover a handful who were running back for the cover of the city.

"Glad you could make it," Doc passed from the next fighting position where they'd been part of the 25% of the Marine force that had been left in their positions during the brief.

"We knew you could handle it," Silva said. "But as long as we're here, how about me and Leif taking out a few of those yo-yos."

Leif was already setting his elbows on the parapet, sighting in on the two trucks.

"If there're any left, you mean." Lerner already got herself two.

As if in response, there was another crack from the direction of Doc and Lerner's position, and the prone man Leif had been about to target went limp, his weapon falling from his fingers. More rounds hit the trucks as Marines manned their positions, and within a few moments, the last living Novacks were knocked out.

That didn't stop the incoming, however. Rounds were reaching the camp from the edge of Prestonville, some 1800 meters away. At that range, small arms were almost an afterthought, more of harassing fire than a grave threat. But the Novacks had more than just their rifles.

There was a flash from the second story of one of the buildings, followed by a whoosh and a smoke trail as a rocket corkscrewed into the base. Leif joined the other Marines in a barrage of fire that hit the building, blowing chunks of the wall away in clouds of dust. The rocket hit the fence and detonated, but the only result was a half-meter rip almost three meters from the ground.

"What happened down there?" Silva asked Doc.

"Those three hovers drove up to the gate. I don't know what the MP saw, but he passed an immediate alert and drew down on them when the first hover just blew up. I don't know if the others did, too, or if the first one took them out with it. The other trucks out there sped up, so we stopped them."

"What about the MP?"

"Gone with the blast," Doc said.

"Fuck. What a shit way to go," Silva said as he fired off a quick burst at the retreating fighters.

"Did his job, though," Leif passed.

The sharp crack of ionized air reached out to them from inside the city. A few moments later, a column of smoke started to form beyond the front line of buildings.

"Somebody just took a hit from Uncle Nasty. With the zapper, too."

"Uncle Nasty" was the nickname the Marines had given the guardian angel gun monitor in geosynchronous orbit 50,000 meters above the city. The gunship was manned by a six-person crew and had access to the wide array of Mbangwa Station's surveillance capabilities.

"Wonder what it was?" Leif asked. "Had to be something big for them to use the zapper instead of the firecicles."

The "zapper" was a hadron beam cannon, and a firesicle was the nickname for the stream of kinetic rounds shot from orbit, called that for the glowing fireshow they created due to heat of passage through the air.

"Whatever it was, it's dead now," Silva said. "You can't hide from Uncle Nasty."

Three quick explosions from deep within the base somewhere reached out to them.

"Sounds like 82's," Leif said. "I guess that's what caught the attention of our guardian angel."

The ubiquitous 82mm mortar was a mainstay for militia forces throughout the empire. Cheap and easy to use with a decent punch, the rounds could take 45 seconds to reach their target.

"They probably fired and scooted," Silva said. "They've got to know what we have upstairs."

"Probably. But that should still help keep their heads down," Leif said as he scoped the buildings for another target.

Ten seconds later, the sounds of three more explosions reached them. The Novack mortar team had stuck around for another salvo, and that might have been a fatal mistake on their part.

"On the other hand, maybe they didn't know," Silva said with a laugh. "Dumb shits."

A Torrington class gun monitor needed about 15 seconds to track and fire upon a position. If the unseen mortar position fired two salvos, then they'd just been on the receiving end of terawatts of a hadron beam, which wasn't the usual weapon of choice for ground support due to atmospheric dispersion, but it did provide for a quicker response than the kinetic weapons.

It was obvious to Leif that the Novack attack lacked a cohesive effort. The vehicle in front of the gate had probably been intended to blow up the gate and knock out the Marines around it, while the follow-on three trucks, filled with fighters, was going to hit the breach and establish a foothold. When the alert MP had stopped the vehicles, the first had detonated too far away from the gate to destroy it, and the three trucks, which were already in motion, didn't have anywhere to go and had been sitting ducks for the Marines.

Now, with the rest of the Marines, MPs and Seabees falling into their positions, the attacked broke down. Once the last fleeing fighter was cut down, the incoming fire from the city slackened. Five minutes later, a single Lancer buzzed the city, but it left back to Mbangwa without finding a worthy target.

There were still Novack out there in the fight, but the initial thrust had been crushed.

****

Leif fired another burst from his M-31, fifteen .40 cal magring rounds arching across to reach a three-story white building, blowing a hole in its facing wall.

"Did you get them?" Gunny Dream Bear asked.

"Not sure. Made them duck, though," Leif told him.

Leif patted the stock of his M-31. He loved his Stahlmont, and the MAW he'd used at the smuggler ambush had been a fun toy, but the M-31 he'd been given shortly after the initial assault was beaten back gave him a longer effective range—up to 2800 meters—and a much bigger bang for the buck. The .40 cal round was massive, and as a magring round, it had the velocity to punch through most armor. It was almost a shame to waste the rounds on personnel.

Almost.

The Novack attack on the camp hadn't been stopped, but neither had they breached the base perimeter. The combined force of 2/14, Charlie Company, and the Seabees, who had enthusiastically joined in the defense, was more than enough to keep the Novacks from crossing the wide-open spaces between the camp and the city. There just wasn't any cover for them, making the space a giant kill zone.

They weren't giving up, though. They kept up a slow but steady stream of small arms, mortar, and rocket fire. Uncle Nasty pounced on the rocket and mortar fire, so the Novacks couldn't sustain any single position for long without getting hit, but it was up to the snipers and HMG gunners to keep the small arms fire at bay. At almost 1800 meters beyond the fence, the first of the buildings was too far the Marines' personal arms to be overly effective against an individual or other point target. But that also meant the Novack fire was ineffective as well.

Still, as gunny had pointed out to the team, a seeing-eye round fired from two klicks away hurt just as much as a well-aimed round from two-hundred meters.

Leif wasn't a machine-gunner by trade, but all Raiders were cross-trained to fill multiple missions, and with the Charlie Company filling in alongside 2/14's rifle companies, each team had been issued an M-31 from the prepositioning stores. Leif got his team's HMG. It was actually a pretty sweet weapon, easy to aim and delivering a devastating kick at the target. He wasn't sure he'd hit anyone yet, but he was making them keep their heads down. And it was pure fun to fire.

Marines weren't supposed to admit that killing was fun, and it might not be the actual killing part that set Leif's blood pounding when he squeezed off a burst from the big gun, but . . .

For Marines, making big booms was better than sex . . . almost.

Leif fired off another burst just for the hell of it, taking off a corner of the same building. They'd just taken fire from the building 30 seconds before, and he was sure that any non-combatants who might have been in it were long gone by now, so, no harm, no foul.

"Did you see anything else?" Gunny asked.

"I thought I saw movement, Gunny."

Wyntonans were known for being poor liars, and the gunny harrumphed and said, "Yeah, I'm sure you did." He left it at that. It wasn't as if they were ever going to run out of rounds with all the stores in the camp.

Silva, sitting back in their position eating his MDRM, just snorted, his mouth full.

The Novack assault was turning into a big bunch of nothing. The MP at the gate was the only Imperial KIA. Another MP had been wounded, as had a Seabee who took a round in the foot a couple of hours before. None of the rounds that had impacted inside the camp had done major damage, and no one had been hit by them.

The Novacks, however, had at least 32 dead, and except for the atomized car bomber, their bodies still lay where they fell. There were undoubtedly more inside the city. At some point, they had to realize that they couldn't prevail, not unless they still had something up their sleeves.

****

Three hours later, the Marines found out what that was.

"What the fuck is that?" Silva asked, his head snapping up from where he'd been close to nodding off.

Leif unslung his Stahlmont so he could use his scope and glassed the edge of the city. He couldn't see anything, but the rumble sounded suspiciously like . . .

"I thought Intel said they didn't have armor," Leif said.

"They've got those old Anteaters," Silva reminded him.

"Yeah, old. And those are personnel carriers. That sounds like something bigger."

"Do you see anything yet?" Silva asked.

"All hands, be prepared for enemy armor," came over the net.

"See, what did I tell you?" Leif asked.

Gunny Dream Bear slid into their hole and edged to the front, glassing the city with his binos.

"There!" he shouted, pointing ahead and slightly to the right where Palmer Avenue dead-ended in the open area between the city and base.

Leif swung over his M-31 and saw, well, he didn't know quite what it was. It wasn't any known military armor, that was for sure. It had been some sort of construction equipment, that much he could tell. The construction-yellow paint that still showed through attested to that. But there had been massive amounts of added material to act as armor, enough to hide exactly what the original equipment was. A small white flag, looking like little more than a torn sheet, adorned the right front quarter of the vehicle, stuck on like an afterthought.

"I don't see a weapon on it," Leif said.

"Neither do I," the gunny added.

The . . . *thing* stopped for a moment, several puffs of black smoke rising up from behind it as it idled.

"What kind of engine does it have?" Silva asked.

"Biodeisel, probably," Leif answered. "Like that one truck back at their militia camp."

Home was still a somewhat backward planet in many aspects, and larger mining and construction vehicles were biodeisel where more modern power systems were not as efficient. Leif had been surprised to see such vehicles on a human world, but from the size of that thing, it may have been the most cost-effective and practical way to move the mass.

"No, shit! Will it explode if we hit it?" Silva asked.

"Burn, maybe, but not explode," Leif said, with a little uncertainty.

He didn't think it would explode, but he wasn't going to bet his paycheck on it.

"So, come on, buddy. Let's see if you go boom," Silva said.

Without a visible weapon, the ROE kept the Marines from firing. Just sitting there, it was not a proven threat. Leif knew that a hundred weapons were trained on it at the moment, however, waiting for a reason to engage it.

With another puff of black smoke, the vehicle lurched into motion, crossing into the open area. Leif's finger tightened on his M-31, taking in the slight slack in the trigger.

"All hands, all hands, hold your fire," came over the net.

"Shit," Silva muttered.

"It does have that white flag, and we don't have any incoming from the dipshits in the city," the gunny said. "Maybe someone wants to talk."

Leif hadn't noticed that the sporadic harassment had died off, but he didn't give that much weight. There were other ways to talk aside from coming up in some frankentank. He edged off the trigger, however, waiting to see what came up. Not that he thought his M-31 would have any impact on the thing. Armor-piercing or not, his .40 cal rounds would have a difficult time getting through that mass of metal.

At least Uncle Nasty is our guardian angel. He'll have this thing targeted.

The vehicle slowly rumbled forward, and Leif could see the ruts the twelve wheels created under the huge weight of the thing. More smoke puffed out as the engine, designed for something not nearly so massive, struggled to move it.

"We've got company," Silva said. "At the edge of the city."

Leif tore his gaze away from the beast approaching. Silva was right. At least fifty fighters on benny bikes, APV, and line hovers appeared between the buildings and stopped to watch.

"Gunny, are we cleared?" Leif asked. "They're armed."

"Wait one," the gunny said, then a few moments later added, "That's a negative. As long as their weapons are slung, we need to see what's happening here."

Leif picked up his Stahlmont again, and using its better scope, checked a couple dozen of the newcomers. Each one had weapons holstered or slung. He didn't like it, but he put them out of his mind and focused back on the vehicle.

The thing had covered about 500 meters, and with his Stahlmont scope, Leif was able to pick out more details. It was obvious that this was a hasty modification without regard to niceties. Pieces of metal and ceramics were applied in a hodgepodge fashion with bulk seemingly the main intent. He tried to spot what could be a gunport, but there was nothing, only a small slit about halfway up, right about where a . . .

"I can see a driver's slit," Leif said as he realized what it was. "Just to the left of the hunk of yellowish ceramic halfway up."

He couldn't tell if it was an open slit or if there was some bulletproof glass in there, but there certainly weren't centimeters of armor plating. If it came to it, that was going to be his target.

"Really?" the gunny asked. "Yeah, I see it. Let me send that up."

"Others have spotted it, too, and it's being promulgated now," he said twenty seconds later.

Leif checked his Battle-I, and sure enough, the slit was now highlighted as a potential area of vulnerability.

"Vehicle approaching NSB Sunrise, come to frequency one-oh-one-point-five and state your purpose here," a voice blasted out over the camp PA system as the thing reached 500 meters out.

The thing kept up its slow approach.

"Vehicle approaching, we cannot understand your broadcast. Come to a halt and do not approach any closer."

It chugged along.

Leif dropped his Stahlmont and brought his M-31 to bear on the target, ready to let loose.

"If you continue, you will be taken under fire. Halt!" the voice almost shouted.

Finally, the vehicle slowed to a halt, a little over 300 meters out. It sat there idling. No one came out.

"What the hell's happening? Just drop the fucker," Silva said. "They're up to no good. I can feel it in my God-loving bones."

Leif's mistress stirred. She felt it too.

Two MPs left the East Gate and started out to meet the vehicle, their own weapons slung.

Pretty ballsy of them, Leif had to admit.

He was feeling uneasy, sure that the shit was going down. If the Novacks wanted to talk, there were better ways to do this.

When the MPs were 100 meters out, the vehicle gave a lurch forward, black smoke puffing up as the engine strained.

"Halt, or you will be taken under fire!" the voice shouted over the PA again.

If anything, the vehicle sped up. The two MPs stopped, then turned and started sprinting back to the gate. Almost immediately, the mass of fighters still in the city started pouring forth, zipping on their assorted bikes and ATVs in a confusing mass as supporting fires reached out from the city.

"Weapons free. Focus on the fighters and leave the vehicle to Uncle Nasty," came over the company net.

Leif swung his M-31 and started engaging. Smoke rose up, this time shot from grenadiers hidden within the buildings, obstructing the Marines' views. Leif didn't stop firing. He had almost unlimited ammo, so he poured rounds into the smoke, along his final protective fire PDF, knowing that Staff Sergeant Ted Yellow Bird, Third Team's HMG gunner would be doing the same, and combined, their fire would form a wall of lead.

He caught the light of a firesicle from the corner of his eye as the monitor opened up, and he smiled, knowing the vehicle was toast, but the firesicle was too short, only a few rounds.

While still firing, he risked a glance. The vehicle was still advancing, and the monitor wasn't firing.

"All hands, we've lost comms with the monitor. Missilemen and HGM gunners, shift fire to approaching vehicle," came over the ops net.

Leif shifted fire, aiming at the slit in the front. Several Taipan and Dagger missiles flew out, impacting right on target. Any single one should have been enough, and pieces of armor broke off, but the vehicle kept advancing, heading right to East Gate. Leif could see his tracers reach out to the front, impacting all around the slit, but he couldn't tell if any rounds were making it inside. A hypervelocity Dagger hit high and ricocheted up and over it, flying out over the city.

"Stop that sucker," Silva yelled at Leif.

"I'm trying!" Leif yelled back as he slammed home another belt and fired.

Fire enough, and one of the rounds would have to find its way through.

"Stop!" Gunny said, putting his hand on top of Leif's M-31.

"What?" Leif said, his heart pounding with adrenaline.

"Look!" the gunny said, pointing.

A Marine was outside the wire, running and dodging. Leif has seen moves like that before on the televised pitchball fields. There was no mistaking it. Private First Class Hexter Bon-Kingury was single-handedly charging the vehicle.

"Shift your fire," someone shouted over the tac net. "And cover that Marine!"

Rounds started kicking up around Bon-Kingury as the Novack fighters spotted him, but the same smoke that obscured the Marines' vision had the same effect on theirs. Still, that was a lot of incoming, and Leif twisted his HMG to pour fire into the fighters, who had seemed to double in number.

"Go you bastard!" Doc yelled at Bon-Kingury in excitement from the next fighting position.

Leif kept up a steady stream of fire, but he kept glancing to his friend, expecting to see him cut down as he ran forward. There were just too many rounds aimed his way. But with his patented final burst of speed, he vaulted up onto the front of the big vehicle as it closed to within 150 meters. Now shielded from the Novacks by their own vehicle, he started to make his way to the slit when a burst of rounds hit near him, making him pull back. Rounds fired from the camp by some overly excited Imperial.

"Cease fire on the truck!" someone passed over the net.

Bon-Kingury waved back to the camp, then started forward again. Leif didn't know what kind of visibility whoever was driving the vehicle had, but he doubted it was very good. They probably didn't know that the Marine was on top of them.

"Come on, Ball," Leif urged him on.

Another burst hit the front of the vehicle, eliciting a chorus of yelled and passed "Cease fires."

"You fucking idiots. He's on our side!" Silva shouted.

The PFC reached the slit, bent over and took a look inside. He immediately snapped back out of the way, hugging the body of the vehicle. He looked over to where the Raiders were positioned, gave a thumbs up, then reached into his battle vest and pulled out two small objects.

"He's going to burn them out," the gunny said.

Leif was still keeping up his fire, but he had to watch as Bon-Kingury popped the release on the two grenades, bent over, and rolled them into the slit. He pulled back, then waited a terribly long five seconds that seemed to stretch out for hours before the grenades detonated, the light of a thousand stars bursting from the slit of the vehicle. At 4000 degrees C, nothing could withstand the heat, not even rhenium latticed armor or halfnium carbide plates. The M-166 grenades wouldn't burn for long, but they'd burn long enough to do some damage.

"Get some, Ball!" Leif shouted.

PFC Bon-Kingury gave another thumbs up to the Raiders and started to jump off the vehicle when another burst from inside the camp cut him down mid-jump, his finely tuned body sprawling awkwardly as it fell to a heap on the ground.

"Shit!" or "fuck!" a hundred voices rang out.

"You fucking idiots!" Silva shouted, standing and looking over to the north from where the fire had originated. "Couldn't you see him?"

"Get down, Puff!" the gunny said, pulling on the sergeant. "We've still got targets."

Anger filled Leif. He'd lost friends before, but not like this. For Bon-Kingury, perhaps the most capable Marine he'd ever met, to get cut down by friendly fire filled him with rage. His mistress boiled forth, and he was barely able to restrain her from making him run to find out who had shot his friend. It took a huge effort of will to turn the rage to the Novacks, the ones who had used a white flag as a ruse.

His anger grew laser-focused, and he poured .40 caliber fire out over what was now a killing zone. The Novacks didn't lack courage. They kept coming, hoping their speed and numbers would overcome the Marines. Leif wasted no respect for the enemy. If they kept coming, he was more than happy to kill them. As the smoke drifted away, he began to become more selective, aiming instead of just spraying.

Until there were no more targets on the ground, and he shifted to the buildings.

"That's enough, Leif," Gunny finally said, putting his hand on Leif's shoulder. "That's enough."

Leif started to pull away, his mistress still part of him, but the gunny's hand was firm, and that penetrated. He took a deep breath, then pushed his mistress back down. Out across the killing field, bodies, bikes, and ATVs littered the ground. He turned to his right. The Novack vehicle had slowed to a stop, probably another 20 meters beyond the crumbled body of Bon-Kingbury.

"Is he . . . ?" he asked Gunny Dream Bear.

The PFC was not in First Platoon, so Leif didn't have bios on him in his Battle-I. Neither did the gunny, but the gunny could ask Captain Yelz or Master Sergeant Lin. The gunny just shook his head.

Down in front of the East Gate the bodies of the two MPs lay. They'd been cut down before they could reach safety. Along the defensive positions, Leif could see a few corpsmen moving. More Marines had been wounded or killed. And for what?

The Novacks had to know they'd had no chance. Even with the monitor out of the picture, and Leif was sure that was no coincidence even if he didn't know how the Novacks could manage that, just the imperial ground forces could turn back an attack ten times the size of the one that just occurred.

None of this made any sense. The Novacks couldn't be that stupid. Something else was going on here, something bigger.

But as a sergeant of Marines, that wasn't his concern. Give him an enemy, and he'll kill him. It was that simple. It was just that now, he had more of a desire to crush each and every Novack who dared to raise a hand against his fellow Marines.

Chapter 20

"You got everything you need?" First Sergeant Timiko asked the four of them in the makeshift OP they'd erected.

"A regiment of grunts would be good," Silva said. "Other than that, we're good."

"The rest of 14th Marines will be here soon," the First Sergeant said. "They've embarked, just waiting for the word to go."

"What's the hold-up?"

"The hold-up is trying to figure out what the hell just happened. Sixteen coordinated attacks on Marine, Navy, and militia positions? And no one, not the IIA, not NIA, knew what was coming?"

Leif had been wondering much the same over the last day. Within a single hour, 16 different attacks had taken place on former Fremont, Jin Long, and Parker worlds. All had been beaten back except for the one on Camp Ikitu on Banderling, home to the Third Maintenance Battalion, Fourth Marine Division. The 3,000-plus Marines on Camp Ikitu had been overrun. There was no word on survivors.

Prior to eleven of the attacks, there had been a seizure of smuggled weapons. Each smuggling attempt had been anonymously reported, and each had been successfully thwarted by Marine or militia units.

One such smuggling attempt was to be suspected. Two could be a coincidence. But eleven? Didn't that raise some alarms?

Leif didn't believe in coincidences. Like how the comms with the monitor had failed just at the Novack truck was about to ram the gate. The monitor was back online now, with no clue as to what happened. Coincidence? Leif knew it wasn't. All of these were connected, and to him, it reeked of foreign influence. He was no fan of Special Agent Tambor, but he thought she was right. Given their support to the initial coup attempt, even as lukewarm as it had seemed, he'd bet an ibent steak dinner that the sassares had their fingers in this as well.

Not that anyone was asking him. He was just a dumb grunt, staring out through the fenceline, waiting for another Novack to do something stupid enough to rate a couple of bursts from his HMG.

Chapter 21

"Any word on the Patrases?" Leif asked Gunny Xan.

"Still working on them. The squid engineers don't know squat about tanks."

"It would be nice to have the big beasts rolling up and down the wire," Gunny Dream Bear said.

It was somewhat ironic that the Marines were depending on Navy engineers to try and get the six M-66 Patras heavy tanks online. FNB Sunrise was more than a simple logistics base. It also served as a prepositioning center, one large enough that sometimes things got lost in the shuffle. The six tanks, all "B" models some 30 years old, had been packed away, ready to be broken out in time of need.

For the Marines and MPs, now was that time of need, especially if the Novacks had another of their makeshift beasts, but the tanks couldn't just be fired up and rolled out. They had to be brought back online. The big problem with that was the tanks were so old that much of what was needed was so out-of-date that it wasn't readily available.

Three systems engineers from Mbangwa Station braved the insurgents' missiles, riding a gig in on a death spiral, to see what they could do to get the tanks up and running. Two days later, the Marines were still waiting.

Not that the fight had progressed much over the last week. The Novacks probed, and the Marines pushed back, never at risk of letting the insurgents gain a foothold since that first breach during the initial attack.

None of this made sense to Leif. The Novack rebels knew that the Navy was firmly in imperial hands, and that the monitors could rain down a fiery hell upon them if they made another move. Except for the attack on Camp Ikitu, not one of them had succeeded, and the entire Marine Corps was ready to clean up the rebels once and for all as soon as they were given the imperial OK.

Rumors were rife, but no one knew what the rebels' endgame was. Their uprising had been crushed, so now what were they going to do?

And when was the emperor going to unleash his hounds?

Sure, the rebels were still technically imperial citizens, and yes, with the Novacks on Sunrise, at least, they showed no signs of being willing to surrender. Digging them out would take at least a Marine regiment, maybe upwards of a division, and there would be collateral damage. But this was the Fremonts'—and the Jin Longs' and Parkers'—second time in a year. There had to be consequences for that.

A chatter of automatic weapons fire reached the OP, and five heads swiveled in that direction. The MPs were getting hit again. Seven of them had been killed over the last week, to go along with one 2/14 Marine. The rebels didn't seem willing to commit to another all-out assault, but they sure seemed to want to remind the imperial forces that they were still out there.

The rebel weapon fired once, twice, three times. Normally, the rebels would fire a mortar or automatic weapon, then displace before Uncle Nasty could react. They'd learned that lesson quickly.

A ship could fire energy weapons almost instantaneously, but those weapons were designed for the vacuum of space. In an atmosphere, the beams were absorbed and dispersed over distance. That was why Navy ground support was heavily weighted to kinetic rounds. From tiny 300-grain anti-personnel inerts to the huge 3,000 kg HE rounds, a Navy monitor, manned by only a crew of six, could mess up an enemy's day.

The downside was the lag from acquiring a target to the rounds on deck. In this case, nineteen seconds.

When the rebel machine gun started its third burst of fire, all five Marines stopped to watch.

"You don't think . . ." Silva started to say before trailing off.

The MPs returned fire, and the rebel gun fired yet another long burst.

Leif looked up in the sky, for once willing an enemy to fire again. It did—or at least half of a burst which was cut off when firecicles lit up the sky as they slammed into the ground, just out of sight of the Raider OP.

"Get some, Navy!" Silva shouted, lifting a hand to high five the others.

The wyntonans called it "The Mother's Rejects." The humans called it "Darwinian Selection." Whatever the term, the stupid of any race didn't live to pass on their stupidity genes.

Chapter 22

"Hey, Puff. You doing OK?" Leif asked Silva.

The staff sergeant frowned, then said, "I'm all right. I just must have eaten something bad today for breakfast."

"You don't look good. I mean, even for a troll."

Silva grimaced and gave Leif a half-hearted finger. At that moment, a mortar round landed 30 or 40 meters behind their position, and the staff sergeant didn't flinch. The mortars had been an every fifteen-minute occurrence for the last two weeks, but Leif calling his friend a troll would normally have resulted in some sort of "ghost" or "casper" comment back at him.

"I think I must have eaten it, too," Doc said, tapping her belly. "Feeling a little queasy myself."

"Like I keep telling you, put some Spice on it. It'll kill whatever germs get mixed up in the chow."

"Your fucking spice, the shit in the chow. I'll puke all the same," Doc said with a laugh.

"Don't talk about chow," Skate said. "As soon as we get back to Iwo, I'm heading to Champs and getting me a double bacon and swiss burger so big, so juicy . . ." she said, miming bringing the burger to her mouth, then chomping it. She dramatically ran her forearm over her mouth as if wiping away the juices.

Silva took that moment to heave, vomiting across their position.

"Fuck, Puff," Skate shouted, trying to kick off some of the vomit that had hit her leg.

He gave her a strange look, as if he didn't understand what happened before his eyes rolled back in his head and he collapsed, out cold.

Doc immediately sprang into action, lunging across the position to grab Silva, lay him down, then tilt his head so he wouldn't choke on his vomit. A split second later, he puked again. Leif tried not to gag as the acrid smell hit him.

Doc gave him a quick assessment, then said, "Hell, he's tachy. We need to get him to sickbay."

"I've got him," Leif said. "Let gunny know."

Silva wasn't tall, but he was a solid mass, and Leif was the strongest of the three.

"Tell Chief that he's got coffee-ground vomit," Doc said.

"Which means?" Skate asked, turning her leg over to get a better look at the splatters.

"Blood in the stomach, most likely," Doc said.

"From something bad at breakfast?" Skate asked.

"Probably not," Doc said. "They'll figure it out at sickbay."

Leif bent over, grabbed an arm, and then slung Silva over his shoulder in a fireman's carry.

"Keep your head down, Leif," Doc said as he stood and started out of their position.

They'd hardened the position, to include cover to get in and out of the back. The rebels did have snipers that took the occasional pot shot at anyone they spotted. Leif, being the tallest Marine, had to duck to keep his head below the cover.

Silva was easily 130 kg, but Leif had no problem carrying him the 300 or so meters to the battalion aid station. He stopped dead in his tracks as he reached it. At least fifteen Marines were on the ground in front of the station, two corpsmen attending to them.

One of them looked up, saw Leif then yelled back into sickbay, "Chief, we've got another one."

He pointed to an open spot on the ground and said, "Put him there."

"But he needs to be seen. And Doc Yeltsov said to tell you he's got coffee-ground puke."

"Look, sergeant, I'll get to him when I can. But we've got thirty-one—"

"Thirty-two," the other corpsman interrupted.

"Thirty-two. We've got thirty-two who've come in in the last hour. We're kinda slammed here. So, drop your buddy there, and we'll get to him."

Two more corpsmen came out of sickbay carrying a stretcher. The corpsman who'd been talking to Leif pointed to six who'd had their vitals taken. They looked at three of the readouts before rolling one onto their stretcher and taking her inside.

Leif wanted Silva to be checked now, but he was out of his element. He knelt and carefully placed his friend at the designated spot on the ground.

"Hang in there, you damned troll. They'll take care of you," he said quietly, giving the unconscious Marine's arm a pat. "See you back at the position."

Leif gave one last look around, then started to head back to Doc and Skate. As he was leaving, another Marine was stumbling up, slightly weaving as he walked. He gave Leif a look of anguish, then bent over to puke.

"You OK there, Corporal?" Leif asked.

Hell, Leefen, of course, he's not OK! He's puking his guts out.

The corporal held up a hand as he puked again. He straightened up, wiped his mouth, then said, "Not feeling at my best, but I'll be all right."

"Do you need any help?"

"No, I'll make it."

Leif watching the corporal stumble on. Thirty-two . . . no, the corporal made it thirty-three . . . Marines were down with some sort of bug. Out of 1,600 in the battalion and Charlie Company, 33 didn't seem like too many, but Leif had a sinking feeling in his stomach that this was only the tip of the iceberg.

Chapter 23

Twenty-four hours later, the iceberg had crashed full onto the Marines. Not just the Marines, but the MPs, too. Fully half of both units were out of commission, and the beleaguered docs at the medical clinic, who had taken over for the battalion and regimental surgeons, were struggling to make heads of what was sweeping through the camp. They were streaming test results up to to the naval hospital on Mbangwa Station, but so far, there wasn't a diagnosis. All tests were negative.

Leif had a slight sore throat for a couple of hours, and he thought he was coming down with the mystery disease, but it passed. He was now on the vastly thinned line of defense, alone in the position he'd previously manned with Silva, Doc, and Lerner. Now, three Marines covered both positions: Leif, Forintik, and Lerner.

When people started dropping, the command initially suspected a bioweapon, and they expected a massive attack to take advantage of their depleted numbers. The only saving grace was that the probes and attacks had dwindled in frequency. Either the rebels were marshaling their forces for the final assault, or whatever was hitting the Marines and MPs was hitting them, too.

So far, only humans were falling sick, at least among the Marines. Leif didn't know what was going on throughout the rest of the base. All 18 non-human Raiders were among the Charlie Company's 57 combat-effectives.

Leif adjusted the mask on his face as he watched the monitor screens. He was sweating under the seal, and it itched something fierce. But all hands were required to wear them around the clock now. It was (water under the bridge) now for him, he thought. He'd carried Silva back to the battalion aid station, so, he'd been already exposed to whatever was striking Marines down.

Still, better safe than sorry.

Movement on one of the monitors caught his attention. It was from a scan down Murphy Boulevard, one of the main routes leading to the East Gate. Two humans, probably a man and a woman, marched down the center of the road, holding a sign. "Probably" because Leif couldn't tell for sure they were bundled up so much, masks and robes hiding their features.

The sign said, "Stop the murder now!"

What? We're not even doing anything.

He pushed the feed to the CP. The combat AIs were analyzing every feed, but his orders were to forward anything out of the ordinary. As good at the AIs were, Marines felt better with actual eyes overseeing them.

Leif watched the couple as they reached the intersection of Murphy and Ninth Ave. They stood silently, unmoving for a good three minutes before they turned around and walked off.

Chapter 24

Twenty-seven hours after he was stricken, Staff Sergeant Lars "Puff" Silva, Imperial Marines, died at the Naval Medical Clinic, NSB Sunrise.

Chapter 25

"I'm up," Leif passed to Forintik. "Get some rest."

"Roger that. Wake me in four hours, OK?"

"You can take longer if you need to. It's been quiet."

"Four is enough," the qiincer said before cutting the connection.

The two Marines were the only ones left from Second Team. Twenty-five Raiders in total were still healthy—the 18 non-humans and seven humans. Another forty-five wyntonan and qiincer Marines from 2/14 were untouched as well. Among the civilian workers, more than two thousand tokits and fewer numbers of alindimars and hissers, were back on the base, none showing signs of the disease. It was obvious by now that only humans were being affected by the bug. It could be a natural mutation of a known disease, but IIDCA, who had taken over from the naval hospital had yet to find a cause. Leif was betting that this was a bioweapon, but one that might have turned to bite the rebel hands that created it.

That didn't explain why the hospital was having problems identifying it. Anything the rebels could develop would be based on known science, and the Imperial Disease Control Agency should be able to determine what was the infecting agent and then assign a treatment.

Until then, Sunrise was under quarantine. No one was going to land on the planet or take off until they knew what they faced. The quarantine also affected communications. Leif didn't have time to go to the ISO and call home, but he didn't know how much of what was going on was public knowledge, and he wanted to let Soran know he was OK.

Leif now had more feeds to monitor, but it was relatively quiet beyond the wire. Two mortar rounds had landed inside the base a few hours ago, but they'd taken no other fire. Small numbers of people hurried to and fro in the city, all wearing various forms of biomasks or with their faces covered with scarves.

One of his feeds pinged, and Leif brought it to center. A lone tokit, in the blue overalls of public services, was sitting on a street cleaner, running it down Eighth Avenue, as if nothing was amiss. He reduced the feed back to its normal position. Leif doubted the tokit was a threat, but he tagged him for the other feeds to follow.

His stomach rumbled. With so many down sick, food services was interrupted, so they were down to MRDRs, emphasis on the "*Minimum*" Required Daily Rations. They did provide the calories, but taste was not a factor. Not even Granny Oriano's spice mix could save them. With a sigh, he unwrapped the blue bar and took a bite, ignoring that "blue" was the code for the evening ration, as now it was late morning. They all tasted like cardboard to him anyway.

Another of his feeds pinged, and he looked up, trying to swallow the bite of the MRDR. A human male, face uncovered, was marching directly at the East Gate. The man looked vaguely familiar, and Leif hit the face recognition.

"Dragon-CP, this is Post One-One-Three," he almost shouted as he pushed the feed to the battalion CP. "I've got Horatio Fremont walking up to the East Gate. I repeat, Horatio Fremont!"

"Post One-One-Three, did you say Horatio Fremont? As in *the* Horatio Fremont?" the voice asked, the disbelief obvious.

"I've just pushed it to you. What do you want me to do?"

"You . . . wait one," the voice said. Twenty seconds later, he came back on the net and said, "If he's coming to the gate, get him and restrain him. If he tries to back off, you are authorized to use lethal force to stop him. We're sending a team to your position."

"Roger that," Leif said, his blood starting to pound.

Horatio Fremont had been the heir apparent to the Fremont Clan. His theft of imperial funds and his attempted arrest had been the trigger for the attempted coup. He'd been among, if not the most, wanted criminal in the empire, and here he was, just walking up to the East Gate.'

"Forintik, sorry to wake you, but I need you to cover me."

"What . . .?" she asked.

"Check your twelve-alpha-six feed. That's the Fremont heir. Battalion wants me to collect him, and I need you to cover me."

There was a short pause, then, "That is him. What do you want me to do?"

Post 113 was twenty meters off the main gate, giving the Marines (now *Marine,* singular) inside good observation and fields of fire over both the gate and the Perimeter Road. Forintik was manning Post 115, fifty meters down Perimeter Road.

"I need you to go to Post One-One-Four. If Fremont tries anything, then you need to be in position to drop him. He's not to get away."

Meaning, if he takes me out, you take him out.

"Roger that. I'm on my way."

Leif watched the perimeter monitor, and a few moments later, Forintik emerged from the post, then hurried to Post 114. With her moving into position, he backed out of his own position, ducking down by habit to keep out of sight of any snipers.

If they're out there, I'm going to give them a big fat target.

Leif took a deep breath, then stood straight, exposing himself as he left the cover and marched over the East Gate. Usually, the gate would be manned by two MPs to oversee entries and exits. Post 113, which Leif was manning and was more easily defended, was now the de facto East Gate.

Horatio Fremont reached the gate before Leif did. He stood there, shifting his weight from one foot to the other, wringing his hands.

"You have to take me in," he shouted before Leif made it to the gate. "I demand medical treatment as a Prisoner of War under the Pretoria Accord."

Leif didn't say a word as he scanned the area beyond the fence. He didn't see anyone, but he could feel eyes on him. The buildings of the city were only 1800 meters away, so he was still within the extended range of any potential rebel with a weapon.

"Hey, I'm talking to you!" Fremont shouted.

Leif turned to focus on the man, then said, "And why should I let you in? You've led a rebellion against the empire."

"And you imps poisoned us like rats! We're dying," he said before bending over and going into a coughing fit.

Fremont's answer took him by surprise. *They* had poisoned the rebels?

"What makes you think we did any such thing?" Leif asked.

"Who else? Your fucking emperor isn't going to allow any dissent, even if he has to resort to genocide!"

"You think the emperor did this? You're high. You infected us, but it looks like you didn't control it well enough, and it got back to you. That's what happened."

"Bullshit! We did no such thing!"

"Sergeant, what the hell are you doing there? Quit arguing with the fucker and get him inside the fence. We've got a team on their way, ETA three minutes," a new voice came over his comms.

Leif lowered his Stahlmont to cover Fremont and said, "I'm going to open the personnel gate, and you're going to come through. If you run, I'll cut you down."

"You stupid fuck! I came to you! I need the antidote, and you have to give it to me. I'm not going to run."

Conscious of the CP watching him, he kept Fremont covered, then sidestepped to the personnel gate to the side of the main gate. It had already been coded to him, and he ordered it open, waving the rebel forward with the muzzle of his rifle. Fremont looked unsteady on his feet, but he walked through and onto the base proper.

"On your face, hands locked behind your head," Leif told him.

"Is this fucking necessary? I'm not going to do anything."

"I said, on your face," Leif ordered.

With a sigh, Fremont slowly got to his knees, then lowered himself to the ground. "Happy now, imp?"

"Let's keep it zipped," Leif said.

"I need medical treatment."

"I said, zipped!"

Leif did a quick scan outside the fence. Two people had appeared along the front line of buildings, and their attention focused on what was going on at the gate. Neither had any weapons that Leif could see.

Movement caught Leif's peripheral vision, and with his nerves taut, he jerked around, drawing down, but it was the three battalion Marines, two wyntonan and one human.

"Daya, Sergeant a'Hope Hollow," the wyntonan corporal said in Uzboss as they came up. "Honors."

"Daya"

"We'll take him now, Sergeant," the human staff sergeant said, his voice muffled by his biomask before turning to Fremont and saying, "You, stand up."

"He just told me to get down," Fremont muttered before he started to rise.

He got to his hands and knees and had to pause for a moment, dry heaving. The staff sergeant jumped back a couple of meters. The heaves stopped, and Fremont slowly got to his feet.

"Slaptie him, Gangon," the staff sergeant told the lance corporal, who stepped forward, pulled the unresisting Fremont's hands behind his back, and slapped on the restraint.

"Let's go," the staff sergeant ordered.

"I demand medical treatment," Fremont said. "I'm a Prisoner of War, and you're bound by the Pretoria Accord. You have to give me the antidote."

Leif watched them leave. They'd long figured that whatever was striking down the humans on the base was also hitting those in the city. Leif was sure this wasn't natural, that it was a hitherto unknown bioweapon, but that the rebels had been sloppy with it, accidentally infecting themselves. But Fremont accused the empire of unleashing it against them. He could be lying, of course, but Leif believed the human. Not that the empire was behind it, but that Fremont believed it.

If it wasn't the imperial forces, and it wasn't the rebels, then who was it?

He gave one last look out to the city as he started to turn to go back to his post, but then froze. The two people had grown to a couple of dozen, and more were arriving. Six or seven had already started to walk to the gate. Two people were carrying others in their arms, another was pulling a still body in a small cart.

Eyes had been on them the entire time, but not to take him under fire. They'd been watching to see what would happen to Fremont. And now they wanted in, they wanted an antidote that didn't exist.

"Dragon-CP, this is Post One-One-Three," he passed as he made sure the personnel gate was locked again. "I'm going to need a lot more help here."

Chapter 26

"Right here, sir," the alindamir communications tech said, pointing to the secure cubicle.

"Don't call me sir. I work for a living," Leif said by rote, barely hearing his words.

He was nervous, wondering what was going on and still in shock. He'd been told fifty-two minutes ago that he, Sergeant Leffen a'Hope Hollow, Imperial Marine Corps, was in command. That wasn't supposed to happen. It *never* happened. Until it did.

Every single human on the base save Private Lorenzo Jones, a rifleman in India Company, was down with the hammer, as they were calling the disease. Not all were incapacitated, at least 100 percent of the time. Captain Kelly-Soronson had been the one to tell Leif to get to the CP, for example, but by the time he got there, she was already half-conscious, raving about goats getting into the crops. A good percentage of the humans had lucid moments, but they didn't last long.

Leif sat down in the seat, looking at the almost featureless console in front of him. It was hard to believe that this simple piece of gear was the heart of secure communications across the breadth of the empire.

The alindamir petty officer leaned over his shoulder, her chest pressing his back, as she entered a string of code. He caught a whiff of the cinnamon-like smell common to the race. There weren't yet many alindamirs in the Marines, and none in the Raiders, so Leif had never been around many of them. They'd been in the Navy in small numbers, however, longer than wyntonans had been in the Corps, almost all taking technical positions in communications, navigation, nano-engineering, and propulsion.

"Please put this into your mouth," she said, as the console came to life.

Leif looked at the small, flat piece of plastic, shrugged, then did as she asked him. She pulled it out, then looked at the 2D screen.

"Access Denied. Unauthorized Clearance," blinked in red on the screen.

The petty officer muttered something in what sounded like one of the alindamir languages, then inputted another code. Her skin flashed from a light rose to a deeper maroon.

The message remained the same.

She pulled back, her hand to her throat as she subvocalized to whoever was on the other side. Leif stared at the blinking message. Of course, he didn't have clearance for this level of comms. He didn't belong here.

Why don't they just send in some officers? he wondered. *Put them in biosuits, to keep them from catching the hammer, and let them run things.*

The alindamir, Petty Officer 3 Hook, he saw from the nametag on her chest, leaned back and entered a new code. A moment later, the message disappeared, and the screen turned a soft lilac.

"I am sorry about that, sir. NS6 hadn't cleared you in the SYX-77 cue."

Leif didn't know what an NS6 or SYX-77 were, and he didn't ask.

"As soon as I close the hatch, your circuit will be open. You may speak freely then."

I'm not a sir.

She flipped a switch by the edge of the hatch and slipped out. The door closed with a whisper. Immediately, the screen flickered and a Navy commander looked out at him.

"Ah, Sergeant Hope Hollow. Finally. I'm Commander Warren, and I'll be your commanding officer for the moment. Maybe for the duration, if the crud doesn't find its way here."

"The 'crud,' sir? You mean the hammer?"

"Is that what you call it? Yeah. The hammer. UC-1066, to be official."

Leif had watched enough holovids and the recent trend to medical themes that he knew "UC" stood for "Unidentified

Contagion." Did the "1066" mean that there had been 1065 of them before?

"I see that you've officially taken over command of NSB Sunrise, Sergeant."

The entire base? Not just the Marines? Leif wondered, feeling even more out of his depth.

"Yes, sir. I have . . . but I don't know what I'm supposed to be doing. I'm a sergeant, sir, not a colonel."

"I know, son. But you are the ranking military member on the base. I'm afraid it's fallen onto you. But that's what I'm here for. I'm going to bring you up to speed, and I'll remain in close contact—"

"But sir, with all due respect," Leif interrupted, "can't you just take a shuttle down and take over? With a biosuit, you should be—"

The commander held up a hand to stop him.

"I know this is a little overwhelming. Hell, did I just say 'little?' I meant this is fuck-ten overwhelming. To answer your question, no I can't just take a shuttle down. I'm not at Mbangwa Station. I'm not in the Sunrise system. I'm at a small research station, one that I can't tell you the location."

Leif looked at the commander in confusion. What he was saying didn't make sense.

"I . . . look, I've got a full brief to send to you, but here's the salient points. Over a third of the empire had been inflicted with the crud, and it is spreading rapidly. The military had been especially hard hit. Every major base and station, and 94% of the Navy ships have been compromised. Earth, Wayfare, Saint Liam, Last Chance, Galveston—"

"Galveston? That's a Fremont world."

"Yes. Your point?" he asked, looking confused.

"The Novacks, did they do this?"

Given the epidemic in the city, Leif had already begun to doubt that, but he wanted confirmation.

"If they did, Sergeant, they let it loose among themselves. Every former Novack world has been hit hard."

"So, who did this? It isn't natural, right?"

"No, it's not natural. But as far as where it came from, well, we don't . . ." the commander paused as if to think of how to proceed. "Hell, Sergeant, you've got the clearance now. Initial indications are that this is the first volley from either the sassares or the leera. I'm betting on the sassares."

"But that means war," Leif said.

"One they're winning the first battle. So, if I can continue?" the commander asked, looking at Leif. When Leif didn't say anything, he said, "All the major human population centers have been hit. Whatever is doing this, it seems to only affect humans."

Leif thought back to his sore throat. It could have been coincidence, but he'd wager wyntonans were affected, just not to the same degree as humans.

"We do have isolated pockets of uninfected humanity. Most on are ships, Navy or commercial. Some are on small stations. And, of course, there are pockets on most, if not all worlds, that either weather patterns or something else we don't understand has kept them from being infected."

"And the imperial couple?" Leif asked.

"I can't tell you that."

"Can't, or won't?" Leif asked, reaching up to touch his Knight Extraordinaire pin.

The commander didn't seem to mind being questioned like that from a Marine sergeant.

"I don't know myself. Earth has been hit bad."

"What about a cure, sir? How long before we have one?"

"I don't know that, either. We don't even know what the vector is yet. Whoever designed this was genius. There are too many dead-ends, red-herrings, from what I gather. All of them are taking time and effort to unravel."

"The IIDCA can't figure it out? With all their resources?" Leif asked.

"And where is the IIDCA headquarters? Nairobi, right? Nairobi is a ghost town now."

"But there are other labs scattered around the empire, right, sir?"

"Yes, and they're working on it. Every resource is being put on this. Failure just isn't an option. We've already lost too many as it is."

On Sunrise, over two hundred humans had died. More were in very bad shape. The few alindamir and hisser medical techs and nurses were doing what they could, but without a doctor left unstricken, everything was via the medical AIs and comms with doctors off-site.

And those doctors never mentioned that this epidemic was not just here on the planet's surface? Why not?

"How many, sir. How many have been lost."

"At the moment, maybe ten percent," the commander said soberly.

"The mortality rate is ten percent? I was afraid it would be worse."

"Ten percent of the total population. And that's going to grow unless we crack this." The commander shook his head and seemed to gather his thoughts. "Look, Sergeant. I'm sending all of this to you. The purpose of this call is to give you your marching orders. The command doesn't think NSB Sunrise is going to be a major target if there is follow-on conventional military action. There just aren't enough forces there to be a center of gravity."

"We have lots of war supplies, sir."

"Granted. And those will be your main concern. Your written orders should be sent within two hours, but I want you to start marshaling bodies now. You're authorized to swear in temporary militia for the duration, and you've got 2,000 tokits there and--"

"Tokits, sir? As fighters? I mean, they've got the heart, but I was there at the palace when they were slaughtered."

"Use tokits, use anyone you can. You have to secure the base. That's your mission. That and caring for your sick the best you can."

And how am I supposed to do that?

"I know this is a tall order. But I've got the report here on you. You've attracted notice at the highest levels. You're a Knight Extraordinaire, Sergeant. Protector of the Empire. Now, it's time to protect."

His mistress stirred for the first time during the comms as he fingered the lioness head with crossed swords on his collar. Neither one would help him manage the task facing him.

But neither would let him give up, either. A warrior was a warrior, no matter what was asked of him.

Chapter 27

"That's sixty-five Marines. Twelve qiincer, two hissers, one human, and forty-five wyntonans," Petty Officer Third Class Oana Ulo, the next ranking military member left on the base, said. "Navy personnel are at one-hundred-and-thirteen: twenty-two hissers, twelve tokits, fourteen qiincers, sixty-four alindamirs, and two noxes. Twenty-one of the Navy are Seabees."

"Noxes? You've got noxes?" Leif asked the alindamir petty officer, surprised.

Noxes made up the fourth "great race," who, along with the humans, sassares, and leera, controlled most of the explored galaxy. The noxes were almost tribal in nature, owing more allegiance to each grouping than to their race as a whole.

"They're imperial citizens," Ulo said. "They've got the same rights as any other citizen."

Leif knew that there were colonies of noxes within the empire, all swearing allegiance to the Granite Throne, but he'd never even considered the possibility that any would be serving in the military.

"And the MP regiment? Anyone there?"

"It was totally human. No one."

That was a blow. Most, if not all, of the remaining sailors were technicians. If the base ever had to be defended, he needed people who knew how to handle weapons, and while the MP militiamen weren't Marines, they were essentially combat soldiers.

"And of the Navy personnel, how many can handle a firearm?" he asked hopefully.

A wave of blue, then purple swept over her face as her chromatophores reacted. When alone with their kind, the colors constituted more than half of their communications, but around other races, they tried to keep their skin a single, neutral color, the chromatophores activating only under emotional highs and lows.

She took three sharp breaths, almost like a weight-lifter in the gym, and her face turned back to her normal light green. "We alindamirs are not trained in personal weapons. We're technician-track, all of us. The Seabees have had some firearms training. Of the rest of us, maybe the noxes or the qiincers."

Leif was expecting that answer, but he pressed on. "If we arm you, and it comes to that, will you fight?"

The short-lived tost'el'tzy would not lift a finger to harm a living creature, but Leif wasn't sure what alindamir culture would allow.

"We will do our best, Sergeant. I must warn you that we aren't . . ." she paused, and a wave of orange passed over her face ". . . among the most aggressive of the races."

"But you will destroy an enemy ship, killing hundreds," Forintik said, her first words since the meeting started.

Ulo looked at the qiincer for a moment, then nodded. "It's one thing to enter the command into the weapons station. It is another to physically face an enraged human who wants nothing better than to render our bodies into compost."

True enough. Easy to push a button. Harder to stand firm when the rounds are flying. But if they'll try, that's better than nothing.

"Corporal Forintik, I want you and . . . take Corporal a'Bord," he said after a moment's thought, choosing the battalion wyntonan he'd met when Fremont had surrendered. "I want every sailor to be issued a weapon and famfire it."

"What should we issue them?" she asked.

The base had thousands of weapons in the prepositioning stores. Some were undoubtedly older models, but they should all work.

"Take a look at what we've got and you decide."

Hah! Delegating authority, Leffen a'Hope Hollow. You need to do more of that.

Letting Forintik decide was probably a good idea. She couldn't fly, or at least, stay aloft long with heavier weapons. She carried the M-77 carbine, but there were other lighter weapons in the arsenal, and she should be more familiar with them than Leif was. Looking at Ulo, he thought the lighter the better.

Forintik nodded, and Leif checked off that box. He knew she'd get it done.

But that still left his biggest problem.

He turned to the second alindamir in the conference room, Mr. Bowanna Efeelo. Effeelo was an IS2, technically the civilian equivalent to a first lieutenant, and so, senior to Leif. No one had suggested that he, or any of the other higher-ranking civilians, however, be in charge.

"Mr. Efeelo, do you have the numbers I asked for?"

Waves of discordant colors swept across the alindamir's face, the same waves flashing across his hands. For a moment, Leif could picture his entire body flashing like bar signage back in V-town on Iwo.

"That's not so easy, sir," the alindamir said.

"Why not? You've got records. Just pull them up."

"It's the tokits," he almost hissed out as more colors flashed. Leif couldn't speak alindamir color-talk, but he knew the guy was upset. "The contracted ones. I have the base workforce, but I can't get a number of the rest. I've asked, but they won't tell me. I can't plan anything, sir, unless they tell me."

"Do you have any estimates?"

"From the contracts on file, maybe two-thousand. But I can't vouch for that. No one can. I only know for sure the ones who're here on the imperial rolls."

"Then what do you have for the base personnel," Leif asked, keeping his voice calm.

He wanted to yell. The pressure was weighing heavily on his shoulders, and this guy, an IS2, no less, was acting like a little *ada*. But he knew if he did yell, the alindamir would shrink back into his shell, and Leif knew he needed him. He couldn't manage the civilian workforce himself.

The alindamir handed Leif a piece of plastisheet. He looked over the numbers. They were lower than he'd have guessed. Two-hundred-and-sixty-one. Alindamirs, tokits, hissers. Nineteen noxes, which still struck Leif wrong. No tost'el'tzy, which was no surprise. No wyntonans, which was.

"Same thing I asked Petty Officer Ulo. Can any of them handle firearms?"

"Weapons?" the alindamir asked, as even more colors flashed.

This guy's having a problem controlling his emotions, Leif noted. *I'd better keep my eye on him.*

"Sir, our contracts specifically state that we will never be used for aggression!"

"I'm not asking you that. We aren't going to invade the city and take it over. But if we're attacked, what is your ability to resist?"

"None, sir. We don't fight. It's in our contract."

"Let me get this straight. If we're attacked, and they are here inside the base, what will you do?"

"Rely on you to protect us. That's—"

"In your contract. I get it," Leif said, anger starting to build.

"And if we can't protect you?" he said, trying to keep calm. "If we're all killed trying to protect you? Then what?"

"Then we let whoever it is take what they want. We're *non-combatants*," he said, as if lecturing a particularly dense child.

Leif started to protest, but then gave up. The alindamir's position made no sense to him, as if a sassares or leera attack would somehow spare the civilian workforce. Already, seven of them had been killed by the Novack rebels' mortars and rockets. He needed to talk to the commander and get some advice.

"Mr. Efeelo, I want you to track down how many contractors we have, then I want to see your plan for making sure everyone is fed and supported. That includes the humans. We don't know how long the quarantine will be in effect, and I need to let Commander Warren know where we're at."

The colors faded from the alindamir's face as he sat down. This was evidently more in line with what he was used to.

The humans were another issue. There were over 2,000 alive, almost all comatose or semi-comatose. The non-human medical staff, all eleven of them, were kept busy making sure all of them were connected to life-support trundles. The hospital didn't even have that many, but once again, the prepositioning stores came in very handy. They had 800 more trundles still in the containers.

The trundles weren't absolutely necessary to keep the sick humans alive, but they made it much easier for the eleven medical staff by monitoring each person and keeping them nourished.

"You can ask the tokits yourself, Sergeant," one of the sailors, whose name Leif hadn't caught yet, said. "There are three waiting outside who want to talk to you."

"What? Three? Who are they?"

"Who are they? Who knows? They're tokits," the sailor said.

This time, Leif was unable to stop from rolling his eyes. "Send them in. Maybe they've got some answers."

Leif leaned his head back and closed his eyes. He'd been in command for less than a day, and he was already sick and tired of it. Give him an enemy, tell him to kill said enemy, and he'd be happy. This . . . this . . . this stuff was mind-numbing. The emperor himself had once offered to get him commissioned, and he now he was doubly sure he'd made the right choice in turning him down.

"Sir?" a soft voice asked.

Leif opened his eyes, realized he'd almost drifted off, and sat back up. Three tokits were standing on the far side of the conference table. The others in the room were avoiding his eyes except for Forintik, who had her normal grin-of-superiority.

"Sorry about that," he muttered.

The three tokits bowed their heads twice in unison.

"Are you in charge of the tokits here?" he asked the one in the center.

The three exchanged glances with each other, then the one on the left said, "There are none above the rest, as Nonnana taught us. Each of us are in charge of the greater whole. But, if we may be so bold as to assume your meaning, then we three are able to represent the tokit family here."

Leif's direct contact with tokits had been largely limited to the hustlers on Iwo, trying to sell fake Rolexes and Wen Zhous, steering Marines to certain bars, and like attempts to separate Marines from their BCs. Those tokits spoke standard—that is the individual words were standard, but often, what they said didn't make sense. Evidently, that pertained to these tokits as well. They weren't in charge of the rest of the tokits, but they represented them? No, that they were "able" to represent them. Leif didn't know what that meant. And were they really all part of the same "family?"

He tried to make sense of that, then shrugged. He'd just act like the one on the left was in charge.

"How many of you are there here?" he asked.

The tokit on the right immediately said, "Nine-thousand, four-hundred-and-sixty-five."

Leif's mouth dropped open, and he looked over to Efeelo. The alindamir looked equally shocked. He'd told Leif there were about two-thousand of them on the base.

"You've got nine thousand of you here?" Leif asked.

"And four-hundred-and-sixty-five," the center tokit said.

"Nine-thousand contracted tokits?"

The three looked at each other, trilling softly in their native language for at least twenty seconds while the rest of those in the conference room waited.

"We have nine-thousand, four-hundred-and-sixty-five here," the one on the left said, spreading her arms wide. "On Sunrise. Are you seeking how many are in this system?"

"On Sunrise? You mean on the entire planet?" Leif asked.

"On Sunrise. New Wister, the Fertile Plains, Lamont, City of Dreams—" the one in the middle started before Leif cut him off.

"I mean here, on NSB Sunrise."

Why would I care about how many of them are on the other side of the planet. Of course, I'm talking about the base.

"Within the boundaries of this base, four-thousand, nine-hundred-and-twelve," the one on the left said.

The tokit on the right trilled something, and the one on the left corrected herself. "Four-thousand, nine-hundred-and-eleven. Rrinlrey Peerst Orn Sepmith is on *ryryron*."

None of that made sense to Leif, except for the number: 4,911 tokits.

"Four-thousand, nine-hundred-and-eleven are here, on base," he said.

"Yes," all three said in unison.

That was still more than double what he'd thought. The question was what he was going to do with that figure.

Tokits were not known for the martial prowess. There were some in the Navy, but none yet in the Corps. About the same height as a qiincer, they lacked the qiincers' streak of nasty. They'd made a place for themselves in the empire as a model workforce.

Still, Leif had been at the palace when hundreds of them, armed with kitchen utensils and anything else they could grab, took on the advancing rebels. They'd been slaughtered, but they'd slowed the assault. Without that delay, Leif was sure the throne would have been seized. An individual tokit might not amount to much as a fighter, but other than the odd hustler, and even then, there was never just a single tokit. They always had numbers.

Commander Warren had told him to use all of his assets, even the tokits.

"Can you tokits handle firearms?" Leif asked.

"They are just tools," the one in the center said.

"Is that a yes?" Leif asked.

The three said "yes" in unison.

Leif turned to Forintik and said, "I want them armed."

"We don't have that many carbines," the qiincer said.

"Give them handguns. Heck, give them knives. Just do what you can. Take another twenty Marines to help you."

"That's about it for now, then," Leif told the rest. "We've got a lot to do, so let's meet back here at seventeen-hundred. I'm going to want a progress report." He turned to the tokits and said, "That means you, too. Can you make it."

The three bowed their heads twice, hands reaching to their foreheads on the second bow.

"And I can't just keep saying 'Hey, you.' What are your names?"

"Yryingling Tesiry Wyxynrrlig Sessarery," the first one said, which Leif caught maybe 20%. He did worse with the other two, although he could swear the middle tokit had a "Smith" jammed in there somewhere.

"Do you have something easier for us to use? What did the humans call you?"

"Yingling."

"Smith"

I knew I heard that!

"Horse."

"Is it OK if I use that?" Leif said, not missing the irony of his feelings when the Marine Corps initially trying to humanize their wyntonan names.

The three didn't seem bothered by it, though.

"That's it, then," Leif said. "See you all at seventeen-hundred."

Leif hated meetings. Twenty hours after being put in command, however, and he'd already scheduled four.

What have you done with the real Leefen a'Hope Hollow, and when can I get him back?

Chapter 28

"But I don't want to go, Sergeant. I want to stay here with you," Private Lorenzo Jones said, his voice almost breaking.

"Orders, Jones. It's coming from above."

"But I don't run, Sergeant. Can't you tell them I have to stay?"

Leif reached out and place his hand on the private's shoulder, then said, "Look, Private. You carried half of the sick to the hospital, but you didn't catch the hammer. Doesn't that seem a little odd to you?"

"I . . . I've always been healthy, Sergeant. I don't get sick much."

"But you're the only human out of more than two thousand?"

"I don't know why. But that doesn't mean they should take me away from the battalion. What if we get attacked? Some of the others, they think the leera are behind all of this. What if they come? You'll need me."

Leera? That's the rumor? I'll need to address that.

Leif had not mentioned that it might be the sassares or leera who'd engineered the hammer, but it was a logical conclusion in an information vacuum.

"And I'd be honored to have you here. But the scientists, they need to find out why you didn't get sick. What if there's something in your body that keeps the hammer at bay? Don't you think that the rest of the empire needs it?"

"Where're you from, Jones?" he asked, changing tack.

"Saint Liam."

One of the worlds hit hard, Leif remembered, trying to keep his face expressionless.

"So, say there's something in your blood that is fighting the hammer. Don't you think your family back on Saint Liam would want that?"

"Well . . . yeah."

"I know you're a good Marine. Sergeant Wonput told me that."

Wyntonans were not very good liars, and the only reason he knew Sergeant Wonput's name was because he'd looked it up when Jones was the last human standing. He was sure the private would see through his lie.

"He did?" Jones said. "I tried hard, you know."

"Everyone knows you're a good Marine, and you'd stay here and fight if it came to it. But they need you now. The empire. Humanity."

The private stood quietly for a moment, then said in what was barely a whisper, "Am I gonna be a lab rat, Sergeant?"

"No!"

Yes, you are, son. I'm sorry.

There was a flash in the sky, and both Marines looked up to see the ship appear, coming in on its approach. It was the military version of a Hesterling yacht, capable of landing on the surface of a planet and traversing the black. Normally, they were used only by flag-rank officers. This one was picking up a private, someone who might be a key in fighting the hammer. Neither of them said a word until it landed and the hatch hissed open.

"So, what do I do now?" the private asked.

"The ship is unmanned, and so everything's on autopilot. You don't have to worry about anything. Just relax for the trip, check out the entertainment, and dial up some good Navy chow."

"And you don't know where I'm going?"

"No, I don't."

"Well, I guess I gotta go," the private said, taking a big breath. "I'll be back, though, when they're all done with me."

"We'll be waiting," Leif said.

There were undoubtedly other humans who were exposed but had not contracted the hammer, and they'd be being gathered up to try and unlock to the key to the disease. Jones was not the only one. But as the Marine disappeared inside the ship and the hatch closed, Leif was pretty sure he wouldn't be seeing the private again.

Chapter 29

"How are we on the cylosponastin?" Leif asked Katako N.

The hisser, a certified nurse now in charge of the hospital and keeping the humans alive, said, "More than enough in the medical prepositioning supplies, Sergeant. It would need to be suspended into a solution with any of the lipid solubilizing agents, however. I'd need authorization to break into the Class VIII supplies."

Leif didn't understand most of that, but he understood that they had enough of the drug to help out the humans in the city, and that he'd have to authorize the drug being broken out of the prepositioning supplies.

"And can you do that? Put it into solution?" Leif asked the hisser from the main hospital out in Prestonville.

"If we have the drug, yes, sir," the hisser said.

"Give them what you can spare," Leif told Katako N.

After both the coup and the attacks on the base, it was still difficult for Leif to think of the Novacks as anything other than the enemy. But even as enemy, he couldn't ignore them. The cylosponastin didn't cure the hammer, but when given in mist form, it helped stabilize the sick. The death rate among the humans had slowed down, so maybe it was helping.

"Thank you, sir," the hisser said, grimacing and flashing his teeth—something that had looked aggressive to Leif when he'd first observed it, but was more in line with a wyntonan or human smile.

"I'll let you figure out how to deliver the drug to them," Leif told Katako N. "Let me know when it's done."

"And if we can help in any other way, let me know," Leif told the other hisser. "I don't know what we can do, but it doesn't hurt to ask."

The hisser hesitated, then said, "If you can spare any medical personnel, that would be most appreciated, most deeply appreciated."

Leif started to tell him they couldn't spare anyone. The bulk of the medical personnel, and all of the doctors and the naval hospital, had been human, and now, Katako N had a staff of 23 to try and keep over two thousand humans alive until a cure was developed. Most of the intravenous feeding and drug administration was done automatically, but still . . .

But then he gave the hisser another look. He wasn't an expert on the race, but the hisser's rotund, heavy-set body looked worn out. Tired. At least that was his take on it.

"How many people do you have at your hospital?" he asked. "Not humans. People who can care for them."

"Thirty-one."

"And are they all medically trained?"

"Twelve," the hisser said.

Hissers made a significant proportion of medical personnel in the empire. Leif didn't know if they were particularly good at it, or if it just worked out that way.

Sunrise, however, was . . . *human centric*, some people would say. Xenophobic, others would call it. There weren't many non-humans on the planet when compared to others. With the hammer cutting down humans, then there wouldn't be many left to care for the sick.

The hisser, whose name Leif hadn't caught, had twelve people to try and keep two-million humans alive. There were other hospitals in the city, but they would be staffed the same. And he didn't even want to think of what was happening across the rest of the planet.

"Katako N, can we spare anyone to assist . . . I'm so sorry. I know you told me who you are, but I didn't catch your name."

"Volt Y, sir."

"Katako N, can you see if we can spare anyone to help Volt Y get set up? Don't put yourself in a bind, but if you can?"

He knew Katako N and his staff were working overtime. Humans were crammed into every bed at the naval hospital and filled thousands of cots in two warehouses that had been commandeered. All of them had to be hooked up to the trundles. The staff were stretched thin. But he had to ask.

"I will see who I can send, Sergeant. We'll work something out."

"Thank you. I'll let you two work out the details."

The two hissers left, chattering in their native language, and Leif rubbed his eyes with the heels of his hands. He'd been up for almost 40 hours straight, and he was mentally and physically exhausted. But there was always more to do. And now, it looked like he had to worry about the Novacks as well. This was too much for a Marine grunt.

"OK," he said, sitting back up. "What's next?"

"We're at 72% famfired—" Forintik started before Leif's earset buzzed.

"Sergeant a'Hope Hollow," Corporal a'Bord said. "We've got an issue down at the LZ."

"By the Mother, Orelian," he snapped in Uzboss. "You're a Marine NCO. Just take care of it! I've got too much to do to take care of every little thing."

There was a moment of silence, then the corporal said, "I think you really need to get down here."

"Why?" he said, frustration and fatigue taking over.

"A ship just landed. It was cloaked or something, then suddenly, there it was, landing."

"A ship?" he asked. "What kind of ship?"

"It's sassares."

A stunned Leif sat there for a moment, trying to process what she'd just said.

"Sassares? Are you sure?" he asked.

He'd been speaking Uzboss with her, but "sassares" was the same in any language, and when he said it, the others at the table caught that and were now looking right at him.

"Well, I've got a sassares officer standing in front of me right now, and he wants to speak to whoever is in charge here."

"Holy shit!" Leif muttered aloud in Standard.

Sassares? What are they doing here?

"Stand by, Orelian. I'm on my way."

Chapter 30

The sassares turned to Leif as he came up. Clad in his peach-colored uniform, his cuff was the color of a sere-blue—roughly equivalent to a Marine major or Navy lieutenant commander. The sassares ranks didn't align exactly with the human, with colors differentiating each one, but Leif knew that as a sere-blue, this guy was probably in charge.

Sassares looked remarkably like humans. Take the sere-blue out of uniform, put him in a pair of jeans and a shirt, and let him walk around Nairobi, and Leif doubted he'd give him a second glance. Humans said they could easily tell the difference between the two races, but to Leif, they looked alike. He'd often wondered if there was a link between that similarity and the fact that the two races were the most powerful in the galaxy.

"Sergeant a'Hope Hollow," the sassares said, hand out human-fashion. "I'm happy to finally meet you."

Leif had been around humans enough that he automatically took the sassares' hand.

"Do I know you, sir?" Leif asked.

"No," the sassares said with a laugh. "We've never met. But your deeds are known in the Hegemony. An Imperial Order of the Empire. Knight Extraordinaire. These are accomplishments, especially given your position among the monkeys as one of their dung races."

Leif bristled at the term, and his musapha stirred, but he kept his face expressionless.

"I was pleased to learn that you were here, and after the unfortunate affliction that struck the monkeys, that you were elevated to a position of authority."

He gave a quick glance to Corporal a'Bord, who shook her head slightly. She hadn't told him.

So, how did he know who I was?

"What do you want, Sere-blue . . ." he prompted.

"Forgive my manners. I am Sere-blue Beleena," he said, "commander of the *corana*. . . well, you would call it a monkey cruiser."

Leif looked over the sassares' shoulder to the small skiff that sat on the pad, two junior sassares standing at attention on either side of the single hatch. Another person, of a race Leif didn't recognize, stood between them, holding a massive beam weapon of some kind.

"Of course, my *corana* is in orbit. My other position is that of ambassador at large, and I do hope that is the position that I will be fulfilling."

"How did you get past the Navy, sir?" Leif asked.

"Please. The monkeys had one frigate operational. I took care of it."

There wasn't a doubt in Leif's mind as to what he meant. But why hadn't Leif been given warning?

Then what the sere-blue said sunk in. He'd just essentially admitted to destroying a Navy ship. This was war.

His musapha started to rise, and he had to consciously push her back down. He had to know that the sassares wanted.

"You caused the hammer, didn't you? You started the plague against the humans."

"That's what you call it? The 'hammer?' Appropriate, I must say. But to answer your question, yes, we developed it."

He's admitting it? What next? Does he want me to surrender the base? I won't!

"The monkeys have an annoying propensity for building ships, for arming legions of soldiers. After the Chin Longs failed to take down the emperor, we needed something to reduce their advantages. So, we created a new weapon, one engineered to be only effective against the monkeys."

Leif's mind was reeling. This was too much to take in.

"So, you decided to kill them," he said.

"Kill them? Not at all. Oh, there will be collateral damage. Extensive collateral damage. Think of it as pruning. But we will need the monkeys to work their old worlds-—with us in charge, of course. Many of them will survive, once we reverse the weapon's effects."

That gave Leif a glimmer of hope. The hammer was reversible. He had to get that message to the commander.

"Of course, if we need to, we can make it lethal whenever we want," he said with another laugh.

"And the Novacks? They were your allies, but from the looks of it, you poisoned them, too."

This time, the sere-blue leaned his head back and let out a huge belly laugh.

"Allies? They were tools, nothing more. We wanted the monkeys to fight with each other, to winnow down the numbers. The fact that some monkeys were complicit in their own doom is perfectly delicious."

Leif was trying to wrap his head around what the sassares had told him over the last few minutes. It was overwhelming.

"How did you spread your . . . your *weapon*, to get everyone infected?" he blurted out.

"Timing, Sergeant, and patience. We delayed activation to have the most impact. Once each human was infected, our agents lay quiescent, undetectable, until all were activated at the same time.

"It was difficult, though. Monkeys are everywhere, and we realized we could not infect every single one of them, so we focused our effort. The large population centers, yes. But military targets were our priority. Supplies going on ships. Equipment getting on base—"

"The smuggler we took down. It was a Trojan horse," Leif said before he could stop himself.

"See, you're smarter than you let on to be," the sassares said. "Yes, the smugglers were one of the methods we used to spread the weapon among the ships and bases. Call it more direct targeting. Not once did the monkeys catch on. For all their conquests over races like yours, they are too gullible. They believe they are infallible. And to take another monkey historical reference, that is their Achilles heel."

"Conquests?" That's strong wording. It wasn't quite like that.

Leif knew that not every wyntonan would agree with that, however. Some regularly used the word.

He stared at the sassares for a long moment. The person was so at ease, so sure of himself. He probably had reason to feel so sure. The sassares military was not broken up into branches. There was no Navy, no Army, no Marines, and they stressed flexibility among their servicemembers. A sassares might be part of flight ops off a hangar, then switch over to being an infantry rifleman the next day, like the sea raiders of the wyntonan past. If the sere-blue was the commander of a sassares version of a Navy cruiser, then he'd be able to put 1,200 to 1,500 fighters on the ground under his command. And Leif, with 65 Marines and 113 sailors, could not stand up to them, even with all the civilians augmenting him.

"Why are you here talking to me, sir? Do you expect me to surrender the base without a fight? If you do, then you're sadly mistaken," he said, hoping to buy some time until he could get the commander on the comms and ask for reinforcements.

"Surrender? Oh, my dear young boy, I don't want your surrender."

"Then what do you want?"

"I want you to join us. I want you—all of you—as part of the Hegemony!"

Chapter 31

Leif stared at the sassares sere-blue in shock. Whatever he'd expected to hear, that sure wasn't it.

"Join you? As in becoming part of the Hegemony?" he asked.

"Of course. You aren't human, so what loyalty do you have to them? They conquered you by force. They discriminate against you, call you 'dung races.' You are ruled by a young monkey who calls himself emperor. You have no say in your future."

"That's crazy," he blurted out.

"Is it?" the sassares asked as if telling the obvious to a second tri-year ada. "They don't call you dung races? They don't have an emperor ruling from the Granite Throne?"

"Well, yes, but the Proclamation of Sentient Rights—"

"Just words. Does it really make you equal?" the sassares interrupted.

"No," he had to admit, as much as it hurt to do so. "But we are getting there. The emperor has given his word, and he's trying to address those issues."

"Bah! Even if he's serious and not lying, he's a baby monkey surrounded by older monkeys, monkeys who want to keep things just the way they are."

At least the proclamation is an effort. You sassares have never even given equality lip service. You've got three subjugated races, and then there's the Lost Ones.

The Lost Ones might be rumor, Leif knew. There was no evidence that they even existed. But most citizens in the empire believed that there was a lost race who helped raise the sassares long, long ago, only to be slaughtered by their proteges.

The sassares sere-blue turned and motioned to the person with the beamer.

"This is Bine," he said as the person trotted up. "Do you know who, or should I ask *what*, he is?"

Leif wasn't an anthropologist, but he knew most of the races ruled by the four powers. This person presented as male (although that didn't mean much—with several races, the females were the larger and more powerful than the males). Looking vaguely like a large, muscular qiincer, but without the wings, he moved with a feral grace, and Leif's musapha took notice.

The sassares had just said he wanted Leif and the others to switch allegiances and join the sassares Hegemony, however, so whoever this was, Leif didn't think he was going to attack him.

For now.

"I don't recognize your race," Leif told Bine.

"You should. He's a supposed citizen of your empire," the sassares told him.

Leif whipped his head back to take in Bine. He wasn't a

. . .

Oh, by the Mother. He's a torku!

The empire consisted of eight "native" races: humans, wyntonans, qiincers, hissers, tokits, tost'el'tzy, llyena, and torku. The last two were special cases. The llyena existed within the empire, aware of it, but living their lives on permanent ignore. There was no formal interaction between the llyena and the rest of the empire, or any other race, for that matter. The torku were different. From a technological standpoint, they were millennia behind the other races. Humans had essentially "uplifted" the other races in the empire, some more than others. By the time they'd discovered the torku, however, there had been some anti-imperial sentiment, and the decision was made to leave the torku as they were, to naturally develop as they would. The charter stated that once they achieved space flight, only then would they be taken into the fold.

The torku's system was placed under naval protection to keep people out who might want to exploit them for commercial or religious purposes. Each year, they arrested people who broke the interdiction for both reasons.

There weren't even holos of the race, but there were some early descriptions, and those fit the person standing in front of him.

"I see you recognize him now. Yes, he's a torku. It seems as if they don't appreciate being held under subjugation, unable to join the rest of the galaxy. All because of human hubris. They are now a valuable and honored member of the Hegemony.

The torku never said a word during the exchange. He only stared at Leif with the intensity of a wasilla on a stalk.

And if this sassares had a torku with him, then the protection around the torku homeworld was out of action.

"So, you want the wyntonans to break from the empire and join the Hegemony?" Leif said, his eyes still locked with the torku.

"There is no empire. Or soon won't be. So, why not join the winners as equals?"

"Why do you want us? We're only one world."

"We want all races in our brotherhood . . . ah, that sounds facetious even to me. I'll be blunt. You wyntonans are warriors. You've suppressed that, but for once, the young monkey emperor was right in bringing you out of those ridiculous restraints. We can use you for taking and holding ground."

"Fighting who? Humans?" Leif asked, as his musapha stirred again.

Leif didn't know if that was in anger or excitement about fighting humans, and he felt guilty for that.

"Initially, probably. We cannot infect all of them, so some of the vermin will have to be dug out and exterminated."

"And after that? After there are no more humans?"

"There are other races, my young wyntonan. Closer in the spiral arm."

"Noxes and leera."

"Them. And beyond the leera? Who knows what lies out there?"

It was audacious to think that there was no sentient life beyond the leera. There was no proof that there was, but the galaxy was vast, and this galaxy was just a pinprick in the universe. From the looks of it, the sassares had grand designs beyond just explored space.

"And we want you with us. Will you join the Hegemony?"

"Just me? I mean us here? I'm just a sergeant. A nobody."

"Hardly a nobody, son. You're a person of note on your home planet. When we found out you were here, plans changed, and this dusty trash bin of a monkey planet became our first conquest, a blueprint, if you will, for the future. I was diverted to come here. If you willingly join us, that will go a long way in convincing your people to join us as well."

Soran has said something along those lines. Not about joining the sassares, but that his opinions would hold sway among the People. He didn't believe her, and he didn't believe this sassares.

"And the rest? The qiincers? What about them?"

"That was a little tougher, but the sere-blacks have decided to bring them in as well. They can fly, and they've also proven themselves in your military."

"Hissers? Alindamirs?"

"Possibly some. As slaves, along with whatever monkeys survive."

"Tokits?" Leif asked.

The sassares laughed again as if this was the funniest thing he'd ever heard, then said, "Are you serious? Tokits? More vermin."

Leif didn't even ask about the tost'el'tzy. He knew what the answer would be.

"And if I don't agree. What then?"

"Why then, I'll kill you. All of you," he said without rancor, as if saying he was going to lunch or that it was sunny today. "And we'll look for someone else who can see the future and wants to be part of it.

"Remember, too. What we developed for the monkeys, we can tweak for others."

Leif nodded his head. At least the sassares was being honest.

"Can I have a little time? I want to talk to some of the others."

"I thought you were smarter than that, son. But you would be a catch, and that would be noted in the higher registries. I'll give you ten hours. Don't disappoint me."

He immediately spun around and marched back to his shuttle. The torku stared at Leif for a moment, smiled, then spun on his heels and followed.

For a moment, Leif was tempted to unsling his Stahlmont and take the sere-blue out, but that wouldn't serve a purpose. The sassares cruiser would raze the planet, killing everyone still alive.

"Well, Orelian," he said to the corporal, who'd stood silently throughout the entire exchange. "What in the Mother's name do we do now?"

Chapter 32

"Still nothing, Sergeant," the hisser comms tech said, sticking her head in through the hatch."

"Keep trying. There has to be a way to break through the blockage," Leif said.

The lack of comms was only one of the problems facing him, albeit one of the most important. The sassares had a stranglehold on the communications, so, they were cut-off from the rest of the empire. As soon as the sere-blue's skiff had taken off, Leif had tried to raise Commander Warren, both to tell him what he'd learned from the sassares and to ask for help. The entire communications system had been shut down, however. They were on their own. Leif didn't know if Mbangwa Station was in human or sassares hands. He didn't know if the empire still functioned at all.

It wasn't just the interstellar comms. Even on base, all individual or unit comms were down as well.

"I guess we're on our own, then," Leif said, trying to keep the feeling of helplessness that threatened to overwhelm him out of his voice.

"So, what are we going to do?" Katako N asked, purples and indigos slowly swirling across her face.

Leif had called in an improvised staff meeting to determine just that. Katako N from the base, Forintik from the Raiders, Corporal Jenuun a'Wood from 2/14, and at the last moment, a representative from the contracted workforce. He expected one of the three tokits from before, but a single old female with a typically long name that he missed showed up, telling him he could call her "Star."

Leif checked the time and said, "We've got nine hours and twenty-seven minutes to respond to the sere-blue. I'm still trying to get comms with Commander Warren, but from the looks of it, we might be on our own."

"You said the sassares commander was from what kind of ship?" the alindamir asked.

"He called it a *corana*. Said it was like a Navy cruiser."

Leif had tried to look up a *corana* to find out its capabilities and manning, but the ethernet was knocked out as well. Even back home in Hope Hollow, Leif had never been out of reach of the net, and he felt naked without it. If he had a chance, he'd go to the library and try and look it up. As long as someone had pulled the information before, it should be in the library main's cache.

Wait. You don't have to do it yourself. Delegate!

"Denitok, go to the library and see what you can pull up about a *corana*. If there's nothing in the cache, pull up anything you can find about sassares cruisers," he told the qiincer, one of four runners he had standing by.

We can traverse the galaxy, but I need messengers like the ancient serta.

The PFC nodded and slipped out the hatch.

"The cruiser, how many onboard?" the alindamir asked. "How many of them are we facing?"

"On a cruiser? I think maybe upwards of about fifteen hundred or so. How many of those are dual-hatted for ground ops, I don't know. Do either of you two remember?" he asked the other two Marines.

When he mentioned "fifteen hundred," the alindamir's face broke out into rapid swirls of red, pink, and yellow. Leif didn't need to understand the alindamir's chromatophoric language to know she was upset or scared. Probably both. This was too much for Leif to grasp, much less for a nurse.

"What are we going to do?" she asked, voice verging on panic as she wrung her long-fingered hands. The cinnamon smell around her grew in intensity.

Neither of the other two Marines corrected him. In fact, neither had said much since their arrival. Leif had called this meeting so they could figure out what to do, but looking at them, along with Katako N and Star, they were waiting for him to make a decision. They wanted to know what to do.

Come on, Leefen a'Hope Hollow! You tried to pawn off a decision to the commander. When you couldn't reach him, then you tried to bring in these guys. That's not how it works. You're in command, like it or not, so command!

He knew what he wanted to do, but this wasn't just him. It wasn't just his team. There were over 4,000 people who would be affected by his decision, not even counting all the sick, defenseless humans, both on base and off. The sassares said that some would be allowed to live after the rest had been "pruned." How many would die?

He could fight, and the Marines, at least, would fight with him. But to what end? He didn't see how he could defeat the sassares equivalent of a Marine battalion, not with what he had to fight them.

Leif tried to open his comms again, but there was nothing. If he only knew what was going on out there, that would allow him to make a better decision. For all he knew, a Marine regiment was on its way to the rescue, and all Leif had to do was hold out. Or, the rest of the empire had already been crushed, and he was fighting for something that no longer existed.

One of the battalion Marines opened the hatch, looked around, and came in.

"Sergeant Hope Hollow, we issued all the carbines and handguns, but they won't come close to arming all the tokits."

"Don't worry about us, Lance Corporal," Star said. "We'll do fine with what you can give us."

The lance corporal gave the tokit a quick glance, then turned back to Leif and asked, "What do you want us to do now?"

Eight sets of eyes swiveled to lock onto Leif's. The real question was what was he going to decide. This wasn't up to them. This was his call. Were they going to lay down their arms and join the sassares, or where they going to fight, no matter the odds?

And he knew there was only one real choice.

"Get everyone fed and armed. We're going to fight!"

Chapter 33

"Blow it," Leif told the tokit, pointing at the chow hall. "We need the fields of fire. Mines alone won't do much if we can't cover them."

"Yes, sir!" the tokit said, the glee evident in his voice before he turned and issued the orders in their native tongue.

A trill of excitement rose from his team. They loved to blow things up.

Leif started to remind them this wasn't a game, that they probably wouldn't make it through the upcoming battle, but he shook his head. If they were all on borrowed time, then the tokits might as well enjoy something.

And he couldn't fault what they'd done over the last six hours. Leif had seen the singletons, the beggars and scammers back on Iwo, and those outliers had tilted his opinion of the race. That had begun to change when he's watched the tokits take on the rebels at the imperial palace, but he'd never grasped how industrious they were. He'd heard the general consensus that they were good workers, but it wasn't until he'd seen them scramble to help prepare the base that he'd really begun to appreciate just how good they were.

Leif, Forintik, and a'Bord had put together an operations order. It wasn't as detailed as the extensive orders coming out of a battalion or higher-level Three Shop, but they didn't have the time nor resources to do anything more than the broad-brush strokes. The details, like blowing up the Area 1 Dining Facility, were being done on the fly as they became clear.

The base had a defensive plan even more detailed than a battalion operations order, but it supposed a full security compliment and orbital support, none of which suited Leif's small force. The base was just too big, so he wasn't going to try and defend it. He was ceding 90% of the base to the sassares, defending that portion with only the existing automatics. Keeping the main defenses around the armories and Class V supplies, he shrunk the perimeter to match his forces. He'd have liked to shrink it even further, but there were too many tokits, and he needed the warehouse space to stash the unconscious and semi-conscious humans.

The thought of them reminded Leif to see how that move was going. "You," he said to a tokit private, one of the few in 2/14, "Go find out how many more humans need to be moved."

The runner took off to find out, and a wyntonan PFC stepped up, ready to run his next message.

Leif wished he hadn't had to waste personnel to move the humans, but he couldn't leave them outside his constricted perimeter. The hospital might be lovely perched on its hill, surrounded by huge trees, but it was not defensible. Five hundred tokits had been assigned to Katako N to effect the move, and Leif wanted those 500 back as soon as they finished.

Leif might lack Marines, but he had more supplies than he knew what to do with. He was going to give it a good shot, however. According to the inventories, he had over two million mines of various types, and he was trying to get as many out as possible in the time left to him. Those 500 tokits would be a big help in that.

Other working parties, each led by a Marine, were emplacing crew-served weapons around their perimeter, giving them interlocking fields of fire, while still more, mostly tokits, were hardening each position.

There was a general feeling of excitement in the air as their fighting positions began to form. Leif understood that, especially among the younger Marines and the civilians. With the weaponry being emplaced, with the mines being laid, it didn't seem possible that anyone, even an entire sassares cruiser crew, could breach their position.

What the newbies were not considering was that the sassares were not going to simply march into their fire. They had weapons, too, and they'd be taking out the imperial positions, one-by-one, and each gap in the defense made it that much easier to take out the next one.

Leif and the other Marine vets understood this, however. None of them had a false sense that they were going to easily turn back the sassares.

There was a huge blast, and Leif spun around to see the chow hall disappear in a column of smoke as the tokit crew trilled their delight.

I just gave them the order, what, five minutes ago?

As the smoke cleared, only rubble—very small pieces of rubble—remained. The new minefield going in on the other side of what used to be the chow hall could now be covered with fire.

OK, then, what's next on the list?

His stomach growled, and he wondered if he had time to stuff something down his throat. Leif had just about decided to run over to where the MRDRs had been stacked when he spotted two Marines heading right at him from two different directions. Lance Corporal a'Bang the Drum was vigorously waving a long arm to get his attention. Corporal Kikenit saw that, unfurled his wings, and took to the air to beat the lance corporal to him.

I can always get something to eat later, Leif told himself as he waited to find out what new emergency required his attention.

✳✳✳✳✳✳✳✳✳✳✳✳✳✳✳

Leif wiped the sweat from his forehead with his arm, then reached down to grab the lifting handle on top of the spade. It was hot, too hot for him, and the physical activity didn't give him a chance to cool off.

"OK, on three! One . . . two . . . three!"

He strained to stand, then shuffled three steps to the side, helped (or hindered. he couldn't tell), by a dozen tokits.

He knew he didn't need to be spending his time with grunt-work, but the tokits had struggled to get the artillery piece lined up. He took a step back and looked it over. It was . . . well, *ancient*. The targeting comp was missing, the elevating cylinders had long seized up over time, and there wasn't a rotational base. It would have to be aimed by hand, physically horsing it around and using it as a direct fire weapon.

The piece was so old that it wasn't even in the inventory. Leif doubted it would even fire, but the tokit engineer had rigged up a firing mechanism that he said would work. If the shells they scrounged up were actually compatible. If they were still viable. Like as not, the shell would explode in the breach. But it was worth a shot.

"Sergeant Hope Hollow!" one of the alindamir sailors shouted, running up to him. "I've been looking for you!"

Leif straightened his back, wincing at the sharp stab of pain in his back. He took a deep breath, then turned to face the sailor, waiting to hear his message.

"Corporal Forintik," he started, mangling her name, "Needs you at the east gate."

"Did she say why?" he asked.

"I think it might be the tokits. But I don't know."

The tokits who had just begun to harden the howitzer stopped working and looked up when they heard "tokit."

The tokits had been more useful that Leif had expected, willing to do whatever needed to be done. Their numbers had been inflated with tokits who had been previously working for the Novacks but had come to the base to assist in the defense. Frankly, Leif was grateful for their help, and he couldn't imagine what was Forintik's problem.

He trusted her, though, so he said, "I'll be there momentarily."

"Are you OK here?" he asked the team around the big gun.

"Thank you, sir," the mechanic said. "We have it."

Leif hesitated for only a moment. He probably should assign a Marine to the gun. Maybe one of the battalion Marines had been from the arty detachment.

Just one more thing to get done, he told himself, adding it to his growing mental checklist. More things were being added faster than he could check them off.

But that could wait until when—if—the mechanic could actually get the thing to fire. He turned and broke into a trot, the alindamir sailor following. He rounded the armory and stopped dead in his tracks. The road to the east gate was full with a line of tokits, stretching back at least as far as the nearest buildings in the city. He tried to make a quick estimate of how many there were, but the best he could do was "a shitload."

He gathered himself and ran to the gate where Forintik and four other Marines had held up the line. Star, (at least that was who he thought she was—he still wasn't that good at telling the race apart), was trying to explain something to Forintik. The qiincer spotted Leif and greeted him with uncharacteristic relief in her voice.

"Sergeant, we're getting overwhelmed here," she said.

When the first tokits from out in the city had arrived, there had only been a couple of hundred. Leif had decided to let them in and left Forintik to handle the situation. But the trickle had become a torrent.

How can there be that many tokits out there?

"Star! What's going on?" he asked.

"They wish to help," she said.

"But . . . but so many of them? Where are they coming from?"

"We are many here on this planet."

"Yes, but . . ."

"Sergeant, we don't have room," Forintik said.

Which wasn't exactly true. Leif had contracted their defensive AO, but far more could be crammed inside. But he knew what she meant. Too many people without purpose would be a hindrance when it came down to a fight. Leif had to be able to move forces quickly from one spot to another, and those forces would be held up by the crowds.

And it wasn't going to be safe. They didn't have enough covered positions as it was. More people inside would only increase the casualty rate when the sassares attacked. Leif had to stem the incoming tide.

"Star, why are they all coming now? Can we turn them back?"

"They are coming to take a stand, Sergeant a'Hope Hollow. They will fight."

"But we don't have room for them. I don't have positions for them."

She twitched in what Leif now knew was the tokit version of a shrug. The tokits might show deference bordering on worship to Leif, but not all the time. Star was not going to act. He had to make sure she understood the consequences.

"Without positions, they will be slaughtered. Most of them. All of them," he amended, considering that the sassares would overrun the base, and he'd already heard the sere-blue's position on tokits.

"Our strength is in our numbers, Sergeant. We may not be as strong on an individual basis, but in great numbers is great strength. We do not fear death. We fear *Loscan*, should we not do our duty. We do not fear *Almomop*."

Leif knew that *Loscan* was the tokit hell. He'd never heard of *Almomop*, but it could be heaven or enlightenment or—

It doesn't matter what it is. Just fix this! You've got too much else to do in the next five hours!

"How many more are coming?" Leif asked, wondering if there was someplace he could stash them that might give some protection.

"As many as can in the time we have," Star said. "As I told you, Sergeant a'Hope Hollow, our strength is that we are many."

The other three tokits had been very specific in numbers, and Leif was sure Star knew as well. If she was evading a direct answer, then he was back to a shit load.

Leif looked down the line of patiently waiting tokits. Their spirits seemed high, as if they were going to a child's summer camp. They didn't seem to realize the gravity of the situation.

There are a lot of them, though. If they were Marines, trained and armed . . . Hell, Leefen. As long as we're wishing, how about a full-strength battalion and an orbital gunship?

"And if I don't let them in?"

A look that Leif would swear was disappointment crossed her face, and she said, "Then they will wait here until you need them."

Which will make them even more vulnerable.

He looked over the line again, a lot of tokits from the gate to the city. There were undoubtedly more back there, hidden from his sight by the buildings.

"Forintik, Star, this is what we're going to do . . ."

Chapter 34

A sharp clap, followed by a rolling thunder, chased Leif, Star, and Corporal a'Bord from the machine shop where Leif had situated his CP. High in the sky to the east of the base, a ship was descending.

"Ayah," a'Bord said in Uzboss. "That thing is huge."

"Ayah," Star repeated.

Leif was too focused on the sassares ship for the tokit's use of Uzboss to register. A'Bord was right. The ship was huge. Maybe not by the standards of interstellar transport, but for a ship that could make landfall, it defied belief.

Large ships had three major problems with landing in a gravity well. The first was that it took an inordinate amount of power to bring large mass down under a controlled descent. The second was that the ship's structure had to be beefed up to handle the landing and takeoff as well as the gravity while on the ground. And third, the exhaust from a large ship would fry anything on the ground.

"I want everyone under cover, now!" he shouted at his five runners, who immediately took off to pass the word.

The sassares cruiser looked like it was coming in to land at the shuttle pad, which had baffles suitable for shuttles and yachts, but it wouldn't be too hard to let it drift over the base and cook the imperial forces.

He looked back up at the cruiser. Humans had large ships, much larger than this one, but they docked at stations, with cargo and passengers ferried to the surface by shuttles or elevators. The sassares like things big, however. Their cargo liners were the largest in the galaxy, and some of their military ships dwarfed any in the Imperial Navy. The sassares military had far fewer ships than the Imperial Navy, but the total tonnage was not that far apart between the two navies.

"Do we fire?" a'Bord asked.

Leif hesitated for a moment despite already making his decision an hour ago. Still, the thought of taking down the cruiser was tempting.

"No. Let it land."

If he had the right weapons, he'd take the shot. But the anti-air weapons within the battalion and what they'd found in the bunkers were designed for aircraft, shuttles, fighters, and reconnaissance craft. They'd do nothing to a cruiser except make the crew mad.

They'd found more than 50 ship-killer missiles, eight of which were designed to be fired from land-based launchers. They didn't have any launchers though, so the missiles were just big paperweights.

The three sat in silence as the sassares ship swung in to land. She was at least 150 meters long, maybe 200 meters. That was twice as large as any human ship Leif had seen that could make planetfall.

"Four hours. The sere-blue gave me ten to make a decision, and we've got four hours left," Leif said.

"Hopefully we still have the full ten," a'Bord said.

The big ship slowed, spun on its axis, then gently lowered the final 200 meters. A single puff of hot wind reached the three, but nothing else. Leif should have realized that the sassares would have solved the problem of their exhaust. They wouldn't be wanting to scorch any of their worlds every time they came in for a landing.

"I'd better go see what he wants," Leif said after one of the forward hatches recessed back into the ship and two guards posted themselves on either side.

"Do you want back-up?" a'Bord asked.

He considered it for a moment, then said, "No. Not this time. But put Dylanan in position. If something happens to me, take out whoever he can."

Private First Class Dylanan a'Central was the best shot remaining among the Marines, and he'd been designated as a sniper for the upcoming fight. None of the wyntonans were as good as the best human snipers, for reasons Leif couldn't figure out, but a'Central was still pretty good with a weapon.

The shuttle pad was an annex to the main base to the north, and Leif had contracted his defensive AO well inside the gate to it. He didn't want to show the sassares a route through the base outside of his AO, so, followed by a'Bord and Star, he headed to the East Gate, the only working entry. He handed the corporal his Stahlmont and Springfield. He almost gave her his vic as well, but then decided he'd feel too naked going out there with nothing.

"I guess this is it," he said, turning to leave.

Star reached out and took Leif's hand, bringing it to her forehead, saying, "Be smart, Sergeant. We need you back here."

Leif resisted the urge to pull away his hand. The gesture bothered him, even more so with Star than when tokits had done it before. She wasn't some nameless person to pass through his life. He'd only known her for six hours, but that was enough for him to consider her a peer, and the hand-to-the-forehead thing smacked him of subservience. It would be on Home, at least, and he was a creature of his culture.

"I'll be back," he said, carefully disengaging his hand.

Leif was pretty confident of that. The sassares had an overwhelming advantage in combat power, and while he didn't trust the race more than any other, he knew they didn't have to lay a trap for him personally. The sere-blue would be waiting to see if he'd join them.

The battalion Marine silently let him through the gate, and Leif said, "If I come back running with the sassares on my ass, I'm not going to be showing you my ID. I trust that's OK with you?"

That was sure lame, Leefen. You can't do better than that?

The PFC laughed, however, and said, "I've got you covered, Sergeant."

Leif realized he didn't even know the Marine's name, and he was wyntonan. Once more, he felt in over his head. He had neither the training nor experience to be commanding the battalion, even one as depleted as this one.

He pulled himself erect, puffing out his chest, and started marching along the perimeter fence. Crazy, yes, to be worried about his posture, but he couldn't help himself. His view of the ship was blocked for the first 200 meters, but he knew they'd be watching him. He wanted to project confidence to the watchers.

Leif felt exposed, and not just because he'd given up his Stahlmont. Without comms, he was out-of-touch, totally on his own. A'Central would be covering him, and others would be watching him, but that didn't give him a warm and fuzzy.

He reached the bend in the perimeter fence, and the sassares ship came into view. It maxed out the main shuttle pad, the far side hanging over the edge. Leif revised his initial estimate. It had to be 250 meters long if it was a millimeter. That was an awful big hunk of engineering to land like a shuttle and still be an effective warship in the vacuum of space.

It was still a good 500 meters off, but it seemed much longer as Leif closed the distance. He'd been sure that he was in no immediate danger, at least until he'd given the sere-blue his decision, but his skin crawled, sure he was at the crosshairs of a sassares weapon.

He reached the civilian gate of the annex—and it was locked. He stood there stupidly looking at it as if he could open it through telekinesis. This was ridiculous. When they contracted their AO, cutting off the main way in and out of the annex, no one had thought to make sure the civilian entrance was open.

Leif looked over to the ship, wondering what to do next, and there was activity. One of the guards had turned and was talking to someone inside. A moment later, four guards trotted out. One was the torku, and to Leif's surprise, one was a wyntonan.

What, no o*manto? Leif thought sarcastically.

If there had been a way to support the only aquatic race in the galaxy, he was sure the sere-blue would have done it. Anything to prove the sassares were welcoming of others.

The four formed a quick square, and a moment later, the sere-blue appeared at the hatch. He took a moment to survey the scene, sweeping his visions slowly around until he ended up on Leif.

With the activity at the ship, Leif had come to a very relaxed parade rest, trying to exude confidence, as if he'd never intended to enter through the gate and approach the ship.

Sere-blue Beleena gave Leif the briefest of nods, then stepped down the ramp. As soon as his foot hit the tarmac, the four guards stepped off. Impressive on the surface, especially as it was obviously just put together when Leif stopped at the gate, but to the wyntonan, it put the sere-blue in the inferior position. Leif was there alone, unarmed. The sere-blue was being escorted by four armed guards. In the way of the People, that gave Leif the upper hand.

Doesn't matter how we think of it, Leif told himself. *What matters is how the sere-blue thinks of it.*

He waited patiently while the five made their way to him, walking over the tarmac, past the terminal, and across the loading and unloading area. Heat radiated up around them in tiny mirages, and that made Leif very aware of the sweat that was dripping down his back. An itch started to grow, right between his shoulder blades, and he had to fight back the urge to scratch it.

It took three long minutes before the sere-blue arrived. His four guards split in a move that would have made the Marine Corps' Silent Drill Team proud, and the sere-blue stepped up to the gate.

"You've been busy since I left you," he said.

"Idle hands make idle minds," the humans say, Leif said.

The sere-blue frowned, making him look even more like a human, and he said, "You don't have any humans there with you. Except for the dead and dying. But it's sad, that even now, you're reduced to using monkey sayings. Surely, you wyntonan's have your own homilies?"

"*Assateen ot moranta borg moranta wyvor be.*"

The sere-bleu raised a single eyebrow, waiting.

"When one is without a task, the task one chooses is mischief," Leif translated

"Touché, Sergeant, touché," he said with a smile and half nod of his head. "But that doesn't belie the fact that you've been busy building up defenses. That isn't a good sign for our future cooperation."

"And you said I had ten hours to make up my mind. It's only been six," Leif said through the gate.

"I was perhaps being generous with ten hours, and given your activities, which look suspiciously like hardening a defense, I thought I would come back a little early and find out your intentions."

Leif said nothing as he tried to weigh his options. He wanted to delay, to give them more time to get ready for the inevitable.

"And what are your intentions," the sere-blue asked with the sharp bite of honed steel after a long silence between them.

Leif knew that the facade of civility was about ready to crumble, and only a complete capitulation would appease the sere-blue. No request for more time to consider. No meeting in the middle proposal.

"During our history classes at boot camp, we were taught about a human general back in one of their many world wars on Earth. His army unit was surrounded by one of the old European forces, the Germans, if memory serves me right. The German commander, assuming the result of a fight would be obvious, and thinking he was acting honorably to save lives and keep the town from being destroyed, asked for the general's surrender."

"And what does this little monkey history lesson mean to me, Sergeant?"

"A logical general, knowing what he faced and understanding the odds, would accept the offer. Lives would be saved, American, German, and the French civilians in the city. Do you know what this general's response was?" Leif asked.

"OK, I'll play. What did the monkey general say?" the sere-blue asked, clearly running out of patience.

"Nuts."

"What? Nuts?" the confused sere-blue asked. "What does that mean?"

"That means no, we are not joining you. We are not surrendering. If you want the base, you're going to have to take it from us."

The sere-blue gave Leif a long, hard stare, then broke out into a laugh. "You think I want this base? I was here for

162

you, to see if you had a gram of intelligence. I should have known better. The monkeys call you a dung race for a reason. No, I don't want this base."

Leif raised his left eyebrow, waiting for the other shoe to drop. "I don't want the base, but I want you . . . dead, now, as it seems. There are other targets we will approach to make our case, but you are now out of the equation."

"*Tomak*," the wyntonan guard whispered, probably to low for the sassares to hear, but loud enough for Leif to pick it up.

A tomak was a larger, semi-aquatic version of the grazpin Leif used to hunt as an ada. They were noted for being mindless eating machines, and while grazing on the seagrasses, they were prey for the *lett*, sinuous parasites that would latch on the animals, sucking their blood. If enough latched onto a single tomak, they would suck enough blood to kill it. The lett would then leave the dead body and latch onto the next nearest victim.

When used as a pejorative, the meaning was clear. Leif was a victim, stupidly letting the parasitic humans suck away his life force.

"I am disappointed. Not for you, of course. But this would have been a reflection on my abilities. Wiping out your feeble force will hardly compare to the honor I would have received."

At some unseen signal, the four guards conducted an about-face, ready to escort the sere-blue back to the ship. The sere-blue gave a wry smile, and started to turn, only to stop, and face back to Leif.

"And what happened?" he asked.

"Sir? What happened where?"

"The monkey general who didn't surrender. What happened to him?"

"Him? They won, that's what happened. They held off the German forces."

Sere-blue Beleena's eyes opened wide, and he laughed again, deep belly laughs that shook his body.

"He won? Monkeys and their fairy tales." He spun around, and the five started their march back to the ship.

"Yes, he won," Leif muttered before he spun around as well and took off at a run. He had a battle to fight.

Chapter 35

"No more prep for the Marines," he told Corporal A'Bord. "I want all of them in their positions now."

"We're not ready," the corporal said.

"We don't have any more time. You can keep the sailors and the civilians working, but I want the sailors ready to fall into their positions and the civilians ready to pull back."

"The runners?"

"Not them. They need to be in position, too," Leif said.

It had been a hard decision to make, to put civilians directly in harm's way, but he needed every trigger-puller ready to fight. He'd accepted the inevitable and authorized civilian volunteers, mostly tokits from the contractors, to act as runners to relay orders and get information back to Leif at the CP.

"Sergeant," Star inserted herself, trying to catch his attention for the third time in less than a minute, this time grabbing his wrist.

"I don't have time now, Star," Leif said, snatching back his hand. "Whatever it is you have to take care of it."

The tokit was becoming an annoyance, and he didn't need that right now. He'd welcomed her into his inner circle, but now, when the shit was about to go down, he regretted his largess. He didn't even know who she was, what place she had within the rest of the tokits. He hadn't seen the first three tokits who he'd thought were leaders of some kind since the sere-blue's ultimatum, only Star.

"I need a runner," he shouted, and one of the rushed up. "Go to Lance Corporal Doon and tell him—"

Star grabbed his wrist again, pulling him around with surprising force for a person half his size.

"I need to speak to you now, Sergeant!"

Leif was working on adrenaline, and his nerves were taut. He instinctively almost struck the tokit, but after taking three deep, calming breaths, he bent over until they were almost eye-to-eye.

"You've got twenty seconds, Star."

"The sassares ship. I never knew it was going to land at the annex."

You're interrupting me to tell me that?

"Neither did I. But it did. So, what?"

"It's close. In the annex," she said, as if her meaning was clear.

"Look, Star. I don't have time to play guessing games. If you've got something to say, then say it. If not, then get the hell out of my way."

She blanched in the face of his anger, but she said, "There are tunnels from the base to the annex."

"Which we blocked."

That had been one of his first orders. He didn't need to contract his AO, but then give the sassares an easy route into his lines.

"Which we can unblock. Then, it wouldn't be far to the shuttle pad," she said. "Maybe three-hundred meters?"

Something began to tickle the back of his mind, but he was amped, and whatever it was remained just out of reach.

"And . . . ?"

"Grierson AAG has a tunnel team," she said.

Grierson was one of the major corporations hired to rebuild the base. The fact that they had tunnelers . . .

Oh, by the Mother's mercy!

"How long would it take this team to dig a tunnel to the pad, say, under that ship?" Leif asked as he understood what she was getting at.

Obvious relief flooded her eyes, and she seemed to gain confidence.

"About five hours. Maybe more, maybe less."

That long? I don't think that's enough time.

If the sassares attacked—when the sassares attacked—Leif didn't know how long they could hold them off. The five hours was actually quicker than he'd thought, but it probably wasn't quick enough.

Still, it was an option. And if they could get something tunneled to under the sassares ship, they had more than enough in the prepositioning supplies to rig up something nasty.

Anything was better than nothing, and it wouldn't be taking any Marines off the line. This was the easiest decision he'd had since taking command.

"Do it. Take whatever you need, and get it done."

Chapter 36

"What's your name?" Leif asked the runner, a tokit who looked too young to be given the task.

"Rransol, sir," he stammered.

Leif had given up trying to keep the civilians—and more than a few of the sailors—from calling him "sir." It wasn't worth the effort.

"So, Rransol, do you understand what you need to do?"

"Yes, sir," the tokit said, his voice soft.

"Why don't you tell me?" Leif asked.

Without comms, this message was too important, and the messenger would be in danger. There was a very significant chance that he wouldn't make it, and if he was cut down, Leif needed to know.

This is surreal. I'm probably sending this young kid to die, and all I'm worrying about is if the message gets delivered.

Leif had seen more than his fair share of death, but this was different. He selected this young tokit from the other runners, and it was on his orders that the kid was facing danger. It was a heavy responsibility, and it weighed on him, but he had to push it down in the recesses of his soul, almost like when he was denying his musapha. To let it surface would affect his ability to command.

"I need to deliver the message to the corporal, sir. Once I've done that, I need to hang the banner," the tokit said, patting the blue cloth he had wrapped around his stomach, under his shirt. "And I need to make sure you can see it from here."

"Good. You'll do fine," Leif said with a certainness that he didn't feel. "Go ahead, before the battle starts."

"Sergeant, why don't you send some more with him," Whist R, a Navy third class petty officer working for him in the CP asked.

"What do you mean? I don't want to increase the chances that my orders are compromised."

Rransol had memorized the message, so the only way it would get compromised was if he was captured and tortured. Leif thought it better to leave that part unsaid.

"Not with your orders. But as camouflage. You know, just some rats leaving a sinking ship."

Leif started to summarily dismiss the suggestion. He didn't want to put any more civilians in danger, and a group would be easier to spot, but then it hit him. She was right. A single tokit would most likely be spotted, and the sassares might take an interest in him. A group of unarmed tokits, seemingly fleeing the upcoming battle, would certainly be spotted, but would the sassares react? He didn't think they'd bother.

"Good suggestion, Whist R. Get it done, but I want Rransol on his way in five mikes."

"Aye-aye, sergeant," she said before turning to the tokit runner. "You, come with me. We're going to grab some of your friends and get you out of here."

She trotted off with an alindamir's easy stride, the tokits shorter legs working overtime to keep up.

Leif spared a glance to the hisser sailor sitting on the roof of the nearest warehouse. The sailor had his back to Leif and the CP, intent on the view to his front. Leif had chosen the CP because it had reinforced walls and good fields of vision over the east gate and over most of his defensive perimeter. What it didn't have was a line-of-sight to the annex. He'd never even considered the sassares landing in the shuttleport, which in retrospect, he should have. Now, he was down to relying on a sailor sitting on top of a building to give him a warning when the sassares started to debark their ship.

Leif checked the time. It had been twenty-three minutes since the sere-blue had left him at the gate. He wasn't sure why the sassares hadn't started their assault yet. But every minute they delayed was another minute in which to prepare. It was another minute for the tokit tunnel team to get another few meters along.

Part of him just wished they'd hurry up and start, though. His nervous energy was eating him up. He was so amped that he'd even considered a preemptive assault on the sassares ship, just taking all his Marines and sailors and charging into the fray.

Luckily, the rational Leif knew that this was just his mistress making herself known, and that would only hasten the end. They had only the slightest of chances to hold back the sassares soldier-sailors when they attacked. They had *no* chance standing up against the cruiser itself. He still half-expected the cruiser to take off and slag the camp, and the longer they waited for the ground assault to begin, the higher the chance that the sere-blue would decide to take the easy way out.

Unless . . .

No, that only happens in the holovids, Leefen a'Hope Hollow. The Navy isn't coming to the rescue. You need to fight your way out of this with what you've got.

Still, he couldn't help taking a look over his shoulder, hoping to see the Imperial Navy arriving to crush the sassares. The blue sky remained distressingly empty.

"Sergeant . . ." Corporal a'Bord said, catching his attention.

He turned to her. She was pointing over the sailor on the roof. Leif jerked himself around, and the sailor was on his feet facing him, wildly swinging a yellow towel.

The sassares were coming.

Chapter 37

The order of battle didn't look good. Sometimes, better training, better terrain, better intel could trump simple troops on the ground. This wasn't one of those times.

Leif had 65 Marines and 113 sailors of which only the 21 Seabees had even basic combat training. The rest of the personnel on the base were civilians. He had one howitzer and more than enough anti-armor Taipan missiles, hypervelocity Daggers, and HMGs. He'd hoped to have at least one of the Patras tanks available, but despite feverish efforts to bring them online, he didn't have any yet. Facing him were upwards of 1500 sassares sailors well-versed in infantry combat. The sassares would have mortars, HMGs, beamers, eight to twelve tanks, and most of all, a big, stinking cruiser. The ship might be designed for space combat, but its hull was impenetrable with the weapons Leif had at his disposal, and it had several weapons which could be used in an atmosphere.

The ship itself was a weapon. Sere-blue Beleena could just raise the ship and hover over the base, letting its engines cook all the imperial personnel there, and there was nothing Leif could do to stop that.

"That doesn't look like too many," Whist R said as they watched the debark.

It wasn't too many, maybe 200 sailors so far. More were debarking, however. Leif wondered if he should let his mortar teams fire, but he recognized the two counter-battery defense systems set up on either end of the ship. Designed to protect a ship on the ground, they'd pick up any mortars long before the rounds could splash. He had to wait until the sassares left the protective bulk of the ship before he let the teams fire.

"More are coming," Leif said.

"Why don't we attack them?" the sailor asked.

Whist R was a bright sailor, and her idea to send out dummy messengers had been sound, but she wasn't a Marine.

She didn't understand ground combat. Some of the milling sassares were within view, and Leif could employ his snipers to start picking them off, but when a weaker force is faced with a larger, better-armed force, one way to mitigate that disadvantage was to intermix the forces. It was risky, but if the two sides were in close combat, the heavy weapons on the ship would be much more limited in where and when they could be deployed.

Leif had to get the sassares in close to his Engagement Area, his EA, then hit them hard in hopes that the Marines' professionalism and shock would turn the tide. In this vein, as much as he hated to do it, he had to use some of his sailors as sacrificial lambs, to use an apt Earth phrase. Once the attack commenced, Navy teams would take them under fire, trading volume for accuracy. It was only as the attackers reached the outer belt of minefields just beyond his FEBA (the Forward Edge of Battle Area) that the better-disciplined Marines would emerge from their fighting positions and engage the enemy.

Leif took a step back to look at where his single howitzer was hidden. Lance Corporal Toshi, a battalion mortar man, was the gun captain, aided by four tokit mechanics and the engineer who had pulled the gun out of storage and rigged the firing mechanism. Leif was counting on the lance corporal to give the sassares a huge slap in the face, adding to the shock value.

"They're doing something, sir," Whist R said, snapping Leif's attention back around.

Leif couldn't tell how many sassares had exited the ship yet, but it didn't seem like that many. Certainly, nowhere near the 1500 on the ship. But it did look like they were moving. The crump of sassares mortar fire from the teams set up behind the bulk of the ship, reached Leif and his fighters. Leif had counter-battery radar, but no one had been able to find a working counter-battery gun. Leif didn't need to have the radar working. He knew what was coming. The sassares prep fires had begun, and according to sassares doctrine, the assault would be right on its heels.

Leif raised his hand, two fingers outstretched, and the sailor standing on the roof dropped her towel and gave two blasts on the airhorn, the signal for everyone to take cover in their positions. The newly excavated holes would not protect anyone from a direct hit, but they were fairly effective against near misses.

Leif didn't take cover. He had to watch, so he'd had a sandbag barrier built up to offer some protection while he monitored what was happening. It wasn't as good as a dug-in fighting position, but it was better than nothing.

As the first mortars started landing along both the fence line and the base headquarters, the first wave of sassares started pouring around both sides of the ship. Leif hadn't expected much from a sailor/soldier, but their fire and maneuver was on par with even that of Marines. At this range, it looked like squad rushes, with each squad being upright and on the move for no more than five seconds before hitting the deck. It made for an exhausting attack, but it kept fighters out of the line of opposing fire. Half of the possibly 250 strong sassares had blown a break in the annex fence and were bypassing it. The other half stayed inside the annex, which made for a little tougher going, but gave them more cover.

Leif lifted three fingers, and the sailor on the roof gave three blasts. Within moments, fire reached out from the Imperial lines. Leif quickly glassed the sassares advance. Between the sassares' fire and maneuver and the lack of Navy marksmanship, not many of the enemy were falling. He had to make a more spirited defense before he sprang his Marines or the sassares would know something was up.

He'd had a back-up plan, one he didn't want to use yet. He didn't think he had a choice, however. He held up his left hand with one finger, and the sailor on the roof dropped his airhorn and picked up another. The sailor gave two blasts of a piercing whistle.

Almost immediately, eight of his 16 snipers opened up, and seven sassares fell. They managed two more volleys before the enemy battle surveillance picked them out. One-by-one, the automatic weapons base of fire, set up under the bulk of the ship and providing overwatch for the assault forces, started rooting out the snipers, silencing them. Lance

Corporal a'Monti was hit in full view of Leif as the younger Marine was displacing from one position to another.

Leif watched the Marine, a fellow Silver Ranger, struggle to pull himself into cover with his arms, leaving a trail of scarlet in the dirt before he tore his gaze away, steeling himself to the fact that he had already lost men and women, and he was going to lose more before the fight was over.

The two sassares prongs were not advancing equally. The ones outside the annex were covering more ground, and that was worrisome. Leif's plan was to hit all the sassares at the same time to induce panic, but with the sere-blue splitting them up into two forces, that was going to be problematic.

He needed to figure out a way to speed up the sassares still in the annex or slow down the ones who were bypassing it. No easy answer was magically popping into his head.

In ancient times, musapha was thought to be the spirits of long-dead warriors coming back to help the living. Leif wished that was true, and his mistress had been a tactical genius. Anything to help him figure out a solution.

A mortar round landed just in front of Leif position, shrapnel stitching the sandbags and one piece pinging off his helmet. Whist R yelped and slapped a hand to her cheek, bringing it back bloody. She sunk to a sitting position, back up against the sandbags. The skin on her face and hands skin swirled in a myriad of colors that Leif didn't need to get translated. They *looked* like panic.

"Let me see that," Leif said, pulling her close and checking the wound. "Just a scratch. You're fine."

It was a little more than a scratch, but he needed her functional. If she lived through this, she'd recover fine and have a nice battle scar to boot. He pulled out a pressure bandage out of his medkit and slapped it on her, then purposely turned away as if her wound was of no import.

By regulation, he shouldn't have given her his bandage, but not all the sailors had been issued medkits yet.

Another thing I screwed up.

He gave her a quick glance out of the corner of his eye as she shook herself and stood back up, her skin slowing down to pale yellows and rose.

Leif fingered the small gouge in his helmet. He'd hate to get taken out by a mortar. Dead was dead, but a round fired by an unseen enemy was hardly a way for a warrior to meet his end.

Hell, I've got to do it, he thought as the realization hit him. There wasn't another choice.

This wasn't going to be as easy as having an airhorn blast. He motioned to one of the tokit messengers who was huddling with the rest inside a single fighting hole. The man crawled out and ran up to him.

"I need you to go to Corporal Atteen. I want twenty-four rounds at B-3 and B-4. One-hundred-and-fifty-meter spread. Repeat that for me."

"Twenty-four rounds at B-3 and B-4. One-hundred-and-fifty-meter spread, sir," the civilian runner said.

"Good. Go!" he said, slapping the smaller person on the back as he took off. Leif watched him run back for a moment before looking forward again, glassing the advance.

Maybe I should have ordered 36 rounds.

Leif looked around at the other four runners. He could send another, but he held back.

"Let's see what happens here first. Right, Whist R?"

"Uh, right," she almost squeaked.

The sassares base of fire was still putting out rounds, but the Imperial fire had slackened. Either the sailors were getting taken out or they'd lost their initial enthusiasm. Leif had to engage his Marines soon, or the sassares would have gained too much momentum. He could already see a sense of confidence in the sassares as they advanced, spending longer times on their feet as they rushed forward.

What about you, Sere-blue Baleena? Are you feeling confident? he wondered as he looked at the ship, still sitting menacingly on the pad.

It still hadn't fired upon the Imperials as if they were too insignificant to rate such as response. Rather insulting, when it came down to that, but an insult Leif was more than willing to bear.

From behind him, inside the walled basketball courts, two teams of mortars, four total tubes, fired their first salvo, quickly followed by five more. That took a lot of time, enough for a sassares response to be fired, but there still should be time for them to displace out of range of the return fire before it splashed.

The closest sassares counter-battery opened up. Leif couldn't see if it was knocking the mortar shells out, which had minimal evasive capabilities using gravity and movable vanes. Leif counted down the time, reaching 40, 45 seconds with nothing.

Some of them must have made it, he thought, standing higher to get a better view, when the first four rounds hit among a squad of sassares just as they were rising to rush forward. Seven were blown off their feet while one staggered to the side. Only two rounds landed next with little effect other than to keep the sassares down, which was the intent. Still, Leif was hoping for more casualties.

After the fourth salvo hit, this one with only one mortar getting through the ship's counterbattery fire, Leif turned to look over at the basketball courts where the Marine mortar teams were fleeing, tubes on their shoulders. A moment after he looked, the courts erupted in explosions, flooding Leif with relief that it looked like all the Marines had made it out. That relief was short lived when the entire area, almost reaching to the artillery piece and one of the buildings the civilian tokits were taking refuge, went up in a holocaust. At least fifty rounds landed, more than Leif had thought possible.

When the dust and smoke cleared, most of the mortar team was gone. Two Marines got to their feet. Two out of eight.

Leif underestimated the sassares response. He knew he should have had the two teams fire fewer rounds, giving them longer to displace.

It was torture knowing that every little missed detail cost Imperial lives. He vowed to do better. He just didn't know how to do that. For the hundredth time, he wished the Captain or Gunny Dream Bear were here and in charge, not lying in a coma back with the rest of the still surviving humans. It was all on him, though, so he had to man up.

The mortar attack had slowed down the quicker group, but they were still ahead. But they were about to enter the first minefield. To Leif, the ground looked too freshly disturbed, too obvious, but after picking themselves up off the ground, the sassares started their rushes again, but breaking down to four running forward at a time, what the Marines would call fire team rushes. The first team of four to enter the minefield failed to trigger anything, and for a moment, Leif was afraid they'd screwed up emplacing the small but powerful mines.

The second group of four, however, were not so lucky. One of the sailor-soldiers triggered an ankle cutter, taking two of them down, clutching their legs and writhing in pain.

One of them sat up and reached back for help before he was shot and dropped motionless in the dirt.

"Come on!" Leif yelled in frustration. He turned to Whist R and said, "He was non-effective, and it would have taken another of them out of the fight to pull the wounded guy back. We need to think and not blindly act."

Whist R just looked at him, her eyes big. It was probably unfair of him to expect his makeshift group of fighters to be aware of all the nuances of infantry warfare.

The big sassares cruiser finally broke its quiet, but not in the manner Leif had expected. The big energy cannon rotated and fired a blast right into the minefield. An explosion of dirt reached for the sky, falling back to a cleared section. Three more blasts, and the minefield was clear. The ship was an expensive, but effective minesweeper.

With a cheer, the sassares started rushing forward while taking minimal fire from Leif's forces. He was going to have to commit his Marines, but he wanted to hold off as long as possible until he had more in His EA, his kill zone.

The minefield did delay the group long enough for the other prong to figuratively catch up, reaching the base from the annex. Here, the Imperial sailors had a better position and were putting up a little stiffer resistance.

Just a little bit farther, Leif thought.

He looked up to his signalman on the roof, who was watching him intently. It was almost time.

Below and to his left, Imperial fire had almost disappeared, and the sassares were speeding up again. Leif could feel their confidence grow as they prepared to overcome whatever resistance was left. He couldn't wait any longer.

Lifting his left hand, Leif flashed five fingers. His signalman nodded, air horn in hand, and stood . . . only to be cut down by enemy fire. His arm flung up, the airhorn flying up in the air to bounce on the low wall, spin, then tumble to the ground a dozen meters below.

"Get that horn, Whist!" Leif yelled. "Five blasts!"

The sailor, bandage on her throat, looked up at Leif with wide eyes, red and white flashing up her face in waves.

"Now, sailor!"

She scrambled to her feet and ran up the slope, quick as a grazpin. It took her a moment to find the airhorn, but she held it aloft and blew five long notes.

Immediately, the Marines came up from their holes and a heavy fusillade of fire raked the sassares forces, dropping dozens within the first minute as they scrambled for cover. They slowed, and Leif hoped that the assault was broken, but as their base of fire started finding Marine targets, the attack started moving again, closing to within 100 meters of the Marine and Navy lines.

It wasn't just Marines firing. Surviving sailors had regained their fighting spirit and were joining in, but it wasn't enough. With their base of fire in support, the sassares kept pushing forward.

Leif still had one more trick up his sleeve . . . but so did the sassares. Leif had forgotten about the sassares tanks. Sere-blue Beleena hadn't. He'd been holding them back for maximum impact. Leif was so intent on the disposition of the leading edge of the assaulting force in his EA that he missed them powering down the ramp of the ship. His battalion Marines didn't, though. A flurry of Taipans reached out just as the lead two tanks opened fire. The lead tank got out one shot that took out a chunk of fence before it was hit. The second tank fired off flares and managed two shots before it was destroyed. The Taipans were like the mosquitos back at Camp Navarro, swarming to taste blood. The follow-on two tanks sped up, spitting out decoys and firing round after round, but the Taipans kept coming.

Each time a Marine fired, however, they gave up their position, the trail of the missile like a reverse arrow pointing right at them. The sassares base of fire was raking the Marines, dropping them like flies.

Leif couldn't wait any longer. He pulled out a pop-up, aimed, and fired it into the air. It burst into silver sparks, visible to the entire Marine defense.

"Fire the FPF," reverberated from the lines as Marines took up the cry.

The remaining M-31's opened up for the first time, spewing death. The last two mortar teams pumped out round after round. His big hammer, however, was the field gun. Lance Corporal Toshi and the tokit engineer had carefully aimed the gun with Kentucky windage at the base of the ship. The gun, while powerful, wouldn't do much other than scrape up the paint on it, but it was more than powerful enough to take out the base of fire that had set up just under it, safe from Marine mortars, and with their portable barricade, safe from small arms. The field gun might be old, but it wasn't small arms.

The first round blew part the barricade and detonated five meters past, shrapnel tearing through sassares bodies. The shrapnel that had exploded upwards hit the underside of the ship and ricocheted back down, taking out more of them. The second blast essentially sealed the deal. The base of fire had been broken, which freed the Marines and sailors to be more aggressive as they fired into the two masses of sassares, cutting down the infantry and taking out the last two tanks. The mortar rounds started falling, but it was another blast from Toshi and his crew that started the rout. Somehow, one wyntonan and five tokits had horsed the thing around and fired into the kill zone.

First one, then two, then the trickle became a stream as the assault force turned in retreat, chased by more firing from the Imperials. Leif stood up to get a better look, fearing this was a trick.

It wasn't, but the sassares were not going to go quietly. The big cannon on the ship was slow to aim, and it had been last fired to clear the minefield near the East Gate. In his excitement and stress, Leif had forgotten about it, but Sere-blue Beleena reminded him of his overwhelming power when the cannon hummed, then fired a bolt into the camp, over the head of his lines. The ionization of the near miss burned Leif's nose until he realized that the cannon hadn't missed. He ran a few steps back and looked down the slope, knowing what he was going to see.

The artillery piece, Toshi, and his team were gone. They'd paid the price for turning the tide.

The sassares were fleeing the battle, but Leif didn't feel victorious. There might be a hundred dead sassares just in his sight, but he didn't know yet how many of his own troops paid the butcher's bill, only that the number was too high.

And the sere-blue hadn't even hit him with a full force. It had been little more than a probe, a probe that had almost broken the back of the Imperials.

When the sassares hit them again, and they would, Leif didn't know if he had the forces to turn them back.

Chapter 38

Leif was numb as he stood over the wreckage of the howitzer. Most of it was a twisted pile of slag with only the cerraloy barrel recognizable. The ground around the artillery piece had been fused into black glass. Of Lance Corporal Toshi and his tokit crew, there was nothing. They were gone, as if they'd never existed.

Leif didn't know the battalion Marine, and of the five, he'd only met the tokit engineer. He never even got his name. They were erased before he could get to know them, and that had him feeling inadequate to be in command.

"Any of you know them?" Leif asked his entourage of runners, one hisser and four tokits.

"Grastian was my *deltar*," one of his runners said quietly.

Leif didn't know what a *deltar* was, and he couldn't look it up with the sassares blanketing the base, but he could infer it was an important relationship.

"I'm sorry for your loss," Leif said.

"For the whole," the runner said, as the other three tokits immediately parroted him in what was an obvious rote response.

At least it was quick, he thought before quickly berating himself.

Quick or not, they were dead. Civilians, not Marines. Every Marine, and sailor too, for that matter, signed up knowing that death was a real possibility. Toshi knew that. His five tokit crew did not come to Sunrise to fight, however. They were hired by Grierson or one of the other contractors to rebuild a base, not to man an old artillery piece, not to be vaporized when a sassares cruiser unleashed a weapon meant to take down other ships.

Yet, they had all volunteered to man the gun.

Was it worth it? Leif asked himself. *Should I have just surrendered the base?*

Twenty-one Marines, forty-two sailors, and he didn't know yet how many civilians were now dead, and for what? A short reprieve?

His command had only turned back the assault because for reasons only known to him, the sere-blue had sent out a partial force, using the brute power of the ship only against the howitzer and to clear a minefield. Maybe he wanted to make a statement. Maybe he was using those out of favor with him to probe Leif's defenses. Maybe . . .

All the maybes in the galaxy didn't matter. What mattered was that the sere-blue wasn't going to do that again. The next assault would be in earnest. With 1500 originally on the ship, and with close to a hundred dead, he had possibly a thousand or eleven-hundred to commit to the assault, assuming it took a couple hundred to keep the ship running.

Leif was pulling that out of his ass, though. He wasn't even sure how many were aboard the cruiser, and for all he knew, it only needed a couple to man whatever stations had to be manned, freeing up the rest of the sailors for infantry duty.

This whole sassares thing about their sailors and infantry being interchangeable, just trading one hat for the other as the mission changes, was almost incomprehensible to Leif. In the old days back on Home, raiders rowed their *listans* as crew, then hopped out, axe or spear in hand to wreak havoc among their enemies. That was a long time ago, however, and warfare had become much more specialized.

Leif had to assume that while good at both missions, the individual sailor-soldier could not match an Imperial Marine as an infantryman.

Then again, Leif had 45 Marine effectives left, and Sere-blue Beleena had at least a thousand.

"Sergeant Hope Hollow!" Lance Corporal Hulorin shouted as she landed a few meters from Leif and his runners. "The sassares are coming."

By the Mother, what am I doing? I didn't need to come see this now! I still have a job to do.

"Where, and how many?" he shouted, starting to run back to the CP.

"About twenty," the qiincer said, "and they've got their red ribbons flying."

That brought Leif to a sudden halt.

"Red ribbons. You mean their parlay banners?"

The qiincer scowled, then said, "Two long red ribbons hanging from a bar perched on top of a pole. Carrying it like a fucking trophy."

Not a trophy. They want to talk.

"Where are they heading?"

"Looks like to the annex gate. Where you talked to them before."

"Get Corporal a'Bord, Star, and Katako N and tell them to meet me there at the gate," he ordered.

The qiincer nodded, then took off, flying back to the CP.

"Let's move it, he told his runners knowing that he should wait for some security. He wanted, to be at the gate before the sassares arrived, however.

They cut between the buildings and down to the perimeter road before slowing to a walk and taking a left to the gate. The five arrived and were met a few minutes later by a'Bord and Katako N. He looked around for Star, but she wasn't there.

"You two, go stand next to Corporal a'Bord. Try to look like you belong," he told his hisser runner and the tokit who'd lost a relation at the howitzer.

The sere-blue had played the we're-all-inclusive race card at the last meeting, but Leif could play that game, too. He waited until the two took their position, then turned to face the gate. On the other side, still 200 meters out, Sere-blue Beleena, surrounded by his security team, and preceded by a single sassares holding aloft the twin parlay banners, strolled toward him.

Leif tried to pull out from one of his classes back at recruit training the terms of a sassares parlay. Held aloft by a crossbar—a gonfolon, the term suddenly came to him—two bright red banners hung. Red was the sassares color of peace, and when raised, all fighting ceased. For how long, he didn't remember. He didn't even remember if the bearer could simply drop it and end a cease-fire. More, now then ever, he wished he had the simple access to the net that he'd taken for granted all his life.

He tried to calm the tic that suddenly appeared under his left eye. His mistress rumbled deep inside of him, and he was tempted for a moment to let her rise. He needed the surge of confidence musapha brought with her.

What he didn't need was anything else she brought. He had to remain calm and find out what the sere-blue wanted.

For a brief moment, he wondered if the initial assault had proven so costly to the sassares that they were going to cede the field of battle. Watching the sere-blue as his party approached dispelled that little fantasy. The sassares was too cocky, too assured of himself. That wasn't a person about to give up.

Leif waited in silence as the sassares detail halted, leaving the sere-blue to walk up to the gate. Leif swore he could smell the arrogance from the man. No, he was not about to announce he'd given up.

"Made me walk quite a ways, Sergeant. Couldn't you have chosen your last defense a little closer to the spacepad?"

"Couldn't you have brought your ship down a little closer to us?" Leif snapped back before he realized what he was going to say.

Get ahold of yourself, Leefen. Don't let your nerves betray you.

"I supposed I could have," the sere-blue said, sweeping his eyes over the cleared area between the base and the start of the city. "Habit, I guess."

He turned back to Leif and said, "You surprised me, Sergeant. You did better than I thought you would against my probe. I can see why the sere-blacks would like you wyntonans to come to your senses and join us.

"So, I have to ask, have you assuaged your sense of honor enough to succumb to the inevitable? Whether you personally join us or not, your people will. It's really their only choice. All that will happen if you refuse is that you will needlessly die."

Leif's mistress flared, but he knew the sere-blue was baiting him. He was probably right about them dying, but Leif wasn't sure that the People would join the sassares.

I'm not sure they won't either, he had to admit to himself.

"We pushed you back once. If you want to get your ass kicked again, then have at it," he said, pointing to where dead sassares bodies still lay unclaimed on the ground not 150 meters from them. "We haven't changed our minds. So, unless you want to die here on this human world, that is *your* only choice."

"You said 'we haven't changed our minds.' Is that the royal we? So human of you. How many of the others agree with you?" he asked, looking at the tokit, hisser, and qiincer backing up Leif.

Leif wanted to turn around to see their expressions, but he knew the sassares wanted him to do that. He wanted Leif to doubt himself. The thing is, he was doubting himself. He'd been doubting himself since he'd made the decision to fight. If it was just the Marines and the Navy, that would be one thing. They'd sworn an oath to the Granite Throne, to the empire. Leif had sworn another oath to the empress. Their decision was a done deal. On the other hand, however, the civilians, four or five thousand of them, had never sworn such an oath, and the tokits and hissers, in particular, had a long and regrettable history with the humans. Was he right in making a decision that affected them, too?

He wasn't too sure about that.

"I am in command here. It is my decision. But my Marines and sailors know their duty."

"That tokit doesn't look like a Marine," the sere-blue said.

Leif said nothing.

The sere-blue looked at him for a moment, then broke out into a belly laugh, the third time he'd done that in the two conversations the two had had.

"I expected that, Sergeant. And I regrettably respect you for it. The sere-blacks are right to want you. Not just your people, but you. My regret is that your DNA ends here. There is no other option for that.

"However, in the interest in saving lives, all of yours and, yes, some of mine, there is an option."

"An option?" Leif asked, suspicious of anything the sassares might say.

"An option." Sere-blue Beleena turned and looked at the wyntonan in his security detail.

The wyntonan glared at Leif for a long moment, and Leif felt his mistress struggle to break free. It took an effort of will to tamp her back down.

With the bold swinging steps of a male in musth, he sauntered forward. For one of the People to strut like that to another when not in musth or heat was a grave insult, but Leif held his temper. Losing his head would do no one any good.

The wyntonan was big, as tall as Leif, but sporting another 15kg of muscle, and there was a looseness in his walk the belied his size. This was an impressive specimen of the People.

The wyntonan reached the gate, grabbed the vertical bars with both hands, and pressed his face right up against the spacing.

"*Atonya fosteel wynton ymat tú,*" he spit out with a snarl.

In Standard, "I challenge you to an honor duel."

****

"Are you sure you want to do this?" Corporal a'Bord asked.

"No, I'm not, but this is the only way out I can see," Leif answered.

That was a lie. He *did* want to do this. How could he not? His blood was pounding, adrenaline coursing through his body. His mistress kept prodding him, wanting to be released.

"What about the—"

"We don't know if the tokits will ever make it to the ship," Leif said, shucking the last of his body armor. "We can't count on that."

"And if you lose. I mean, not that I think you will. But if you do. We're supposed to surrender to them?"

"That's up to Petty Officer Katako N," Leif said, nodding at the sailor who was standing back, nervously wringing her hands. "Not that I plan to lose."

Leif had made that clear when the sere-blue had thrown down his proposition that if Leif was killed, whatever orders he'd given before were null and void. Katako N, as the senior military member, would be in command, and any decision would be on her. The sere-blue had taken one look at the nervous sailor, then dismissively agreed to his condition. If Leif won, he'd pull back and leave the planet. If Leif lost, it would be up to Katako N to decide whether to surrender or not.

So, now, Sergeant Leefen a'Hope Hollow, Imperial Marine Corps, was about to enter into *fosteel*. Marines didn't do this. Personal combat was not in the SOP.

Hell, wyntonans didn't enter in *fosteel*, at least not for a hundred years or more. Sure, there were rumors that well past the Leif's Silver Range, out in the Great Morass where old traditions held sway among the secretive villagers, *fosteel* was still practiced. But Intikan a'Bay, his opponent, was not one of those on the fringes of the People. His accent was Plains, from the capital.

The big wyntonan had stripped down to his shorts and was going through a series of stylized warm-up positions. *Ros* had undergone somewhat of a revival since the People's assimilation into the empire. According to accepted lore, *ros* fights were to the death. In modern times, however, this was illegal, and practitioners of the ancient martial art wore pads on the arms and legs, and edged weapons were synthetic blanks.

A'Bay wasn't bringing out the pads for this fight. This was going to be for real. Leif could see the excitement in his opponent that even exceeded his own. The wyntonan was one of the *punaran*, a dismissive term for the almost religiously radical xenophobes who wanted to turn back the calendar to the olden times before the People knew of any others. They shunned modern technology, wanting to revert back to the old ways.

Yet you are fighting for the sassares, and you ply the stars in their ships. Not hypocritical, are we?

Leif dropped his shirt, then took off his boots. He started to remove the tokit Nonnana talisman from his neck, but hesitated, looking at it for a long moment. With a shrug, he let it fall back to his chest.

It can't hurt, right?

The tokit he'd sent to stand with the other two gave him a small smile of appreciation.

With only his trousers on, he stretched his own muscles and joints, jumping up and down to warm up as he watched a'Bay. The wyntonan moved smoothly from one kata to the other. Leif knew that he wasn't a dilatant, dabbling in the ancient art. He was skilled, and he'd be a fierce opponent. Leif couldn't underestimate him just because he was a punaran fanatic.

Leif might have never trained in *ros*, but he'd been through the MCIBA 3, the Marine Corps Individual Battle Action, Level 3. It might not be as stylized as ros, but it was the street-fight version of hand-to-hand combat, the eye-gouging, nut-kicking, anything-goes-to-take-down-the-enemy style of fighting.

And Leif had his ace-in-the-hole. He was the only person that he knew of who could control his mistress. He could call forth musapha at will, negating any advantage in experience a'Bay had. Was that ethical? Probably not to the purist his opponent was, but Leif wasn't an ideolog. He was a MCIBA-trained Marine, and he'd use every advantage he had to prevail. He didn't have a choice—he couldn't afford to lose.

Leif, Corporal a'Bord, the tokit, and Petty Officer Katako N were outside the gate, outnumbered by the sere-blue and his entourage. Twenty Marines, sailors, and civilians were lining in the inside of the perimeter fence, giving Leif morale support.

Leif rotated his neck a few times, gave a last few jumps, then stepped out in front of a'Bord and Katako N.

"Are you ready?" the sere-blue asked him. "Do you need more time?"

Leif reached in back of him, palm up, and Corporal a'Bord, acting as his second, place his vic in his hand. He brought it in front of him, gave it a quick glance, then lowered the hand to his en garde position.

"I'm ready now. Let's bring it on."

As the challenged individual, Leif had the choice of weapons or not, and he'd foolishly ceded the choice to a'Bay.

"Never give away any advantage in a fight, and use the ones you had," Gunny O'Neil, his Level 3 MCIBA instructor had stressed, and he'd forgotten that.

A'Bay had chosen knives, and the way he was twisting around his *talid*, and curved blade favored by sea raiders of old, he'd had practice with it. Leif had used his vic to kill two people, but he didn't consider himself a bladesman. His plan was to close in and make the fight hand-to-hand.

"Are you sure? I don't want to step on any wyntonan traditions."

Right. You don't give a shit about our traditions. You're trying to sell your war with the humans to us.

"I'm ready," Leif snarled.

The tiniest quirk in the corner of the sere-blue's mouth was enough to let Leif know the sassares had successfully goaded him, got in his mind.

Tune him out.

"Elder a'Bay, are you ready?"

Elder! He's no elder! Leif thought, opening his mouth to protest until he realized that this was just one more mind game."

"I am ready."

"In that case, there's one tradition we have. Uanamo, please halve the tenlien," he said to the sassares holding the twin banners aloft.

The standard bearer slowly lowered the banners by 45 degrees, the tips of the red banners just brushing the ground.

"By lowering the banners, we allow the agreed upon combat to take place. By keeping the banners aloft, we remind all others that the rules of *Hnomn* are still in effect. No matter what happens, no matter who wins the fight, the rest of us will not take action against anyone else for the duration," he said, taking the time to sweep his eyes past the mostly armed imperials lining the fence.

He's afraid that one of my Marines will take him out if I get killed. No reason to worry, Sere-blue. I'm not going to lose.

"If that's understood, then let's proceed and get this over with. I'm afraid I am not up on your *fosteel* traditions," he said, managing the wyntonan word quite well, "So, is there anything else that has to be done?"

"No. We just fight," a'Bay said.

Which suited Leif just as well. He'd seen fosteel bouts on holovids before, but those were fantasies created for entertainment. He didn't know if there were any traditions associated with them. But a'Bay, who would know if there were any, had said no.

Leif didn't hesitate. He called forth his mistress, feeling her invade his arteries, filling him with power. It had been months since he last set her free, and he wondered why he kept her locked away. This must be how it felt to be a god, to fulfill his potential.

With a roar, he started to close with his opponent as the musapha gave him power and speed and . . . there was something else that tickled his senses, but overridden by the power surge that wanted to rend and tear the puny person who dared to stand in his way, the minion of the sassares.

Leif reached for a'Bay's left arm, the one holding the talid, as it descended, to block it and create an opening for his much smaller vic. But the other wyntonan was impossibly quick, diverting his swing forward, making Leif miss it. At the same time, a'Bay shot his right arm out, palm forward, to hit Leif's left arm at the elbow in a tremendous blow that pushed his arm aside.

A'Bay's talid, diverted to the front, swept down, just missing Leif's leg by millimeters. Leif, still rushing forward, brought the knee up and struck the extended arm before the two fighters broke away from each other.

There was a combined gasp from both sets of observers. They had to have been shocked at the speed of what had just happened, and that neither fighter had been cut. That wasn't to say they were untouched. Leif's elbow was beginning to hurt, the pain breaking through his musapha. There had been a tremendous amount of force in a'Bays' blow.

And Leif knew what he'd sensed. No normal wyntonan could react so quickly and with such force. A'Bay had called forth his own mistress. His body was coursing with musapha.

A'Day must have realized that Leif was under his mistress' spell as well. He paused, a gleam in his eyes before he smiled and quietly said, "*Vieheim.*"

"My enemy," but with an almost respectful connotation.

If he expected Leif to return the salutation, he was going to be sadly disappointed. Leif didn't have time for that. He'd never fought someone under the thrall of their mistress. His big advantage had just vanished, and a'Bay had more knife-fighting training.

But have you ever drawn blood yet? I have.

The two started slowly circling each other, both wary now of simply bull-rushing in. Leif considered the talid. Curved, it was a wicked slicing weapon, but a'Bay needed room to wield it. Leif's own vic was too short to do much damage with its edge, but it was made for stabbing, to puncture through armor and pierce vital organs.

It was clear to Leif that he had to close in, taking away his opponent's ability to wield his sword and giving him the opportunity to bury his vic into the *punaran* fanatic. But how could he do that? A'Bay was holding his talid in front of him at the diagonal, edge facing Leif. If Leif charged in, a simple slice in almost any direction would score.

Leif could feel his opponent's musapha, or rather, he could feel a sympathetic resonance that seemed to heighten his own mistress. Every other time Leif had been under the sway of musapha, he'd felt confidence, he'd felt almost invincible. It was no different now. He wanted to close in and crush a'Bay, but with him under musapha as well, the rational Leif had to take that under consideration. He knew he had to use his mistress, not let her use him, if he was going to survive the next few minutes.

A'Bay feinted a lunge, and Leif immediately reacted, dodging down and to the side, the coming up underneath the slash. But the other wyntonan never completed the lunge, turning his talid to the side. He knew Leif would be wanting to close in, and he had to guess which side Leif would pick.

He chose correctly, angling his talid to his right, the tip catching Leif high on the shoulder. Leif dove out of reach, rolling to come to his feet facing his opponent, ready for the follow-up. A'Bay had extended to try and catch Leif, and he was recovering as well, coming to en garde.

Leif knew he'd been scored, but the musapha masked the pain, and he still had motion in his left arm. His shoulder joint had turned the blade just enough. He was losing blood, but he was still functional.

There were shouts from both sides as the bright red blood rolled down his white skin. Leif tuned them out, putting all his attention on the wyntonan facing him.

He shook his arm, splattering blood and interrupting the flow. He had to keep his grip on his vic dry. A'Bay's eyes lit up, first for drawing blood, then as he realized the blood could make Leif's grip on his weapon precarious. His eyes flicked ever-so-briefly on Leif's hand, and Leif knew he was going to focus his next attack on the arm. Leif, or maybe his mistress, forced his body into action before he'd thought out what he had to do next, instinct taking over.

With a shout, Leif flicked his knife-hand at a'Bay's eyes as he stepped in, splattering bloody droplets. He was too far away to connect with the vic, and a'Bay's eyes widened as he saw his chance, turning his talid to the horizontal and slicing up at Leif's exposed arm, knowing Leif couldn't withdraw it our-of-range at the time.

Leif knew that too, and he didn't try to pull back. Instead, he pushed forward, shortening his opponent's swing, and as the talid dug into his forearm, he used his momentum to swing his right leg in a roundhouse kick, connecting at the side of a'Bay's left knee.

The wyntonan's leg buckled, the ligaments and tendons destroyed, throwing off the rest of his swing. Leif planted his right foot, and while a'Bay flailed to keep his balance, Leif kicked again with his left, right between a'Bay's legs, who folded with a grunt.

The talid's blow had knocked his vic from his hand. Leif pounced on it with his right hand. A'Bay was struggling to get up, pushing against the pommard of his talid, the tip of the weapon in the dirt. As Leif closed in, a look of resignation came over his face, but he still tried to fight, whipping up the talid with a supernatural effort that almost defied gravity, the tip of the weapon missing Leif's face by millimeters.

Leif wasn't going to give him a second chance. Without the talid propping him up, his opponent fell heavily to the ground, and as he tried to get up again, Leif stepped on his sword arm and thrust his vic into a'Bay's throat, driving the tip into his temporal lobe.

Intikan a'Bay shuddered once and died. Held up by Leif's right hand, Leif pulled his vic back, and the body flopped on the deck, bright red blood spurting obscenely twice before the flow evened out.

Leif's left arm had taken a deep cut, but still, his mistress kept the pain at bay. Without another glance at his fellow wyntonan, Leif marched up to Sere-blue Beleena, who instinctively took a small step back, hand straying to the cover of his holster. The sere-blue's guards tensed up, ready for action.

"Sere-blue Beleena, I have defeated your champion in *fosteel*. As you agreed, you will now board your ship and depart Sunrise, leaving us in peace."

The arrogance flowed back into the sassares, and he gave another of the belly laughs that Leif had begun to hate.

"So, you think I'm going to be governed by some backward race's inane traditions?" he said, gaining confidence.

"You gave your word," Leif said, hope beginning to fade.

"I lied. And now you will die."

He shouted something in his native language, but before anyone else could respond, the sassares carrying the tenlien barked something out as well, shaking it for emphasis as he raised it to the vertical.

That stopped the sere-blue. He slowly turned around and told Leif, "Under the shadow of the tenlien, we have a temporary truce, and never let it be said that Isoma Beleena broke that. You have thirty minutes to make your peace with your gods."

With that, he wheeled away and strode off, followed by his security team.

Leif stood there for a few moments, trying to corral his mistress and forcing her back down. Musapha took a lot out of a person, and he had to be functional. She rebelled, but she had no choice. Leif was too strong.

As she left, the pain surged through him. With a gasp, he fell to his knees, his arm on fire. As if a signal, his Marines and sailors broke into motion. Corporal a'Bord and Petty Officer Katako N rushed to his side. The medic took one look at his arm before calling for a pressure bandage.

"What do we do now, Sergeant?" the corporal asked and she helped him to his feet.

"What do we do? We fight, Marine. We fight."

Chapter 39

"They're not being subtle about it," Lance Corporal Tesoomo D, the surviving hisser Marine, said.

With Leif operating at less than 100%, the lance corporal was acting as his aide-de-camp, bagman, bodyguard, and assistant, all rolled into one. Less than 100% was an understatement. Leif was barely functioning. He was drained, and all he wanted to do was to curl up and go to sleep. Even his mistress was quiet. With the sassares assault looking like it was about to kick off, however, he couldn't afford to zone out. He had to remain alert.

Leif was still in command, but he'd turned over many of his commander-on-the-ground duties to Corporal a'Bord, even if Oana Ulo was senior to her. No disrespect intended, but he wanted an infantry Marine instead of a Navy petty officer to lead the fight.

Leif wasn't completely out of it, though. Perched on top of the building where his lookout had been, he had a full view of the sassares ship as well as most of his defensive perimeter. Five qiincer sailors were with him, huddled behind the low wall running along the edge of the roof, ready to fly to a'Bord or anyone else to relay his commands. Four civilian tokit runners were with him as well.

Tesoomo D was right about a lack of subtlety. The sassares were making no attempt to hide their intentions. Sere-blue Beleena, having had his champion defeated, wanted to make a statement. He was going to ram his forces down the Imperials' throats, crushing any opposition. For the last half-an-hour, his troops had been debarking their ship on the far side, using the ship's bulk to give them cover. If Leif still had any mortars left, he could have wreaked havoc among the assembled troops—then again, if he had an imperial gunship overhead, he could have vaporized the sassares ship and crew. Leif had waited in impotent frustration as the sassares assembled for their assault. He hated ceding the initiative to anyone.

The sassares sailors, now acting as ground troops, could debark on any side of the ship, but there was only one vehicle ramp, and Leif had a direct line-of-sight to it. The ramp lowered, and the first of the sassares armor appeared, slowly coming down the ramp, a ground guide making sure it cleared the ramp struts. Before the first vehicle had reached the ground, the nose of a second appeared at the top of the ramp.

The sere-blue should have lifted his ship and rotated it so that the ramp was facing away from the base.

Leif didn't hesitate. He was going to punish the sere-blue for his complacency. The range was a good 1,500 meters, which should be child's play.

"Wave the yellow banner," he told one of his civilian tokits who then ran to the east side of the roof and waved the "banner," a gym towel that had be hurriedly dyed yellow.

Ten seconds later, there was the sharp crack as the Patras' 105 mm gun spoke. An instant later, the first sassares tank erupted into a fireball, the turret spinning into the air as if in slow motion, clanging against the side of the ship before bouncing off. There was another crack from the Patras, and the second sassares tank was hit. It careened to the right until it crashed into the ramp strut.

A cheer rose from the defensive line, but a moment later, the ship's cannon hummed, and a pulse of focused energy hit the side of the base gym, incinerating Private First Class a'Noradyne and the Patras. When the tokit crew managed to get the first Patras online just an hour ago, the PFC, along with a Navy cargo handler, had volunteered to operate the tank's fire control AI. Without someone to drive it, the tank was little more than a bunker, unable to maneuver. A'Noradyne was supposed to fire once, then hightail it out of there before the inevitable response, but he'd stayed long enough to fire twice. He'd taken out two tanks, but at the cost of his and his Navy driver's life.

Another sassares tank nosed down the ramp, pushing the second one off the side as it continued to the ground. A second followed a moment later, and the two turned to join the ground troops on the far side of the ship.

Leif was relieved. From what he'd been able to glean, a sassares cruiser normally carried two platoons of four tanks each, but they could carry three platoons. One platoon had been destroyed in the initial assault, and it didn't look like there were any more hidden on the ship. That meant that the sere-blue's remaining armor had just been cut in half.

There was a roar of five-hundred sassares throats on the far side of the ship, and a moment later, bodies started flowing around both sides of it, running forward into the assault.

"Here they come," Leif said, stating the obvious.

Immediately, Marines and sailors started opening up, and sassares bodies began to fall. Leif had set up as many fighting positions as he could, most armed with tokit contactors, but very few of them were armed with assault weapons. At these ranges, their handguns and carbines were ineffective, so the tokits were hunkering down and waiting.

Leif had hoped that so many bodies would confuse the ship's scanners, but when the Marines and sailors commenced fire, they revealed their positions. The ship only had its one big beam weapon that would work in a gravity well, and it took almost 20 seconds to arm, but the sassares had set up a another base of fire with automatic weapons that keyed on the Marine positions.

What had looked like a mad rush that had given Leif hope quickly converted to a series of mutually supporting rushes. These might be part-time infantrymen with other sailor duties aboard the ship, but they understood fire and maneuver. And by using the buildings first in the annex, and then in the base itself, they had cover.

Leif was kicking himself for not razing the annex when he'd had the chance. He'd never considered that a cruiser would land there. But some of his weapons had good fields of fire into it. One of his M-31 HMG's, manned by a battalion Marine with a sailor as his A-gunner opened up down one of the avenues of approach, mowing down several sassares troopers and causing the rest to jump for cover.

Leif moved to the far west side of his building to get a better view.

"Come on, take the bait," he muttered.

And they did. One of the two tanks was called up to knock out the machine gun nest. Leif caught a few glimpses as it moved between the buildings and into the undefended part of the base.

"And you displace now," he said, waiting for the HMG crew to move and wishing for the thousandth time that he had comms his troops.

There was another chatter of a string of automatic fire from his team, a blast from one of the tanks, then silence from the Marine gun. Leif prayed that the two-person crew had displaced before the tank fired on them. Leif couldn't afford to lose his crew-served weapons, and staying too long in one place was a sure way to get killed.

The sassares tank, all weird angles and protuberances, so unlike the smoother lines of a Marine Patras, surged forward. Buttoned up, Leif didn't think the crew heard the crack of the Taipan being fired, nor the directional jets that steered the missile at them. Leif didn't see it hit, but he heard the secondary explosion and the black smoke which rose over the base headquarters.

Despite his dogged fatigue, Leif felt a small surge of excitement. The plan to lure the sassares tank to where the Taipan gunner had a clean shot worked. Three of the four sassares tanks were knocked out of the fight. Combined with the first platoon of armor, his small group of Marines and sailors had destroyed seven of eight of the tanks.

One more to go.

As if linked to his thoughts, a second, then a third Taipan was fired. The sassares tank, which had jumped forward to come to the aid of the stricken tank, reversed course immediately, spitting decoys into the air. The first missile bit on the decoys, detonating 30 meters from the tank. The explosion might have disrupted the tank's shield of countermeasures. Whatever the reason, the second Taipan, ran true and struck the tank low on the treads. Leif could just see the tank through a gap in the buildings, and the single tanker the sassares favored popped the hatch and scrambled out of the way.

There wasn't a secondary explosion. As with all modern armor, the AI would be attempting to repair any damage, and the tank could fight automatically under the control of the AI—not as well with as with a tank commander, but well enough to hurt the Marines. When there were no further missiles, Leif was afraid that his Marines might have assumed the last tank was permanently out of action.

"You," Leif said to the next qiincer runner. "I want you to find someone with a Taipan, and I want that last sassares tank hit again. We need to see it burn."

"Aye-aye, sir," the sailor said as she gathered her feet under her and started to pulse out her wings. "Uh . . . who do I ask? And what's a Taipan?"

Think, Leefen, and be clearer when you speak. She's a sailor, not an infantryman.

"A Taipan's an anti-armor missile. Like what took out those two enemy tanks. But one of them isn't destroyed yet. You just find any Marine down in that direction," Leif said, pointing over the west side of the roof. "Give them my orders, and they'll get it done."

Without his Battle-I, Leif didn't have an ordnance count, but there should be at least eight more Taipans distributed among the Marines.

The sailor darted to the edge, leapt off the roof, and disappeared from sight for a moment until reappearing some 100 meters away as she flew to relay his orders.

Two different, almost muffled blasts reach the roof, and Tesoomo D said, "They're in the minefield."

Leif darted to the south side of the roof, and he could see a sassares enveloping force within the minefield in front of where they'd blown the chow hall. Several bodies, or parts of bodies, were scattered on the ground, while more sassares were taking cover.

"Remember, hold your fire," Leif muttered.

Leif had created what looked like a weak spot in his defenses, away from both the annex and the east gate. The sere-blue would know he was understrengthed, and it would make sense that if he went light in any area, it would be away from the two logical avenues of approach. Leif hoped the sassares would see it and maneuver around to attack from the rear. To further the subterfuge, the tokits construction crews had built two dummy positions with unmanned weapons on automatic that had taken the advancing sassares under fire before being quickly destroyed. The mines and the two positions would hopefully make it look like they'd found an exploitable gap in the defense where the Marines, without enough bodies, were relying on mines to secure that flank.

Stopped for what Leif hoped would be assumed as a minor setback, and without a line-of-sight to the ship so it could be used as a minesweeper, the sassares deployed three minebulls, unmanned detectors that could pick a path through a minefield. With a "clear" path, the sassares infantry started to follow the minebulls, all in a nice column as they hurried to close in and assault the Imperials from the rear.

Making them easy targets.

With forty or fifty sassares exposed, the four hidden positions opened up with sweeping enfilade fire. At least half of the sassares were hit in the first burst of interlocking fire. Others hit the deck and attempted to take cover where there was none. More were hit as they tried to hug the dirt before the bulk broke and ran back to the far line of barracks. More than a few strayed off their path in, only to detonate the same mines they'd already bypassed.

Less than two minutes later, Leif counted 31 dead or seriously wounded sassares, taken down by tokit workers who had set the stage, and four Marines with Navy a-gunners who did the killing.

He felt a surge of elation that almost stripped his fatigue away.

Almost.

It was a small victory that had gone exactly as planned. But there was still a much bigger force facing them coming in from two directions, and once the force to the south reorganized, they'd add that third direction, and those sassares wouldn't be fooled again.

A massive explosion rocked the base, the shock wave shaking those on the roof. Smoke billowed up to the north, just 400 meters away. The base chapel, which anchored part of his defense, was gone. While Leif had been focused on the minefield to the south, the sassares to the north had pushed farther and faster than he'd expected. Cursing his lack of battle intel, he had to assume that he'd lost those positions, and there was a breach in the lines. The sassares would pour in, and he didn't have much of a defense in depth. He just didn't have enough fighters. All he could do was to shift what he had and hope they could plug any holes.

"Fly down there and tell Corporal a'Bord to shift a squad right to close off the breach," he told one of the Navy qiincers.

The qiincer nodded, the jumped over the edge of the roof, and took off, gaining height as she flew. She hadn't made it half-way when she suddenly folded up mid-flight and tumbled to the ground, slamming D Street to lie in a motionless heap. Leif waited a few moments to see if she would get up, but it was obvious she was dead. The messenger was gone, but the message had to get through.

"You," Leif shouted to the next qiincer, "Get those orders to the corporal."

The sailor stood, allowed the pseudo-haemolymph to spread his wings, then folded them close to his chest as he sprinted to the edge of roof and dived off. He plummeted to the ground and only snapped opened his wings at the last moment. Keeping just a meter above the ground, he jinked and juked as he flew between buildings to carry out his orders. Leif waited until he appeared on the other side of the buildings, landed, and entered the corporal's hardened fighting position. A moment later, one of the corporal's runners appeared and ran off to relay the orders to get the squad moving. Only then did Leif edge back.

He sat down for a moment and rubbed his eyes, a headache pounding away at him. It was always rough after musapha, but this time it seemed worse.

No time for this.

He triggered his medbot to release a small shot of painkillers, afraid to take too much. No one had really studied the effects of human-developed medications on the post-musapha wyntonans. Not every human even thought musapha was a real condition, placing it along the same lines of human berserkers or running amok. "Real" in the sense that those wyntonans would fight harder, but only because of psychological factors.

I need to make sure someone figures this out. It would sure help, he thought, before he laughed out loud, drawing a weird look from Lance Corporal Tesoomo D. *Yeah, like I'm really getting out of this alive.*

He gave the Marine a thumbs up, and turned back around to look over the AO. The volume of fire was rising as sassares closed in. With most of his forces in built-up positions, and the sassares maneuvering to keep their approaches covered, Leif couldn't see much. But the fight was getting intense.

He instinctively pulled up his Battle-I's display again, but there was no change. It showed a map of the base, but with all the Marines' individual telltales and the transmissions of the drones being blocked, there was nothing overlaid on the map. He couldn't tell who was where.

How did they fight in the old days? he wondered, his frustration rising. *I don't know what's happening with my Marines.*

He reset his display, hoping against hope that something would break through the sassares jamming, but there was nothing. He was still fighting blind.

No, not blind. I can still watch, I can still listen. Make do, Leefen a'Hope Hollow. Just make do.

He closed his eyes and listened, trying to gauge the volume of the fire and from where it was being fired. The battalion Marines' M-88s, which relied on mag-rings, were essentially silent, the crack of the round as it exited the barrel audible for only a few tens of meters. His surviving Raiders had a variety of weapons, as did the sailors. The tokits had been armed with handguns and carbines, but they had yet to start firing in earnest. What he could hear were the sassares, who relied on a chemical slug-thrower, the reports evident even from this distance. From what he could hear, the main thrust was coming from the north, and it was getting closer. A few rounds were reaching them on the roof.

Leif looked down over the edge. He had a decent view of the positions toward the east, but not as complete to the north. He'd thought the main assault would be to the east, which is why he'd chosen this roof and put Corporal a'Bord there.

Six hundred meters away, four sassares edged around the side of a building, in full view of Leif. Their attention was focused to their right, toward those positions.

"Screw it," Leif said, unslinging his Stahlmont.

He'd told himself he needed to stay out of the fighting, to keep focused on the big picture, but the picture he saw now was that four of the enemy had slipped through the lines and was getting ready to hit his troops.

He didn't need his bandaged left arm. Using the low wall for a support, he sighted in on the four, right hand hovering over the trigger.

"What do you got?" Tesoomo D asked, kneeling beside him.

"Zero-two-zero. Second building to—"

"I see them," the lance corporal said, laying the handguard of his M-88 on the wall, using it for support.

"I'm taking the lead. You take the guy in back. On three."

"Total ten . . . uh, roger that, Sergeant."

"One . . . two . . ." he said, starting to squeeze the trigger, ". . . three!"

Almost as one, the two fired. A moment later, the lead and trail sassares dropped as both Marines fired again. The two remaining sassares dove to the rear, scrambling to clear the corner of the building. Leif fired twice more, awkward with using his non-dominant right hand. One of the enemy stumbled and went down, but he scrambled back up, dragging a leg. Both made it around the corner and out-of-sight.

"Total ten, that felt good," Tesoomo D said, breathing hard in his excitement.

Leif gave him a look, and he realized that the lance corporal was frustrated. He didn't want to be up here babysitting a sergeant. He wanted to be down then with his battalion buddies.

Leif knew how the lance corporal felt.

"You know I need you here," Leif said. "This is where you can do the most good."

He wasn't sure if he was telling the lance corporal that or if he was trying to convince himself.

"Sorry. Is it that obvious?" the lance corporal asked. "It's just . . . I mean, down there, those are my friends."

There was another blast to the north before Leif could respond. He could see sassares infantrymen assaulting through. His positions there must have been knocked out.

"Is it time to go with the red?" Tesoomo D asked, gripping his M-88.

Leif looked over at the tokit huddled on the roof against the wall, clutching the red banner, and looking at him with fearful eyes. Two rounds pinged off the edge of the wall, making him cringe farther down.

Leif didn't know. His mind wasn't at 100%, and if felt like he was struggling through mental quicksand.

Should I? Where are the tunnelers?

He checked the time. From what they promised, they should be under the ship by now.

"Any word from the runner?" Leif asked, then kicked himself.

He'd be the first to know if the runner was back. He looked at his last two messengers. He could send one of them, but time was getting short. With sassares inside the camp, it wouldn't be long now. From the sounds of the firing, they might already be past the tunnel entrance.

Looking back over to the ship, he could see more ground-pounders milling around the back side of it. From the ship to the east, the open ground between the base, the city, and the annex was like a pitchball field. It was designed to protect the base from a ground attack, after all—there was zero cover. Only this time, it worked against the Imperial force. The sere-blue could tell the beamer gunner to fan out the beam, then burn the entire area. Sending anyone across would be a suicide mission.

"No, not yet," Leif said. "I can't."

More rounds hit the top of the wall, showering the six with chunks of plasticrete. Leif ignored it, moving forward to see the stretch of the original defensive line along the perimeter. It was still holding out. Corporal a'Bord was holding it together. As he watched, she popped up out of her position and ran to one of the remaining crew-served weapons, physically horsing the crew around by the collar and pointing out a new target.

Leif couldn't see what she was pointing at, but the two-person wyntonan and hisser crew spun around and started firing.

"Keep it up, Orelian," he said, as she sprinted back.

Two steps from her position, she flung up her arms and fell forward, hitting the ground and skidding forward to the edge of her hole.

"No!" Leif shouted, as a set of hands reached out and dragged the body into the position.

Leif fell back, eyes closed for a moment. He'd been counting on her, but this hurt even deeper.

Well, that's it, he thought as he probed his mistress, hoping to find a bit of moisture in that dry well.

Like a long-lost lover, she stirred, a promise of what was to come. But she was weak, depleted.

"Corporal a'Bord's down," he told Tesoomo D. "I'm heading down there."

"But your arm," the lance corporal said, pointing at his bandaged and immobilized left arm.

"I've got two," Leif said, holding up his right.

"And the red signal?"

Leif looked at the tokit.

"Do you know what to do?" he asked.

"Yes, sir. I know."

"Can I count on you?"

The tokit edged up and glanced over the top of the low wall. "Yes, sir. I'll do it."

The tokit's red banner was only a back-up. The plans were already in place.

"What's your name, son?" Leif asked, wondering why he hadn't asked before.

"Two Foot, sir."

Leif laughed, making himself dizzy. The tokit was about two feet tall, but then again, all of them were about the same height.

"What is your tokit name?"

"Toofita Bryngyng Yel Rombel, sir."

Well, Toofito Bee . . . Two Foot, I'm counting on you."

He turned to Tesoomo D and said, "He's got it, but I want you to stay here—"

"Not gonna happen, Sergeant. Corporal a'Bord told me to stick with you no matter what."

Leif didn't have the energy to argue. He reached deep to call forth his mistress, but only a wisp of musapha answered, barely giving him anything.

"Let's go then," he said, standing up and immediately stumbling as a low rumble filled his senses.

What's wrong with me . . . ? he started before it hit him.

There was nothing wrong with him. He looked over at the ship, and dust was rising around it. The ship was intact, but it has settled somewhat, partially buried in the buckled pad.

The tokits had set off the first charge, the slow, earth-moving charge, made from barrels of construction explosives, the ones used to excavate dirt.

"Get some!" Leif shouted, moving to stand at the edge of the rood, right hand on the retaining wall, as he prayed to see damage.

Alarms sounded, painfully loud, even as far away as he was from the ship. Take-off lights started rotating. Some of what he could see of the second assault wave of sassares were struggling to their feet and trying to run. Understandably. If the ship took off, they'd be fried. Just like what was left of the defense would be fried when the sere-blue turned the ship around to remove what had been a troublesome pain in his ass. Leif knew there would be no more ground assaults to prove a point. Things had progressed far beyond that.

"Is it flyable?" Lance Corporal Tesoomo D asked.

"I don't know," Leif said, hoping, praying that it was too damaged.

But spacefaring ships were made strong, and dual space/atmospheric ships even stronger. With scraping groans that reverberated across the base, the ship started to rise.

"Come on guys!" Leif shouted. "Now!"

As if in response, a flash of blindingly white light that seared itself into Leif's brain flashed under the sassares' ship, followed a moment later by a boom that knocked him to his knees. Stars filled his eyes, but he squinted, and through his tears, he saw the ship fall back to the ground, its formerly clean silhouette bent, sparks shooting out from rents in the ship's skin.

Several tons of the high explosive RDX-8, formed into a massive shape charge, and thanks to its wonderful, glorious brisance, had shattered a chunk of the ship, just as the tokit engineering foreman had promised it would

"You did it! By the Mother, you fucking did it!" he shouted.

Then he remembered Two Foot.

"Now, Two Foot, now!"

The tokit stood up, climbed on top of the wall, and started wildly waving his red banner.

Leif, his eyes still smarting from the flash, looked back at the ship. Bodies, maybe a hundred, lay still around it. Leif didn't know whether they were felled by the blasts or the ship's engines. It didn't matter. Others were getting to their feet and running, some away, some toward the ship. Some of the troops already engaged inside the base started retreating, running pell-mell back to their husk of a ship. They were the engineers and mechanics in their other duties, but Leif was pretty sure that nothing short of years in the yards could hope to get that thing functional again.

Another rumble reached him, and he turned to the city. A shouting mass of people was emerging, led by a familiar figure, flying at their head. Without comms, Leif wasn't sure how many tokits Corporal Forintik had under her command, but they kept coming and coming. There had to be thousands of them, all running as fast as they could to close the distance to the ship. And with sparks still shooting out, the ship's beam cannon was out of action.

It took the panicking sassares a few moments to recognize the threat, and to their credit, many of them started to organize, but too few. The shock of losing their ship was too much for too many of them to react in a tactically coherent manner.

The organized few took a toll on Forintik's tokits, tens, maybe a hundred falling, but the flood of bodies was too much. They were not going to be stopped.

"Marines! Iwo Jima!" Leif shouted, a command that flowed down lines of the survivors.

Marines and sailors flowed out of their positions, raking the sassares who'd turned to face the mass of tokits coming from the city. Another thousand tokits, many who'd been patiently waiting inside some of the buildings and waiting for the word, rushed to support the others.

The tokits from inside the base and 1200 of the ones with Corporal Forintik had been armed with handguns and carbines pulled out of storage, some of them quite obsolete models. But a round from a century-old Beckham PT-40 would kill just as well as a round from a modern M-88. As they closed to within a hundred meters, the tokits started firing. Most of them had minimal training, and their accuracy suffered, but pure mass of fires, supplemented with the remaining Marines concentrated fire, started having an effect. And when a tokit dropped, another was there to pick up their weapon and fight on.

A well-disciplined defensive posture could have turned back the tokits, regardless of their overall numbers. But the sassares were in shock at losing their ship, at having an easy mission go so wrong for them so quickly. And all they could see were thousands of tokits closing in on them. Leif doubted that they could see that most of the tokits were only armed with knives and tools.

First a couple, then more surrendered, standing and holding their hands high over their heads. Some were still cut down, and Leif didn't know if that was from the crossfire or on purpose. Other sassares fought on, only to be overrun by the mass. Leif hadn't considered those armed with tools to be more than a facade, to spread the target choices among the sassares, but in close, those tools were deadly.

Fifteen minutes after the initial explosion, the firing finally died down. Around two hundred sassares had successfully surrendered and were standing next to the annex while Marines and sailors searched them.

Another shower of sparks shot out of the ship, and with a loud crack, part of it settled down farther. Flames reached out from inside, hungry for oxygen. Sassares shouted, in fear or anger.

Almost immediately, Leif's comms came alive.

"Any Imperial military forces, any Imperial military forces, come in," a voice said.

Leif had forgotten all about his comms, and because of that, he'd never turned them off.

Several of his Marines started to respond, but Leif cut them off with his command mode. "Person calling, this is Sergeant Leefen a'Hope Hollow, Imperial Marine Corps, commanding forces on Sunrise."

"Sergeant?" the voice asked in surprise, then Leif heard her say, "Colonel, I've got the sergeant on Sunrise!"

A few seconds later, another voice came on the net. "Is this Sergeant a'Hope Hollow?""

"Yes, sir."

"We've been trying to reach you for four days. What's your situation there?"

Leif looked out over the battlefield. Bodies littered the area in and around the annex. Buildings inside the base were destroyed. Down below him, someone had laid Corporal a'Bord's body alongside her fighting position.

Leif didn't know how many people he'd lost yet, but they'd been hurt hard. They might have lost more than the sassares, despite winning the field of battle.

He hesitated a moment, then passed to the unseen colonel, "The sassares have been defeated. The Imperial Marines and Navy hold Sunrise."

Chapter 40

"How many of the wounded are effectives?" the Navy chief on the other end asked.

With comms open again, the chief, who was clad in a full hazard suit, could pull up the bios on all the military personnel with Leif. He knew how many were alive and how many were KIA, but he couldn't tell who of the wounded were combat effective.

"I don't have an exact number, Chief. We've got some still getting treatment. But as of the moment, I've thirty-two Marines and sixty sailors. I might get another dozen or so after Katako N clears them."

"Katako N? A hisser, then. Not a doctor," the chief said, making another entry into his notes.

"A nurse. We don't have any doctors here. I mean, we've got the ones with the rest of the stricken humans, but none who are conscious."

Leif yawned, then cut it short. He was still suffering from the effects of musapha, but he was at least functional now.

"And how many civilians?" the chief asked.

"I don't know how many tokits we had. Maybe six or seven thousand, and I don't know how many—"

"Not tokits," the chief said. "Humans. How many are still alive."

"I don't know," Leif said, taken somewhat aback.

Hundreds, possibly up to a thousand, of tokits had died in the battles, and Leif would have thought that was relevant. Humans had died, too, about 15% of those stricken, but until there was a cure, they were out of the picture. Aside from their sacrifices, the tokits were a vital component of the base's security now.

Leif never would never have guessed that the tokits would have been so necessary to winning the battle, first with the sapper tunnel, then in overwhelming the surviving sassares. But he knew that without them, Sere-blue Beleena would have overrun the base.

"I don't have a count, Chief," he said, failing to hide the hint of anger that had crept into his voice. "We sort of had our hands full here."

If the chief noticed his sarcasm, he didn't let on, saying, "We're going to need those numbers as soon as you can get them."

He pushed back on the faceplate of his biohazard suit, settled it better around his shoulders, then made another entry. Leif could see his face through the faceplate. The man looked haggard, with several day's worth of a scraggly beard. Leif suddenly realized that the human had probably been in his biohazard suit for days now. The suits were bulky, and they weren't designed for long-term wear. Eating and elimination of wastes were complicated and laborious processes. If the chief seemed abrupt, then maybe the suits had something to do with that. Leif decided to cut the man a little slack.

"Hey, Chief," Leif said. "What's going on? I mean, what's the situation out there?"

Leif was using the generic "out there." He didn't know where the human even was. He could be up on Mbangwa Station, or he could be back at Naval Headquarters on Ganymede, for all he knew.

The chief leaned back for a moment and closed his eyes, then leaned forward again and said, "It's bad, Sergeant. The sassares hit us pretty hard with the crud. Our head doc thinks they got over eighty-five percent coverage, and the mortality rate is hovering around twelve percent."

That hit Leif in the gut, almost taking his breath away. With about fifty billion humans in the galaxy, that meant 500,000,000 had been killed, and who knew how many others might pass away?

"By the Mother," he whispered.

"Yeah, you can say that again," the chief said.

"And the military? Are we fighting them?"

The chief looked at him for a long moment with a distrustful look in his eyes, and Leif suddenly felt guilty. There was no reason for him to, but it was what it was.

Then the chief shook his head and said, "Fuck it. You've proven yourself.

"You Marines have been pretty hard hit. There were a couple of human battalions that were aboard ships that are intact . . ." he said, pausing as he seemed to realize what he'd just said. "Sorry about that. I meant, a couple of battalions were aboard ships that were never infected. Most were out plying the deep. But the bases were all hit hard. Only you casp . . . you wyntonans are left in any numbers."

Leif narrowed his eyes as the chief started to say "caspers."

"The Navy's down to a fraction of our ships being operational. Most of the ships' crews were hit hard, but some managed to escape infection. They've been in running battles with the sassares Navy, trying to keep them occupied. If they fuckers would just coordinate, they could end us right quick.

"Luckily, they're commanders are so anxious to make a name for themselves that cooperation isn't their thing."

Sassares had a reputation of being a cutthroat race. Leaders at the upper echelons of society were in a constant battle of wits and politics to make black, which formed the basic sassares governing body. And it was from this group that someone was selected to become the next member of the triumvirate every couple of years.

Leif has seen it with Sere-blue Beleena. The sere-blue had been more conscious of the appearances of how he'd take the base rather than strict tactical considerations. He'd paid for that mistake with his life.

"Are we going to win?" Leif asked.

"I don't know, Sergeant," the chief said, suddenly sounding very tired. "The doc says that even if we find a cure tomorrow, it's going to take a long time for us to get folks back on their feet. By that time . . ."

By that time, the sassares will have defeated whatever forces we have left.

Chapter 41

The next two days were hectic. Leif struggled to get the damaged defenses repaired, dealing with the surprisingly difficult task to take care of the dead, both imperial and sassares, and figuring out what to do with a couple hundred prisoners, all the while responding to a never-ending string of requests from the Naval headquarters which was now evidently in command of his . . . not battalion. They were too small to be considered a battalion. *Detachment.*

He still didn't know who was his headquarters or where it was located. The senior officer he'd seen was a commander. All the humans were clad in biohazard suits, which meant wherever they were had been compromised. Leif had tried to get an alindamir petty officer to give him more information on what was going on, but after the chief had opened up, the rest were more tight-lipped.

Without Forintik and Star, Leif would have gone stark raving mad. The corporal was given the task of rebuilding the defenses. Their headquarters did not expect an immediate attack, but he had to prepare for the worst. If the sassares Navy prevailed, then they would return, and the next ship wouldn't put itself in the position to be taken out by tokit sappers.

Star became Leif's liaison with the tokits and hisser work crews. Seven hundred and fourteen civilian tokits, twenty-three hissers, and a noxes were killed in the fight, yet the mob of tokits now working seemed to have grown. Thousands were busily cleaning up the aftermath of the battle.

"Sergeant a'Hope Hollow, you're wanted in the comm shack," his duty comms watch passed.

Hell, what do they want now? A count of the bottles of booze in the O'Club?

"I'm on my way," he said.

"Sorry," he told Corporal Forintik. "Mama calls. Just do what you think is right."

"Then, I'm going to move the line up to Bravo Street," she said.

"Yes, yes. You're in charge," Leif yelled over his back as he started to trot to the comms shack.

He'd had to relocate his headquarters to one of the armories because of the comms. The armories were hardened against electronic surveillance, and each armory had secure spaces.

He entered the front hatch to, "Sergeant a'Hope Hollow!" from a waiting tokit, a foreman from her brown overalls.

"Talk to Star!" Leif shouted as he hurried past the tokit and disappeared into the cool recesses of the armory. The door at the very rear led into a space where few had authorization. Leif leaned into the scanner, had his retinas read, and the heavy door whispered open. He made his way past several heavy crates of nuclear warheads and to the back where the comms suite, his desk, and the duty desk had been set up. It was a little cumbersome, but the previous comms suite had been in the basement of the base headquarters, a building that had been destroyed during the battle.

The destruction of the base headquarters had served no tactical purpose to the sere-blue. Leif had abandoned it as he contracted his lines. He was pretty sure that the sere-blue had destroyed it just because he could.

"What do you have?" he asked Corporal a'Roland, the duty NCO.

Leif was down most of his force, but he kept a corporal or petty officer, along with the comms tech, inside the armory at all times.

"You need to stand by," the corporal said, pointing to the comms.

Seaman Orantono L was one of the three comms techs to survive the battle, and she was on a four hours on, eight hours off schedule, with no other duties assigned. She spoke into her pick-up, "Sergeant a'Hope Hollow is here now," before standing up and giving him her seat. The alindar who Leif had tried to grill for answers was on duty at the other side.

He was often on duty, which made Leif wonder just how many bodies were functioning over there.

"Wait one, Sergeant," the sailor said. "I'm patching you through now."

A moment later, the view changed to a plain white room. A civilian human operator sat there without a biohazard suit.

"Please wait for the acting minister."

What? A minister?

Leif unconsciously sat up straighter in the seat.

"Do you know what this is about?" he asked.

"The acting minister will tell you," the man said before leaning away from the pick-up as if making a reading, something Leif knew was a dismissal.

Sorry to intrude on your day.

Leif was surprised that a minister wanted to speak with him, but he wasn't in a very conducive frame of mind. He was tired, dead tired. Physically and mentally. He'd never fully recovered from his musapha, which had him worried. Normally, a couple of hours, and he was as good as new. And now, with still a million things to do, he was stuck here, waiting for some politico.

When he saw Assistant Minister for Special Operations Montrose—no, Acting Minister Montrose—step into view and sit at the console on the other side, he forgot his fatigue.

"Minster Montrose, congratulations on your promotion," he said.

"These are not the circumstances for congratulations, Sergeant a'Hope Hollow. And I need to ask you to clear your room and set up a cone."

By the Mother, what an idiot. Of course, she's acting minister because of the hammer, not because she was picked for promotion.

"You heard her," he told the other two, turning away from the pick-up.

Orantono L leaned over him and pulled up the instructions for the cone, then followed a'Roland out the hatch.

As soon as it closed, Leif said, "Activate security scramble november-three-eight-niner-yankee-echo."

A small red spinning ball appeared in the right of his 3D screen.

"I read november-three-eight-niner-yankee-echo, Authorization yellow-dog-taco-river," the acting minister said.

A moment later, the red spinning ball turned to green.

"I read that you were hurt. How is your arm?" the acting minister asked without preamble.

Leif lifted his left arm, which was still bandaged. "Doing well. The nanites are doing their job."

His arm wasn't 100%, but he wasn't going to go into details. He had full motion, and that was good enough.

"Are you physically capable for another mission?"

What? Are the sassares coming back?

He wasn't sure they could . . . no, that was pussyfooting around. He *knew* they couldn't stand off another assault, not without reinforcements and Navy support.

"Yes, ma'am," he said, keeping his misgivings to himself.

"Good, because your reestablishment of communications came at a good time for me.

"First, I want to tell you that I've seen the reports on what you've done. I'm proud of you, Sergeant. To not only hold off a sassares corana, but to destroy it? Wonderful innovation there."

"It was the tokits, ma'am?"

"What? The tokits? But I was under the impression that there were only a few of them in the battalion."

"The civilians, ma'am. They destroyed the sassares cruiser, not us. And they attacked the survivors. Without them, I don't think we would have survived."

"The tokits? I never would have . . . I'd like a full report from you when you have the time, Sergeant. I evidently didn't receive a very complete picture."

Leif had only given the Navy commander a preliminary verbal report, and the full report had become OBE. He had mentioned the tokits contributions to the commander, but whoever had then given an accounting of the battle to the acting minister had evidently left quite a bit out of it.

Leif had downloaded footage from the drones, which despite not being able to transmit, had still recorded. He had one of the techs run them through an editing AI to cobble together a montage of what had happened. He hadn't thought of sending drones along with the tunnelers, so he didn't have a firm grasp of what went on, or why two of them had stayed behind to detonate the explosions, but what he had should have given a good picture of who did what.

"But that's not why I needed to talk to you. Like I said, your reestablishment of communications is very fortuitous. I need you for a mission. I want you and fifteen of your Marines ready to leave Sunrise in another," she paused, looking at her slate, "another eight hours.

"You'll be taken to a secret location, and I need you to provide security to the people there."

"Ma'am? Leave my command here and provide security? Where am I going?"

"I can't really tell you where. This should be a secure net, but if you don't know where and something happens to you . . ."

"I can't give anything away."

She nodded.

"But can I ask why fifteen other Marines?"

"There will only be space for a total of sixteen. The ship that is inbound is not a Navy ship. I can't say whose."

IIA.

"It will not land where it can be spotted, especially on a Novacks planet."

"I don't think the Sunrisers are very happy with the sassares anymore. They were hit with the hammer . . . I mean the crud . . . just as hard as we were."

"Still, this is the way it's going to be. You'll do a transfer from the shuttle to the ship, then be taken to your destination."

"What kind of destination? I need to know in order to pick my team."

She hesitated a long twenty seconds, and Leif could almost see the thoughts banging around inside her head.

"It's a lab. One that doesn't look like a lab. On an asteroid. Or rather inside an asteroid. It isn't a particular target at the moment, as far as we know, but the sassares are making the rounds to all known human installations."

One working on a cure. But why secure it with sixteen grunts?

"Why not station a Navy ship there?"

"And show the sassares that there is something there to protect?" she snapped.

Leif could see the fatigue in the woman, and he realized that she must be exhausted. She must have a huge weight on her shoulders, far more than he could ever imagine.

"Sorry about that," she said, sitting back and rubbing her eyes. "We do have a few ships guarding dummy sites, but we can't afford to spread our remaining Navy around too thinly. They are doing a tremendous job in keeping the sassares Navy occupied, but it's only a matter of time before we run out of crews."

"I understand, ma'am." Then something she said struck him. "You said we're going up on a shuttle? Is Mbangwa Station intact?"

"Partially. It was hit bad, and power generation has failed. The survivors are living on canned air. But the crews are scrambling to put it back together.

"The shuttle is automated, so it doesn't need guidance from the station."

"Understood, ma'am. Is there anything else I need to know?"

Marines were fond of detailed operations orders. This was barely a commander's statement of intent.

"That's all I can tell you at the moment. Upon your arrival, the commander will give you a more detailed brief. Just be ready for your shuttle."

"Taking 16 Marines from the base will leave it pretty vulnerable, ma'am. In case of another attack."

He didn't say that even with another hundred Marines, to include officers and SNCOs, they would still be vulnerable.

"At this stage of the war, Sergeant, I'd sacrifice the entire planet if that meant your destination could accomplish their mission."

"Understand, ma'am. We'll be ready."

"So, unless there is something else?"

"No, ma'am. I've got it," he started, but then, "Well, there is one thing."

"What is it?"

"The emperor. Is he alive?" he asked, his heart lodged firmly in his throat.

"The palace is prepared for a biological attack with overpressure and filters, so during the initial sassares seeding, the palace center was not infected. Later, when the attack was initiated, I was with the emperor on a . . . suffice it to say that we were isolated. When we realized what was happening, he was taken to a safe facility. So, yes, he's alive."

Probably the same place you are. Off of Earth, I'm guessing.

"And the empress?"

Her eyes clouded over, and she said, "The empress is in a coma. We pray that she'll recover."

UNNAMED ASTEROID

Chapter 42

"Total ten," Lance Corporal Tesoomo D said, pointing to the screen. "There it is, our new home."

Leif snapped awake, then stretched out his legs. He was still tired, unable to take more than catnaps ever since they'd come aboard.

The "ship" they'd taken barely deserved the term. The 16 Marines were crowded into the single compartment in small, cramped seats, a tiny galley in the back next to a funnel attached to the bulkhead that acted as a toilet. Not that the galley served real food. It was all MRDRs and reclaimed water.

At least he'd recovered from his musapha, and he'd had an opportunity to study more of the drone footage from a copy he'd made for himself. Enforced inactivity had some benefits, it seemed. Not many, but some.

The other Marines in the ship started to stir as well. Leif had twelve of the surviving Raiders with him. He wished he had Forintik with him as well, but he'd left her in charge of the remaining military personnel. She'd proven herself to be a skilled manager, and she'd been the only logical choice to leave in charge. Star had agreed to assist in any way she could.

The other three Marines had come from 2/14. Lance Corporal Tesoomo D had insisted that he come. He'd been a valuable assistant to Leif during the fight with the sassares, but he still smarted from being left out of the direct combat, and Leif figured he owed the Marine one of the spots.

One of the other battalion spots was PFC a'Knight. The other was HM Korindtut, a Navy corpsman. A'Knight had come recommended by Corporal a'Roland, and Leif had chosen the tokit corpsman. Korindtut might not be the most martial Marine or sailor from 2/14, but neither of the two non-human Raider corpsmen has survived the battles with the Novacks and sassares.

Leif had become a big fan of the tokits, but it still struck him odd to see the short corpsman in uniform. They just didn't look the part to him, no matter how willing their attitude.

The ship was approaching the single "caterpillar" docking tube that protruded slightly from the rock surface of the asteroid. The only other sign of habitation was a single array that seemed to spring out of the rock.

"That's a QN-5104," Korindtut said.

"A what?" Tesoomo D asked.

"A QN-5104. It's a comms array. My dad and uncle used to install them for Quixote."

Leif recognized the company, of course. Quixote, LTD, was one of the larger space construction firms in the empire.

"So, we're going to some sort of communications station? How many people are in there?" Lance Corporal Hulorin asked, sounding unsure of herself.

All eyes turned to the corpsman.

"I don't know. My dad just built them. He didn't man them after. I think just a small crew, though, in case something goes wrong. Most of what they do is automatic."

"Well, let's see if we can raise them," Leif said.

He moved to the tiny control panel at the starboard bow and opened up the Bravo-band comms.

"Station . . . uh, communications station, this is commercial packet Areon Light," he said, using the callsign given to him before they left Sunrise's orbit. "Please acknowledge."

Silence.

"I say again, communications station, this is commercial packet Areon Light. Please acknowledge."

Again, silence.

"Are they dead, do you think?" Lance Corporal a'Tin asked.

"If they are, we came along ways for nothing," Leif replied. "I say again, communications station, this is commercial packet Areon Light. Request docking clearance. Please acknowledge."

The comms remained stubbornly quiet.

"Areon Light, please initiate docking," Leif commanded the ship before turning to his Marines and saying, "We'll just have to go take a look. First Team, you lead. Second, Fourth, and then Third. Normal clearance SOP. We've done this a hundred times, so no mistakes."

Leif had split the 16 of them into four teams. There hadn't been enough room to rehearse movements in the tiny ship, but with twelve of them being Raiders, Leif was sure they knew how to work together. He'd considered spread loading the battalion Marines among the others, but in the end, he put Tesoomo D, Doc, and a'Knight together with him as Fourth Team. He was at least familiar with Tesoomo D, and that left the other three teams with only Raiders.

The ship came stopped about 20 meters from the surface of the asteroid—too close for comfort, but it was a pretty small craft.

"Here comes the caterpillar," Hulorin said, looking out a small porthole in the main hatch.

On the front screen, Leif could see the caterpillar accordion out, reaching for the ship. In settled around the hatch, completely covering it as the flanges sought a seal. After 20 seconds, the red exit light switched to green.

"This is it. Don hoods," Leif said.

The "hoods" were emergency survival suits designed to keep people alive in case of a breach in a ship. Designed to keep a person alive for up to 30 minutes, they supplied O2 and kept the head and torso warm. Arms and legs were unprotected.

Leif had been concerned about Doc. The hoods were designed to conform to various body-types, but the tokit was much smaller than the others. He needn't have worried. Doc's hood shrunk down to fit his body.

The hoods were not combat EVAs, but Leif had no idea who or what was waiting for them inside the asteroid. A caterpillar was a sturdy piece of equipment, but it was a choke point. A simple explosive detonation while the Marines were transiting the caterpillar would expose them to the vacuum of cold space. The hoods would keep them alive long enough to fight their way in or get back to the ship.

"Give me a shout and a thumbs up," Leif told them.

From front to rear, each Marine sounded off that they were in their hoods, after which Leif gave the order to open the hatch. First Team dove out and disappeared from view, followed a moment later by Second. Leif, standing at the head of Fourth, watched down the caterpillar as his Marines pulled themselves along the length of the tube, expecting any moment for them to be hit. The caterpillar curved slightly, so he didn't have a full view of the two teams as they opened the airlock door that led into the asteroid, then entered, closing the door behind them.

"We're inside," Corporal a'Noon passed. "No sign of . . . belay my last. We've got one, no two bodies. No one alive. The space is clear."

"Hold on and don't touch anything. We're on our way," Leif passed back.

"Let's go," he told his team, diving head first out of the ship, moving from artificial gravity to null-G. Leif liked being in zero-gravity, but the transition, when part of his body felt the pull of the artificial gravity while the rest of it was in zero-G, was always a little disconcerting. He tried to make the transition as quickly as possible.

It took only a few seconds to pull himself along the length of the caterpillar, twisting around to let his legs take the shock of arriving at airlock. He hung on one of the handles that lined the lock until the other seven had arrived.

"We're cycling," he passed.

"Clear!" a'Noon said.

The lock was supposedly foolproof, and cycling could not commence if there were anyone in the lock or if the inner door was not sealed, but while Leif didn't like to consider Marines as fools, they had a tendency to render anything so labeled "foolproof" as a misnomer. He wanted verbal confirmation.

Within moments, the air inside the lock had been vented back inside, and the outer door opened. The seven

Marines and one corpsman moved inside, once again with artificial gravity giving them an up and down.

As soon as the inner door opened, Leif cracked his hood, and immediately regretted it. The smell of death permeated the room. Corporal a'Noon motioned Leif over to a small console. A dead human—a very dead human—slouched in one chair, his bloated body straining against the confines of his work overalls. Any more rot, and Leif thought the slumping body would slide off to lie on the ground. Time had done no favors to the body, and Leif couldn't see what had killed him.

"Doc, take a look and let me know what you think of him," he told Korindtut, glad he was a grunt and not a corpsman.

"Anything else?" he asked the Corporal a'Noon.

"Yeah, in there," she pointed.

There was a single hatch beyond the control console. Leif went through it into the crew's living quarters. Or dying quarters. A single female body lay on her back on the bottom bunk, hands crossed over her chest. The light blue sheet under her was stained with yellow and white bodily fluids that had leaked out of her corpse. The rest of the room was spotless, and the low notes of music seemed at odds with the sight before him.

Leif could imagine the scene. The women dying, her partner placing her with respect on the bed before going out to the control room to die. He just didn't know why they died. If it was the hammer, then how did it get into a sealed compartment? And even if it was the hammer, not every human died from it . . . unless they'd died for lack of care?

How long has it been? Is that long enough for a human to starve to death?

"So, what are we here for?" Lance Corporal Hulorin asked. "Just a comms site?"

Leif didn't have an answer. This, whatever it looked to be, was still not a lab. Either they'd been brought to the wrong location, or there was more to this place than met the eye.

"I'm going to find out," he said, heading back to the other room just as part of the rear bulkhead recessed into the wall.

Marines immediately drew down, taking whatever cover they could.

"Is that you, Sergeant a'Hope Hollow?" Private Lorenzo Jones, United Federation Marine Corps, asked, stepping out into the room.

****

"Why didn't you let us know where you were when we entered, sir," Leif asked Commander Warren.

"Well, you still had your hoods on, so we couldn't be sure, and since you were . . ." he said, trailing off.

We weren't human, you mean.

"But Private Jones here, he said he recognized your weapon, and since we were told you were coming, well, we knew we had to make contact," the commander said.

A beaming Jones, the only human without a biosuit, stood by, obviously happy to see Marines again. A small smile cracked the corner of Leif's mouth. He'd been sure he'd never see the private again, but here he was, recognizing Leif by his Stahlmont. Leave it to a Marine to be such a firearms nut.

The galaxy was a small place.

But then again, maybe not so small. As the commander had told him, they'd initially been thrown together due to proximity from a galaxy-wide perspective, so it made sense that when the command wanted Marines at the lab, then they would be the closest to answer the call.

And lab it was. There was no mistaking the white painted bulkheads, the individual laboratories with equipment that Leif knew nothing about but certainly fit a layman's perception of what labs had.

He was somewhat surprised to see all the personnel, except for Jones, in biosuits, however. The commander hadn't been in one when they'd first communicated. When he asked, the commander had simply said they were in the "testing phase."

"I have to ask, what's with the two bodies out there," Leif asked the commander.

"Those two *bodies*, Sergeant, are Doctor Hari Nutasaya and Lem Stokely," Dr. Manuel snapped. "I'll have them treated with respect."

Leif's mouth dropped open in surprise. Dr. Manuel had been introduced as the project head, but the older human hadn't said much to him while the commander brought him up to speed.

"I meant no disrespect, Doctor. But if I'm here to provide security, then I need to know what's going on."

The doctor struggled to her feet, picking up her cane and leaning on it. She was breathing hard, and Leif could see small amounts of condensation on her faceshield grow and contract with each breath.

"You take care of this, Mike. I can't waste any more time here."

"I didn't mean to upset her, sir," Leif said once the two were alone again.

"She's . . . she'd been under a lot of stress. And Doctor Nutasaya was one of her closest friends."

"What happened to her? The doctor out there, I mean. And the man."

"They thought they had a breakthrough, but time is of an essence, so Doctor Nutasya volunteered to be a guinea pig."

Leif had no idea what a guinea pig was. An Earth pig, yes, but that didn't make much sense to him.

"She did what?"

"Why, she had the crud virus injected into her. As you can surmise, the so-called breakthrough didn't work. They adjusted what they thought went wrong, and Lem volunteered."

By the Mother, that's horrible! Brave, though.

"So, why were they out there? Like that?" Leif asked.

"Camouflage. If the sassares came, the hope was that they would see the two and assume this is just a simple comms array. It is a comms array, by the way. That part isn't fake. But it serves to hide the lab."

Leif thought that could possibly work, but it wasn't clean. It wouldn't explain the bodies and how they died. The sassares probably knew when each location had been seeded, and they'd know this one wasn't.

Maybe they'd assume that a supply ship brought the virus in.

But the bodies were in a pretty advanced case of decomposition, maybe too far from when the virus was activated, and that made him wonder again about the timeline.

"The crud doesn't kill everybody, right? And it hasn't even been that long."

"Like I said, it didn't work. Made it worse. I'm a little vague on the concept, but it had to do with destroying their own defenses before trying to genetically splice their coding with a section of Private Jones' DNA."

Over the last thirty minutes, as Leif was being brought up to speed, he was getting the impression that the commander didn't command much. He was a Navy medical service officer and not a physician, much less a scientist. Stuck in the middle, he wasn't part of the research team, nor was he really a Navy officer. He was more of a liaison between the Navy and the rest of the personnel and the facility itself.

And that disheartened him. Leif was hoping to have an officer to, well, *officer*. He wanted someone in command. And now he realized that nothing had changed. He was still in command, for all intents and purposes.

Everything was still on his shoulders.

Chapter 43

After the rush to get to the lab, the next several days were downright boring. The biggest decision made was to switch out the facade in the outer rooms. Leif had been bothered about the inconsistencies with the timelines, and while the commander had balked, any excuse to seal the two bodies up and bring them into the freezer was jumped on by Dr. Manuel. She said they deserved as much.

The Marines scrubbed down the spaces, incinerating the sheets and clothing, then running the scrubbers on high to get rid of the smell. Once the space had been cleaned as well as possible, Tesoomo D and Doc Korindtut took their places as the array crew. None of the humans could be spared, and Leif thought it would work better with non-humans anyhow. The wyntonan Marines had an air about them that screamed warrior, so, it came down to a tokit and a hisser.

The two donned civilian overalls, ditching their uniforms. They found a pair that fit Tesoomo D, but Doc's had to be altered to fit his frame. Then they spent a full day going over the array manual, learning what they needed to do and how to work the galley, head, shower, and entertainment system. They needed to make the array spaces look lived in.

To Doc's surprise, the vast library had tokit holovids, so they were spooled up and ready to run. Doc insisted that he "check" them to make sure they were authentic, and after two days of watching, he admitted that they were and told Tesoomo D he'd also found hisser music drums and holovids, which, of course, the lance corporal had to check out as well.

If anything could convince Leif that the tokit and hisser were truly in the military, that might be it. A real Marine would take any opportunity to legally fuck off.

Leif was only a little jealous. He and the others could use the distraction as well, but he'd decided that once they were set up, only Doc and Tesoomo D were allowed in the array spaces. He didn't want to leave any clue that there were more Imperials inside the asteroid.

The humans had a self-contained entertainment center as well, but it was located in the lab's second level, and the Marines were not allowed past the first. They couldn't even use the net as the lab was completely shielded.

So, the Marines did what they've always done: they hurried up and waited.

****

"I need your tokit," Dr. Manuel told Leif. "Send him to Lab C."

"Excuse me, ma'am? You mean Doc?"

"He's a physician?" the head scientist asked, obviously surprised.

"Not a physician. A corpsman," he said, and when she still looked blank, he added, "Like a medic."

"Oh," she said with a dismissive wave of her hand. "Not a doctor, then."

Dr. Manuel had never warmed to the presence of Marines in her kingdom. Trapped between the outer array spaces and the inner lab spaces, the Marines congregated in the bunk spaces and galley, and she'd complained to the commander about them being "underfoot." Not that any of the humans spent much time in the area. They were working around the clock, and more often than not, they caught catnaps at the workstations.

"What do you need him for?" Leif asked. "He's got an assigned position out here."

Like watching holovids in the array spaces, he thought, not that he would voice that.

The scientist didn't like the Marines, and Leif didn't like her in return. He wasn't just going to hand over Doc without knowing why.

Her eyes lit up for a moment, and she said, "We're on a new path that shows promise, and we need tokit DNA to test this out."

Leif didn't know much about what Manuel's team was doing in the lab—other than trying to find a cure. This was just one operation. He didn't know how many others there were, only that they were in constant communications, sharing data and ideas.

"Why tokit DNA?" Leif asked.

Her momentary excitement disappeared, and even through her biosuit, Leif could see her condescending expression as she said, "Because tokits' DNA is the closest to humans," as if she were explaining stars to a child.

Really? Tokits and humans?

Leif wasn't sure why that surprised him so much. The two races didn't look that much alike, not like humans and sassares, for example. If that was true, however, then maybe her request made some sense, even if she had worded it as an order, not a request.

"I can't order him to give up DNA samples to you," he said, more for formality's sake than anything else.

He knew Doc would volunteer, but he didn't want Manuel to think he was under her control. His boss was the commander, not her.

"He will do what he's told," the head scientist said. "We're on the verge of a breakthrough, and we need a control."

"I thought you were on the verge of a breakthrough the day we arrived," Leif slipped out before he could engage his brain.

Dr. Manuel stared at him in shock before gathering herself up and saying, "Just get him to me in five minutes, Sergeant!"

She wheeled around and returned to her restricted spaces, not waiting for his response.

Way to go, Leefen. Pissing them off.

What he'd said was true, though. Ever since they'd arrived, the scientists were always on the verge of a breakthrough, but one that never developed. Frankly speaking, Leif didn't know what the hold-up was. Human medical science was supposed to be one of their strengths. True, the sassares' knowledge of the biological sciences was supposed to be the best in the galaxy, but the humans were right up there, and they should have been able to develop a cure by now. Leif had overheard a couple of the scientists discussing the "layered boobytraps" they were encountering, but still . . .

"Are you going to do it?" a'Noon asked.

"Where is Doc?"

"Where do you think?" the corporal asked. "Watching come tokit epic in the array bunkroom."

Leif wanted to tell Manuel to shove it, but he knew he wouldn't. He couldn't let his petty conflicts get in the way of the mission, and without a doubt, the mission was what was going on inside the labs. Leif and his Marines were just a sideshow.

"Tell him to put his show on pause and get his ass back to the lab. The vampires want to suck his blood."

Chapter 44

"What are they cheering for?" Leif asked Commander Warren as he peered through the window into the lab's second level.

"They've had some breakthroughs," the commander said.

"We've heard that before," Leif said.

"I think it might be serious this time. One of the other teams out there thought they might have cracked the crud coding, and our tests here seem to be bearing that out."

Leif was not a biologist, so his grasp on the problems with the crud was not very detailed. He knew there were two issues. The first was to develop a genetic defense against the effects of the virus. This was where the gene-splicing came in. The second problem was the little booby-trap the sassares had managed to insert into the virus. When faced with a defended cell, the virus morphed into another form to continue its assault, and so far, it always morphed into something far more deadly than the original. That was why four of the volunteers to be guinea pigs (Leif now knew what the phrase meant) had died instead of just contracting the hammer.

If the scientists could freeze the virus into one form, then they were confident that they could not only create a vaccine but could work to neutralize, then eliminate it.

That was about the depth of Leif's understanding. He was happy to leave the science to them and let him worry about the security of the asteroid. Not that he'd had to do much. After the switch from the bodies to Doc and Tesoomo D, the Marines had been sitting on their collective asses doing a whole lot of nothing. Leif had run some drills, but there was a limit to what he could do in the restricted space allowed to him.

"So, we might be out of here soon?" Leif asked.

"Not too soon. They still need to run the simulations, then do a live test."

Meaning, try and infect another one of them.

Leif would rather face a platoon of sassares infantry than let someone infect him with some sort of weaponized virus. Leif had seen horrible mutilations of people in battle. He'd also seen two of the bodies of volunteers, and they gave him the shudders far more than any battlefield remains.

"And then, we would need to step up the manufacture of the vaccines, distribute them. Do you know how many humans there are, and how spread out we are? We're talking a huge logistical challenge here. Most of the human resources we would normally use for such an emergency are stricken themselves. We'd have to figure out a work-around."

"Which we're doing, of course," he said. "People are putting together the plan now."

For the first time since the Marines had arrived, the commander seemed in his element.

"Then, once the vaccines are administered, how long before those stricken are well enough to function? How much of their lost capabilities will return? All of these are unknowns, and all the while, the sassares will probably step up their pace. It's obvious they want our worlds intact, but maybe blow up a few, like Earth? Just to fire a shot across the bow? To tell us to back off? I'm not sure we have the forces to hold them off if they try."

Leif hadn't considered that. The thought of Earth destroyed hit him harder than he expected. He wasn't human, and Earth wasn't his home. But he'd seen the Serengeti, he'd seen Lake Victoria and the Imperial Palace. He couldn't imagine them gone, no more.

He'd assumed, without thinking it through, that once a cure was developed, everything would be magically fixed. The Marines would be back at full strength. The Navy would surge out like an avenging angel to smite the sassares demons.

It wasn't going to happen that way. It would take time, and the sassares wouldn't likely give them that time. Leif didn't know how many Imperial ships were combat effective, either those that were never infected and manned by mostly human crews, or those where the human crews had the hammer and non-human crews took over.

The sassares Navy was never as large as the Imperial Navy, but the sassares ships were generally bigger and more powerful. With the hammer, Leif was sure that the Imperial Navy was no longer the larger of the two. Could they hold off the sassares long enough for the humans to recover? Leif didn't put the odds of that very high.

"We can deliver the vaccine," Lance Corporal Hulorin said.

"You? The Marines?" the commander asked.

"No. I mean all of us who aren't human. Hisser, alindamir, tokit, qiincer, wyntonan. We did a pretty good job of keeping you humans alive on Sunrise."

"They did, sir," Jones said. "You should have seen them. The hisser lieutenant was running it, but they had a tokit on each guy around the clock."

Private Jones, who'd been poked, prodded, and had samples pulled out of him, had been spending every moment he could with the rest of the Marines. After his interactions with Manuel, Leif could understand the private. Even the commander, who was officially part of the lab personnel, liked to spend as much time as possible with the Marines.

"Of course, we'll have to rely on our non-human citizens," the commander said. "There might not be enough to put someone on every person," he added with a laugh. "There're a lot of us."

"There's a shitload of tokits, sir," Jones said.

Leif was just about to weigh in when the overhead lights started flashing red.

"Where's Tesoo?" Leif shouted, jumping to his feet.

"Playing five-up-three in the bunkroom," Corporal a'Noon answered as she ran to join Leif at the main console.

"Get him out there, now!" Leif ordered.

"Is it . . . ?" the commander asked, looking at the display where a flashing red icon was making its way to the center.

"Yes, sir. It looks like we've got company!"

Chapter 45

The lab was dark. No lights, all unessential machinery turned off. Dr. Manuel had balked at turning off all equipment, telling Leif that they were essential to the mission, and they were so close to having a solution. Leif had started to argue, but one look at her convinced him that if he wanted to shut off everything, he was going to have to do it himself, and then only after he'd shot a few scientists.

The only illumination in the room was a single flat screen, which showed the array station. Doc and Tesoomo D were sitting at their control console, waiting for the sassares' arrival.

The sassares had hailed the station two hours before. Leif had decided that silence wasn't an option, that it would raise more suspicion, so Tesoomo D had answered. He'd answered some rote questions and assured the sassares that it was only him and Doc there.

They'd been told to shut down the array and wait for them. Any attempt to transmit a message would be dealt with "most harshly." Leif had expected that, and as soon as the ship was spotted, he'd piggybacked on normal traffic to inform higher headquarters. He could still contact headquarters via the snake transmitter that had been bored through solid rock to emerge on the other side of the asteroid, but even if it was spook gear, no one could give him assurances that a sassares ship didn't have the means to detect the transmission even if not the message itself.

Time had dragged on, and without blowers, the temperature inside the lab was heating up. Sweat trickled down the back of Leif's neck. It was almost a relief when the sassares ship docked at the end of the caterpillar.

About 30 meters long, this was not a capital ship. In the Imperial Navy, it might be a skiff or a scout, barely a man-of-war. Still, the medium-sized meson cannon running the length of the ship was more than powerful enough to blast the array and the lab—and everyone inside of them—into their component atoms.

"Here they come," Tesoomo D said, more for Leif and the rest rather than for Doc. The two stood and moved to the airlock.

Leif had eyes on the ship itself, then a single pickup inside the caterpillar. Eight sassares sailors, the officer with a sidearm and the enlisted with the main sassares battle rifle, pulled themselves down the caterpillar, speeding to the airlock, then with a deft twist, turned and landed feet-first.

"Looked better than us when we came," A'Noon muttered.

By treaty, all airlocks worked in the same way. A sassares sere-silver, the equivalent to an Imperial petty officer, worked the controls, venting the air and opening it. All eight crowded inside and started cycling.

"They might handle null-G looking fine, but that's stupid. All of them in a single cycle? What if Doc just tossed in a grenade?" Hulorin asked.

"Then whoever is left on that ship fries us all," Leif said before turning to the commander and asking, "You don't know how many they'd have left onboard?"

The commander shrugged and said, "Like I told you, I don't know much about ships. I'm not a line officer."

No, but you're a freaking Navy commander.

The inner door opened, and the sailors marched out, four flanking the two Marines, three backing up the sere-orange.

"Can we help you, sir?" Doc asked in his most unassuming voice . . . which Leif had to admit was pretty unassuming.

The officer swung his finger, sweeping it around the array. The four split off to search the spaces, while the three stepped up to take their place protecting the sere-orange.

"What is this place?" the officer asked.

"This is C-A-one-three-six-four-four-three, sir. Under Imperial contract to Toulamare and Dejesus. I can show you our license, if you want."

The sere-orange flipped a dismissive hand and asked, "Why aren't you on the charts?"

"Charts? We are, sir. Under communication relays. Class one-zero-zero-eight," Doc said.

"Din, can you get our license?" Doc told Tesoomo D, who gave a brief nod and started to back away, only to freeze as two of the sassares leveled their rifles at him.

"Jentut, look at them! What do I do now?" Tesoomo D said, raising his hands, and sounding quite frightened.

"Not bad," a'Noon whispered. "He looks like he's about to shit in his pants."

The sere-orange said, "I don't need your license. So, you're here alone?"

"Yes, sir," Doc said. "We're done our tour, and we're supposed to go back, but there's been an emergency out there. Some kind of plague. So, we're stuck here for now. Sir," he added, his voice rising slightly in pitch.

He started to wring his hands as the sassares searched the spaces. One of them came back and said something in their language.

"Don't we have a translator here?" Leif asked, looking around.

Dr. Manuel reached over and entered a command, just in time to hear the translating program kick in at the end of the sere-orange's sentence, ". . . like what?"

"Like something curled up and died in there."

Hell, I thought we cleaned everything up.

"He says something smells bad in your personal space," the sere-orange said.

Doc looked over at Tesoomo D and said, "I told you to clean up after yourself, Jentut. We're not slobs." He turned back to the sere-orange, tapped his nose, and said, "Sorry sir. We get nose-blind in here after a while."

The sere-orange looked at Doc for a moment, then said, "A tokit in charge over a hisser. Interesting."

He gave the space a sweeping glance, then said, "You do know that the humans are no longer in charge, right?"

"The plague, sir. We know about that. So, we have to wait until someone can come relieve us."

"But they won't be . . . *rista*, I'm not even going to bother with these two," the sassares said, turning to one of his sailors.

The translator caught the "*rista*," translating it to "shit."

Every race uses the same word, Leif thought.

"Are we going to blow this place?" one of the sailors asked in their language, the program translating it.

"No, it's a communications relay. We're going to want to be able to use it. Log it in, and let's get ready for the next target."

He turned to Doc and said, "We're going to leave you now. I want you to keep running this station, and someone will come back later to take over. Understand?"

"Yes, sir. I understand."

"Hell, it's working," Commander Warren said quietly inside the lab. "I never really thought it would."

The gods of chance were a fickle lot, however, and as if to punish the commander for jumping the gun, one of the sailors looked down at his scanner, stopped, then swung toward the hidden hatch into the lab.

"Sere-orange, I've got an anomaly here," the translator said.

"What kind?"

"I don't know. Like there's a space back there."

"Get ready," Leif hissed at his Marines, stepping back and unslinging his Stahlmont.

The sailor stepped up to the bulkhead, placing his scanner against it as the sere-orange took a couple of steps forward to see the results.

Tesoomo D, forgotten and obviously not a threat, reached under the table and pulled out his M-88 which he'd taped to the underside, thumbing the power. His first round took out one of the three standing around the officer, his second hit another in the shoulder.

"Go!" Leif yelled to the Marines waiting by the hatch.

PFC Baban a'Indigo hit the emergency release, blowing the hatch out, which caught the sassares with the scanner in the chest, flattening him. The Marines poured through the hatch, taking out the officer before the four inside the berthing space took cover and started firing back.

Leif, Lance Corporal Hulorin, and PFC a'Knight followed the rest, darting across the space, ignoring the firefight. The PFC stumbled and fell face-first to the deck, but Leif and Hulorin made it to the airlock. The sassares had left the caterpillar pressurized, or this wouldn't work.

Qiincers were at home in null-G, and Hulorin flew down the caterpillar, Leif on her ass as he pulled himself along the handholds with his right hand while his still tender strong hand held out his Springfield .45.

A sassares sailor appeared at the door, looking down the caterpillar to see what was happening. The man must had focused only on Hulorin flying right at him, somehow missing the twice-as-large wyntonan behind her. The sassares snapped off a couple of shots at her, which made her juke upwards, and that left Leif with a clear shot. With one last pull, he shot forward, bringing up his right hand to grasp his left in a combat stance, and as he flew, he fired three shots, center mass.

The sailor gave Leif a surprised look as he slowly started to tumble, and Leif, his momentum unabated, continued forward and through the door, crashing into the sailor whose blood was spreading up in large globules as they arched away.

Shit, Null-G!

Leif had expected to hit the ship's interior and roll, not knowing that the sassares didn't use artificial gravity for smaller vessels. He bounced off the body, which sent him off at an angle as he struggled to orient himself. He hit the bulkhead and tried to kick off, but his rotation kept him from getting a good push. As he spun around, he caught a glimpse of another sailor diving for a console of some sort.

From Leif's perspective, the sailor was upside down and above him. He'd fired his .45 so many times that the ballistics of the round were embedded in his brain—ballistics under gravity, not null-G. He had to stop the sailor before he set off an alarm or whatever he was going to do, and he didn't have the time to try and calculate out how he needed to adjust his point of aim.

He had to trust the gods of war. As he bounced off the bulkhead, he fired three more times, the recoil from each shot altering his own trajectory. Two shots missed the sassares sailor. One hit him in the temple just as he turned a key on the console.

The console lit up before bright red blood drenched it.

Leif managed to bring his legs under him before he hit the opposite bulkhead. In control again, he pushed off for the console. Leif couldn't read sassares script, but if form followed function, then the key turned on some sort of communications net. Leif couldn't hear anything, so all he could do was hope that it required some input. He reached out and slowly turned the key back, powering down a few of the lights.

Movement flickered in the corner of his eyes, and he pushed back, spinning to face Hulorin, who was stumbling in, her left wing deflated and leaking a yellowish fluid.

"Cover me," he mouthed to her before he started a quick search.

Sounds of firing that had reached them through the caterpillar died down, and a few moments later, a'Noon and four Marines came through the door, relieving Hulorin.

"Two down," the corporal said. "A'Knight and Tesoo."

"Clear the aft," Leif ordered.

Less than a minute later, the corporal gave Leif the all-clear. The sassares ship was theirs.

****

"Doctor Manuel, give me a hand," Doc Korindtut yelled as he crouched over PFC a'Knight, his fingers buried in the Marine's thigh.

The laboratory director had just tentatively entered the space, followed by three of her staff. Leif had just returned as well, bringing with him Hulorin, who was pale and unsteady on her feet.

"I'm not a physician," she said, blanching at the PFC's blood pooling under him, then at Tesoomo D's body, over which someone had spread a lab coat.

"I don't care what you are. You know anatomy. I need you to close off his femoral artery so I can get him stabilized," the tokit snapped. "Now," he yelled, when the scientist hesitated.

She gave her three staff a worried look, then stepped up and knelt beside Doc, running her hands alongside his and into the wound on a'Knight's thigh. She shifted her position as Doc withdrew his hands and opened the medkit a'Indigo had carried with him. Sure hands selected one of his magazines, slapped on the air needle, and injected the PFC. Leif could almost see the color flow into a'Knight as nanites flooded his body and he relaxed.

Doc monitored his medscan for a few moments, then pulled out a tube of Knitwell.

"I'm not going to try and sew it, John," he told the PFC, who looked like he was beyond caring as the pain-blockers took effect. "I'll just give you a little shot of this to hold you until the nanites do their thing."

"Doc, when you can, Hulorin's going to bleed out," Leif interrupted.

The corpsmen took one look, then said, "She's not bleeding out. That's pseudo-haemolymph fluid, and her system's bifurcated."

"What?" Leif asked.

"Bifurcated. The fluid reservoirs are not connected to each other. I'll get her fixed up, but out here, it's going to take awhile for her to be able to reconstitute the fluid enough to be able to fly again. But now, Sergeant, let me deal with John."

Leif wasn't used to being cut off by an HM, the equivalent to a Marine lance corporal, and this sense of authority from a tokit was surprising. He felt like he'd been shut down pretty effectively.

The corpsman stuck the dispenser nozzle into the wound on a'Knight's thigh, then as Dr. Manuel removed her hand, filled the gap with the organic and semi-intelligent glue.

"Does it hurt?" Leif asked Hulorin.

"No, Sergeant. I just got fucking shot, and it feels like a nice massage," she got out through clenched teeth. "Why would you think it hurt?"

Shot down for the second time in 30 seconds by junior enlisted, Leif still had to suppress a smile. He knew she wouldn't appreciate it, but her snarky reply, so like a qiincer, convinced him that she was going to be OK.

He motioned Corporal Tellinine over and told him, "Watch Hulorin here until Docs done with a'Knight." He then turned to her and said, "You heard the Doc. You'll be OK."

"Then that makes my fucking day."

Leif turned his head so she wouldn't see him smile, but it faded when his eyes landed on Tesoomo D's body. The hisser had been cut down in the first volley when he took on all of the sassares himself. By drawing attention to himself, however, he'd given the rest of them the chance to rush through the door without the sassares cutting them down at that choke point.

"Total ten, Tesoo," Leif whispered.

Commander Warren was standing over Doc and a'Knight, next to a now-beaming, if bloody Dr. Manuel, who was looking pretty proud of herself. Leif still had work to do, so he walked over and pulled the commander aside. The man was technically his commanding officer, and he needed to know what was going on.

"Sir, both the space and the ship are secure. I don't think they got out a warning, but I can't be sure."

"What? You're not sure? What are the chances?" the commander asked, raising his voice excitedly.

"I don't know. I think one of them opened a channel, but I shot him before he could speak. But I just don't know."

"So, what do we do now?" the commander asked.

You're the officer. You're supposed to tell me.

"We're clear for the moment, but longer term? Even if no warning was sent back to their command, they're going to realize that there's something wrong with the ship, sir." Leif said. "We need to get rid of it.

"Are there any explosives aboard this place?" he asked.

"Explosives? Like a bomb? This is a research station, Sergeant, not a Navy base."

Which is ironic coming from you, Navy Commander Warren.

"Do you really think they'll come back?" the commander asked Leif.

"What would you do if you lost a ship?"

"I guess so," he said, looking worried. "I wonder if we'll have to leave. We're so close to a vaccine."

Leif took a moment to survey the space. Four of his Marines were gathering the sassares bodies, lining them up against the far bulkhead. He'd have to insist to Dr. Manuel that they be put into cold storage until someone much higher up on the food chain figured what to so with them.

PFC a'Knight was happily mumbling something under the influence of the drugs his nanites were filling him with. He looked to be out of immediate danger, but he needed advanced medical care not available here. Doc was now assessing Hulorin.

They'd fared better than they could have hoped for, and the immediate danger was over. But it wasn't the immediate danger that worried him. It was what was coming.

Now, he had to get rid of the sassares ship, and with just grunts, scientists, and a Navy officer who knew nothing about the Navy, he needed help that he wasn't going to get here.

"I've got an idea, sir. I'm going to report what happened here, then try and see what we can do."

****

"I think we're there," Willis Lafferty, the lab tech who maintained the equipment said.

"Turn the green knob in a clockwise direction until I tell you to stop," Irina, the human on the other end of the comms said. "I want to see the readout before you fire her up."

Leif watched as Lafferty slowly turned the knob. When Irina said "Stop! Right there!" Lafferty pulled back.

"Move the pick-up a little closer. I'm getting some glare."

She studied the display for a few moments. Leif couldn't make heads nor tails of what was written there.

They were lucky that the sassares did not rely on verbal commands to the same extent that humans and the rest of the empire did. No one on the station spoke Omaja, the sassares primary language, so there would have been no way to get the ship underway if they did. As it was, Irina, the Intel expert on sassares ships on the other side of their comms link, had to check and recheck each step along the way. What might take a sassares helmsman two minutes had taken Irina and Willis over two hours to set up, two long hours where the dead crew's higher headquarters might check in for a status report.

"I think we're there, too. If we're right, the ship will leave you and travel to the next destination on their itinerary."

"Won't they try to contact the ship?" Leif asked, bending over to stick his head in the pick-up's view.

"Probably. The sassares are more independent than our own Navy, though," Irina said. "So, it might take them longer to get around to checking. As long as the ship is within its scheduled route windows, they shouldn't be too concerned."

That would never happen in the Imperial Navy or Marines. His own headquarters had been in meltdown mode wanting a report from him after the fight, this despite the fact that they had been able to observe everything that happened on the monitors except for what went on inside the sassares ship.

As a Marine NCO, he thought there was a lot to be said about the sassares way. Not that he would voice that to anyone up the chain, especially given the current situation.

"Ivanov," a voice used to command asked from just out range of the pickup. "Will this work?"

Irina turned her head and said, "It should. At least that's what the manuals say."

Leif hadn't seen Irina's boss, nor did he know his name. Evidently, this was a highly secure location, and probably not because of the hammer. He was sure they would have hidden Irina as well if they could have.

"Can you repeat what you said about how much time we'll have?"

"Roughly thirteen seconds. They don't use our timing," she said before Leif could ask why 13 seconds and not 10 or 15.

"And all I have to do is flip this switch," he said, reaching out to touch the toggle.

"After Willis arms it, yeah. You'll have ninety-one seconds to do that, or we'll have to go through the last five steps again."

"OK, then. Are you ready?" Leif asked Willis.

"Yeah," he said, twisting his body awkwardly to get his head facing the hatch.

Leif had needed Willis' basic familiarity with equipment to be Irina's hands here on the ship, but the human had almost no experience in Null-G. Leif had two Marines ready at the ship's airlock, waiting to pull him back from the ship and into the station. That left it to Leif to trigger the sassares ship's departure.

If Lance Corporal Hulorin weren't hurt, he'd have had her trigger the ship's systems. Qiincers handled Null-G better than the other races in the empire. But with her out of action, that left it to the Marines, who all had been trained and had experience. The most experienced was the senior Marine, one Sergeant Leefen a'Hope Hollow.

"Commander, we're about ready. I'll be sending back Willis now."

He turned to the door where a'Noon and Corporal Pastichet were waiting and gave them a thumbs up.

"Good luck," Irina told them.

"Go ahead," he told Willis, who took a deep breath, then entered in a string of numbers that Irina had given him.

Immediately, the lights flashed lilac, the sassares color of warning. Leif grabbed Willis by the collar and jumped for the main hatch. Willis struggled to maintain an even keel which just made it more difficult, but Leif was stronger and manhandled the human.

"Here you go," he told the two corporals. "Get him back.

"And thanks, Willis," Leif shouted as the two pulled the human down the caterpillar. He flipped on his hood as he watched them reach the airlock on the other side and start cycling.

"We're in," Corporal a'Noon passed after a too long wait, Leif's nerves rising. His musapha sensed the danger and tried to wake, but the last thing Leif needed now was to feel invulnerable.

He had fifteen more seconds before the outer airlock door, the one the caterpillar side would reopen, fifteen more seconds before he could flip the toggle. He pushed back to the command console, something too small and too simple to seemingly run a space-going ship.

"Twenty-five seconds, Sergeant," Irina said.

Leif would be leaving the pick-up on the ship, and he guessed Irina or others would monitor it as the ship plied on with its assigned route. He'd voiced concern about that, thinking that if the sassares found the ship, they would see a human-made pick-up, but Irina had assured him that wouldn't be a problem and left it at that.

For the hundredth time, Leif wished the research station had something that could be rigged as a bomb, or that Irina could program the ship to blow up. She had laughed at him when he suggested that, saying that was pure Hollywood. Real ships weren't rigged to self-destruct.

Leif had given Willis a condescending smile when he'd adjusted his body position prior to arming the switch, but he found himself doing the same thing. He set his feet to give himself a strong push, and took several deep breaths, pushing down his mistress who read his fear and wanted to surface.

"Fifteen seconds, Sergeant. Don't be afraid. You can do it."

Leif wanted to snap that he was a Marine, that he wasn't afraid, but in truth, he was. Facing another soldier in combat was one thing, getting cooked by the sassares' gamma stream was another thing altogether. Dead was dead, but this one scared him.

"Here it goes, Mother help me!" he said, flipping the toggle and pushing off, heading not at the hatch itself, but at the bulkhead strut across from it.

Deep purple lights flashed, and a raucous alarm filled the ship. Normally, after flipping the toggle, the ship would commence to move out, but with the hatch open, the engines wouldn't fire. The ship would close the hatch, then test for integrity before the engine sequence would kick in. That was what gave Leif his thirteen seconds.

Leif twisted in space, hitting the bulkhead feet first, then immediately pushing off for the hatch. If he missed, he'd either clip the edge and tumble out of control in the caterpillar, unable to clear it before being washed with enough ions to cook him. If he hit the bulkhead more solidly, then he'd never make it out of the ship, and he'd be settling in for a long and lonely journey with who knew what waiting for him on the other end.

He shot forward . . . and he was going to clip the edge of the hatch. He shot out an arm, grabbed the edge as the hatch was closing, and adjusted his trajectory, slowing him down, but just missing the edge and giving him a chance to make it to the airlock at the far end of the caterpillar.

There was no room for error now. He reached out for the passing handholds, but there were millimeters too far. He needed more speed, but he couldn't get that without something to grab.

Behind him, he heard the hatch close. The ship would be checking for atmospheric integrity, then the engines would kick off. Ahead, only ten meters away, was sanctuary, but it might as well have been a klick away.

His mistress struggled to free herself, and this time, Leif didn't fight her. Mustapha flooded his body as he drifted tantalizingly closer. He felt more than heard the ship's engine power up just as one finger caught a handhold and he yanked with augmented strength, sending him rocketing to the end and slamming into the open airlock as light filled the caterpillar, the bones of his hands visible for an instant before the outer lock door closed.

Leif slammed into the deck as artificial gravity grabbed at him. Looking back down the caterpillar through the window, he could see the stars of open space as he took in several deep breaths, trying to take inventory. His skin tingled, which couldn't be a good thing. But he was alive.

"Are you OK, Sergeant?" an excited voice came over the net.

Leif struggled to his feet, then looked out the window in the airlock door. At the end of the caterpillar, all he could see was black space.

"I'm fine. A little sunburned, I think, but I'm OK. The ship is gone."

He barely had time to rip off his hood before he puked all over the deck.

Chapter 46

"Hey Mr. Hollow, you're sure looking in the pink today," Corporal a'Noon told Leif with an exaggerated human accent as she flopped in the seat beside him.

Leif gave her a crooked little finger, the wyntonan version of a human flipping the bird. The rest of the wyntonans thought his pink-tinged skin was pretty funny, telling him he looked so human now.

He'd been lucky. Doc had given him the once over, and he'd only taken minor damage that a specialized nanite infusion was now correcting. He was already a couple of shades lighter than he was before after almost getting his ass fried. He'd still need a complete checkup once he was in a Class A medical facility, and he'd probably need a full body scrub, but he'd be fine for all practical purposes within a day or so, and he'd have a full recovery after the scrub.

Luckily, like all races, the sassares followed the standardized protocols. Ships did not engage interstellar drives at full power within 10,000 klicks of inhabited stations. Without a hard EVA, the walls of the caterpillar would not have protected him had the ship taken off at full power. Even a split-second of exposure would have killed him on the spot.

Feeling grateful that he'd suffered no permanent damage did not mean that he appreciated being the butt of the others' ribbing.

I'm a sergeant, by the Mother, and they should give me respect.

If anyone was a grumpy as he was, it had to be Lance Corporal Hulorin. Doc had patched up the through-and-through wound in her left middle wing, but the pseudo-haemolymph that allowed her to pump up her three left wings would take at least a week before there was enough built up to allow her to fold the wings and much longer before they were strong enough for her to fly.

PFC a'Knight was in an induced coma. Doc was sure he'd recover, but his leg was too mangled for the standard medkit nanites to repair. He needed surgery, and even then, it was no sure thing. By keeping him in a coma, Doc was increasing the chances that surgeonbots would be able to save the leg.

Leif now kept four Marines on guard in the array spaces at all times. They'd seen no sign of sassares in the three days since the fight, but that didn't mean that another ship wasn't on its way seeking revenge. If the sassares didn't come within the next five days, they'd be home free, and the Marines could leave this floating hole and get back to their fellow Marines.

Two things had changed since the attack. The first was that since their location was almost assuredly compromised, the government wanted them out of there. The second was that a tentative cure had been developed and was in initial trials, much to the dismay of the scientists. They wouldn't say it in front of the Marines, but they were pissed. To a person, they thought they would have gotten the breakthrough, but it had happened in another lab.

At the moment, with someone else getting the credit and with orders to pack up shop, most of the scientists were drunk. This was supposedly a dry station, but with scientists with lab equipment at their disposal, anyone who thought it would remain a dry station was crazy. Two of the scientists had even brought out moonshine for the Marines, but Leif had put his foot down. No one was getting drunk while they were still at the station.

Leif's stomach rumbled. The food on the station was surprisingly good, even if he'd long run out of Soran's spice mix. Only a'Indigo still had any spice left . . . if anyone could call that processed city shit real spice.

Still, I'd take some of he offered it, Leif had to admit to himself.

He stood up to go into the galley when the door to the lab rattled. There were two thuds, then finally, it opened, and a human who'd had a few too many spotted him.

"Hey, Sergeant. The emperor wants you!"

Leif frowned, then turned to continue to the galley.

"Sergeant Hollow! Really, on the PF-80. You're wanted now."

Six sets of eyes swiveled to lock on the human. The PFS-80 was a highly classified, highly secure communications suite. It was supposedly impenetrable to hacking. The Marines had been using their T/O PF-245 to communicate with their headquarters, a nice piece of gear, but nothing to the level of an 80.

That didn't mean His Imperial Majesty, Forsythe the Third, Protector of the Empire and Servant of the People, was sitting on the other side, just waiting to chat with a Marine sergeant. But if this wasn't some drunken prank, and if he really was getting a call on it, then it was someone important.

The commander stuck his head out of the hatch and said, "You heard him, Sergeant! Get your ass in here!"

He'd obviously been tipping a cup as well.

Five sets of eyes now swiveled to Leif.

"I'm coming," he said.

Prank or not, he had to find out.

The scientist, a red-haired, slightly overweight human male in his 30s who Leif had seen plenty of times but never caught his name, held the hatch open so Leif could walk through. The heavy smell of moonshine enveloped Leif as he walked past the man.

It wasn't as bad inside as Leif imagined. Most of the lab hatches were closed. Lara, whose father was a Marine and who was one of the few science-types who'd taken an interest in them, was slouched on a chair asleep, but another ten or so were standing, waiting for Leif, their interest palpable. Leif began to wonder if there was something to all of this.

He was escorted through the B-level to the C, the commander stopping at the hatch. Leif stopped to wait for him, but the commander told he wasn't cleared.

Hell, what's going on?

Dr. Manuel was waiting for him outside a heavy hatch. As he approached, she scanned her eyes, and the hatch swung open on a whisper, quiet for something so massive.

"Sergeant . . ." she started before falling silent.

"Ma'am?"

"I . . . oh, forget it. Just take your call. Sit down and state your name. The AI will connect you."

Leif looked inside the secured space. It didn't look like much, certainly not impressive for something so high-tech. A single black chair was placed before a lone cam pickup perched on a white stand. There was nothing else. No screen, no holo stand, no displays. Nothing.

Leif sat down and said, "Sergeant Leefen a'Hope Hollow. Imperial Marine Corps."

Immediately, a portion of the wall flickered once before revealing a 3D screen with an image of Earth floating in the background. "Stand by, Sergeant a'Hope Hollow," a surprisingly pleasant female voice told him.

"Yes, ma'am," Leif said automatically before giving a rueful smile. Most AI's purposely had flat voices, but this one was very realistic.

The screen switched to a series of landscapes, a soft melody playing in the background. When the scene switched to the Cañon Majesté on Last Chance, he realized that it was showing scenes from throughout Imperial Space, not just on Earth. He leaned forward, hoping to see an image from Home.

If Home was in the rotation, it hadn't made it before the screen cleared, revealing Acting Minister Montrose, still in a biosuit, still looking tired. Leif was a little disappointed. Not because he had anything against the acting minister, but the drunk had said "emperor."

"Sergeant a'Hope Hollow, it's good to see you. How's the gamma exposure?"

Leif was mildly surprised that she knew about that, but for all he knew, his record flashed on the screen the moment she signed on.

"Just a little bit of an itch, now, ma'am. I'll need a scrub later, but I'm good to go."

"Good, good. First your arm, now this. You need to take better care of yourself, Sergeant. We won't want potential recruits to think being a Marine is dangerous," she said with a laugh.

"I promise to duck next time, ma'am."

This is surreal, trading jokes with a minister when the empire is in such a messed-up position.

"We're trying to get a medivac for PFC a'Knight, but shipping's at a premium now, as you can imagine."

What's going on? She doesn't need a PFS-80 to tell me this? What's the real reason?

"Ma'am, with all due respect, why are you calling me?"

There was a pause, and she scrunched her eyebrows together as if trying to parse her words. "I just wanted to take a moment and have a quick chat first." There was another pause, then a deep breath before she continued. "Sergeant a'Hope Hollow, you have done an admirable job as a Marine, and you've developed quite a following."

What kind of following? What's she talking about?

"I know you were in the first group of wyntonans to enlist in the Corps, and many considered that just a political move by the emperor, that your people had no place in the Marines."

Leif felt his body tense up, wondering what was coming next.

"You—well you and others—have proven, however, that this was not just a political statement, a stunt, so-to-speak. You've proven that you belong in the Corps. Not just belong, but that you're needed. But serving isn't a one-way street. Those of us in positions of power have to be sure that you are being served as well. I hope we've done that. I hope *I've* done that."

I still don't know what she's getting at.

"But one thing is clear to me, Sergeant. It's that wyntonan and humans need to band together. Not just us, but alindamir, qiincers, tost'el'tzy, hissers, tokits, too. We are stronger together, we are *better* together."

She paused again, started to say something, then cut it off before starting again. "I believe that from the bottom of my heart, and I hope you come to the same conclusion."

Now Leif was really lost. This was so . . . so weird. A minister was giving him a pep talk, complete with kumbaya overtones? Nothing was making sense.

"I don't have any more time, but please, think of what I've said, Sergeant. We're stronger together."

"Of course, ma—" he started, but her image cut off, to be replaced by a single image of the imperial seal while the anthem played softly in the background.

A moment later, Emperor Forsythe, the leader of the empire, appeared on the screen.

Leif was shocked at his appearance. The emperor was young, only in his early twenties, but he looked like he'd aged twenty years, his hair speckled with grey, wrinkles at the corners of his eyes and on his forehead. More than that, he looked dead tired, his eyes dull.

All of that was expected, Leif guessed. With the empire's very existence imperiled, with the human race at the verge of extinction, the load upon his shoulders was unimaginable. Leif felt a surge of . . . not pity, but maybe understanding. Although nowhere near the level of the emperor's responsibilities, Leif had felt in over his head since the humans had been infected.

"Ayala, Leefen a'Hope Hollow," the emperor said in Uzboss, his accent almost flawless. "May the Mother guide you."

"Ayala, Forsythe a'Earth," Leif said. "May the Mother guide you as well."

"Forsythe a'Earth?" he said with a weak laugh and a smile that gave a hint at the man Leif had known and admired. "I like it.

"I know you must be wondering why I've asked for this conference, and as you can imagine, my time is pretty much accounted for now, so, I'll cut right to the chase.

"The empire is in dire straights. There's no way around that. Most of the humans are infected, and the sassares are overpowering what's left of our Navy. If the Navy falls, then so does the empire and everything we've tried to accomplish."

Leif could hear the bitterness in the emperor's voice.

"We humans alone cannot hope to hold off the sassares. That's a fact, and no spin can change that. We've made some breakthroughs in treating the crud, but we need time, time that we simply don't have. Unless . . ."

"Unless what, sir?"

"Humans cannot hold back the sassares, but we're only 28% of the empire. The *empire* can hold them off, though. Wyntonan, the qiincers, the alindamir, and even the tokits can contribute."

"Sir," Leif interrupted, mouth engaged before his brain could hold him back, "Don't underestimate the tokits."

The emperor's eyes opened wide, his mouth dropped open, before he said, "Of course, not. They are good workers, good supporting actors. Full citizens."

Leif had seen the tokits in action, and he'd slowly changed his opinion of them. They were more than mere workers. But it wasn't his place to argue with the emperor now, so he shut up.

"But back to my point. If the rest of the empire holds firm, we can hold back the sassares long enough for the humans to return to the military."

Leif deeply respected the emperor. He'd given his oath to the man. But even he, who had championed equality among the races, was telling Leif right there that he needed the other races to hold off the sassares long enough for the humans, the *real* sailors and Marines, to get back and only then defeat the enemy.

"I understand that, sir," he said.

And I understand that you still give primacy to humans.

He respected, even admired the man, but that somehow made his disappointment at the emperor's implied meaning worse.

"But what has that got to do with me, Your Majesty? I've sworn an oath to you. I am a Knight Extraordinaire, sworn to the empress. I will fight for the empire to my dying breath, but I'm only one person."

"Sergeant, you are more than one person," the emperor said. "And I am counting on that.

"The sassares know their key is to subvert the other races in the empire. They've already done it with the crud, which they did right under our noses," the emperor almost spit out, his anger palpable. "And now, they're petitioning the other races. A sassares battleship, with a sere-black aboard, has appeared in orbit above Kandelhan on a diplomatic mission. They are demanding that the wyntonans officially cede from the empire and join them."

Leif's mistress almost took over at those words, and he stood up from his seat, spitting out, "That's bullshit! I saw how they treated the Novacks. We can't trust those assholes, Your Majesty!"

The emperor didn't seem taken aback by his outburst. He smiled and said, "I was hoping to hear something like that from you, but I'm more than pleased with your vitriol."

Leif stood there, clenching and unclenching his fists, before he slowly sat back down, telling the emperor, "I'm with you, Your Majesty. But like I told you, I'm just one person. I am at your service, but I don't see how I can change anything."

"You are more than just a person. You are Sergeant Leefen a'Hope Hollow, the most decorated Marine on active duty. You've made quite a name for yourself."

"Among my fellow Marines, maybe."

"Not just among the Corps. Everyone knows who you are, and back on Kandelhan, you're somewhat of a hero."

"We don't make heroes from the military, sir. We gave that up three centuries ago."

This time, the emperor gave a full-throated laugh, and for another moment, he was the young emperor, full of dreams and hopes for his empire.

"You really don't know, do you? Your people do know who you are, and they take pride in you. I want to send you back to your people, and I want you to do your best to keep them in the empire. Right now, we humans need the wyntonans, but I hope that you believe the wyntonans need us as well. That they need the empire to achieve what is best for them."

Leif realized that the wyntonans and the rest of the "dung races" were still second-class citizens within the empire, but he was positive they were better off with humans and the emperor than they would be with the sassares. With the empire, things were slowly getting better. With the sassares, things would be undoubtedly worse.

Maybe they could pull back and stay neutral, but his gut told him that the sassares would take neutrality as being against them. The People would have to take sides, and for their sake, Leif would do whatever he could to try and open their eyes to the consequences of making the wrong choice.

Not that I can do much.

"Your Majesty, I will go wherever you send me, and if that is back to Home, to Kandelhan, so be it. I'll do my best, although I think you're overestimating my influence."

"And I think you are underestimating it, Leefen. But I appreciate your willingness."

The emperor looked off-screen for a moment, then nodded and said, "Give me a minute, Sascha."

"I need to go, but I've hired a noxes ship to pick you up and take you to Kandelhan."

"A noxes ship?"

"That's the only way to get you there with that battleship in orbit. The Navy is stretched thin, and even if I did have something available, it's arrival would instigate a fight. Right now, the noxes are neutral, so their ship shouldn't cause a problem.

"First Lieutenant a'Black has also agreed to go, and I'll try and send a couple of others," the emperor said to Leif's relief.

He was glad to know that this wasn't landing solely on his shoulders. With An as an officer, she would be in charge, and that was welcomed.

"I'm not going to try and tell you what to do or what to say. I'll leave it up to you. My only advice is to be honest, and speak from the heart."

"I'll do that, Your Majesty."

"I wish I could tell you how much I appreciate this. How much the empire appreciates this. But I have to go.

"I wish you the favor of the Mother in all you do," he said in Uzboss as he stood up.

"Your Majesty!" Leif almost shouted, stopping the emperor in his tracks.

"Is there something else?" the emperor asked, giving a quick glance to whoever was waiting for him.

"The empress, sir. How is she?"

With the emperor speaking to him without a biosuit, Leif had to figure they had clean facilities.

The emperor stopped, and his shoulders slumped. "She's infected. Still in a coma," he said in a low voice.

"But the vaccine. You said you had it."

"We're manufacturing it now, but it will all go to the military first. We need to reconstitute our Navy."

The empress was one person, and no one would miss a single dose, but Leif understood. The emperor never acted in a vacuum. Every action was scrutinized. It was the appearances that mattered, to no matter how much the man wanted his wife at his side, the emperor had to not only make priorities but show them.

"When she does wake up, please give her my respects," Leif said.

The emperor gave a slight smile, then said, "I will, Sergeant. I will."

HOME

Chapter 47

The shuttle came on on final approach to its assigned landing pad. Leif anxiously watched the display as they got closer. He hadn't been home for over a year, and despite the gravity of his mission, all he could think of at the moment was seeing Soran and Jord, his son, for the very first time.

"That looks so flip," Private Jones said excitedly.

"Just another city on another planet. There're thousands of them," Lance Corporal Hulorin said, her eyes buried in her pad.

"You can at least look, Lance Corporal," the private said, refusing to let her dampen his mood.

Leif ignored them both. He'd been surprised when Jones had asked to come with him when he'd informed the others. Leif had automatically refused, thinking the private still had to give up body parts on demand, but the commander told him Jones had been detached from the research effort. He'd still been about to refuse, but just as he was opening his mouth to say no, something came over him, and the "no" turned into a "yes." He hadn't been quite wasn't quite sure why he'd agreed. This mission was for wyntonans, not humans.

It wasn't until Corporal a'Noon had asked if he was going to take Hulorin, too, that he realized he was using Jones as a window prop. He wanted to present a picture of racial harmony. Three races were better than two, and four was better than three, so the qiincer and Doc were added to the party. If Tesoomo was still alive, he'd have made it five races.

The baffles popped up, and the shuttle settled gently on the ground. He was home, and none too soon. The trip on the noxes commercial transport had been disconcerting, the lighting too low for Leif and the other tthree. There had been little contact with the ship's captain or crew, and the four had mostly stayed in their staterooms on the transit.

The hatch slid open flooding the interior with a clean, bright light that lifted his spirits even higher

Their harness snapped free, and Leif hurried to the hatch and paused, taking in four huge draughts of air and the aromas of home. There was no mistaking the hint of spice in the air, nor the sweet smell of tonsir blossoms, which should be in full bloom throughout the capital.

"Are you going to get off, Sergeant? Or are we just going to head back to the noxes' ship," Hulorin asked.

Leif didn't know how much of her snark was the normal qiincer manner or how much was because she still couldn't fly and only just been able to fold her wing. Frankly, he didn't care. He was home!

The baffles recessed back into the tarmac, and a ground shuttle headed for them. Leif climbed down the steps, resisting the urge to kneel and kiss the ground.

"Ayah, Sergeant a'Hope Hollow," a wyntonan shouted out in Uzboss as the shuttle pulled to a stop. "Welcome home!"

"Ayah," Leif answered, peering past him to see if Soran was in the shuttle. She wasn't.

"I'm Lyon Raster," the man said. "I'll be your *pangform* while you are here. If you'll board, I'll take you to the terminal."

Raster? Not a'Raster?

Leif had heard that a growing number of wyntonans were dropping the "a" honorific, and the thought that just one more tradition was going by the wayside was disheartening. Technically, the "a" just indicated "from," so it had no real meaning, but it was the way people were named for centuries.

To cover his unease, he turned to the other three and translated for them, "This is our pangform. He wants us to board to go to the terminal."

"What's a pangform?" Jones asked.

"It's . . . well, not a servant, and not a handler as you humans would say. Maybe a cross between the two? He'll take us to where we need to be, but if we need something, he's our guy."

"So, if I tell him I want a Coke or a Sassy, he'll get it?" Jones asked.

"Yeah, I guess so. I'm not sure we have Sassy here, though."

"Sweet!"

The four loaded the shuttle, and within moments, it was whooshing into the terminal. Leif was surprised at the number of people there, to include the media. Not just local. Several of the bigger news organizations were crowding the entrance, none using human reporters, of course. JBS, the sassares-backed news company was there, which was surreal. JBS and ICN right next to each other while humans and sassares were at war.

Leif only gave them a passing glance. His attention was focused on the tall woman holding the hand of small ada in the front of the mass of people.

"Stay with a'Ras—with Raster," he told the other three as he bolted from the shuttle and ran up to Soran, giving her a hug.

"I've missed you so much," he said before Jord hit him in the thigh and said, "My mama!"

Leif laughed, gave his wife one last squeeze before letting her go and kneeling, to pick up his son. Jord's eyes grew large, his face screwed up, and he let out a piercing scream, much to the delight of the gathered crowd.

It wasn't so delightful to Leif.

"It's OK, Jord. It's me. Dada!" Leif said, trying to calm Jord, who was having none of it.

The little guy pushed away against Leif's chest, trying to get as far away from him as possible.

He screamed, "No! Mamma!"

Leif tried to hold the struggling ada and calm him down, but it was a lost cause. Jord whipped his head back and forth, pushing away from him.

"Let me," Soran said, reaching between the two and taking their son into her arms.

Leif stared in shock as Jord's cries settled into whimpers, tears streaming down his cheeks as he looked fearfully at his father.

"That's your dada, Jord. You know, from the camcam."

Leif could see that Jord didn't believe her, and it broke his heart. This was not what he'd envisioned for when he'd finally see his son.

"Sergeant," Raster said, taking him by the upper arm. "We need to get going. You're expected."

Leif wanted to whip his arm free. He needed to convince his son who he was. Raster gently tugged again, and Leif knew he had to go.

"I'll see you later," Leif said as he let his pangform lead him away from the media and spectators and toward a side door.

"Sergeant Hope Hollow! Why are you here?" and "Sergeant, what's your take on the ultimatum?" were shouted out by the press. Leif didn't answer but ducked through the door and out into a waiting government van.

There was only one thing on his mind as the van sped the four into the capital.

My son doesn't know who I am!

****

"An!" Leif shouted, breaking into a run and almost knocking her off her feet in his enthusiasm. "I mean, ma'am! Look at those silver bars. First Lieutenant a'Black!"

"Good to see you, too, Leefen," she said with a laugh. "It's been a long time, my friend."

"Since Camp Navarro, at graduation. I've been following your career, though. The first officer of the People."

He gave her another hug, and looking over her shoulder, he spotted another familiar face.

"Keijon? Is that you? What is this? A boot camp reunion?"

"Good to see you, Leefen," his fellow sergeant said, coming up for a back-pounding hug.

"You still as fast as ever?" Leif asked, giving Keijo a poke in the belly. "Looks like you've gained a little weight there."

"I can still run your sorry ass into the ground," Keijo said with a laugh. "And who're your friends there?"

Leif turned to look at the three, who were standing uncomfortably, still at the doorway into the small office, not understanding Uzboss.

He switched to Standard and said, "Sorry. This is Lance Corporal Hulorin, PFC Jones, and Doc Korindtut. Guys, these are some of my boot camp buddies. First Lieutenant An a'Black and Sergeant Keijon a'Tanner . . . are you going with Keijo or Keijon these days?" he asked Keijo in Uzboss.

"You know the humans. Hard time pronouncing the trailing N. So, I still use Keijo."

"Sergeant Keijo a'Tanner," Leif said, back to Standard. "Lieutenant a'Black was the trailing series honor grad, and Sergeant a'Tanner here was the fastest recruit in the company.

"So, the emperor told me about you, An. What about you. Keijo? What are you here for?"

"Same thing as you are," Keijo said before switching to Uzboss. "Nice touch there, Leefen, bringing in those three. Shows singularity among our races."

"Did the emperor talk to each of you, too?" Leif asked.

Both nodded. These were crazy times, with the fate of the empire itself at stake, but the emperor thought it important enough to take the time to talk to each one of them. Leif hadn't thought his presence would do much to steer the future, but with so much effort going into this, he was beginning to give his opinion a course-correction. He wasn't convinced he'd have any effect on the Council of Elders, but the emperor had given him the mission, and he had to try.

"Sergeant a'Hope Hollow, if you will come with me," a wyntonan with an access badge said, sticking his head inside the door.

"It's just a preliminary interview and to tell you the plan," Lieutenant a'Black said. "An hour, tops."

"OK, let's go," Leif told his group, but when they turned to follow him, the messenger said, "Just you, Sergeant."

Leif stopped for a moment, about to argue, but An had said this was only a preliminary interview.

"You three, stay here. There's food and drink—"

"I can smell it from here," Hulorin interrupted, wrinkling her nose. "That spice shit you put on your chow is rather overpowering."

"There's water, Hulorin. No spice in that. Anyway, just relax. I'll be back soon."

The messenger stood passively waiting, his face a blank slate, until Leif asked, "Where we going? Right or left?"

The messenger held out a hand to the left, and the two walked silently down the hallway.

"So, pretty crazy, huh?" Leif asked. Anything to break the silence.

"Yes, Sergeant."

That's it? They must train you guys to keep your thoughts to yourself.

He didn't try again, content to simply follow the man into the Council Wing. The man waved his access pass at the lock on an unmarked door which clicked open.

The messenger held it open for him, saying, "Please take your seat, Sergeant. Someone will be with you shortly."

"Someone will be with your shortly," Leif mimicked after the door closed behind him.

Leif was from the Silver Range, and out in the boonies, people were friendlier. It wasn't fair to stereotype Plainsmen, particularly those from the capital as always having a stick up their asses, but the messenger fit the bill.

Probably deleted the "a" in his name, too.

He took a moment to look around the room. It cut the median between spartan and luxurious. A single roa-wood table, four comfortable-looking chairs, and a small counter where a traditional tea set steamed alongside a human coffee dispenser. Leif walked over to the counter and sniffed the tea.

Zamma! I haven't had this in years, he thought as the flowery, yet biting aroma filled his senses.

If he had to wait, he might as well help himself. He poured himself a cup, then sat down in one of the chairs, closing his eyes as he let the aroma take him places he'd long forgot.

"I see you found the zamma, Sergeant," a voice said, snapping him back to the here and now.

Leif jumped up, spilling the tea over his hand and onto the table, as Council Elder Hordun blew into the room.

"I wouldn't mind some myself, if you don't mind," the elder said, nodding at the tea set before he slid into one of the seats on the opposite side of the table.

Leif put his cup down, resisting the temptation to blow on the burns on his hand. He poured another cup, then carefully stretched his arm out across the table to hand it to the elder. Council Elder sniffed, nodded, then took a long sip.

Leif had met the Council Elder seven years before, in the admin building on the other side of the square, just before reporting to Camp Navarro. The elder, newly risen to the position, warned them about the travails they would face as a result of prejudice and politics, but stressed that they had to endure for the good of the People. The elder had kept close tabs on the wyntonan Marines, mostly through his aide, Ferron a'Silverton, but he'd made a few appearances at official functions over the years. Living off-planet, Leif hadn't followed politics as much as he could have, but he knew the elder was gaining clout as a traditionalist hard-liner.

"Sergeant a'Hope Hollow, from all our initial class of Marine recruits, it's you who are here right now."

That wasn't a question, so Leif kept silent.

"I have to admit I hadn't pegged you back then as anyone who would rise to importance. You were one of the last to be approved for the first wyntonan class. If it weren't for that human staff sergeant, Wysoki, you wouldn't have even made it. He saw something in you that wasn't evident to us."

Staff Sergeant Wysoki? Is the elder remembering things correctly? All the guy did was yell at me.

"But here you are, so I guess he was right. And that leads us to this evening, when you appear before the Council."

"This evening, sir?" Leif asked, a hint of panic setting in.

"Yes, this evening. Our . . . *guests* . . . are getting impatient for an answer. It was difficult enough to accede to the emperor's request to have you three address the council before we made a decision. So, no use in waiting."

Leif had just arrived, and he'd thought—he'd hoped—that he'd have time to get oriented and plan out what he'd say. The thought that he'd be appearing before the Council of Elders today was daunting, to say the least.

"Sir, what's going to happen?" Leif asked.

"What's going to happen? With you? You are going to tell us what you think we should do. The council is allowing this because the emperor requested it. We are still imperial citizens, after all."

"And then what?"

"And then what? Why we vote, of course. We either remain in the empire, leave and join the sassares, or we leave and remain neutral."

"Neutral? Sir, the sassares won't allow us to remain neutral. We're either for them or against them."

"So say most of the experts," the elder said with a chuckle. "So, that would be a problem."

"How is the council going to vote?" Leif asked.

That was the burning question.

"I don't know. I guess we'll find out this evening, won't we."

Leif didn't believe the elder wasn't working behind the scenes, drumming up votes to support his own views. He had to have an opinion.

"How will you vote?" Leif asked, surprised at his audacity.

"Me? I haven't made up my mind. I haven't even heard what you three are going to tell us."

Gorring shit. You've already made up your mind. But which way?

The elder was known as a traditionalist, but not like Elders Loroton or Brynttyon. He hadn't objected to the ban on a'aden hunts, for example. And if he was a die-hard traditionalist, he might not be conducive to remaining in the empire. He'd never seemed to have an affinity for humans.

"Either way, we've got trouble," the elder said. "It's either rejecting the sassares or rejecting the humans. If it's the sassares, then the ambassador has assured us that they don't treat enemies kindly. If it's the humans, and they somehow manage to extricate themselves from their current situation, they won't be too happy for those who commit treason.

"Which leads us to you, Sergeant."

"Me?"

"Not just you. The wyntonan Marines. We currently have seven-thousand, four-hundred, and twenty-two wyntonans serving in the Marines. I want to know your loyalties. Is it to the People?"

Leif hadn't expected that question. He'd never even considered it, and now his mind was blank. He couldn't formulate his thoughts.

"If it came to it, would you join our militia."

"Militia, sir?" Leif asked, trying to grasp something on which he could focus.

A huge smile broke out on the elder's face, the smile of a proud father.

"Yes, the militia. The Shield of the People," he said, using a three-century-old term. "Do you remember Merkan a'Tonsure?"

"Merkan? From our recruit class?"

Merkan—Mark—had been a quiet recruit, always lagging a bit behind the other wyntonans, but still a middle-of-the-pack recruit when compared to the class as a whole. Last Leif had heard, he'd gotten out after his first enlistment to come back to Home.

"Yes, him. My brother's son."

Leif almost choked on the tea he'd just sipped. Like all Council Elders, he went with his call-name, Hordun. But his full name was Hordun a'Tonsure. It wasn't a common surname, but not so rare that Leif had thought anything of it.

"Colonel a'Tonsure is now the commander of the militia, with a cadre of over a thousand ex-Marines."

"Former Marines," Leif said automatically as he tried to wrap his mind around what the elder had just said.

The elder waved a dismissive hand like a granny keeping a fly out of the spice mix.

"And we've trained over ten thousand militia. I told you this seven years ago, that it was imperative for you to learn from the humans, because in the future, we were going to need fighters. Sooner than I'd hoped, that future is now."

Leif was a proud Marine, but Merkan? He was a colonel, and Leif wasn't even asked to be part of this militia. He had to ask.

"Sir, with all due respect, why wasn't I asked to be part of this militia? I've proven myself."

"Because you proved yourself is why. I was better served with having you right where you are. You, Lieutenant a'Black. A few others. You were in the public eye, and when we banned a'aden hunts, that created a large population of angry tri-years, all who wanted to prove themselves. When it was leaked that enlisting would serve the same purpose, well . . ." he trailed off, looking exceedingly pleased with himself.

He was behind the banning of the hunts! Or maybe he just saw an opportunity.

"And you say this militia is eleven-thousand-person strong? How am I just now hearing about it?"

"Don't be naive, Sergeant. How empty is the Great Morass? I could hide a division in there and no one would blink an eye.

"But enough of that. I've got another meeting with the ambassador. Back to my question. To whom is your loyalty."

"I am loyal to my People, sir. But I have also sworn oaths the emperor and empress."

"And if those two are diametrically opposed?"

"I hope I never have to make that decision."

"Well, you'd better think on it, Sergeant. In about four hours, you may have to choose sides."

Chapter 48

"It has to be you," Lieutenant a'Black said.

"But you're senior. You're the officer."

"And you are the one with the Knight Extraordinaire. You're the one with the Imperial Order of the Empire. People want to hear from you, not me."

Leif looked over at Keijo, eyebrows raised in a question.

"She's right. It has to be you. But we'll be there to support you."

One of the ubiquitous messengers had just told them that due to constraints, only one of them would speak to the council. Leif had said it should be An, but she and Keijo seemed to think that he should be the one.

He wasn't so sure. Never a good public speaker, he was stressed out about speaking in front of not only the council but most of the entire planet and anyone else who wanted to listen in. Couple that with worrying about Soran, who he'd only seen for a minute after their arrival, and Jord's rejection of his own father, and he was not in a good place to somehow convince an entire race to remain loyal to the empire.

And then there was that mess of a meeting with Elder Council Hordun. Leif couldn't get a feel for which way the wind was blowing, and if the council did reject the empire, then what would he do? Would he foreswear his oaths and fight for his People if it came to that?

Give him a rifle and an enemy, and Leif knew what to do. This was different. This was way above his paygrade.

"I'm not sure—"

"I am," the lieutenant cut him off. "I can make it an order if you want."

That made Leif chuckle, and he said, "Maybe it would be better if you did."

"OK, then," she said, coming to the position of attention. "Sergeant Leefen a'Hope Hollow, I, First Lieutenant An a'Black, do hereby give you a direct order to save our planet by speaking to the Council of Elders."

Leif snapped to an exaggerated position of attention and said, "Mighty ambitious order there, ma'am!"

"That's because I have faith in you!"

"What's all of that about?" Doc asked.

"Oh, nothing," Leif said, realizing that they three wyntonans kept reverting to Uzboss, leaving the other three out of any conversations. "Sorry."

"All joking aside," the lieutenant said in Standard, "it really has to be you. But we can all prep you here now. We've got another hour before we're on."

Leif looked around at the five sets of eyes looking expectantly at him, and he knew he didn't have a choice. This was on him.

"Jones, do you have the downloads?" he asked.

"Right here, Sergeant!" the human said, patting his sleeve pocket.

"Then bring them over, and let's get this thing locked down."

Chapter 49

Leif sat in his chair, nervously going over his speech in his mind. Short and sweet, he wondered if it was *too* short. Somehow, he had to convince the People that the sassares were not honest brokers and could not be trusted. The empire, for all its historical faults, was getting better, and the emperor had vowed to continue that process.

Directly behind him, An, Keijo, Doc, Hulorin, and Jones were sitting as well, and behind them, the spectator gallery. In front of Leif, the 21 seats of the Council of Elders were still empty.

Leif snuck a look down at his pad. The small light remained a steady green. On the other end to the comms link, the emperor himself was listening in. He didn't need to use a military channel. Behind the gallery, six news agencies were prepared to broadcast the proceedings throughout the galaxy. Still, the personal connection was a comfort.

The sassares ship could shut down comms in an instant, but until they did, Leif had that direct link. Just twenty minutes before, the emperor had told him that the tokits had declared for the empire. That gave the empire one race vowing fealty, the sassares, with the torku, one race as well. The emperor didn't think the rest would make a decision until they saw on which side the wyntonans fell.

Movement behind Leif caught his attention. He turned to see workers carrying another chair and small table identical to the one behind which Leif sat.

What's this?

The workers set up the chair and table to the side and even with Leif. The spectators murmured, and Leif looked back and An, who shrugged. She didn't know what this was, either. Two minutes later, it all became clear when the sassares ambassador, a sere-black who was also the captain the battleship in orbit over the capital, walked into the hall. She seemed surprised to see PFC Jones there, and her step faltered ever-so-slightly, but she kept the arrogant glare plastered on her face, refusing to meet anyone's eyes . . . except for Leif's. She didn't go directly to her seat, but walked right up to him, giving a sardonic half-nod of her head.

"Sergeant a'Hope Hollow, I must commend you on your defeat of Sere-blue Beleena. I thank you."

"Thank me, Ambassador?" Leif asked, his mistress clamoring for release.

"Of course. Beleena had risen too fast. He was not capable, and you have rid us of his cancer. I hope we'll be working together again in the near future, but this time in a more mutually cooperative way."

"I am loyal to the emperor."

"And I respect that. But your Council of Elders may have other priorities. So, we shall see," she said, giving Leif another nod before going and taking her seat.

If the sere-black had intended to fluster Leif, it worked. He lost his train of thought as he tamped down his mistress. As a sere-black, Leif knew the woman was at the top of her game, and Leif was a grunt sergeant, not a politician, but even knowing that, Leif could not control his thoughts. He was angry, and anger could cause him to make mistakes.

He was still fuming four minutes later when the Council of Elders marched in to take their seats. All were present for the meeting, even Elder a'Restiv, whose health had been an issue. She looked unsteady, helped by a young staff member to her seat.

The council had no single leader. The meeting chair rotated, and today, it was Elder Brynttyon who took the center seat. The elder had fought against the a'aden hunt ban, but had lost out. Now, Leif knew Elder Hordun had helped pass the law with ulterior motives.

A Council of Elders open meeting was extremely informal when compared to like meetings of other races. Elder Brynttyon looked at his scanpad for a moment before announcing, "This is the third meeting we're conducting to consider the choices laid before us by Ambassador Unt. As requested by Forsythe the Third, we are here now to entertain comments by his representative, one of our own, Leefen a'Hope Hollow. Sergeant?"

And just like that, it was on him. For once, he'd rather that the People were not so direct and to the point.

Leif stood and said, "I am Sergeant Leefen a'Hope Hollow, Imperial Marine Corps. I come from the Silver Range, having joined the—"

"I think we all know who you are, Sergeant," Elder Restiv said. "If you can get to your comments?"

"Uh . . . yes, of course. Let me see. I am representing His Majesty Forsythe the Third, Protector of the Empire and—"

"And we know who you are speaking for, Sergeant," the elder interrupted him again. "Get to the point, son."

If Leif was flustered before, he was even more so now. He turned to look at his five companions. The three non-wyntonans had been given translator buds, and Jones gave him a thumbs up while all five looked at him in encouragement.

"I know what's at stake here," he said, scrapping a good five minutes of his prepared speech. "I was told by Sere-blue Beleena what the sassares want, just before my small command of Marines, sailors, and civilians killed him."

The thousands of tokit civilians didn't make up a "small command," but Leif was taking a few liberties.

He made a point of looking over at the ambassador who simply smiled back at him.

"The sassares claim to be welcoming us into their fold as equal partners. But I contend that of all the races, they are the least likely to treat others as equals. The Lost Ones weren't treated as—"

"Sergeant, there is no proof that the Lost Ones ever existed, and we on the council are well aware of the rumors. We don't need you to rehash them," Elder Sissop scolded him.

Come on, Leefen. Don't get them pissed off. Just get to the point.

"My apologies, Elder. But I do have a more credible, more recent example of how the sassares treat their so-called allies. They enlisted the Novacks to carry out their attacks on the Imperial forces to keep us occupied while their real attack was underway. Yet, they then backstabbed their allies."

"Hearsay," the ambassador interrupted as she stood.

Leif stopped to stare at her, and Elder Brynttyon said, "Ambassador, we'll give you a chance to speak."

The sassares nodded, then sat back down.

"If I may?" Leif asked, holding up his pad.

Elder Brynttyon nodded, and Leif ran the first download. Images appeared on the holo platform five meters above his chair and repeated on several platforms located throughout the hall.

Leif was one of the figures, Sere-blue Beleena the other. Leif hit play, and the feed, downloaded from the drones, which while unable to download anything at the time, were still recording:

"The monkeys have an annoying propensity for building ships, for arming legions of soldiers. After the Chin Long failed to take down the emperor, we needed something to reduce their advantages. So, we created a new weapon, one engineered to be only effective against the monkeys." the sassares commander said.

"So, you decided to kill them," Leif said.

"Kill them? Not at all. Oh, there will be collateral damage. Extensive collateral damage. Think of it as pruning. But we will need the monkeys to work their old worlds, with us in charge, of course. Many of them will survive, once we reverse the weapon's effects.

"Of course, if we need to, we can make it lethal whenever we want," Beleena said with another laugh.

"And the Novacks? They were your allies, but from the looks of it, you poisoned them, too."

The sere-blue leaned his head back gave a huge laugh.

"Allies? They were tools, nothing more. We wanted the monkeys to fight with each other, to winnow down the numbers. The fact that some monkeys were complicit in their own doom is perfectly delicious."

There were murmurs from the spectators. To his right, the ambassador stood up and asked, "I know it isn't my turn, but may I respond to that?"

Elder Brynttyon nodded.

"We were at war with the humans. Not declared yet, but war none-the-less. The Novacks were never our allies. How could they be? They are human. With the human advantage in numbers, we had to do whatever it took to shift that advantage to us."

"Council, we just heard from Sere-blue Beleena that the Novacks were their allies. And if that isn't enough, I have this," Leif said, bringing up another image, this of a document.

It was very clearly a treaty between the sassares Triumvirate and the Fremont Clan, signed by Perspidian and Sere-black Gandouri themselves, declaring that they were allies in a mutual cause, and that the Novacks would govern whatever humans were left after the war.

"That's fake!" the ambassador shouted. "There was never any such document."

Leif didn't know if there was such a document. He'd only received it an hour ago. He didn't care, either. If it was a fake, it represented fact, and from the rumblings in the hall, it had been effective.

"Elders," Leif said, not wanting to relinquish the momentum, "The sassares sought genocide on the humans, just as they did to the Lost Ones." He hurried on before there could be another objection form Elder Restiv. "They turned on their allies, thinking it 'delicious," I believe Sere-blue Beleena said. And now they want us as an ally? For what?"

Leif turned to the next download:

Sept Blue Beleena was speaking. *"We want all races in our brotherhood . . . ah, that sounds facetious even to me. I'll be blunt. You wyntonans are warriors. You've suppressed that, but for once, the young monkey emperor was right in bringing you out of those ridiculous restraints. We can use you for taking and holding ground."*

"Fighting who? Humans?" Leif asked.

"Initially, probably. We cannot infect all of them, so some of the vermin will have to be dug out and exterminated."

"And after that? After there are no more humans?"

"There are other races, my young wyntonan. Closer in the spiral arm."

"Noxes and leera," Leif said.

"Them. And beyond the leera? Who knows what lies out there? And we want you with us. Will you join the Hegemony?"

"Just me? I mean us here? I'm just a sergeant. A nobody."

"Hardly a nobody, son. You are a person of note on your home planet. When we found out you were here, plans changes, and this dusty trash bin of a monkey planet became our first conquest, a blueprint, if you will, for the future. I was diverted to come here. If you willingly join us, that will go a long way in convincing your people to join us as well," the sassares commander said.

"And the rest? The qiincers? What about them?"

"That was a little tougher, but the sere-blacks have decided to bring them in as well. They can fly, and they've also proven themselves in your military."

"Hissers? Alindamirs?"

"Possibly some. As slaves, along with whatever monkeys survive."

"Tokits?" Leif asked.

The sassares laughed and said, *"Are you serious? Tokits? More vermin."*

"And if I don't agree. What then?"

"Why then, I'll kill you. All of you," Sere-blue Beleena said. *"And we'll look for someone else who can see the future and wants to be part of it.*

"Remember, too. What we developed for the monkeys, we can easily tweak for the rest of you."

This time there were shouts, not just murmurs, as the spectators heard the sere-blue's threat.

Elder Brynttyon ignored them, and Elder Sissop said, "The words of a single commander, one that the ambassador assured me that if he'd survived your battle, he would have been executed. You throw these recordings up to incite us, but I won't let base emotions get in the way of logic and reason.

"You don't like the sassares, and given what you've gone through with them, I can understand that. But what makes you think the empire is any better? We were vassals to them, one of the dung races."

"The Proclamation of Sentient Rights—"

"Bah! Just words. We have always been second class citizens of no value."

"I know some of the history, Elder Sissop. I'm sure you know better than me. But there is one thing I know better than you, Elder, and that is the emperor. I've met with him. I talked with him. I've seen into his heart. He is trying, as is the empress. She gave up family for the good of the empire, for the Mother's sake!"

Which might not be a smart thing to say. For wyntonans, giving up family was tantamount to treason.

Like I'm giving up on family, not being there for Jord? the thought intruded before he was able to force it away. He could not afford a distraction now.

"I believe I am an honorable man. I've followed the traditions. I've hunted a wassila to become aden. But I could never swear to the emperor if I thought him anything other than more honorable than I am. I would not be a Knight Extraordinaire of the empress. I know the Granite Throne and I know the sassares, and to me, there is no comparison. Only one deserves our loyalty, and it isn't the sassares."

Scattered clapping reached out from the spectators, but not enough, nor was it sustained. Leif was hoping for more.

Elder Brynttyon looked around at the other elders and asked, "Is there anything someone wants to ask Sergeant a'Hope Hollow?"

"There's nothing new in what he said. It was just a formality before we decide," Elder Sissop said.

Leif did have one more thing, something he'd been told to use if he thought it would help. And with Sissop's contention that nothing was new, Leif knew he had to say it.

"Elder Brynttyon, I do have one more thing."

"Come on, we've heard enough. The sergeant's had his say, and we need to start our deliberations," Elder Sissop said.

"Another minute or two won't matter, Elder Sissop," Elder Brynttyon said. "I'm sure the ambassador has no objections."

The ambassador flicked her hand in the same dismissive manner that Sere-blue Beleena used to do.

"As you know, we are not the only people faced with this decision. Some of the other races might be waiting to see what we are going to do. One has not. The tokits have declared for the empire."

The hall went silent except for a small yip of pleasure from Doc, who'd just heard this for the first time.

"They understand the choices, and they've made theirs."

"How do you know this, Sergeant?" Elder Brynttyon asked.

"I received it from the emperor himself an hour ago. I can assure you it is true."

There was another moment of silence before the ambassador erupted into the braying sassares laugh that Leif was beginning to hate.

"Tokits? You're going to consider what the tokits do? You saw the holo that the Sergeant showed you. We have no place in our Hegemony for dung races, so of course they'll grasp at any lifeline. It won't help them, though. They're slated to become a footnote of history when all of this is over, as will you unless you make the smart choice."

Dead silence greeted her, and she flinched as if wondering if she went too far. With an obvious effort of will, she plastered her arrogant smile back on her face and sat down.

"Well," Elder Brynttyon said, "That's . . . your point is taken, Ambassador. With that, I am concluding the testimony. Fellow elders, if you will retire to the Heart Room, we have some important decisions to make."

Leif stood as the elders made their way out through the door behind them. Only two elders caught his eye as they left, which couldn't be a good sign. As soon as they were gone, the noise level rose and people broke out into conversation.

Leif turned around to look at the other five. Jones gave him another thumbs up, a huge smile on his face.

Leif didn't share the PFC's confidence. He had so much he'd planned to say. So much he wanted to say, but he'd gone off-script. Leif thought he'd hit the main points, but he didn't know if he'd said what needed to be said, if he'd left out too much.

"Mother, please let it be enough," he said aloud, eyes to the heavens.

Chapter 50

"When do we find out?" Doc asked.

He'd been pretty happy since the meeting, proud that his people had declared for the empire, but his now constant chatter was getting on Leif's nerves. He felt sick to his stomach, wondering what was going to happen. If the council decided on abandoning the empire, Leif didn't know what he was going to do.

Sere-blue Beleena had been pretty clear on what they expected of a wyntonan ally. They'd be used as troops to root out whatever humans were still fighting. That also meant he'd be almost assuredly fighting fellow Marines, particularly now that the humans had a cure. If he refused to foreswear his vows, though, he could end up fighting his own people. This wasn't the kind of choice anyone ever wanted to make.

"That was a pretty big blunder the ambassador made there at the end," the lieutenant told Leif.

"Maybe that's what you get when a single person is ship's captain, ground commander, and ambassador," Leif said. "No one can master all the jobs at that level."

Leif thought the lieutenant was right, though. It had been a big blunder. Was it enough of one, though, to sway the council's decision?

The door opened, and all six stood, waiting to hear a verdict, but the messenger said, "Sergeant a'Hope Hollow, the council requests your presence."

"What do they want to see him about?" Hulorin snapped.

The messenger turned his head to look at her, and Leif expected some snarky reply, but instead, the woman sighed, then said, "I really don't know. They just sent me to fetch him."

"It's OK, I'm coming," Leif said, heading for the door.

"Just a'Hope Hollow?" the lieutenant asked.

"Just him."

"I'll let you know what I find out," Leif told the others before he followed the messenger out of the door.

"Why don't they just call me?" Leif asked the messenger after a few moments.

"Tradition, I guess. The Silver Rock's always had messengers."

The Silver Rock, the nickname for the council building, had been built only fifty-odd years ago, so it hadn't "always" had messengers, but Leif let it slide. He'd only asked to fill up the dead space.

The messenger escorted him deep within the council wing, past the office where he'd met with Elder Hordun, and down a dozen steps to a plain white door, which except for the armed guard standing outside, might as easily been a door for a broom closet. The guard ran a scanner over him, then confiscated his tab.

Sorry about that, Your Majesty. You won't be able to listen in.

His escort spoke through the pick-up, and the door whispered open. Leif took a deep breath, then walked inside. To his surprise, the room looked like a Marine rec room, someplace for Marines to hang out and relax. Five big couches and a dozen chairs were scattered around. The tension was palpable, however, breaking any thought that this was anything but deadly serious.

"Thank you for coming, Sergeant. We have a question for you," Elder Washin said. "If we maintain our loyalty, can the Imperial Navy react to the immediate threat hanging over us?"

The question had already been considered, and Leif was given the answer. He didn't think it was a particularly good answer, and he was tempted to change it. The emperor couldn't listen in right now, after all, but he decided to do as instructed.

"The chances are low. There are only three manned capital ships left in the sector, and they are fighting to protect Allister, Juju Lee, and Oresford-Five."

"All human planets, and we know where we stand when humans are in danger." Elder Sissop grunted. "So, you can kiss that idea off."

"There's no other resources that the empire can give to us?" Elder Washin asked. "Anything?"

"The emperor knows about your militia," Leif said, refusing to meet Elder Hordun's eyes. "He is willing to swear them into imperial service, but beyond that, there just aren't any forces that can respond."

"Like that changes anything," Elder Sissop said. "Hey, Elder Hordun! Your pet army can fly the imperial flag. That should scare off the sassares."

Leif scanned the room, trying to gauge the mood. Sissop was obviously in the surrender to the sassares camp. Washin seemed to be wanting to find an excuse to remain loyal. Leif couldn't get much of a feel for the rest.

Maybe I've been gone too long from my People. I can't read them.

"One last question," Sergeant, Elder Washin said. "What will you do if we decide to join the sassares?"

"I've sworn an oath, and in the Silver Range, our words mean something. I will not foreswear."

Sissop grunted and glared daggers at Leif. Sissop, along with most of the others, were from the Plains, and he took Leif's comment as a personal insult.

Which it was. Leif returned the glare, refusing to back down.

"And if that means fighting fellow wyntonans," Elder Sissop persisted.

Here it is, Leefen. You just have to tell them.

"I will not fight my fellow wyntonans, but neither will I fight Imperial troops."

"And if Elder Hordun's militia decides they want to fight you for being a traitor to your people?" Elder Sissop asked, his voice dripping with scorn.

"Some things are worth dying for," Leif said. "I have an ishta and son, and my son may grow up without me, but he will grow up knowing I was never foresworn."

Elder Sissop rolled his eyes, and for a moment, Leif wondered if he knew how human that made him look. Right then and there, he knew he couldn't blame the elder for his position. The man was doing what he thought was right. He didn't think honor and loyalty trumped life, that was all. For him, the wyntonans living as sassares slaves was better than dying.

Maybe he's right.

"If that's all you have, Elder Washin, I'll leave you to determine our People's fate. May the Mother guide your decision."

****

Eight hours later, Leif was shaken awake by Keijo. "It's time."

"Really? Did I fall asleep?"

"If you're snoring was any indication, then yes, Sergeant, you were asleep," Lance Corporal Hulorin said.

Leif stretched his long arms, then shook his head, trying to wake up. He was surprised that he'd fallen asleep. The fate of his People hung in the balance, and he nodded off?

Maybe it was because he'd finally accepted that what was going to happen was out of his hands. He could only control his own actions, and when he told Elder Washin what he'd do, it was a weight lifting off his shoulder.

He didn't want to die. He wanted to be an ishtatan to Soran, and father to Jord. But he was willing to die if it came to it. He was not willing to foreswear his oaths.

Leif looked to the door where two messenger escorts were waiting for them. He didn't know if that was a good sign or not. Only one way to find out.

"Hey, Doc, wake up," Jones was lightly kicking the tokit. "Let's go on our kumbaya display."

Doc opened his eyes, then jumped to his feet, ready to go with a speed that made Leif jealous. He stretched one more time and joined the others as they left the room that had been their home for most of the last day.

It was a silent group that followed their escorts back to the main hall. No more chair out in the middle in which Leif was supposed to sit. Now, he was just a spectator. The center spotlight would be on the ambassador.

"Going in now to hear the decision," Leif passed back to Earth.

Or maybe not Earth. Leif didn't know where the emperor was. For a moment, he worried that the sassares might have the capability to backtrack his message and pinpoint where the emperor had placed his command center.

Not up to you, Leefen. Worry about what you can affect.

"Roger that," the voice on the far end said. "We'll inform the principal."

If the line was that secure, they should be able to say "emperor." If the line wasn't that secure, then whoever was listening in was not going to be stymied by "principal." Procedures, though, seemed never to change. That was a universal truth.

Leif took his seat. A few spectators made an effort to give him support, but most of the people left his little party alone. They sat alone surrounded by a sea of people.

It took the ambassador twenty minutes to show up, preceded by a sailor holding the gonfalon with the red parlay ribbons, as if she wanted to remind them that she was there under a recognized truce. Leif didn't know if that was showmanship or if she'd had to travel far to arrive at the hall. In the end, it didn't matter. She was there. Within a minute of her arrival, the council filed in, each going to their seat. Elder Restovnn had the chair, though, with Elder Brynttyon having passed it on.

It wasn't required for the spectators to stand, but to a person, everyone took to their feet. All except the ambassador, who lounged in the seat provided to her.

Elder Restovnn was physically frail, and that carried through to her voice. She started speaking, and the drone-mics had to swoop in so her voice could be heard.

" . . . ultimatum given by Ambassador Unt of the Red Hegemony. We have considered this from all perspectives, and in the end, we were not unanimous in our decision.

However, we did reach the threshold required, so our decision is binding."

Once again, Leif didn't know if that was good or bad. If the threshold majority was not reached, then the question would be sent to the public for a general vote. Looking at the ambassador, who was desperately trying to look calm despite the obvious tension in her body, Leif didn't think she had the patience to wait any longer.

"Our decision boils down to a handful of items of note. First, we realize that beyond politics, the sassares are currently at a distinct advantage over the humans in both naval and ground forces. The most likely outcome of the current conflict is that the sassares will prevail."

She paused a moment as if she needed to catch her breath.

"Second, the sassares, through Ambassador Unt, have made it clear that if we turn down their ultimatum, we will be considered their enemy, and our planet and people will be at risk.

"Third, we, as a nation, have a treaty with the empire, and the Granite Throne has met the terms of said treaty.

"Fourth, while the ambassador has assured us of equal status with their race, past actions lend doubt as to the veracity of that promise."

She paused once more, taking a look at the elders on either side of her.

"Despite the first two observations, and because of the last two, we cannot join the Red Hegemony. We will remain loyal to our current treaty."

The hall erupted in shouts, the loudest perhaps being Leif's. He pushed his mic into his throat and passed, "We're staying loyal!" not knowing if anyone on the other side could hear him over the noise.

The ambassador sat motionless for a long moment as people cheered . . . and booed. The decision wasn't totally accepted.

She stood up, and the staff ran the crowd suppressors, dulling the shouts to a low undertone.

"Ambassador Unt, please understand that while loyal to our treaty, we do not have the ships nor ground troops to be of any threat to you. Should you prevail in your war with the humans, our treaty would become overcome by events, and hence null and void. We ask that you leave our planet untouched as you pursue your war."

What? That's not honoring our treaty with the empire. What about our Marines? What are they supposed to do? Stand down?

The ambassador brayed her laugh, then said, "You stupid, stupid people. Dung race? More like a shit-for-brains race. You had a chance to join the most significant advance in civilization, to conquer the galaxy, to find the progenitors and ask why they felt godlike enough to experiment with us. To sully our line with weak races like the tokits, the Lost Ones, the tost'el'tzy. We are going to take back the galaxy and purify our line, and you will be left in the dustbin of history, and not even a footnote of your existence will remain.

"Leave your planet alone? Hah! Before I leave, I will destroy your hovel of a home. You had your chance, and now you've thrown your lives away."

With that, she wheeled around, and with her parlay ribbons preceding, she marched out of the hall, the crowd parting for her as if she was a force of nature.

Chapter 51

"So, will you come join us?" Elder Hordun asked. "Not leaving your Marines, of course, but as a temporary officer. I think your presence would be a morale boost."

Leif wanted to say no. The last four hours, from the ambassador's dramatic exit, to the comms blackout that had cut off his communications with the emperor, to the relocating of the command center, Leif and the other Marines included, to a bunker complex behind the Silver Rock, had been hectic, to say the least. Panic was in the air as plans and recriminations flew back and forth.

All Leif wanted to do was to see Soran and Jord. If this was going to be the end, then he wanted it to be with them.

"With all due respect, why do you think your militia will have any effect upon the sassares ship? The ambassador can simply stay in orbit and scour Home clean."

"We don't think she'll do that."

"Come again? You heard her."

"Yes, she did say that, for all intents and purposes. But she doesn't want to be the one to lose the planet, with all our resources. The sassares are spread thin, and they need the bodies and materials if they want to commence on their manifest destiny. They want to find and take down their progenitor."

"They want to find the Mother?" Leif asked incredulously.

"You heard her. They killed off the Lost Ones, the race who uplifted them. Now they want to go a step further. And they can't do that alone. They need us, or others, at least, and they need our resources. They even need humans and their technology. The sassares are very capable, as they showed with the virus they unleashed. But the humans had capabilities they need as well, and they can't let those disappear."

"So, you don't think the ambassador is going to hit us?"

"Of course, she is. That's why we've been evacuating the cities, to get as many people out of harm's way as possible."

"That's it? Just a slap on the wrist?" Leif asked.

"I don't know," the elder admitted, rubbing his eyes in exhaustion. "Probably not. They wanted to keep only ten percent of the humans around. Maybe that's all they want of us."

Ninety percent of the People gone, just like that, was something too terrible to contemplate.

"Why did the council agree to remain in the empire? I thought Elder Sissop was fighting to give in to the sassares demands."

"Because you were right. Oh, we already knew it, but some of us were grasping at straws. We wanted a reason to submit."

"Keeping ninety percent of us alive is a pretty good reason, I think," Leif said.

"For how long? After we helped them root out the humans, how long would they keep us around? We'd be a threat to them, they'd tweak their little virus, and we'd be struck down."

This seemed surreal with the elder arguing in favor of the empire and Leif having second thoughts.

"And your militia? What's their mission?"

"If they land ground troops, to make their adventure costly. And to protect as many of our People as possible. Lieutenant a'Black has agreed until she receives further orders. I hope you'll agree, too."

Leif had no idea when he'd be able to get off the planet. Somewhere out there, the Marines were being reconstituted as humans recovered. His place was with them, but until that time, he might as well make himself useful. But there was one thing he had to do first."

"I want to see my ishta and son," he said.

The elder shook his head and said, "Sorry, Sergeant. They've already been evacuated. We took them right after you landed."

"Where are they?" Leif almost yelled.

"I think in the old Anagarand mines. She's safe."

Leif ached to see them, but he had to admit that if anywhere on the planet was safe, it was the ancient mine complex. Their safety was more important than his need to see them.

"Well, Sergeant? Or should I say Brevit Colonel?"

Leif knew the elder was dangling the rank as an entitlement, and there was a history of enlisted Marines and junior officers accepting temporary ranks to serve in local militias, but he didn't care about that. He cared about his duty to family, People, and empire.

"Until I receive orders, I'll be happy to help out."

"Great," the elder said, hand out, just as a blast reverberated through the bunker, dust falling from the overhead.

"Sir, it's the Silver Rock. It's gone," a young wyntonan stuck his head into the office and said.

It had started.

Chapter 52

The top of Grazpin Mountain was gone. One minute it was there, the next, a quarter of the mountain was vaporized, smoke and mist rising thousands of meters into the air. Cries of sorrow, anger, and terror rose from those in the bunker with him as they watched the feed.

As a son of the Silver Range, Leif didn't have the same emotional connection to the famous peak that overlooked the capital as the others with him, but it still hit him hard. It was one thing to understand the destructive power of a battleship, but it was another thing altogether to see it in action. Ambassador Unt could destroy the planet if she wanted, and not just with a planet buster. She could systematically take apart the infrastructure and population centers, ridding herself of the People, yet leaving a husk that could be exploited for the benefit of the sassares.

And she still might, despite the party line that the sassares needed the planet in good working order, and they needed the People to work it. As Lance Corporal Hulorin said, the sassares didn't need a living planet to strip it of its mineral resources. Leif didn't bother to add his growing belief that the sassares might be willing to sacrifice the planet as a warning to the alindamirs and hissers who had still not yet declared.

There seemed no rhyme nor reason as to the targets that had been destroyed. The Silver Rock had been a symbolic first strike, destroying the heart of wyntonan government. Most of the building had been emptied, but six elders who had refused to evacuate had been killed. Subsequent strikes, spaced out every five minutes, did not follow a pattern. Anything within direct range of the ship: factories, residential areas, the dirigible port, business centers, and now a mountain top, all felt the sassares wrath. Over a third of the capital was gone, and Leif couldn't even guess at how many lives were lost.

And the death toll was going to rise. The sassares battleship could vaporize the entire capital with one shot, and within a couple of orbits, it could level all the major cities on the planet. But it was obvious the ambassador was playing with them. She wanted the panic, the terror. Leif didn't know if that was to cow the surviving population into something more malleable or was it just torture for torture's sake, a sadist's game before she finally ended it.

Did I do this? Did I let my personal honor drive my People to ruin?

Leif was feeling the heavy burden of guilt. Rationally, he knew he hadn't made the decision to resist the sassares. But he had contributed to it. And that made him complicit with the destruction.

Where's Soran and Jord? he asked himself yet again.

He tried to connect to them as he'd been doing every couple of minutes, hoping to find a crease in the sassares jamming, but nothing. He slammed his fist into the bulkhead. He'd agreed to join the militia, but they were far outside the capital, and there was no way to reach them at the moment. Sitting underground in at least a modicum of safety, but with no mission, no way to help, was driving him crazy.

"I'm going outside," he said, standing up.

"It's not safe out there," Keijo said, grabbing his arm.

"Do you think it's safe in here? If they use a planet buster? If this is the end, I'm not going to face it trembling in a hole like a grazpin. I want to see it coming."

Doc stood up and said, "I'm coming, too."

"And me," Jones said.

Lance Corporal Hulorin looked up from her novel, sighed, and said, "I might as well keep an eye on you three to keep you out of trouble."

The four turned as one to look at the other two Marines. Lieutenant a'Black shrugged and stood up, but Keijo gave his head a small shake, then looked at the deck, refusing to meet their eyes.

"Let's go then," Leif said.

The five made their way through the crowded bunker. The halls were lined with people just sitting and trying to stay out of the way while others hurried from one task to another. No one paid much attention to them, even if Jones got his fair share of looks. All of them had been prominently displayed on the news feeds the day before, but it still must have struck most of the wyntonans as odd to see a human walking about—even more so because the vaccine for the hammer had not been publicly announced.

The exit was a series of filtered airlocks. Leif expected some pushback, but the guards simply waved them through. Three minutes after reaching the exit, they were stepping out into the open, if acrid air, the smell of the destroyed Silver Rock almost burning their nostrils.

"What now?" the lieutenant asked.

"Now? Borderland was hit. Let's go see if there are any survivors who need help."

Borderland was a neighborhood with upwards of a hundred thousand residents. A good 15 klicks away, it would take them a while to walk the distance, but Leif had to be doing something.

The five had to make their way through debris, but after a couple hundred meters, the way cleared out. There was a flash in the sky, followed by the rumble of another strike. Leif looked up, but he couldn't tell where it had hit.

Eventually, the ambassador was going to tire of her game and just end it. Leif had no control over that, so he put it out of his mind.

After twenty more minutes of walking—and five more strikes from the battleship—the sounds of sirens were their guide. While they'd been huddled in the bunker, emergency crews had been out trying to save lives—just one more thing to make Leif feel guilty.

"Come on, let's speed it up," he said, lengthening his stride.

"Hey," Doc said after a few minutes, his legs pumping to keep up alongside Leif. "I never told you how proud I was of you, and how glad I am that you wyntonans have joined us. We're going to beat the sassares."

Doc had been strutting around like an Earth peacock ever since he found out that the tokits had not only declared for the empire but had been the first to do so. It had gotten old after a while, and Leif had started to tune him out. But with his guilty frame of mind, and the stress of what was happening, he snapped.

"Join you? What a joke. What can you tokits do to beat the sassares? Bite their knees?"

It was a low blow, totally unwarranted. Leif had watched the tokits in battle, and no one could doubt their courage. But at the moment, he didn't care. He turned to keep walking when Doc grabbed him by the arm, and with surprising strength, pulled the bigger Marine around to face him.

"You still don't get it, Sergeant. Sure, you wyntonans are larger than us. I couldn't take you in a fight. Two or three of us couldn't take you maybe. But ten? A hundred?" he asked. He pulled Leif's head close to his and almost whispered, "But there aren't just a hundred of us. Try trillions."

He let Leif go, then started marching on. Leif stared at Doc, his friend, in embarrassment. He'd been out of line. There was no call for him to disrespect Doc's race.

You idiot, Leefen a'Hope Hollow.

He stood back up and started rushed to catch up to Doc to apologize. He'd only made it a few strides when the skies lit up in a horizon-to-horizon flash so bright that it almost blinded him.

"Oh, hell! It's the planet buster!"

Standing true to the empire had cost his People their very existence.

"Soran, my love!" Leif cried out, blinking back the stars in his eyes. He wanted to face his doom like a Marine, to curse its approach.

The flash started to fade, replaced by trails of fire that spread out and started to fall to Home.

"What's going on?" PFC Jones asked. "Is that a planet buster?"

"I don't know," Leif said, confused. "Maybe its—"

Leif's comms powered up, and a voice came over the net, "Sergeant Leif Hope Hollow, is that you?"

"Uh . . . yes, that's me. Who the hell are you?"

"Glad to see you're still kicking. This is the Imperial cruiser *Zion* along with the destroyer *Tapir*. You can scratch one sassares battleship."

Epilogue

"I can never express my gratitude to you," Empress Jenifer I, Sovereign of the Serengeti and Protector of the Empire, said into the pick-up.

"It's . . . I mean . . ." Leif started, but was at a loss for words.

The empress looked horrible, to be truthful. She was weak and haggard, but she assured Leif that she was on the way to a full recovery. Leif was not so sure. From the brief he'd received that morning from Marine HQ, the cure was not as effective as it had been hoped. None of the infected Marines were back on full duty. The doctors were hopeful, but the rehabilitation looked like it was going to be a long process.

The Navy had it a little better. Humans were starting to get back to the ships to supplement the non-human crews, but they, too, were weaker and needed more rest than the non-infected crews.

"Don't be modest. You did what so few could do. I guess it was expected, though," she said.

"Your majesty?"

"I mean, you are one of my Knights Extraordinaire, after all. I'd expect nothing less of you," she said, a smile that was just a hint of the women she still was, creeping over her face.

Leif grinned, his hand subconsciously reaching up to touch the small gold lioness pin on his collar. The movement caught Jord's attention, and his small hand grabbed the shiny bauble and pulled it off, bringing it to his mouth.

"Jord!" Leif shouted, taking the ada's hand and pulling out the pin. "That's not for you."

Instead of crying, Jord laughed and bounced on Leif's lap, reaching again for the pin.

"I see you are already raising one of my future knights, Sergeant a'Hope Hollow," the empress said with another laugh before she broke into a coughing fit.

A white-smocked doctor who looked barely stronger than the empress immediately jumped into view and ran a quick scan over her. "I'm sorry, Your Majesty, but you need to rest now."

She held up a trembling hand to stop the doctor and said, "I need to go now, Sergeant a'Hope Hollow. This old body is pretty weak now. But I needed to personally thank you for your service. The emperor thanks you, too, and he'll do that face-to-face when he can."

"Your majesty . . ." the doctor prompted.

"Ah, my nanny is pushing me, so I need to go. The roads are long, but they eventually meet, Mother willing," she said, the last in passable Uzboss before the connection was cut.

"That was pretty amazing," Soran said, rushing over to take Jord. "Imagine that. The empress calling us here on Home."

Jord grabbed Leif's uniform shirt and gave a squawk of indignation as his mother tried to lift him.

"Let him stay," Leif told her.

It had only been that morning that Jord had finally accepted his father's presence, and Leif wanted to soak in every minute of it he could.

"I thought you had another call to take," Soran said.

"Let them wait."

Jord took that opportunity to spit up a stream of breastmilk, covering the front of his uniform blouse. The ada seemed to think it was funny and laughed, which cause another small stream of milk to erupt from his mouth.

"Jord!" Soran said, picking him up.

This time, Leif knew there was no arguing as she tossed him a small towel. He did his best to dab away the milk. His utility fabric was breathable but water resistant, and he thought it didn't look too bad by the time he was done. He'd have to change before his next conference call, but it would do for now.

At least he wasn't as tied up as An a'Black. As the senior Marine on the planet, she was snowed under with meetings. The rest of them, although busy, had it relatively easy.

Soran sat down beside Leif, hugging Jord to her chest.

"So, as I was saying before Jord decided to remind us he was here, that was pretty amazing. The empress!"

It was surreal. Leif was a sergeant in the Marine Corps, yet both the empress and the emperor had taken time to chat with him on more than one occasion. This was not the way things worked.

"So, how do you feel?" Soran asked. "About . . . you know . . . the message you passed."

Leif was happy that they were alive and the immediate threat had been destroyed. But he wasn't sure that he appreciated part of his role in that. When he'd told the council that there weren't any Imperial Navy ships that could respond to Home, he'd believed it. But as the Navy Commander, the XO for the *Zion* and now senior Imperial officer on the planet's surface, told him yesterday evening, it had been a lie. Leif had been fed false information that he was to pass to the council with the full expectation that would be leaked to the sassares ambassador.

It has been a calculated risk. Passing false information that imperial ships were inbound could have resulted in the sassares fleeing, but it could also have resulted in the ambassador deploying a planet buster.

By making the ambassador believe that there were no Navy assets in the sector, the hope was that she would be in no hurry to wreak havoc on the planet. The commander had been beaming with pride that the ruse had worked, and that casualties had been held to a minimum before the two imperial ships had arrived to engage and destroy the battleship.

"Holding casualties to a minimum" was relative, however. The body count was not complete, but the numbers could reach 200,000.

Leif was grateful that the Navy responded, especially as the Tapir had been pulled from defending a human world, which emphasized the point that the emperor considered all the races on an equal footing. Leif didn't know why he had been an unwitting tool, however, instead of being on board with what was happening.

Breaking all sorts of classification rules, Leif had told Soran about it, and she could see he was bothered.

"It worked out, Soran. We're still here, and the sassares aren't. It doesn't matter how it was done, only that it fell out this way."

True enough. Maybe someday I'll believe it.

"Do you think we're safe? Are the sassares coming back?"

He could say something soothing, but this was his *ishta*. He had to be honest with her.

"I don't know. I think they could very well return. It all depends on what else they have to deal with. That's why I want you and Jord to go back to Hope Hollow. I want you to stay there. Don't come back to the capital."

"I know," she said with a sigh as Jord reached up to grab her ear. "As soon as you go, I'll make arrangements to get back home. It might take a while, though, with all the damage. The dirigible port was hit, you know."

"I've uh . . ."

"You've what?" Soran asked when Leif trailed off.

"I've already made arrangements for you. A Navy shuttle will take the two of you home. I'm sorry I didn't discuss it with you first, but it just came up, and I grabbed the opportunity."

Soran tensed, and in a forced calm voice, asked, "And when would this be?"

"This afternoon. At three."

"And you were going to tell me this when?"

"I'm sorry. But this is for the best," Leif said.

"And you? What will you be doing?"

"I'm leaving—all the Marines are leaving—this evening. We're boarding the *Zion* to get back to our units, whatever is still there. The *Tapir* will stay here for a while, so Home isn't getting abandoned," he added quickly as if to downplay the fact that he was leaving.

Soran was quiet for a moment before she softly asked, "Haven't you done enough, Leefen?"

"Most of the Corps is human, Soran, and the Navy isn't much better. We're not going to have mission capable humans in the Corps for some time still. When I said that it depends on what else the sassares have to deal with whether it will be safe here or not, that means what our Navy and Corps can do to keep them occupied. If they're engaged with us, they won't have free time to come dish out revenge. We need to keep them occupied."

"But you can't beat them. That's what people are saying."

"No, right now, we can't. But we don't have to. We just have to keep hitting them, making them chase us, until the humans are back. Not just the humans. We're training more of the People, qiincers, hissers, alindamir. Heck, even the tokits. We're ramping up, and we just have to keep the sassares off-balance enough to give us the time."

He didn't tell her that he'd recommended to the acting commandant that morning that Elder Hordun's entire militia be absorbed by the Corps.

"And then what, Leefen? If you're able to rebuild the Marines and the Navy? Then what?"

He took Jord back and shifted his son to his left arm, and pulled his *ishta* in with his right. This was why he fought. He was loyal to the emperor and the empire. He was loyal to his race. He was loyal to the Marines. But when it all boiled down, his *ishta* and son were why he would sacrifice everything, even his life, to keep them safe.

"Then what, Soran? Then we head into sassares space and teach them what happens when they take on the empire."

Thank you for reading *Devotion,* and I hope you enjoyed it. As always, I also welcome a review on Amazon, Goodreads, or any other outlet. The fourth book in the series, *Fusion,* will be coming soon.

If you would like updates on new books releases, news, or special offers, please consider signing up for my mailing list. Your email will not be sold, rented, or in any other way disseminated. If you are interested, please sign up at the link below:

http://eepurl.com/bnFSHH

Two books were extremely helpful for me in my research for this series:

The Marines of Montford Point: America's First Black Marines, by Melton A. McLaurin

White Man's Tears Conquer My Pains: My WWII Service Story, by Henry Badgett

Other Books by Jonathan Brazee

<u>Ghost Marines</u>
Integration
Unification
Devotion
Fusion

<u>The Navy of Humankind: Wasp Squadron</u>
Fire Ant
Crystals
Ace

The United Federation Marine Corps
Recruit
Sergeant
Lieutenant
Captain
Major
Lieutenant Colonel
Colonel
Commandant

Rebel
(Set in the UFMC universe.)

Behind Enemy Lines
(A UFMC Prequel)

The Accidental War (A Ryck Lysander Short Story)

The United Federation Marine Corps'
Lysander Twins
Legacy Marines
Esther's Story: Recon Marine
Noah's Story: Marine Tanker
Esther's Story: Special Duty
Blood United

Coda

Women of the United Federation
Marine Corps
Gladiator
Sniper
Corpsman

High Value Target (A Gracie Medicine Crow Short Story)
BOLO Mission (A Gracie Medicine Crow Short Story)
Weaponized Math (A Gracie Medicine Crow Novelette,
Published in The Expanding Universe 3. Nebula Award
Finalist)

The United Federation Marine Corps' Grub Wars
Alliance
The Price of Honor
Division of Power

The Return of the Marines Trilogy
The Few
The Proud
The Marines

The Al Anbar Chronicles: First Marine Expeditionary Force--Iraq
Prisoner of Fallujah
Combat Corpsman
Sniper

Werewolf of Marines
Werewolf of Marines: Semper Lycanus
Werewolf of Marines: Patria Lycanus
Werewolf of Marines: Pax Lycanus

Soldier

Animal Soldier: Hannibal

To the Shores of Tripoli

Wererat

Darwin's Quest: The Search for the Ultimate Survivor

Venus: A Paleolithic Short Story

Secession

Duty

Semper Fidelis

Checkmate (Published in The Expanding Universe 4)

<u>Seeds of War (With Lawrence Schoen)</u>
Invasion
Scorched Earth
Bitter Harvest

Non-Fiction

Exercise for a Longer Life

The Effects of Environmental Activism on the Yellowfin
Tuna Industry

Author Website

http://www.jonathanbrazee.com

Twitter

https://twitter.com/jonathanbrazee